Full Circle

Susan X Meagher

By Susan X Meagher

Novels

Arbor Vitae
All That Matters
Cherry Grove
The Lies That Bind
The Legacy
Doublecrossed
Smooth Sailing
How To Wrangle a Woman
Almost Heaven
The Crush
The Reunion
Inside Out
Out of Whack
Homecoming
The Right Time
Summer of Love
Chef's Special
Fame
Vacationland
Wait For M
The Keeper's Daughter
Friday Night Flights
Mosaic
Full Circle

Short Story Collection

Girl Meets Girl

Serial Novel

I Found My Heart In San Francisco

Anthologies

ACKNOWLEDGMENTS

My deepest thanks to the patient souls who read this novel one or more times, providing helpful feedback and suggestions. The many errors they caught are now safely buried. More could have jumped in, of course, but those are entirely my fault.

Dedication

As always, many people helped to bring this book to print, and it's definitely a better read due to their efforts. But my wife's contributions have, as always, been outsized. She listens to each batch of words as they're added to the pile, she encourages me when I hit a stumbling block, she laughs at every joke, and reliably cries at the ending. If I were to design a jill-of-all trades to help produce a book, it would be her. She brings the fun to what can sometimes be a solitary pursuit, and I'm certain publishing a book wouldn't be nearly as pleasurable without her support.

CHAPTER ONE

DEXTER HAVEN-LORD TOSSED HER second suitcase onto the bed, then flopped onto the floral-covered upholstered chair in the corner of the cozy room. She shouldn't have been tired from merely sitting in a comfortable chair for seven hours, but flying cross-country always took a lot out of her.

Getting unpacked and settling in was the smart thing to do, but she'd brought so much with her this time it just seemed like too big a task to even begin.

She was hungry, thirsty, and cranky, but experience had shown that after a short time back home her petty annoyances would disappear. If she could manage even fifteen minutes of quiet, she was certain she'd be up for anything at all. Even the effervescence of a twenty-one…almost twenty-two-year-old girl who sometimes seemed like she was powered by a tiny nuclear reactor.

Dex was almost sure she'd been just as energetic when she'd been Kendall's age, but her impressions of those years were kind of a mess. She made it a habit to focus on the good memories, and there were plenty of them. You could choose to look at struggles as scars that never healed, but that kind of thinking just didn't make sense to her. Tough times could also be a crucible, allowing the pain to harden you in a good way to sharpen your resiliency.

Now she needed just a few minutes to summon up some of that resiliency while Kendall was hopefully making something really tasty to snack on.

After kicking off her shoes and slipping out of her slacks, she moved the suitcases aside and sat on the bed, getting into a decent lotus pose. Sometimes it took quite a while to clear her mind, other times it was as easy as pie. Today, she slipped right into a great headspace. After just another minute she settled into a sweet rhythm with her breath, which now seemed to fill her entire body.

Time usually slowed down, then lost its sharp edges when she began to meditate, so she wasn't sure if it had been five seconds or two minutes, but sounds of Kendall banging around in the small kitchen broke her attention.

Even though she'd been hoping for some time to get centered, she quickly reminded herself that time with her daughter was easily as good for her mental health as her practice, so she opened her eyes and unfolded to put her feet on the floor.

Kendall always wanted to hop into the pool the minute Dex arrived, and tonight was likely going to follow suit. Since she'd been through this drill many times, she'd remembered to put her swimsuit in her carryon for easy access. It was still best to check before she bothered to change, though. Kendall's unpredictability was one constant she could rely on.

Her hand wrapped around the doorknob, but as she eased the door open a scream started, and continued as Dex's momentum compelled her into the kitchenette. Not six inches from her, Tracy Lord stood, naked as a jaybird.

"Kendall!" they shouted as one. Dex hadn't realized her reflexes were good enough to allow her to move backward while the forces of nature were working to pull her forward, but she stumbled a little, then fell, inelegantly, on her ass.

Staring up at a naked Tracy, she could only sputter, "What are you doing in my house?"

Tracy had grabbed a towel and was now trying to wrap it around herself. Sadly, it was a kitchen towel, and she had to choose between covering most of her breasts or all of her nether regions. As Dex would have predicted, if she'd had time to reflect, Tracy tried to do both, failing miserably. Bent over at the waist, with one breast and half of her pubic area completely uncovered, she snapped, "You've done some low things, C. K. Dexter Haven, but pulling Kendall into this trick might be the lowest!"

Tracy slammed the bedroom door, barely missing Dex's foot. Knowing her, she'd first done an assessment of all of the angles, and knew she'd miss before she'd even gotten her hand on the door.

Scrambling to her feet to regain the tattered shards of her dignity, Dex put her slacks back on and stormed into the kitchen, ready to unleash whatever anger she could summon onto Kendall, which usually wasn't much.

But the kid was nowhere to be found. There was only a food-laden tray, along with a very nice bottle of Côtes du Rhone, which was a strange addition. Dex picked up the bottle, revealing a note hidden underneath.

To my dear mothers,

Next month, I'll celebrate my twenty-second birthday. Given that I'll be a college graduate by then, it seems clear that I'm now a grown-ass woman. In honor of those milestones, I'm asking for only one gift—that you get over the childish animosity that still burns in your hearts and start treating each other as women who've now successfully completed their primary maternal roles.

I'm not under the delusion that I won't need lots of mothering in the future. But you no longer need to treat me like I'm as fragile as a piece of porcelain, certain that I'll fracture if you ever say a sharp word to or about one another.

I'd truly love it if you'd spend tonight getting past some of that bull-hockey, as Grammy calls it, and figure out how to be in the same room without vaporizing from your rage.

I'd love this so much that I'm insisting on it. The door is locked from the outside, and I have your keys, as well as your phones. Your only option is to break the glass in the door, which I wouldn't advise. The security company will summon the police while the glass is still falling, and you'll have to explain the whole thing to them. On top of that embarrassment, do you really want to face Libby Dexter Haven

3

and confess that you couldn't have a single conversation to make her precious granddaughter happy? I thought not.

So have a snack, drink some wine, and take a stroll down memory lane—after cursing me out, of course. I can't hear you, so feel free to vent your anger. Just please vent it at me, not each other.

I love you both fiercely, and can't wait to have you with me on Saturday. I wouldn't be the woman I am if not for you. Having you by my side at final exercises would truly be the highlight of my college career—although rocking that high honors cord is nothing to sneeze at, either.

Your loving daughter,
Kendall

Tracy was already back in her clothes, looking like she'd gotten dressed in one minute, in the dark, while high. Her mouth opened, but before a sharp word could be spoken Dex handed her the note, then set about opening the wine.

By the time she had the foil off, Tracy had pulled out a stool to sit at the breakfast bar. Her chin was in her hand, and a very melancholy expression had settled onto her face.

"We've screwed this up royally, haven't we?"

Dex was going to let the wine breathe, but Tracy clearly needed the sedative effect pronto. After pouring a glass and handing it over, Dex said, "Every parent screws up. If the only thing Kendall has to complain about is that we haven't all been in the same room since she was four…" She shrugged. "There are worse ways to screw up a child."

Because of their long hiatus, Dex truly had no idea what Tracy's normal drinking habits were. But if she usually drank great gulps of wine like she was doing right that minute, Kendall's mommies would *both* be rehab grads.

"I know this is the last place you want to be," Dex said, using her most soothing voice, the one she pulled out when she was portraying a kindly mother or grandmother who was speaking from the grave or about to be planted in one.

"Do you think?"

Dex took a good, long look at her, not even caring that it was rude to stare. It was also rude to be sarcastic, but that hadn't stopped Tracy.

It was odd to be inches from a person you'd loved so much, so long ago. While you'd have to be blind to think Tracy Lord was anything other than a very pretty, very bright-looking woman, she was, at this point in her life, truly a woman. Every bit of her girlish self was gone, replaced by sharper angles, more defined muscles in her arms, a few visible veins on the backs of her hands. Definitely shorter hair, with the pale brown strands barely reaching her shoulders now. Her eyes were still blue, but they seemed paler, perhaps a little colder, too. But the thing Dex hated the most was that Tracy had an edge to her, one that had undoubtedly been created by stress, hard work, and worry. Raising a child took a lot out of a person, and it broke Dex's heart that they hadn't been able to share the burden equally.

"I say we call a locksmith. Even if it takes a while for them to get here—"

Dex took the note and waved it in front of her. "By call, do you mean shout until a passing locksmith hears you? Our phones are gone."

"I will wring her neck," she groused, surprising Dex with her anger. "Say what you will, Kendall wouldn't have done this if *you* weren't involved."

"Me? What did I do?"

"I'm not sure, but…something. She gets the manipulative part of her personality from you."

That hurt. It actually hurt enough for Dex to mull over the long list of jibes she could have fired back. But she'd been working on controlling her darker impulses for well over ten years now, and she'd made a significant amount of progress. Reminding herself that every situation was around ninety percent your reaction to it, she simply nodded. "I'm sure Kendall has incorporated both good and bad elements of both of our personalities. But she's her own woman, Tracy. She's not a carbon copy of either of us." Softening her voice even further, she murmured, "She looks an awful lot like you did at her age. Sometimes I tear up just from looking at her." Gently, she put her hand on Tracy's shoulder, touching her for the first time since the momentous evening that marked the most egregious screw-up of her life.

Those clear, blue eyes shifted to gaze at Dex, but they weren't the warm, tender ones that had once welcomed her into her heart. These eyes had seen some things, and they weren't going to be fooled again. Despite all of Tracy's many stellar traits, her nature was unforgiving. After your third strike, you were *out*. And no one would argue that Dex's hadn't been a doozy.

"Why don't you go do…whatever in your room. I'm going to sit here and guzzle this bottle of wine. When Kendall checks in, we'll tell her we've buried the hatchet."

"Will we have?" Dex asked, knowing the answer.

"Of course not. But she doesn't need to know that."

"I really think—"

"You know," she said, sounding like she was recounting a tale to a friend. "I have a patient who has a big tattoo of the forty-fifth president of the United States right over his weak, artery-clogged heart. I'm certain he doesn't know I'd like to cut it off with a scalpel. You're not the only actress around here."

Dex gazed at her for a minute, certain Tracy would be a happier person if she could show her pain, rather than her anger. Of course, maybe she usually did that—or at least did it with people she trusted. One thing was as clear as crystal. Dex was not on that list.

⬦⬦⬦

The minute Dex went into the tiny bedroom, Tracy poured herself another glass of wine. She normally stopped at one, only pushing it to two when she was enjoying a special dinner. But she thought she might drain the damn bottle tonight. She had plans, and not only were they now ruined, she had no way to properly cancel them. Yardley would be frantic, justifiably, but even if Kendall monitored the phones she'd swiped, she wouldn't pick up if a message from Yardley came in. She treated her like the neighbor you hated to run into in the hallway. It didn't matter that the neighbor was a perfectly nice person. You just didn't want to spend more than the minimum amount of time with them.

The tray had been sitting right in front of her the whole time, but it took until now for Tracy to really see it. Kendall had done a nice job, if she'd actually done it herself. It was more likely that Libby had neatly rolled up slices of salami and prosciutto, and carefully sliced various hard cheeses to fit onto crisp crackers. But the part of the tray Tracy couldn't resist was the veiny blue cheese. Of course there was a dollop of fig spread. Of course there was a crunchy baguette, pre-sliced.

Rolling her eyes, she forced herself to acknowledge that she and Yardley were *not* going out for dinner tonight. Given the option of being hungry or diving in, she grabbed a handful of the baguette slices and started to load them up. Damn, that cheese was good!

A memory hit her, of the first time she'd had a bite of a very good cheese. It was in their dorm room, back when she thought the sun rose and set on Dex's shoulders—a period that lasted much longer than it should have, in retrospect.

Dex had to use all of her salesmanship to convince Tracy to even try it, but once she'd gotten past the shock to really let herself savor the complexity, they'd whipped through the whole piece, along with a sleeve of crackers. That memory was overwritten by another. Libby had introduced her to the fig paste, which heightened the flavors while toning down their sharpness. That happened the year Tracy had been ousted from her family, with the Havens stepping in to show her how true generosity of spirit, as well as a lavish dinner, could make Christmas absolutely magical.

Those warm memories were quickly replaced by a near-movie of the day she and Dex had split. How did you make up for losing your partner? Your child's mother? The woman you'd been certain you'd grow old with? You couldn't. You simply couldn't. On that awful day, Tracy had decided she and Kendall would go it alone. And they had—mostly. Dex had surprised the hell out of her by hanging in there, even when limited to monthly weekend visits with their child. While Randy and Libby had been extraordinary grandparents, the hard work, the daily grind, had been on Tracy's shoulders. She'd had to struggle to support herself and Kendall, the child she'd only given birth to because of Dex. After their split, Dex had, of course, landed on her feet. In no time, she'd snagged a great job, a great house, and as many women as she could possibly want. Was Tracy bitter about the way things had turned out? She honestly tried not to be, but sometimes the ugly just seeped out.

∞∞∞

Tracy wouldn't have thought it possible, but you could have too much excellent blue cheese. You could have too much wine, too, but she'd known that. You'd think the daughter of a drunk would be the one to develop a dependance, but that's not how that cookie had crumbled. Neither Randy nor Libby ever had one too many, but Dex had taken to drugs like a bee to honey. Genetics must have had something to do with it, but Tracy's daddy hadn't been able to pass a bar without stopping in to say howdy do, yet she was quite sure this was the first time she'd had three glasses of wine since college.

She assumed she'd eventually finish the damn bottle, given she'd been there for over an hour, and there had been no sign of Kendall's return. It's not like she could share it with Dex…

Taking a look at the rest of the tray, still filled with enough food for two men, she guiltily stood on slightly wobbly legs and walked over to the door of the bedroom. It was mostly open, and she was about to announce herself when she spied Dex sitting on the floor, eyes closed, posture perfect, hands resting on her knees. How could she sit like that? Tracy's hips would have popped right out of the joint if she'd even tried it!

Dex had to have been practicing yoga or pilates or something for quite a while to be that limber. But the fact was that Tracy knew next to nothing about her life.

When Kendall had been young, Tracy had steadfastly redirected the child every time she'd mentioned Dex. Whether Kendall had just kept up that practice because she thought it was what they wanted, or she liked having secrets to herself, she revealed less and less as the years went by.

Tracy had to satisfy herself by imagining Dex's life, and she had probably conjured up an existence that was pretty grand—even for Hollywood. But she didn't blame herself for that. Kendall always shared photos, and there was more often than not a young woman somewhere in the background. The woman changed with the seasons, but Tracy had noted that all of the beauties had remained in their twenties. In the past few years, Kendall had begun to look as old as that year's girlfriend, which was simply unseemly.

But now…now Dex looked like she could have taken over for the Dali Lama. Tranquility nearly poured from her body, which was in ridiculously good shape. When did she have the time to work? A body like hers had to be tended to—doted on, even. Of course, she had money, and some of those models Tracy had seen snippets of over the years had to be fitness trainers or yoga teachers. That's just how Dex's luck went. She'd find a gorgeous young thing who could teach her how to stay limber and youthful while screwing her socks off.

As Tracy continued to gaze at her, she noted that Dex's hair was still that lovely shade of dark blonde, a color that perfectly complimented her eyes, which were a pale brown that could sometimes seem green. Not often. Just enough to make you want to stare into them to watch them transform because of the background, or sometimes her mood.

Going down this road was a very bad choice, and Tracy was about to leave when Dex's lids fluttered open. She looked up like she was truly surprised to see another person in the pool house. "Have you been calling me? I can get…lost," she said, with that warm, tender smile reminding Tracy of the thousands of times she'd automatically responded to it. Tonight she tried not to—at all.

"No, I hadn't called you. I thought you might be asleep, so I just peeked in."

"It's only six o'clock." She glanced at the watch on her right wrist, the graduation present that Tracy had helped Dex's grandparents pick out. It was odd to see her still wearing it. Tracy was sure she had the money to choose something more ostentatious or trendy.

"I believe it's nine in the time zone you're currently in. Are you hungry? Either Kendall or your mom went to a lot of trouble to make us a tray."

"Hungry?" She unfolded herself easily, sticking those long legs out before getting to her feet gracefully. Tracy now had to contend with looking at those legs in snug yoga shorts and a cocoa-colored sleeveless top that barely touched her body. "You know, I thought I was hungry when Kendall picked me up at the airport. I'm going to have to come up with a new word for how I feel right now."

"Come into the kitchen. I've just about drained the bottle of wine, but there's plenty of food." She gave her a guilty grin. "Minus the blue cheese. I ate that like a starving dog."

"I don't keep cheese in the house," Dex said as she followed Tracy back into the kitchen. "It wouldn't last the day."

"I don't either." She laughed a little. "I don't need to buy it since your mom practically force-feeds it to me every time I come over."

Dex assessed the tray, nodding. "This will do nicely." She popped a grape into her mouth, then followed it up with a chunk of Parmesan. "Good stuff." Continuing to plot her course, she said, "Do you do that often? Visit, that is."

Tracy almost told the whole truth, but she pulled back. "Oh, sure. A couple of times a month. A little more in the summer." Dex didn't need to know that Yardley didn't feel entirely welcome at the Haven house, so the visits were slightly less frequent now. Tracy honestly didn't blame Yardley for being unenthusiastic about planning get-togethers. While Libby and Randy were unfailingly polite, they had none of the same interests as Yardley, and afternoons spent by the pool seemed to drag. Lately, Tracy found herself scheduling a visit only when Yardley was busy, or traveling for work. It always hurt a bit when no one lamented her absence.

"I'm glad you see them often. I know they're crazy about you."

"It's mutual," Tracy said, sure she'd weep if she thought of how the Havens had taken her in and made her part of the family. "But I know your mom was part of this plot, and that's…going to take me a while to get over."

"Mmm." Dex seemed taken with a hard cheese that Tracy was unfamiliar with.

"Actually," Tracy continued. "I'd been assuming and hoping that you'd handle this weekend like you did when Kendall graduated from high school. I thought that worked just fine."

Dex turned slowly, and Tracy took a step back when she saw anger flashing in her eyes. But in just a second it seemed to vanish. "Excuse me," she said. "I'll be right back." She disappeared into the bedroom, and Tracy heard the bathroom door close quietly.

She'd used the pool house a few times over the years, so Tracy was pretty sure there were no sharp implements hiding in the bathroom that Dex could use to stab her. But the look in her eyes had made it clear she wished she could—but only for a moment. Was she really that in control of her emotions? Where was the woman who'd gone toe-to-toe with her during every one of their fights? The one who laughed, cried, or shouted forcefully when the need arose? Was she still hiding in there?"

A minute later, Dex emerged, smelling of a nice hand soap. She sat on a stool and carefully popped a grape into her mouth, then turned and faced Tracy head-on. "I'd like to clear something up," she said quietly. "Barring me from Kendall's prior graduation might have worked well for you, but it didn't work well for me. Having it made crystal clear that a huge auditorium was too small to share truly hurt."

Having someone sit there and look you right in the eye while she told you how you'd hurt her was more disconcerting than being yelled at. Being raised by yellers had accustomed Tracy to the boisterous approach. She managed to stammer, "B…but Kendall said you seemed very happy to throw a party for her here. Count your blessings. While you were enjoying a pool party the next day, I was still trying to get rid of the headache I developed from sitting in the sun listening to that gabby headmaster drone on and on."

Dex's chin extended slightly. "I cared about Kendall's feelings enough to hide how hurt mine were." She leaned forward, with those warm sable eyes fixed on Tracy. "I would have sat through six hours of speeches to watch my daughter give the salutatorian address. Seeing it on my dad's shaky video was a very, very poor substitute."

"I'm...sorry. If I'd known it was important to you..." She took in a breath. "You're the one who offered to throw a party. I thought that was enough."

"It's *never* enough," she said quietly, but with feeling. She moved the wine bottle from the tray like it was toxic, then took the food over to the sectional, where she sat on the chaise part of the piece and stretched her legs out. "I know how badly I screwed up, but I've been paying for that mistake for eighteen years. Kendall's right. It's time to treat each other like people who've collaborated on a large, important project from different locations." She was quiet for just a second, and when she spoke again her voice was firm and low. "One day we'll have grandchildren, and I want to make it very clear that I *will* be with them on holidays. That's non-negotiable."

"You're right," she said, moving over to sit on the far end of the piece. "I thought things were working fine, but I will admit I didn't ask if you agreed."

"That's hard to do when we haven't spoken. We have warmer relations with Iran than we do with each other." She gazed at Tracy soberly. "Isn't it enough that Kendall wants us to get along?"

"Yes, yes," she said, needing another sip or two of wine to deal with this new, logical Dex. She got up and poured the last of it into her glass, then returned to her seat. "I haven't specifically asked Kendall about tickets to Final Exercises, but I guess I should have. I've already invited... the woman I'm seeing."

Dex turned slowly and met her eyes. "I turned down a very lucrative gig to be here, and I'm going to be sitting in one of those seats on Saturday."

"What am I supposed to tell Yardley...?"

"Yardley?" Her eyebrows climbed. "Not Yardley Simpkins."

"She's the only Yardley I know. She might be the only Yardley in the state."

Dex looked a little ill. "You had to take up with my former co-worker?"

Immediately angry, Tracy snapped, "Sorry, but I couldn't snare a hot twenty-year-old. Of course, I don't have a beach house, or a body that looks like it was sculpted from marble!"

Dex glared at her for a few seconds. "The career, the house, and the body are the result of a lot of effort. I'll admit I've had some lucky breaks, but I worked to make the most out of them. That's just a fact."

"*This* is why we don't talk. You're infuriating!" She stood and marched over to the door, yanking on it until her arm ached. "Damn your parents and their top-notch carpenters."

Standing there for a moment, she tried to devise another way out. The window over the sink would be a tight fit, but... She put her hands on the counter and pushed herself up to sit. It wasn't easy to get her footing and stand in the tiny sink, but she didn't let that stop her.

"You're not going to fit," Dex said, not bothering to walk over and help.

"Fuck off. I'm not going to sit here all night." The window was small, but with the right angles... After unlatching it, she opened it fully, then slid the screen out and dropped it to the ground. There were shrubs right under the window, but she was sure they didn't have thorns or anything that would injure her if she tumbled onto them, which was a real possibility.

Dex was still sitting placidly, watching like she was catching a TV show that bored her slightly. If she'd get off her lazy ass and help this wouldn't be that hard. But Tracy wasn't about to beg. She would free herself, then march along the side of the house and go directly home.

Dex could wait until Kendall tired of the game and released her—preferably days from now.

Trying to slide your ass out of a small window while your ex watched wasn't really a great way to spend a Thursday night. Getting the first leg out wasn't hard at all, and Tracy was pretty sure she wouldn't be badly hurt if she launched herself onto the bushes. But she didn't want to test that hypothesis, so she tried to get the other leg out so she could kind of slide to a soft landing. She almost impaled herself on the faucet handle, which she realized was shaped like a sex toy, now that she'd gotten up close and personal with it. Dexter's snicker just made her work harder, while maintaining a quiet stream of curse words.

She really hadn't gained much weight over the years, but her hips were a little wider than the window would accommodate. Cursing even louder, she wriggled around until she plopped into the sink, ass first, legs spread wide as they dangled over the counter.

"Would it kill you to help?"

"I did help," Dex said, her voice calm and soft. "I told you you'd never fit. If you'd listened, you would have saved ten minutes of struggle."

Tracy glared at her. "I'm going out head-first. If I break my neck, you'll have to explain to Kendall that you let me fall to my death while you sat on your ass."

Sighing dramatically, Dex got up and walked over to the window. "The odds aren't any better if you go head-first. Really."

"Since I'm not going to sit here all night, I've got to try something. I've got places to be."

Dex held up her hands. "What do you want me to do?"

"Hold onto my legs," she said, thinking that gave her the best chance. "I'll try to extend my arms and kind of…tumble out."

Dex cocked her head as she stared at her blankly. "Have you been rigorously practicing gymnastics? I mean Olympic-caliber training."

"Hold my legs—and your opinions."

This was probably not going to work. But she hated being forced to stay in one place more than she hated looking stupid. Trying a few different angles allowed her to finally get her shoulders out, and she breathed in the sweet, spring air. Just that little bit of progress made her feel like she was nearly out—even though the largest part of her was still inside. "This is not going to be easy. I have to slide around this phallus-like faucet to get anywhere."

"Oh, great. I've never noticed the resemblance, but now I'll see it every time I get a drink of water. Ooo…you're getting close."

"Almost," she grunted, just needing to lose about three inches from her pelvis in the next ten seconds. Her hands were dangling, with nothing to hold on to, and they'd started to tingle. The metal window frame was cutting into her belly something fierce, but she kept shifting around, certain she could get the angle right if she worked hard enough.

Dex wasn't helping at all, but she did have her hands loosely around Tracy's ankles, which reassured her only the slightest bit.

"One more push," she said, gasping when the zipper of her slacks bit into her skin. "Shit!"

"Want me to pull you back in?"

"Push me out!"

Dex must have gotten onto the counter, since her voice was much closer and Tracy could feel some warm part of her against her leg. "That's not a good idea. At best, you'll cut yourself up."

"Push!"

It shouldn't have taken Tracy this long to figure out the only available part to push, but Dex followed orders, putting both hands on her ass and giving her a hearty shove.

"Damn it! My hips will not go through." She took a breath. "Dex? I can't feel my arms anymore."

"Did you…did you have a stroke?"

"No, I didn't have a fucking stroke! I'm upside down and the blood's pooled in my hands. You've got to pull me back in."

"That's easier said than done."

Tracy heard a big thump, which she hoped meant Dex was back on the floor, where she'd have better traction. First, she grabbed Tracy's feet, but that was never going to work. She must have gotten back on the counter, because her hands now gripped Tracy's hips tightly. "Here we go," she grunted, pulling her back in at least six inches.

"Great. Do that like three more times."

"Easy for you to say."

"It's hard for me to say! My head's about to explode from being upside down this long. Hurry up!"

A second strong tug would have been enough if Tracy's arms had any feeling left in them. Then she could have grasped the window frame to help. As it was, they just flailed in the breeze as they tingled with thousands of pin-pricks. Finally, the third tug did the trick, and they became a jumbled mass of body parts in and around the sink and counter. Dex jumped back down and tried to methodically unwind Tracy, eventually getting her onto her back. That helped a ton, and she was able to sit upright in a very ungainly fashion. She must have looked like a dinosaur, with her useless hands flopping about as she used just her abs to sit upright. Finally, her feet hit the floor, and she stumbled around helplessly, certain the tingling would never stop. "What a stupid, stupid idea!"

To her great credit, Dex did not say she told her so. Surprisingly, she noisily slapped herself on the side of the head. "I'm going to check the bedroom. Those windows are much bigger."

Tracy followed her in to watch her put her whole body into the effort, giving the window a yank that had it quickly slide up about four inches, only to come to an abrupt halt, sounding like someone had hit a tree stump with a mallet. Dex grabbed at her shoulder, howling. "I think I dislocated my arm!"

"Hold still," Tracy said, immediately reaching for her.

Dex pulled away, hopping back a few inches while glaring at her like she was mad. "Call a doctor!"

"A fucking Family Nurse Practitioner is as close to a physician as you're going to get, Dexter. Now stop being so damn dramatic and let me examine you."

As Tracy tried to get closer, she could see such a completely puzzled look on Dex's face that it became crystal clear that Kendall had shared the bare minimum about her life. How had she known to do that at such a young age?

Dex gave every indication that she would have preferred a well-staffed emergency room, but was willing to accept what she could realistically get. Truth be told, she'd always been a bit of a baby when it came to injuries—of which she'd had many. Moderation had never been her thing.

"You can honestly tell if I've dislocated it?"

"Of course, I can," Tracy grumbled. "It's not a difficult diagnosis." She forced herself to adopt her professional mien, fully distancing herself from her personal feelings about Dex. Gently, she ran her fingers over the joint, certain that the humerus was resting perfectly in the glenoid cavity. She watched Dex's tense face when she tentatively moved her arm through its normal range of motion. Dex didn't flinch, which would not have been the case if it had been even partially dislocated. "I think you've strained a muscle or two. Maybe even a tendon. We'll get some ice on it as soon as we can." She gently patted her back as she stepped away. "You'll be fine, but sore."

A hint of a guilty smile overtook the anxious expression that had lined her face with worry. "I'm sorry I didn't know you were trained…or licensed or whatever. I knew you did something in the medical field, but I thought you were more like a regular nurse." Her smile grew a little. "I only knew that because Kendall used to take that little medical kit everywhere, and some of the things were legit."

Tracy nodded, touched at the memory of how Kendall had lusted for any authentic supplies that Tracy could share with her. A couple of tongue depressors could keep the child happy for an hour while she examined her dolls and stuffed animals for sore throats.

"In practice, I treat patients as if I were a physician. Many states allow Nurse Practitioners to practice without supervision. Not Virginia, of course." She couldn't stop her resentment from coloring her words.

"Yet another way I'm reminded that I couldn't have the job I'd always dreamed of."

Dex stared at her for a second, then turned away and went right back into the bathroom. Tracy dropped onto the upholstered chair—waiting while she heard the water running.

She wasn't sure if Dex was making her wait just to drive her nuts, or if she was taking time to calm herself, but the driving her nuts part was working perfectly.

Finally, she emerged, once against smelling of soap. What was she doing in there? Bathing in the sink?

Dex didn't sit. She used the tiny amount of open space to walk back and forth in the room, still looking awfully close to the loose-limbed jock Tracy had fallen for. "You have many things to blame me for," Dex said softly. "That's beyond argument. But it's not fair to blame me for your not going to med school."

"Want to bet?"

"Yes, I do. There isn't a question that my parents would have paid your tuition, and free baby sitting was a given. Actually, my mom's only complaint has been that she didn't see Kendall every day. So your not going to med school was your decision."

"Not true. If I'd had a partner…a reliable partner, she would have been home in the evenings. It would have been hard, but we could have done it."

"My mom—"

"Not the same! I would have been so busy that your mom would have basically raised our daughter, which wouldn't have been fair to either of them. I screwed up by believing you'd be the partner I needed to co-parent while I became a doctor. So giving up my dream was the punishment I deserved for being so naive."

"Quiet," Dex murmured, quickly walking into the living area. Tracy followed behind, able to see Kendall standing right outside, her jaw quivering. Her cheeks glistened with tears illuminated by the porch light, making Tracy's heart clench. Dex reached for the door, but the kid didn't unlock it. Instead, she turned on her heel and walked away, leaving them staring at each other.

"Oh, god," Dex murmured. "I hope she didn't hear any of that, but she probably did. The damn window was open wide enough to let the sound travel." She dropped heavily onto the sofa. "God, damn it. Kendall doesn't have any idea of how lucky she truly is. If I'd stayed, she would have had to witness that kind of thing all the time." She stared at Tracy for a long minute. "Doesn't being morally superior to everyone ever get tiring?"

⚬⚬⚬

They sat in silence for the longest time, with Dex beginning to regret her decision to come at all. That was a childish reaction, of course, so she went down the list of very good reasons for making the trip. Foremost was that it was important to Kendall, and she'd always tried to put her first—even when she'd failed miserably. Grammy's warning about the road to hell and the good intentions it was paved with still stuck with her.

She was pretty deep in her introspection when Tracy's voice caught her attention. "I'm not normally like this."

"How's that? Self-righteous? Irascible? Short-tempered?" She really didn't want to be so acerbic, but Tracy was pushing her to her *limits.*

Her head nodded slightly. "Yes. All of that." She met Dex's eyes, holding her gaze for a few moments. "I try not to linger on the past, since my present is honestly very, very good. I usually don't have any trouble being in the moment." Her gaze shifted to her lap. "Having you appear— with no warning—threw me right back to the awful afternoon we broke up." Her lips were pursed, and she didn't speak for another minute. "But even though our parting was devastating, it was a huge mistake to cut all contact with you. If all we'd managed to do was keep each other in the loop about Kendall, that would have been a big help. I'm sorry I was so pig-headed."

Dex tried to really listen, to see past the words to the emotion underneath. "Keeping in contact would have been better," she agreed. When Tracy didn't follow up, she did. "But even if we'd maintained a relationship, you wouldn't have changed your mind, would you? About us, I mean."

"No," she said, not even having to give the question a moment's consideration. "Once the trust is broken…"

"I understand," Dex said, and the truth was that she honestly did. "It took me quite a while to trust myself, so it makes sense it would have been even harder for you."

Their eyes met again, with Dex able to see just a hint of the carefree, inquisitive, optimistic girl she'd fallen so hard for.

"Even though I couldn't let you stay, it wore on me that you didn't have any legal right to Kendall. Our lovely state did everything it could to make sure families like ours couldn't be legally recognized."

"Thanks," Dex said, not willing to go into how powerless she'd felt at having Tracy holding all of the chips.

"I mean that. If we'd been married, the courts would have ordered me to let Kendall see you from the start. I'm sorry it took me so long to allow that."

Nodding, Dex said, "It wasn't a good time. For any of us." Summoning the optimism she'd worked hard to attain, she added, "But things worked out in the end. Having Kendall with me for the last few summers has been the highlight of my life."

Tracy smiled at her. "It means so much to her, Dex. She talks about going from the moment she comes home."

"I didn't know that," Dex said, feeling the emotion well up in her chest again.

"Even though I get a little jealous that you're the favorite, I'm glad you've had that time together."

Dex stared at her. "I'm the favorite? I wish." She shook her head, needing to reframe that thought. "I wish she thought of me more as a parent. She put me into the much older sister or aunt category a long, long time ago."

"Seriously? I've never gotten that—"

Feeling the emotion shake her, Dex said, "When she fell on her skateboard and broke her arm, she let me hold her for about a minute. Then she started to wail for her mommy. If we'd been in LA at the time, I think I would have had to find a private plane to get her home. She was inconsolable without you." Their eyes met briefly. "Things like that have happened at least once during every visit. She gets as much as she can from me, but it's never quite enough."

"I doubt that's because she thinks of you as a sister. Really. She's just used to my patching her up when she hurts herself." Her smile was close to the way it had looked when they were first together. "I have a good bedside manner."

"You have a good—"

A figure appeared at the door, and a moment later the whole frame shook. Yardley Simpkins was banging on the door with both fists, looking like she would be all too happy to break right through the glass. "You might want to stop her from doing that," Dex said, trying to stay cool. "I think that's single-pane glass. Probably not tempered."

Tracy jumped to her feet to stand right in front of the door. "We don't have a key!" she yelled.

Yardley's mouth moved, but the words weren't clear.

"I guess I was wrong about the single pane," Dex said, choosing not to stand.

Tracy went over to the counter and found a pen. Using a paper shopping bag, she scribbled something on it and held it up to the door. Yardley held her hands up, clearly asking for direction or a solution.

Writing again, Tracy once again held it up. Yardley stared at the sign for a moment, then stalked away.

"She doesn't look happy," Dex said, realizing how silly that observation was.

"Where in the hell is Kendall, and how did Yardley know to come here?" Tracy's eyes narrowed. "I know your mother's involved."

"That's pretty likely. I doubt that it was her idea, but Kendall can easily talk her into being an accomplice to just about anything."

Tracy held a hand up. "Don't even remind me of the pony. Who gives a child a pony for Christmas?"

"I got one," Dex said, unable to hide a snicker.

"I'm sure you did. Along with anything else you wanted."

"Hey, we were having a nice moment there. Let's not review every mistake my parents ever made with me or our daughter."

"Sorry," she said. "I just feel so powerless…"

"You are," Dex said. "*We* are. Humans are inherently powerless. We just have to make the best out of our topsy-turvy, out-of-control lives in whatever way we can."

"Put a sock in it," she said, overly dismissive from Dex's point of view. "I'm not a member of your ashram."

Dex softened her voice, allowing some of her hurt to show. "I'm not connected to an ashram, Tracy. I just use a few techniques that have helped me become a more connected, more thoughtful person. Is that really something to make fun of?"

"No," she said, hitting the word hard. "I'm just so frustrated! It's going to take hours to explain this all to Yardley…"

"Why is this such a big deal? Our daughter played a silly prank on us. Full stop. You don't even have to go into the details with a date."

"Uhm…" Tracy was quiet for a few seconds. "Yardley's more than my date." Their eyes met. "She's my fiancée."

CHAPTER TWO

DEX WAS ALMOST CERTAIN THAT she'd been polite enough to express some form of congratulations on Tracy's engagement, but she couldn't have sworn to that in a court of law. She hadn't known Tracy was even dating anyone, so finding out she was engaged to a boot-licker who'd undoubtedly been the chief hall monitor/snitch in grade school had her head spinning.

Tracy was still standing at the door, clearly waiting for rescue. Dex didn't think she'd spoken much, if at all, but she wasn't absolutely sure about that either.

Yardley Simpkins, the human equivalent of tuna on white, not even a wilted lettuce leaf to spice it up. Yes, when you were *very* hungry a plain tuna sandwich was better than nothing. But the optimal choice was to do something to take your mind off your hunger and wait for a meal you could really get excited about. But Tracy had obviously changed her stripes—massively—during their long estrangement.

The girl Dex had known would have been tempted by the tuna. She might have even tried to convince herself that food was just sustenance, and any one meal wasn't all that much better than the next. But at her core, Tracy craved burnt ends with some tongue-numbing hot sauce, alongside a big scoop of gooey macaroni and cheese, or eggs Benedict with runny yolks, doused with Hollandaise. Something so full of flavor, and so messy that it would inevitably drip onto your shirt and upset your tummy. Something with a little risk, and a great big reward.

To want to hitch her wagon to Yardley Simpkins clearly showed Tracy had managed to tamp down her yearnings for the spicy side of life, and that made Dex want to curl up into a ball and cry. But she didn't. She sat there like an adult and waited for Kendall to open the damn door.

It seemed like they'd already been waiting for an hour, but when Yardley reappeared she was still panting with outrage. Given she didn't seem like she had the capacity for much emotion of any kind, a very short period of time might have passed.

Libby stood next to Yardley, studiously ignoring whatever she was saying. As a teenager, Dex had been driven crazy by her mother's ability to appear to be stone-deaf, but it was a tactic that had served her well for years.

As the door swung open, Dex caught Libby's dramatic eye-roll as Yardley burst into the room to throw her arms around Tracy. Prisoners of war weren't welcomed home with such histrionics.

"What happened?" she asked, her voice shaking. "I've been calling you nonstop since seven. When neither you, nor Kendall, nor Libby picked up, I went to your house. This was my last resort. I was set to call the police if you weren't here."

"I'm fine," Tracy said, to Dex's eye mortally embarrassed. She had to really press to get Yardley to even let her go.

"How could you possibly be fine? You've been held here against your will!"

"She's fine," Dex said, breaking her vow to keep her mouth firmly shut. "We had a nice snack, and a good chat." She smiled at Tracy while she tried to wriggle out of Yardley's embrace. "Kendall got her graduation present early, by the way. She *was* going to get a new phone, but I'm going to keep it."

"No, you won't," Tracy said, giving her a smile fond enough to warm Dex's heart. "Kendall knows she can get away with just about anything where you're concerned."

Libby brushed by Yardley to put her arms around Dex. "Are *you* all right, honey pie? I know you hate to be confined."

Libby only called the dog honey pie, so she must have been making fun of Yardley, or trying to appear blameless, which she couldn't possibly have been.

"I'm fine, Mom. This isn't exactly the big house."

"I was shocked, shocked, I tell you, when Yardley arrived to announce that Tracy was missing." Her accent had deepened to the point where she sounded like she was from rural Mississippi, rather than the Piedmont. Her gaze traveled to Yardley. "Anyone would have been *mad* with worry."

Dex pulled away from the hug to face Yardley. "I assume Tracy's car was in the driveway. Didn't you see it?"

"I…I didn't notice," she said, still pretty wide-eyed. This was not the person you wanted in the air-traffic control tower. A little stress made her freak out like a skittish toy poodle. "I was just so worried. Tracy's never been out-of-pocket for so long."

Dex itched to slap Yardley across the face for using corporate-speak outside of work. What was that even supposed to mean? Was Tracy usually *in* her pocket? Ridiculous!

Libby put her arm around Dex's waist and hugged her gently. That simple touch brought her to her senses. What did it matter if Yardley used corporate-speak in her private life? It didn't matter at all. Not at *all*.

A little movement caught Dex's eye and she crooked her finger when Kendall peeked around the corner. "Come in here and take your medicine," she said, lowering and hardening her voice to a point where a stranger might have been shaking in her boots.

When Kendall began to slide past Tracy and Yardley to place herself right in front of Dex, she could see that she wasn't upset any longer. The child had remarkable resiliency, and would usually be upset for a very short time, then just let it go. Dex felt oddly playful and she tickled the kid's sides until Kendall fell to the sectional, with Dex tumbling onto the sofa beside her. She had her arm around Kendall's neck, and finally twisted her around so she could swat her on the seat.

"Ow!" she yelped. "Not fair! You shouldn't be that strong when you're old."

"You shouldn't be that cruel when you're young." Dex stood and pulled Kendall to her feet. "I was just telling your mom that since you got your birthday wish by tricking us, I'm going to return your new phone."

"The X-T-C 12?" Kendall asked, cocking her head.

"That's the one."

"Nana already got it for me," the kid said, giving Dex such a devilish smile she considered giving her another swat. This time with some sting to it.

"Thanks a bunch, Mom. The least you could do is clue me in when you splurge on her."

"Will you people stop dismissing what happened here?" Yardley demanded, displaying a stunning amount of anger—for her. "Tracy was trapped in here all night. Against her will, I might add. And we missed dinner reservations that I made three months ago. It's our *anniversary*," she sniffed, with her angry gaze landing on Dex.

"Why are you looking at me? I had nothing to do with this."

"Doubtful," she said, narrowing her eyes.

For a moment, Dex observed her closely. Some people changed a lot in twenty years. Yardley hadn't. Hardly at all, as a matter of fact.

Objectively, Dex supposed she was a nice enough looking woman: tallish, thinish, with the same chin-length blunt cut she'd had when they'd worked together. The color was also about the same—blandly brown. Only her eyes held your interest, and that was solely because they looked so damned sad. Basset hounds seemed joyful compared to Yardley.

"I was just about to congratulate you on your engagement, but you don't seem like you're in a space to hear that. Why don't we circle-back when we have the bandwidth to do a deep-dive on the topic." Dex knew she was being a sarcastic snot, but she could tell Yardley wasn't listening at all.

"Someone should have set firm expectations, along with accompanying consequences for Kendall," she said, still gazing hotly at Dex. "It's unconscionable for a child to pull a stunt like that and not be punished for it."

Dex could see that Kendall was about to get into it, so she stepped in before she could utter a word. "Maybe we didn't raise our daughter the way you would have, but that horse has left the barn. If you're planning on being a member of the family, you'll find the path much smoother if you treat Kendall like a fellow adult." She took in a breath, recognizing she was about to blow. "You don't lecture a fellow adult like a naughty child."

"Dex. Please," Tracy said quietly. "Let's put this to bed right now."

"Since my bandwidth is stretched pretty thin," she said, looking only at Tracy, "that's probably a good idea."

"Good. So we'll see you at Final Exercises?"

"Dex will be at dinner tomorrow night," Kendall said, giving her mom a narrow-eyed glance.

"Dinner?" Dex asked.

"We're all getting together for a meal before the valedictory address," Libby said. "If you don't come along, you'll be the odd woman out."

"Fine," Tracy said, sighing in resignation. "I'll change the reservation. We'll see you at five."

Dex stared at her. "You're having dinner at five? That's two o'clock in the afternoon for me."

"The ceremony's at eight, so we've got to eat early." Her smile made her look a little playful. "Maybe they'll make you some pancakes."

"Oh, no. If I'm having breakfast, I'm going for biscuits and gravy. Can't find good ones to save my life in LA."

"We'll see you both tomorrow," Libby said, still sounding like an actor in a *very* amateurish production. "And we're *so* sorry for the mix-up tonight, Yardley." She grasped Tracy and kissed both of her cheeks, then stepped back and merely directed a mild smile at Yardley.

"Mix-up," she grumbled, taking Tracy's hand and walking out without another word.

Dex plunked herself down on the sectional. "I do declare that Yardley Simpkins has developed a bit of spunk." Adopting the darkest expression she could manage, she added, "Don't you hate spunk?"

※※※

Yardley was making far, far too big a deal about the evening, but Tracy wasn't sure how to calm her down. Even though they'd known each other for a full year, Yardley had never had a single significant emotional outburst. Usually, she reminded Tracy of a cute bloodhound: loyal, devoted, slavishly attached, slow to rile up. But tonight the bloodhound had treed a possum—barking her fool head off even though the possum knew it just had to sit up in the branch and laugh at her until the dog was exhausted.

Yardley not realizing that Dex and Libby had been making fun of her was kind of maddening, but Tracy had to admit that the majority of Yardley's charm came from her ingenuous personality. She wasn't technically naive, but she assumed people were being straight-up with her, which made her miss almost all sarcasm entirely—which was both Libby and Dex's stock-in-trade.

They walked along the side of the house, with the neighborhood as silent as a church. When they got to Yardley's car, parked at a haphazard angle, she opened the passenger door, obviously waiting for Tracy to hop right in. "I'll drive you home."

"My car's right *there*," Tracy said, not pointing out that Yardley would have had to carefully exit her own vehicle not to put a ding in the door. "This evening honestly didn't upset me much, Yardley. I'm perfectly able to drive myself."

"Come to my house," she said, gazing at Tracy with those deep-set, dark eyes. "You're not working tomorrow, so you don't need your car. Come on," she urged, really seeming to need this.

"All right." When you partnered with a woman who made relatively few demands, it was churlish to refuse a simple one.

Tracy got into the car and started to put her seatbelt on. The visor was down, and she flipped up the cover for the mirror, almost gasping at how she looked. When this whole fiasco had started, she'd just taken off her clothes to put on a suit for the swim Kendall had promised. In her haste to get dressed, she'd buttoned her shirt wrong, with the placket not matching up by a couple of inches. And hanging upside down for what seemed like hours had made her hair resemble a bird's nest, which was a very bad look. What a shit-show tonight had been.

Yardley got in and carefully adjusted all three of her mirrors. Given they were automatic, and set at the position Yardley had programmed, her weird little tic always wasted a couple of minutes' time. Normally, Tracy didn't mind, but tonight it made her grind her teeth. She spent a moment trying to convince herself to cut Yardley a break. Dealing with rapidly-changing situations wasn't her forte, and it was cruel to get angry at her for not doing something she was truly incapable of.

"Did you know Dexter was going to be there tonight?" Yardley asked, clearly forcing herself into a modulated tone.

Tracy gazed at the side of her face, wondering what was going on inside her head. "If I'd known, why would I have been in that room?"

"I'm asking a simple question. I don't want a question in return."

What the fuck? Tracy hadn't gotten the slightest impression Yardley was angry with her. If she had, she never would have gotten into the car. "I'm not sure why you've got that edge to your voice, but let me assure you that Kendall tricked us into having to talk. She knew I'd refuse to have Dex at Final Exercises, so she tried to force the issue. Do you honestly think I'd voluntarily spend the evening with Dex, given I didn't want to share the oxygen in Charlottesville on Saturday?"

"I don't want her here," she said stiffly.

"I don't, either. You have my blessing to put her on the next flight to LA."

Yardley turned to regard her for a moment. "I've never liked her. *Never.* From the day I started at Virtus, she's had it in for me."

Okay. This wasn't anger. This was long-held hurt feelings. Tracy could deal with that. "It's one weekend," she soothed. "You and I have known each other for a full year, and we haven't seen hide nor hair of Dex."

A flicker of a smile showed as she started up the car. "I like it when you sound country."

"I don't sound very country," Tracy insisted. "Now if you want to hear country…" She trailed off, knowing neither of them would ever listen to her mama rattling off her very long list of nonsensical, yet colorful expressions.

Yardley played with the damned rearview mirror one more time before backing up. "I believe you didn't plan this or want this, Tracy. So why was Dex nearly naked?"

"Uhm…I guess people would have considered her naked two hundred years ago, but an exercise top and Lycra shorts are widely accepted here in the twenty-first century. Especially on a warm night in your own home."

"Okay." She finally pulled out onto the street. When she stopped at the first dark intersection and looked both ways—twice, she finished up her thought. "Then why do you look like you got dressed in the dark? Is that how you went to work today?"

Despite how she'd acted so far tonight, Tracy truly was pretty easygoing. But that question pushed a button that made her temper start to heat up. "Ask the question. Don't beat around the bush."

Yardley gave her a quick glance. "I did ask a question. Your shirt's buttoned wrong, it's half-tucked in, and your zipper's nearly all the way down."

"It is not!" She grabbed at it, realizing that while the button was still fastened, the zipper had obviously been forced down while she'd been twisting around against the window frame.

"Then why do I know you're wearing pink and green striped underwear?"

"Jesus," she grumbled. "You're asking plenty of questions, but you're still not going for the one that's got you so irritated."

"I already did," she said primly. "I clearly asked if that's how you looked at work today. I implied nothing else."

"Then, no," Tracy said, refusing to play the game. "I did not go to work looking like this."

"Great. That's very good to know." Giving her another look, she said, "Given how you're acting, I assume you don't want to go to my condo."

"Thank you for asking about my intentions," Tracy said with exaggerated politeness. "I'd like to go back to Randy and Libby's to get my car. Then I can go home, where I won't annoy the fuck out of myself by continuing to imply questions I'm afraid to ask."

Yardley did an abrupt, wide swing on the quiet street, something so out of character that Tracy gasped. In a half-second they were headed right back to the Havens'. On the very short drive, Tracy kept reminding herself that Dex was not responsible for this really shitty night. But it was awfully hard to make herself believe that.

∞∞

Kendall was honestly unable to tell how upset Dex was. She was one of the most independent people she knew, and Kendall was certain she hadn't enjoyed being trapped in the pool house. But she'd gotten so into meditation and yoga that she rarely showed a great deal of emotion— positive or negative. That was probably good for her, but it often made her hard to read.

Kendall had no memory of the early years, but Nana had confided that Dex had once been beset with self-hatred and recriminations. Kendall was almost certain those years had been volatile, but both of her moms had tried to shield her from the stress. They still did, which was why she'd tricked them into at least being in the same room before they had to face each other at Final Exercises. Her intention had been to give them a neutral, private spot to at least attempt being polite to one another. Whether that had worked was a question Kendall didn't honestly have to ask. She'd be able to tell—probably by tomorrow night.

"So…" Dex said, staring at the door Tracy and Yardley had just walked out of. "It didn't occur to me this morning that by the end of the day Yardley Simpkins would be even less happy to see me than Tracy would. Life is a cornucopia just bursting with surprises, isn't it?"

"I don't know her very well, but Yardley looked like she wanted to kill you," Kendall agreed. "Shouldn't she have wanted to kill me?"

"I guess I bested you in that competition," Dex said, walking over to close the door. She grabbed a bottle of water and sat on the sectional, sticking her bare legs straight out in front of herself. "So tell me how you two came up with this foolproof plan." Her brow furrowed slightly. "I know you were in on this together."

31

Kendall sat next to Dex and rested her head on her shoulder. "It was my idea. Nana only helped by making the snack tray and donating a bottle of wine that I know Mom likes."

"I was perfectly willing to do more," Libby said, taking one of the stools by the counter. "But you had it all well in hand."

"When did Yardley enter the picture? She said it's their anniversary… I was afraid to ask of what." She gave Nana a grin. "Lesbians tend to celebrate a lot of anniversaries, and I was worried this one might be x-rated."

"I'm not usually skittish about that sort of thing," she said, looking quite thoughtful, "but I truly cannot picture Yardley doing anything in bed that one would want to *recall*, much less celebrate."

That made Dex laugh so hard her shoulder lifted up to dislodge Kendall's head. Dex and her grandmother could crack each other up for hours when something really hit them right.

"Let's not even think of the possibilities," Kendall said, her stomach starting to roil. "I'm certain this anniversary is a g-rated one. They met a year ago at some charity thing."

"Hmm. I can't picture them together, and that's after I saw them with my very own eyes." Dex gave Kendall a hearty slap on the leg. "I hate to be unkind, but your mom deserves better."

"Agreed. But Mom claims she loves her. She's dated other women, of course, but Yardley's the only one to stick around for more than a summer."

Libby picked up the bottle of wine and tilted it back and forth. "Did Tracy drink this whole thing?"

"You might not have noticed, but I never touch the stuff," Dex said, sometimes a little thin-skinned about her sobriety. "I hope she doesn't drink that much, that fast, on a routine basis…"

"She doesn't," Kendall assured her. "Those two can make a bottle of wine last for three days."

"Amateurs," Dex said, chuckling softly. "So what's with this dinner tomorrow?"

"Mom wanted to have a small celebration," Kendall said, "just for the family. But she didn't want to have to cook. So she made a reservation at a new place in town. Yardley has some weird food allergy, so arranging the whole thing took her a while. It's a fixed menu, by the way, so you have to choose between chicken or fish."

"Do we have to go?" Dex asked, sounding like a child. "Wouldn't you rather go somewhere we know we like? Somewhere we can order whatever we're in the mood for?"

"Yes, but Mom wants to do this, so I gave her my blessing. Be a team player." She poked Dex in the side, with her elbow getting a good amount of resistance. "How do you even have time to work? You must be in the gym all day."

Dex smiled at her. "Just an hour. It's not the time you devote, it's the quality"

Libby got up and pulled a glass from the cabinet, then filled it with ice water from a container kept in the fridge. "So? What did you think?" she asked, with her normal accent back in place. Kendall had no idea why she'd adopted such a syrupy drawl around Yardley, but it was now gone.

"About what?" Dex asked.

"About seeing Tracy, of course. Was it awful?"

"It was…surprising. But that was the point, wasn't it?" She gave Kendall a return poke in the side.

"I suppose," she said, with the sadness that had hit her earlier starting to return.

"Hey," Dex said, scooting around to face her. "I'm really sorry you heard us fighting."

"It's all right," Kendall said. "I just didn't know that mom had wanted to go to med school. It's really strange to hear that someone you think you know backwards and forwards has this whole other life you don't know about…"

Libby jumped in quickly. "You know your mom very, very well, honey. While it's true she thought she'd be able to go to med school, I personally couldn't see how that could ever work. She is essentially doing the job she wanted, and she didn't have to suffer through years of a residency. In my opinion, it all worked out for the best."

"Doesn't sound like Mom agrees," Kendall said, really feeling skittish about this.

"I can't know how she feels about her career," Dex said, "but I certainly wouldn't take anything we said to each other tonight too seriously. I think we were both getting out some feelings that got trapped a long, long time ago."

Kendall nodded. "I shouldn't have tricked you guys, given I couldn't possibly have known how you'd react. I just wanted you both at my graduation, and I knew I couldn't convince you to talk beforehand. I felt like you needed—help."

"I wish you weren't right about that, but you were," Dex admitted. "The good news is that your plan worked. There was no bloodshed, although Tracy certainly was being awfully cavalier about her safety for a while there." She tugged on Kendall's hair. "Locking her in here was pretty cruel, kiddo. Your mom has a little bit of claustrophobia."

"I didn't know…"

"She tried to get out by pushing herself through that tiny window, Kendall. I'm surprised you didn't hear her howl when she got stuck."

A stab of guilt hit her hard. "I was in the house, so I wouldn't have heard her if she'd been screaming."

Dex put her arm around her and leaned her head close. "I understand your desire to have your mom and me bury the hatchet. But I'm disappointed in you for not keeping tabs on us. If she'd really hurt herself, and we couldn't call for help…"

"I'm really sorry. It didn't occur to me that you'd *need* to get out. I screwed up."

"Locking people into a room in any situation isn't wise, honey. Like I said, I understand why you did it, but you would have felt awful if your mom had hurt herself."

"Lesson learned," Kendall said quietly. Why couldn't she have parents who yelled at her? Disappointing them was so much worse.

※❈❋

They'd all gotten settled around the pool when Kendall's text notifications started to go off repeatedly. She looked at her phone for a second, then said, "Got a little party sitch going on. You don't mind if I take off do you, Dex?"

"By all means. Are you coming back here afterwards?"

"Don't think so." She got up and moved over to kiss Dex's head. I'll come by in the morning. Cool?"

"Very. Have fun."

"Oh, I will. Good crowd's already gathered. Bye," she said, giving her grandparents a kiss as well.

"I had that level of energy when I was her age," Dex said, watching Kendall nearly bounce on the way into the house.

"No, you didn't," Libby said. "You had a baby keeping you up half the night."

"Oh, right. My timeline was off. I guess I should say that I had that level of energy before Kendall was born."

"Maybe more," Libby said thoughtfully.

A quiet snore caught their attention. "Randy? Wake up, sweetheart. Go on into bed," Libby said. "I'll take Muffin for her final walk of the night."

"Are you sure?" He looked pretty vacant from Dex's perspective. "You know I don't mind."

"Skedaddle, sweetheart. I'll be up in a bit."

"All right. I'm perfectly awake, but I'll give in—as usual." He lifted his hand in a small wave, then sauntered into the house.

"He's bone tired," Libby said, turning to Dex. "He just got back from a trip to Colorado yesterday, and he hasn't adjusted to the time change yet." Gentling her voice, she said, "How are you really feeling about tonight? I know you wouldn't say anything negative about Tracy while Kendall was here, but now that she's gone…"

"I have never spoken badly about Tracy, Mom, and I'm not in the mood to start now." She shrugged. "I assume we'll go back to our radio silence after this weekend…"

"Talk to me, sweetheart. I know that seeing her had to affect you."

Dex let herself think for a minute, gazing at her mother as she leaned over to put the dog on her lap. Dex had just seen her in March, but she'd been fighting a bad cold that weekend, and everything about her had seemed off. But now she was back to normal—upbeat, and in charge. You'd think that a woman who was married to a man who was a pretty big deal at a major corporation would take a backseat to him, but that had never been true for Libby.

Kind, sharply intelligent, generally easy-going, Dex knew she'd lucked out in the mom department. And her dad had lucked out as well. Libby was statuesque and elegant, a natural blond with classically beautiful features. Not to mention the ability to talk to anyone about anything. You could take her to a party where she didn't know a soul, and if you didn't keep an eye on her, the whole night could pass by without even a sighting. Dex had almost lost her once at a premiere, eventually finding her making arrangements to meet up with a couple of animators for an afterparty in Burbank.

"Well," Dex said, "I wasn't crazy about the format of the meeting, but I'm glad we were able to talk. It was much easier to do it here than it would have been at Final Exercises. So…overall I'm fine." She met her mother's eyes. "But it did make me feel a little…odd to have you be part of the scheme. Springing that on me seemed unkind," she said, choosing the adjective carefully.

"I can see that, and I'm sorry if I hurt you, sweetheart." She took in a breath. "My problem was that I knew Tracy wouldn't agree to meet. And if Kendall was going to trick her, I felt like it wouldn't be fair to give you the advantage."

"The advantage…"

"Yes. You'd have time to prepare yourself mentally, but Tracy wouldn't have." She gazed up at the stars for a moment, then said, "I've always tried to treat you and Tracy the same. I never wanted her to feel like I would automatically favor you."

"Well, you'd be forgiven if you did. You *are* my mother…" She was teasing, and knew that Libby would realize that.

"Proudly," she said, smiling. "But I'm the closest thing to a mother Tracy will ever have. I've always wanted to make it very clear that she can trust me."

"I'm sure she does. Well, I'm not really sure of anything when it comes to Tracy, but she'd be foolish if she didn't, and she's never been foolish. But…I still think you could have told me in advance. I'm an actress, for goodness sake. I could have easily made her believe I didn't know anything beforehand."

Libby cocked her head, gazing at Dex through narrowed eyes. "Could you really? I know you make your living with your lovely voice, but are you technically an actress…?"

"You know what I'll never get around here?"

"Bored?"

"A big head. You're supposed to be astounded by my talent. I've made millions of children weep."

"That's a very odd accomplishment, but I'm glad that making small children cry has been so lucrative for you, sweetheart. Working at Virtus would have driven you mad eventually, so I'm very glad you found that you had the gift for giving children nightmares."

Well used to the gentle teasing that had always been backed up by unlimited love, Dex got to her feet. "Time for that walk, Muffin."

"You'll take her? Sure you don't mind?"

"Of course not. It's only eight o'clock in my mind. Although each hour I was stuck in the pool house should have counted for two."

Libby stood up and ruffled her hair fondly. "You and Tracy sat in the same room for the first time in years and years, without bloodshed. That was an accomplishment."

"I know," she sighed. "But it took a lot out of me."

"Sure you can take the dog?"

"I think I can manage all five pounds of her. Come on, Muffin," she said, grasping the leash her mom handed her. "Want me to keep her in the pool house tonight?"

"I'd rather not upset her routine. I'll leave the back door open."

"Okay. I'll set the alarm. Is the code still my birthday?"

"Always will be." After kisses were exchanged, Dex let the little dog lead her toward the front of the house. When they rounded the corner, she saw a modest SUV in the drive. Muffin was as interested as she was, and Dex peered into the driver's side window to see Tracy, with the seat fully reclined, sound asleep.

"What should we do?" Dex asked Muffin. "Do we wake her up?"

The dog was no help at all, so Dex followed through with the walk. Muffin had a range of about a hundred feet, and they were back at the car in five minutes. "I think we've got to wake her up. If nothing else, she'll get a stiff neck from lying in that position."

She knocked at the window, quietly saying, "Tracy…Tracy."

"Sound sleeper," she commented, starting to knock harder. Her knuckles were aching by the time Tracy turned her head and blinked up at her, looking thoroughly confused.

Slowly, her seat moved to a more vertical position, and she rolled down the window. "I didn't trust myself to drive home after draining a whole damn bottle of wine."

"Where's Yardley?" Dex found herself unable to say the name without a certain distain.

"Home, I guess. I turned off my phone."

"Let's go," Dex said, opening the door. "I can run you home, or get you set up in the guest room in two seconds."

"How would you run me home? You'd have to keep my car to get back here."

"Then I could borrow my mom's car."

"Then I'd have to get back here to pick mine up tomorrow. Why go to so much trouble? I'm probably okay to drive now…"

"Is 'probably' good enough? If Kendall felt like you do at this minute, would you want her to drive?"

"Winning argument," she said, giving Dex a wry smile. After rolling up her window, she got out and tried to make herself more presentable, but she'd had a tough night, and her clothing underscored the point. "I feel like I've been rode hard and put away wet."

Dex tenderly coaxed a few hanks of hair to return to the proper side of her part. "You've looked worse." She smiled and amended. "I meant to say that you look just fine. Come on. Muffin's already excited about sleeping with you." As they walked around to the back yard, Dex said, "Want to talk about why you're here alone?"

"Nope."

"You *do* go on," she teased. Muffin's little muzzle was right up against the door as Dex opened it. The dog scampered in, leading the way up the stairs to the guest room.

"All set up for company," Dex said, observing a set of towels neatly folded on the bed. "I'll see if I have any T-shirts still in my room."

Tracy grasped her arm to hold her in place. "No need. Thanks much for the hospitality, Dex. Will you leave a note in the kitchen in case your parents are up before I am? I don't want your dad to shoot me."

"You know he couldn't hit the side of a barn with that shotgun. But I'll leave a note just the same." She wanted to hug her, the feeling so strong she could taste it. But their last hug had been an awfully long time ago, and Tracy had given no indication she'd changed her mind about her final words at their parting.

You're out of my life.

⊗⊗⊗

There was something kind of nice about being on West Coast time when all around you were tuned into the East Coast vibe.

After getting Tracy set up in the guest room, Dex had settled down onto a chaise by the pool. Being alone, outside, in the deep nighttime darkness was one of her favorite things, and being at her parents' let her indulge in a way she couldn't in LA. Of course, LA was a perfectly lovely place to sit outside at nearly any time of day, but it didn't have the sounds or the smells that Virginia had, and those were what soothed her.

The pool filter gurgled softly in the background, and she closed her eyes and tried to breathe in every possible scent.

Her father was quite the gardener, and since he'd stepped down as Senior VP for Governmental Affairs at Virtus earlier in the year, he'd had more time to devote to his hobby. Of course, since he was a lifelong workaholic, he'd immediately started to do contract work for the company. But he tried to keep that to only twenty hours or so a week, leaving him plenty of time to putter.

The stately, gently swaying dogwoods that surrounded the pool had been a terrible choice in many ways. Their leaves dropped early, leaving the pool filter gasping, their flowers made a righteous mess, and having tree roots near a water feature was almost begging for trouble. But the entire family was in agreement that planting the trees twenty years earlier had been a stroke of genius. They provided a good deal of lovely, light shade on a hot summer day, the leaves created beautiful shadows on the water, and if you squinted you could believe you were lying on the bank of a small, blue lake.

Two of the trees were now filled with lacy white flowers, and the other two sported big, pink, teacup-sized blooms that Dex was thrilled to see. Her father had taunted her with them when they were video chatting the previous week, and she'd been sure they would be spent by the time she arrived. Seeing them earlier that night had nearly made her tear up, and she felt a deep certainty that they were a harbinger of a great visit.

But being locked in a room with Tracy hadn't gotten the weekend off to a promising start. While Dex had known they'd see each other at the graduation, she assumed they'd wave politely from a good distance. But the distance had been nil tonight, especially when she had both of her hands on Tracy's butt. She still wasn't sure how she felt about the evening, with so many highs and lows that she knew it would take her a while to sort it all out. Of course, the weekend had just begun, so who knew how many more climbs and dips the roller-coaster would take.

Her gaze shifted down to the pink and white azaleas, also blooming up a storm. Sometimes she had to stop and remind herself that her move to LA had been the best for everyone. But despite its often perfect weather, the flora in LA was sadly lacking, and she found herself yearning for home the minute she learned the crocuses had broken through in the spring.

She would have scheduled her visit for a couple of weeks earlier, but Kendall's graduation took precedence. So since she'd skipped April, her favorite month, she'd decided to extend this visit to spend a good long time with her favorite daughter.

She still wasn't certain how long she'd stay, but booking a one-way fare gave her all of the flexibility she needed. She had no jobs scheduled until a project set for August, and was seriously thinking of backing out of even that one to free up her entire summer. The gap in her schedule had been a choice. A choice she was lucky enough to be able to make. She had enough money in the bank to sustain her lifestyle for quite a while, so if she decided to indulge in the pleasures of a summer in Richmond, she didn't have to worry about a thing—except having to keep a wide berth from Tracy and Yardley, a pairing she had an impossible time understanding. She'd had friends who had made very odd choices in their romantic lives, but this one might have taken the very bland cake.

CHAPTER THREE

IN DEX'S OPINION, EIGHT IN THE morning was the perfect time to hop out of bed. She bustled around in the small kitchen, getting some coffee on to brew. After gulping down a cup, she considered going out by the pool to meditate for twenty minutes—her morning minimum. But when she peeked outside, she saw the lawn service getting ready to fire up their mower. Annoyed at having them start so early, she took a look at the sun's position, then realized it was eleven—not so early at all.

She satisfied herself by placing her yoga mat on the kitchen floor, then got into a lotus position to clear her mind. But she found it was taking her longer than normal. Thoughts kept racing through her head: images of the night before, memories of her and Tracy's Final Exercises, the silliness of their alma mater insisting on calling graduation by a name no one understood, even her empty belly. But after focusing on the burr of the commercial mower for a while, she finally got her restive mind to settle down. Some time later, when she took her final deep, cleansing breath and opened her eyes, she saw that she'd been still for over a half hour—quite an accomplishment with the lawn service guys blowing spent blossoms around with a leaf blower that could have been heard in DC.

When Dex opened the door, she felt like she could nearly bathe in the sweet, fresh air that caressed her body. In LA she was just blocks from the ocean in Manhattan Beach, a spot most people would rank higher in desirability than Richmond, Virginia. But the air near her house, although clean and salty, wasn't her thing. She loved the scent and the feel of the heavy, humid breeze of an early summer morning in Virginia.

The lawn guys were packing up, so she carried her mat over to the pool. Instead of using the deck, she set up on the newly shorn grass, preferring a little cushioning when she could get it.

Even though she'd been working out religiously for ten years, her joints often reminded her that she had to give them as much gentle care as she could.

Her warmup was now rote, and she started to whip through it with very little thought. She was just getting into it when a shadow blocked the sun. Looking up, she saw Kendall gazing at her speculatively.

"Got another mat?

"No, but I'm sure we could find something that would work." She sat down to take a good look at her. "I didn't space on plans we'd made, did I?"

"Nope." She sat down in the grass, wearing a similar outfit, but her yoga pants went all the way to her knees. Her thin top was a pretty shade of green, kind of like a new leaf. "I'm going to hang out here for the weekend. The vibe at home isn't great."

"Is your mom still angry—?"

"Yes, but not at me. I'm not sure what happened, but Yardley rolled up at nine this morning, loaded for bear."

"Loaded for bear," Dex said, chuckling. "Is that one of your mom's expressions?"

"I guess so," she said, shrugging. "I never know where anything comes from."

Dex knew she should keep her curiosity to herself, but now that the bandage had been ripped off a wound that had been consciously ignored for nearly twenty years, she found herself desperate for details. "So? Are they fighting?"

"They were fight-whispering, which is the worst. I packed up my stuff and hit the road. But I left a note," she added, batting her eyes at Dex.

"Mmm. Maybe you should double-check later. If your mom was expecting you to stay home…"

"We'll see. I don't know what time she got in last night, but she seemed to have a hangover this morning. She had that squinty-eyed thing going on."

Dex almost informed her that Tracy had stayed with them, but she didn't want to reveal anything Tracy wanted to keep to herself. Instead, she focused on the part of Kendall's comment that concerned her. "Is that…common? The hangover, I mean."

Kendall reached over and tugged on Dex's hair. "No, it's not. She doesn't drink as much as I do. You don't have to worry about her."

"Now I'm worried about you!"

"No need. I've never, ever gone on a binge, I never do shots, I've never thrown-up from drinking. I'm practically a model for moderation."

"When it comes to alcohol," Dex added.

"Yup. Weed has always been my thing."

"No vaping," Dex said sternly. "You promised. Edibles only."

Kendall smiled at her. "It just so happens that the thing you want me to do is the thing I like to do. Nothing better than popping a gummy and waiting for it to hit me. It's always a surprise," she added, chuckling.

"Hey, don't make it sound like I *want* you to do edibles. I just think they're the least harmful way to ingest the least harmful mind-altering substance." She scooted off her mat and tossed it to Kendall. "Today, let's alter our minds through our bodies. Follow my lead."

"No chance of that, but I'll give it a whack."

෧෧෧

Dex and Kendall spent the afternoon as they often did, watching some old, binge-worthy TV. Kendall was currently stuck on *Parks and Rec,* with Dex pondering why she considered a show that had been on not long ago an oldie. But kids Kendall's age had very odd notions of what "old" meant. It seemed that around thirty days was the sell-by date for popular culture.

Kendall lay sprawled out across the sectional, with her feet in Dex's lap. For nearly twenty-two years Dex had been the designated foot-rubber, and as she worked some nice-smelling lotion into the baby-soft skin, she reminded herself to enjoy the experience. Some day, Kendall

45

would have some goofy guy sitting next to her, and she'd be embarrassed to have her old mom playing with her tootsies.

Kendall laughed hard at a line, the sound always so cheerful. "I love April. That deadpan look she gives Andy cracks me up."

"Oh, yeah, Aubrey Plaza's got great timing." She pulled on a little toe. "So…what can you tell me about your plans for China?"

"Not much. Other than the fact that I'm going, I don't have a lot more to say."

"Ahh… So you're just going to pack a rucksack and hit the road. Unencumbered by even a familiar face."

Kendall laughed. "I'm taking more than a rucksack, if that means backpack, and I'm not going alone. That wouldn't work for me."

"Okay. Then who are you taking?"

"I'm not *taking* anyone, but I'm working on the other girls in my major, hoping I can talk one of them into traveling with me." She showed that cunning smile again. "They're all at least half ethnic Chinese, and I'm hoping I'll fit in a little better if my traveling companion looks like she might be a local."

"You've got this all figured out, don't you." Dex watched her daughter's gaze move quickly around the screen. She got into a show more deeply than anyone Dex had ever met. Even as a tiny baby, she'd stop crying in a second if you turned on the TV—to any show in the world.

"I've been planning this for a year, so…yeah. It's time to explore the big, blue marble."

"But you're not really planning on doing that. You're going to a single country to teach English."

Kendall shrugged. "I'm sure we'll travel around. You can find super-cheap flights all over Asia."

As it always did when Kendall talked about her very vague plans, Dex's stomach started to ache. "Have you made *any* concrete plans? Like choosing which city to go to? Booking a flight?"

"Nope. I've only got two people who I might have a chance of convincing to tag along, but they both want to be where their grandparents are. Problem is, I don't want to go to either Beijing or Shenzhen. I'm leaning toward Nanning."

"Never heard of it. Will I like the food?" She raked her fingernails across Kendall's instep. "Because I'm going to be on your doorstep within a month—at the latest."

Laughing while she pushed away, Kendall said, "It's mostly Cantonese, which isn't your favorite. But there's like eight million people in the metro area. Same size as New York. A lot of ethnic Thai and Vietnamese live there, since it's close to Viet Nam," she added, as though Dex had just forgotten that.

"Why does Nanning appeal to you?"

Smiling, Kendall said, "It never snows, and I've always wanted to see a monsoon. Seriously," she insisted when Dex gave her a suspicious glance.

"A monsoon sounds like fun—when you're considering it from Virginia."

"Probably true," she said, her pensive expression showing she was at least considering Dex's point. "But I won't know for sure until I'm in the middle of one, will I."

⁂

That afternoon, it started to rain the minute they got into Kendall's car. "Will you drive?" she asked, batting her eyes at Dex.

"I guess I can."

"Trade," she said, jumping out of the car to run around to the passenger side.

Dex took her spot and clicked her seatbelt. "Why did we do that? You didn't just pop a gummy, did you?"

"No!" she said, laughing like that was a ridiculous question, which was slightly soothing. "I don't want to get my new shoes wet. This way you can drop me off in front."

"What would you do if I wasn't here?"

"Carry my shoes in my hand, then try to dry my feet before I went into the restaurant. See how much easier this is?"

"For you," Dex said, giving her an exaggerated glare. "I've got nice shoes, too."

"But yours are dark leather. If they're wet it won't be obvious." She patted her leg. "Trust me. I've thought this through."

"Clearly," Dex agreed, often feeling like a younger sister just trying to keep up.

The restaurant wasn't too far away, and it was in a fairly residential neighborhood, which made it kind of perfect for parking. After Kendall hopped out, Dex found a spot about two blocks away. She raced for the restaurant, with the flimsy umbrella Kendall left for her not doing much more than keeping her hair dry.

The front door to the place was wide open, with a heavy velvet curtain giving the restaurant a welcoming, vaguely homey look. Dex parted it and stepped in, finding herself right behind Yardley Simpkins.

"*Lord*," Yardley said to the hostess, looking exasperated. "L-o-r-d. Tracy. It's a big group," she added. "I think eight or nine…"

"Haven," Dex said, leaning over her shoulder. "The reservation will be under Haven-Lord."

"Ahh, here we go," the woman said, smiling at Dex. "I'll show you both to your party."

"Do you really not know your fiancée's name?" Dex asked. As the words left her mouth, she realized she'd said them in a way almost guaranteed to annoy. That hadn't been her intent, but…there it was.

"I'm well aware of Tracy's name, and any decent reservation system would recognize it. What kind of a system requires a middle name to find a table?"

Dex just nodded, then peeled off to the left as soon as she spotted the seat she wanted—between her grandmother and Kendall. "Here I am," she said, bending to kiss Grammy's cheek and give her grandfather a hug when he half-stood. "Wet shoes and all."

"You look fantastic," Grammy said, smiling at her with delight. Dex took her hand and held it gently.

"If I ever looked half as good as you—"

"You might be able to finally land a girlfriend," Grammy said, laughing at her own joke. Dex laughed too, finding her grandmother funny even when the jibe was pointed at her.

⁂

Refusing a drink when their server passed by, Tracy downed some more water, still not fully hydrated from guzzling so damn much wine the night before. Her day hadn't been a total wreck, but she'd definitely had better ones.

Apparently, Yardley had thought better of her snippy tone of the night before, and had gone to the house at six a.m to apologize. Of course, Tracy hadn't been there, and she'd had her phone turned off. After Yardley had driven all the way out to the Havens', whatever scheme she'd concocted had been confirmed to her annoyingly suspicious mind. She'd been waiting on the porch when Tracy returned home, and after Kendall had taken off like a thief in the night they'd spent an hour yelling at each other—a first. But they'd finally sorted things out. Or at least it had seemed like they had. It was hard to tell with this new, volatile Yardley.

The fight had left Tracy unsettled and cranky. She wasn't exactly angry, but if Yardley had to go on one of her fairly frequent business trips, Tracy would not have minded. But no trips were planned, and when Yardley sat down next to her, Tracy could tell in one second flat that she was still out-of-sorts.

"Well, that was embarrassing," she said, with her normally fair skin flushed.

Tracy was still angry enough that she didn't actually want to know what had gotten to Yardley this time, but she couldn't completely ignore the comment. So she gave her a raised eyebrow, showing only the mildest interest.

"Why would I have to use your middle name to have the hostess know where you were seated?"

Tracy gazed at her for a second, puzzled. "Why would you or anyone else even know my middle name? I stopped using it decades ago."

49

"You use it every day!" Yardley was staring at her like she'd lost her mind.

"You just tell me the last time I told anyone my name was Tracy Lu. I bet my own mother doesn't remember it."

"Haven," Yardley said, enunciating both syllables. "Your middle name is Haven."

"I don't have a middle name, Yardley. I dropped it when I legally changed to Haven-Lord when Kendall was born. This shouldn't be a surprise. Why are you making it into a thing?"

An arm settled around Tracy's shoulders, with Randy clearly having heard the tension sparking in the air. He was the perfect chosen-father, always ready to shield her from the mildest threat. Tracy reached up and gripped his hand, then spent a moment wondering what had gotten into Yardley so thoroughly. The woman hadn't even said hello to anyone before she took her seat. It should not have taken a genius to see that the Havens were very social, very polite people. Yardley was never going to fit in if she acted like she was there to meet Tracy for a solo date.

They were going to have to go over a clear set of guidelines for how to interact with the family. That might have seemed like an odd way of moving through life, but it worked. Yardley had very few instincts about social interactions, but she was eager to fit in, and did her best to memorize any tips Tracy could give her.

Now Yardley was staring at her like she was thoroughly puzzled. "You're saying your name is…hyphenated? If we were seated in alpha order, you'd be with the H's?"

"Yes. That's how the alphabet works." She scowled at her for a second. "I'm sure I've told you my name, for god's sake."

"I thought you did that for Kendall. So you'd have the same name."

"I did. We did. We're all three Haven-Lords."

"Why did Haven have to come first? You're the one who had the baby."

Tracy leaned over to place her lips right next to Yardley's ear, with Randy's arm falling away. Whispering hotly, she said, "I'm well aware. For the record, Dex didn't care what order we went in. But I wasn't about to be called Lord-Haven. That would have made me sound like I was trying to sneak into the royal family."

"Ridiculous," Yardley grumbled. "The whole world has to revolve around the..." She at least had the manners to say the name at the quietest possible volume. "Havens. You were never married, you lived together a *very* short time, and Dexter barely lifted a hand in raising your child."

"Outside," Tracy snapped, standing to grasp the shoulder of Yardley's jacket, tugging hard.

Randy looked up, clearly startled. His mouth moved to ask a silent question. "Need help?"

Tracy bent to kiss his head, whispering, "I'm fine. Thanks." Then she marched through the restaurant, past the pleasant woman at the front desk, through the curtain, to stand under the narrow awning that fronted the building. The annoying rain splattered her shins as it hit the sidewalk, adding to the perfection of the afternoon. Yardley didn't look so full of herself now. Eyes downcast, she plastered herself up against the window next to Tracy.

"Listen to me." She had to work on keeping her voice quiet enough so the woman at the desk couldn't hear her through the curtain. "You know almost nothing about how it was between Dex and me."

"I think I—"

"You truly don't. The only reason we didn't marry was because we *couldn't*. Dex wasn't on the birth certificate because the state prohibited it, and she's not Kendall's legal parent because the state went out of its way to prohibit second-parent adoptions. All of that bullshit was rammed through the legislature just to make gay people feel like shit!"

"I'm gay too, you know. I fully realize whatever progress we've made has been recent."

"Well, you don't know anything about how Dex felt to mother a child that the state intentionally prohibited her from claiming. It was unconscionable. That's why *I* decided we'd all have the same name. That let Dex take her to the pediatrician, and all of the other things a legal parent does. I'm *very* glad we did it." She poked Yardley right in the chest. "Don't try to give me a hard time about something you know nothing about."

"I've seen Dex in action, so I know quite a bit about her. You wouldn't think she was such a star if she'd finagled a promotion right out from under *you*!"

"Dex doesn't need to finagle a thing," Tracy snapped. "Good things just happen to her, but that doesn't make her a bad person." She backed up and spent a moment gazing at Yardley. "I don't understand why you're jealous of a woman you'll probably have to spend ten minutes a year talking to."

"I'm not jealous!"

Tracy glared at her for what felt like a solid minute. "If you can't see that you're jealous, you're blind."

"I am *not* jealous," she said, her voice low and firm. "I'm also not going to be lectured. I've devoted this entire weekend to Kendall, even though it's clear she doesn't care if I'm here or not. It's bad enough that tomorrow's supposed to be eighty-five and rainy. We'll be outside for hours in the heat, all for a kid who's ambivalent about my presence."

Tracy hadn't wanted to bring up the seating arrangements until the last minute. But there was no reason to pussy-foot around about them now. Might as well let Yardley vent her spleen all at once. "You're going to be in air-conditioned comfort. Kendall only has four tickets. Two for her grandparents, one for me and—"

"One for Dexter."

"That's correct. Dex is her mother, and she deserves to be close."

"And I deserve…what?"

Tracy only considered her answer for a second. "You deserve a day to do whatever you want. I'll call you when Dex leaves town, which I assume will be Sunday or Monday. Maybe we can get back to normal when your panties aren't in a twist."

"You're banning me?" she said, slack-jawed.

"Of course not. But I'm not going to fight in front of my family, and I can see this isn't finished. I think we both need a few days to cool off."

"Oh, I'm cool. I'm plenty cool," she snapped, turning to stalk away, with the rain streaking her mid-blue jacket in seconds. Tracy watched her leave, on the verge of tears, then turned sharply when something came into her field of vision.

"Oh, it's you," she said, truly not wanting to face Dex at that moment.

"I didn't mean to spy on you, but the server wants to put the order in. I pegged you for the chicken, but I had no idea what Yardley wanted."

Tracy looked up at her, always surprised that Dex was only an inch or an inch and a half taller. "Screw the special menu. We can order whatever we want. Yardley's alpha-gal syndrome is no longer an issue."

"Alpha what?"

"Yardley's allergic to mammals," Tracy said, purposefully ignoring the silly grin that had quickly settled onto Dex's mouth.

※※※

Tracy peeled away to walk directly to the bathroom after they'd gone back inside. The space was generous, with a separate area for checking your makeup. Short stools faced a wide mirror, and she sat down to comb her hair, which the humidity tended to make flyaway.

Just a moment later, Grammy entered the room and put her purse on the narrow counter. "Now, *this* is what a powder room should look like. David and I are going to have to come to this place often. An interesting menu, excellent cocktails, and a proper rest room."

"Thanks, Grammy. I agree this place is very promising. We'll just have to see if the food lives up to the setting."

"I couldn't help but notice your fiancée's not by your side, sweetheart. Has Yardley been called away?"

She said that so matter-of-factly. Like it was perfectly common for some business emergency to come up on a Friday night.

"Honestly? We're not…getting along very well at the moment. It's best that she left, but I wish she hadn't had to."

"Mmm. In sixty-seven years of marriage, David and I have probably had over a hundred of those kinds of spats." She laughed softly. "I recall none of them. We've been getting along better and better as we age. Or maybe we just don't hear the comments the other whispers in a bout of pique."

Tracy laughed along with her. "Maybe I should take to wearing ear plugs."

"Never a bad idea, sweetheart." She put her hand on Tracy's shoulder. "I have no idea what's gone on between you and Yardley, but if I had to attend a dinner with David's first love, I'm sure I'd be less than pleasant. You might want to give Yardley a little room to have a tantrum or two."

"Gramps had a first love?" Tracy asked, having always assumed they were college sweethearts.

"I'm afraid he did. He'd been in the ROTC, and he was sent for special training in North Carolina. I suppose they thought the Korean Conflict might get much worse..." She blinked a few times as she gazed at herself in the mirror, then touched her perfectly arranged pale blonde hair, making sure the pins in her chignon were set. Tracy suspected she ran by the salon on a daily basis, but she had no proof of that.

"Anyway, the girl, *Norma*, wasn't willing to wait for David to return. I met him when he came back to campus the following year, still broken-hearted." She waited a beat, usually having perfect timing. "For two shakes of a lamb's tail, that is. I never would have met him if he hadn't been gone for a year, so I feel oddly fond of the Korean Conflict." She looked at Tracy for a moment. "That's probably not something I should say aloud, is it. Millions died..."

"It'll be our secret," Tracy said, helping Grammy to her feet. "Thanks for the pep talk," she added, bending to kiss her cheek. "Now I'm going to wash my hands, then go eat my lamb—without having to hear how one bite of it might kill Yardley."

"Might what?"

"Long story. If you're interested in Yardley's food allergy, I'll tell you after dinner."

"Oh, my, there are so many other interesting topics we could cover..."

"I couldn't agree more, Grammy. Let's go see how many stars this place merits."

⊗⊗⊗

The grand and great-grandparents departed after dinner, and Tracy certainly couldn't blame them. Driving over an hour to get to Charlottesville, only to listen to a valedictory address by a musician she was sure they'd never heard of just wasn't the kind of thing any of them were into. But she was, and she was glad to see that Dex was equally committed.

The three of them drove up together, the first time they'd been in the same vehicle since Kendall was a child. Now the child was driving them, and Tracy had more than one moment where time seemed to wrap around her in a non-linear fashion.

"Do you remember who our valedictory speaker was, Dex?" Tracy turned slightly to see her.

"I remember he was an old white guy. He seemed like a grouch. Actually...I think he was a professional grouch. I'd never heard of him, but I think he was pretty famous."

"That day was a blur. I was mostly trying to block out hearing Kendall scream 'mommy!' every two seconds. Your parents nearly had to wrap duct tape around her to get her to sit still."

"You could pay me back by screaming 'Kendall' tonight. I wouldn't mind," Kendall said, showing a sunny smile.

"That would be interesting," Dex said thoughtfully. "Most of what I recall is being angry you didn't get class honors for passing all of your finals. Doing that while toilet-training a toddler should have merited some kind of award."

"I did more than pass!"

"Agreed. You kicked ass. And just ten days later we celebrated our little bundle of joy's second birthday. Best month ever."

"That's so hard to imagine," Kendall said thoughtfully. "You two were, for all intents and purposes, married, with a toddler, when you were my age. I don't know what I'd do if I was in your situation."

55

"You'd do just fine," Tracy said, patting her gently. "You've got grit."

"Not much of it. I still cry like a baby when I hurt myself."

"Only when you hurt yourself badly," Tracy insisted. "It has to be at least a grade-two sprain for the tears to come."

"I can vouch for that," Dex said. "And I'm also certain that you'd do just fine if you decided to have a baby. It's easy!" she said, clearly joking. "Well, actually giving birth sucked for your mom, but it was all sunshine and roses for me."

"It didn't suck for me, either," Tracy said. "Horribly painful? Yes. Interminable labor? Yes. An episiotomy that itched and ached for weeks? Definitely. But it didn't suck." She rested her hand on Kendall's shoulder for a few moments. "The day you were born was the best day of my life."

"Aww…you're both going to make me cry." Kendall cleared her throat, seeming like she was already at the crying stage. "It means so much to me to have you both here. This weekend is turning out better than I could have hoped for."

"I'll admit I made yesterday rougher than it had to be," Tracy said. "But I'm proud of us. The Haven-Lords definitely have grit." She turned to gaze at Dex again, amazed at how normal it seemed to have her sitting in the backseat. Life was a series of constant surprises—if you were lucky.

⧉

Tracy was feeling decidedly upbeat when Kendall dropped her off at home. While it was still extremely strange to have a very adult, very sober Dex back in the fold, she'd grown used to her amazingly quickly. Of course, that was partially because Dex was being so mature, and so remarkably polite about the whole thing. Tracy was sure she wouldn't have been so kind if Dex had been the one to put up a stone wall between them, refusing to crack it open even a chink. But Dex acted like they'd lost touch for no good reason, and were now happily joining together to celebrate Kendall's milestone.

If Tracy had been asked how Dex would behave, she would have guessed the outcome fairly accurately. Dex had always been and would always be a well-mannered Southern woman. Even if she thought you were a total asshole, you would likely never know for sure.

Her musings had muted her awareness of her surroundings, and Tracy flinched when she heard a car door close.

"Sweetheart," Yardley called out, dashing across the street, still wet from the night's earlier rain.

Tracy was just about out of gas. While Dex had been on her very best behavior, it was still draining to be around someone you'd parted with so dramatically. But Yardley was her fiancée, and that put her in a different category. A category that required more patience.

"Hello," Tracy said, warily. Even though she was willing to listen to Yardley's thoughts, she wasn't going to engage with her if she was still acting irrationally.

Yardley came to a stop, still at least ten feet away. "Are we speaking?"

Tracy gave her a long, assessing look. Yardley usually seemed like a district attorney, a public health official, or a seasoned aide to a senator. Someone who knew her stuff, and wasn't afraid of voicing an opinion, but who didn't need or want the limelight. She gave off the aura of a very adept, important background player. Tonight…Tracy couldn't get a good read on her. Probably because her behavior had been so out-of-character. When someone's actions took you by surprise, their follow-up was likely to be unpredictable, too.

"I wasn't happy with how you behaved tonight, Yardley, but it wasn't an extinction-level event." She tried to show some affection through her smile. "Are you still angry with me?"

The relief that flooded her expression was actually kind of cute. "I wasn't angry with you," she said, the words rushing out in a second. "I was just… I've been feeling very out-of-the-loop, and having Dexter show up has brought up all sorts of things…" She stopped, with her features slowly going slack. "I have no idea what's going on with me."

Tracy gave her a wry smile. "I can relate. I keep feeling like the last eighteen years haven't happened, but then I look—*up*—at my daughter and realize they most definitely have."

"Can I come in?"

"Sure." Tracy extended her hand, and Yardley took it with obvious relief. "Do we need to go over what happened?" She squeezed Yardley's hand briefly. "I'd rather not…"

"All I want to say is that I apologize. Jealousy isn't common for me, but it's obvious that's what I was feeling. I regret making a scene. Actually, I regret the whole evening—and last evening, too."

"It's all right. I think everyone is under some extra pressure." They started to climb the few steps to the porch. "That will continue to grow tomorrow, I assume. The graduation's going to be hard for me, and having a big party is stressful, too. You're going to have to bear with me."

Tracy took out her keys and got the front door open. After they stepped inside, Yardley wrapped her in a soothing hug before she could get the door closed.

Letting her guard drop, Tracy soaked up the comfort Yardley could usually be relied upon to deliver—just like a faithful pet. If they could both chill a little, and let their affection show, things were going to be just fine—even with Dex temporarily clouding the picture.

⁓⁓⁓

Even though they'd been sleeping together for the better part of a year, Yardley kept almost nothing at the house. Her little kit of a pair of pajamas, a toothbrush, her preferred soap, and a wide-toothed comb was kept in the closet, and when she took the little bundle into the bath Tracy was oddly reassured. Yardley was the one who needed a great deal of structure and habit, but Tracy had to admit she'd grown to like the patterns. Being able to rely on someone to do the same things the same way was soothing in ways that surprised her.

A few minutes later, Yardley emerged, looking neat as always. Hair combed, cheeks pink from a good wash, perfectly-fitted pajamas properly draped over her broad shoulders. Their eyes met, and Tracy started to smile when Yardley did. She patted the other side of the bed while tossing the sheet away. "Come on in."

With a contented smile, Yardley slid into bed and lay on her back. As Tracy rolled over toward her, Yardley slipped an arm under her head.

With a sigh, Tracy put her arm across her waist and snuggled close. "Today took a lot out of me," she said. "I feel like the day was thirty hours long."

"I know," she soothed. When she bent her arm, Tracy tumbled against her body, feeling like she'd been wrapped in a safe, protective cocoon. The skittish, irascible woman who had appeared at the restaurant was gone, replaced by the very comforting soul Tracy had learned to trust and rely on. She'd been looking for a cool, calming, predictable presence in her life since the day she'd been born, and the little blip that had flashed across the radar screen earlier that evening was just a freak thunderstorm that had completely cleared out. Now there was nothing but clear skies in the forecast as she felt her body relax from head to toe.

⁂

Tracy stood at her front door the next morning, with her arms tucked tightly around Yardley's waist. "Are you sure this is how you want to spend your day?"

"Definitely. You know I'm not much of a cook, but I'm very, very good at getting things organized. By the time you return, you'll think a professional caterer had been here."

"I've bought *everything*, Yardley. Truly. If you can just make up some platters of veggies and cheese and put the dip in bowls…"

"Everything will be ready. I'll put the umbrellas up, sweep the patio, and arrange the chairs you rented into nice groupings. When you get home, we'll fire up the grill and be able to start cooking."

"Oh, Randy was already here to get the fire started. His friend will be along at some point to put the meat on. Neither one of them likes help," she added, making that crystal clear.

"Got it. Once you're home, I'll sit on the sidelines until it's time to clean up. Then I'll get right on it." She smiled, with the haunted look her eyes had carried the day before entirely gone. "No one ever wants to fight me to clean up."

"Thank you," Tracy sighed, hugging her tightly. "I feel less stressed already." She pulled away and gently touched Yardley's cheek. "Are you

59

sure you're not being this thoughtful just so you don't have to hear us all singing the 'Good Ole Song?' I know your little Blue Devil heart has a hard time hearing us proclaim how great we are."

"I could handle it," she said, with her gentle smile showing. "It's kind of like when someone who normally rides the bench comes in and nails a three-pointer. You know they're not going to take your roster spot, so you can afford to be magnanimous."

Tracy gave her a slap on the butt, then stuck up the index and middle finger of her right hand, while pointing the same fingers of her left to the ground, creating a VA. "Get ready for a house full of Hoos, sweetheart. Love you."

"Love you too. Give Kendall my best."

"Will do," Tracy said, tossing her keys into the air on the short walk to her car. Her mood was a hundred percent better than it had been just twelve hours earlier. A thoughtful, rational decision to sweep the bad feelings away without further discussion had been the perfect choice. All of the resolution, with none of the strife.

❧

After a long drive, distant parking, a shuttle bus, confusing security lines, and a humid morning that promised a thunderstorm, they had Kendall where she needed to be. Once they found their seats, Dex was finally able to relax. She was on the aisle, with Tracy next to her, her mom to Tracy's right, then her dad. Her grandparents were inside, watching the ceremony from their seats in an air-conditioned room, and Yardley was, thankfully, elsewhere. Now all they had to do was get the show on the road so they didn't get caught in a downpour.

Regrettably, that wasn't really how universities handled events. Rushing never seemed to be on the agenda.

Tracy was chatting away with Libby, seeming like that was their norm. They'd gotten along great from the start, and Dex was honestly thrilled to see that their relationship had grown and deepened even more through the years. It didn't seem like a mother/daughter dynamic. Instead, they appeared to be close friends who found the same things funny, liked the same foods, had a penchant for sappy romantic comedies, and current literary fiction. Dex had learned that they sometimes traveled together, sneaking away for long weekend trips so Libby could work on her extensive genealogy quest. Dex had been thrilled to learn that Tracy seemed to enjoy traveling all over the south to take photos of old tombstones, since Dex might have been called to assist if she hadn't.

Dex turned around once again, seeing the graduates jamming together to take their walk along The Lawn, many of them holding massive mylar balloons. Kendall had one, too, but she swore it was solely so they could pick her out in the crowd. It was a big orange K, and Dex thought it would probably be a help, since most kids carried cartoon or action figures.

The band had been playing Pomp and Circumstance for a good ten minutes, and Dex was about to ask them to vary the selection when the color guard finally started down the steps of the Rotunda. In a flash, all of the guests were on their feet, each of them straining to catch a glimpse of their beloved graduate.

Tracy didn't seem to understand that Kendall wasn't going to pass by for a while, since she was on her tip-toes, trying to see over the heads of the very tall people behind them. She gasped and grabbed Dex's arm, squeezing hard. "Is that her?"

"I think she would have mentioned that she was carrying the standard," Dex said, unable to see how Tracy thought the average-sized girl with fairly dark hair was their child.

"Oh, she might be the valedictorian for all I know. She tells you more than she ever does me."

Dex thought that was probably true. It wasn't that Kendall was closer to her. That wasn't accurate in the least. But talking on the phone seemed to be easier for the kid than looking you in the eye. Some of their best talks had been when Dex was driving back to Manhattan Beach from Burbank or Hollywood, with Kendall chattering away like a magpie, making the trip seem much faster than it really was.

When the color guard reached the seating area, the band launched into the *Star Spangled Banner* and everyone—or most everyone—joined in. Dex wondered if the crowd at Berkeley, where she'd wanted Kendall to matriculate, was as overtly patriotic.

She'd been sure Kendall's very progressive political ideas, as well as her desire to learn about China's vast and deep history, would be a much better fit at a school in California. But Kendall always went her own way, and she'd only applied to three places—a shockingly low number, in Dex's opinion. She'd gotten into all three, and even though Oberlin or Wellesley had seemed better choices to Dex, Kendall hadn't hesitated to head to UVA. Dex was almost sure Kendall had simply wanted to follow in the family footsteps, and when you thought about it, that wasn't such a bad thing. Today, her child would become a fourth-generation Hoo, which really did thrill Dex.

Finally, the procession of graduates reached the crowd, and the excitement level went way, way up. Dex couldn't recall what order they'd gone in when she'd graduated, but she recalled it being more organized. Today, people from every major were mixed up, with Ph.D. candidates intermingled with masters and bachelors. Some kids wore only a black gown and a black mortarboard, with no honors or affinity cords or stoles. Others had added every possible flourish, each making their personal statement about the whole endeavor.

It took forever, but Dex finally spotted a big orange K in the distance. It was shiny Mylar, and as it got closer, the clouds parted for a minute or two, with the weak sun hitting the balloon, making it gleam. "There she is!" Dex called out, leaning over so her father could hear.

Tracy's hand was on Dex's arm again, surely leaving a bruise. But she didn't care. The most important person in her world, her little cookie, was just a few feet away, looking positively radiant. Dex was desperate to pull her from the crowd and hug her until she squealed, but she'd promised herself she'd behave. They'd have plenty of time to gush over the new graduate later.

Tracy must not have made the same vow, because she elbowed Dex in the side after she'd reached out and slapped Kendall's raised hand when she walked by.

"She saw me!" she said, elated by that tiny bit of contact.

That was exactly what every one of the last seven or eight years had felt like to Dex. Just seconds of joyous connection as Kendall purposefully pulled away to make her own way in the world. It was undisputed that her doing that made it clear they'd done a damn fine job of raising her to be independent. But sometimes Dex wished they'd helicoptered the hell out of the kid so she'd never, ever want to strike out on her own.

❈❈❈

The speeches were kind of interminable, even though they were limited. The whole point, Tracy knew, was to have the graduates walk past their families, while being cheered for wildly. No names were called. No diplomas were in hand. It was simply a tradition that the university had kept in place even as the number of graduates grew and grew and grew.

Finally, they all got to their feet again to sing the "Good Ole Song." She'd been dreading it, knowing she couldn't get through it without sobbing. But if you couldn't sob when your only child graduated from your alma mater, what in the hell were you waiting for?

The band began to play the opening strains of *Old Lang Syne*, to which some enterprising students in the nineteenth century had appended new lyrics, and she caught Dex's smile, one that seemed full of old memories. Everyone slipped an arm around the person next to them, and they swayed as they began to sing, with Tracy feeling not the sadness she'd expected, but the glee of celebrating their daughter's accomplishment.

Then everyone chanted in unison, breaking up the song right in the middle. "Wah-hoo-wah, wah-hoo-wah! Uni-v, Virginia! Hoo-rah-ray, hoo-rah-ray, ray, ray-UVA!"

She felt light as air for a second, with the chant echoing all around her. Then the second verse started and all of the sadness hit her at once. She was crying like a child by the end of the first line, and having Dex's arm around her waist didn't help one damn bit.

What though the tide of years may roll, and drift us far apart.
For alma mater still there'll be a place in every heart.
In college days we sing her praise, and so, when far away, in memory
we still shall be at the dear old UVA.

That was the damn truth. Through the years, she and Dex had been tied together tightly, even though they were so very far apart. Their love for their child, their connection to their home, and the bonds of their alma mater held them together via invisible strings. They would always, always be Hoos.

❧

The garden party was kind of a mess, but it was a traditional mess. And Dex loved being tied to a place where no tradition was too small to celebrate with gusto.

It took quite a while to find Kendall, but that shiny orange "K" eventually led them to her. After the four of them hugged Kendall until she gasped, Dex went to fetch her grandparents. It took a while to corral them and walk them over, but her group had stayed exactly where she'd left them.

This interlude was just a way to let people link up with their graduate and meet some of their friends and professors. Kendall had quite a few of each, and Dex was so grateful that the storm no longer threatened. They were able to stay outside and wring every bit of joy from the occasion, even though they now had to go to Kendall's actual graduation, which promised to be a much shorter affair. But they would call Kendall's name, and she'd march across the stage to accept her diploma. That was worth another hour of sitting on a plastic chair. Easily.

❧

The Department of East Asian Languages, Literatures, and Cultures was one of the smallest, and their diploma ceremony was squeezed into an auditorium that was just now being cleared of the slow-moving astronomy students.

The ceremony was really pretty brief, much to Tracy's pleasure. There were only eight graduates in Kendall's program, and she strode up onto the stage like the confident, upbeat kid she was. When the dean shook her hand and offered a brief hug, Tracy turned to see tears streaming down Dex's cheeks. Without taking a second to think, she grasped and held her tightly, beginning to sob as well. "Our baby's all grown up," she whimpered.

"I want to start over," Dex murmured. "I want to fix everything, and do it right this time. No screw-ups," she added, with her voice shaking hard. "I'd give anything in the world to be right here to catch every minute of her precious life."

Tracy felt herself nodding decisively. "I want that too," she whispered. "For all of us." She was truly on the verge of losing it, and for the second time that day found herself so very thankful that Yardley was back in Richmond, neatly placing cheese cubes on trays. If she'd been jealous yesterday, today would have sent her 'round the damn bend.

CHAPTER FOUR

SEATING FOR THE DRIVE HOME had turned into a free-for-all. Somehow, Dex wound up alone, in Kendall's car. She was also the last to leave Charlottesville, spending a few minutes wandering around campus after her parents and grandparents had gone. Nothing major. Just a little reminiscence, since she didn't think she'd be back on campus any time soon.

Upon reflection, it seemed that everything was kind of like it had been, while being radically different. But that's how many things were after twenty years. Similar, but not the same. She wasn't exactly melancholy, but she could have gotten there without much help. But today was a celebration, and she decided to clear her mind of old memories and focus on her sparkling new graduate. With great luck, one day she'd return to watch a fifth generation Haven-Lord become a Hoo.

When she got to Richmond, she went on auto-pilot, finding her way to her former home without a moment's thought. It was truly as if she'd been gone for a short vacation, every turn burned into her memory.

She and Tracy had moved into the cute little row-house just after they'd graduated. Her parents had paid for their apartment in Charlottesville, and when they'd moved to Richmond, they found them a small, old home that they could fix up over time. It had been incredibly generous of them to handle the substantial downpayment, getting the monthly mortgage down to a number Dex could handle. Her parents were the kinds of people who liked to share their good fortune with others—especially their only child.

Since Dex had been unceremoniously kicked out of that starter home long before they'd completed all of the upgrades, she knew it was going to look different. But when she pulled up across the street, she sat in the car for at least five minutes, just staring at it.

Still painted a nice marine blue, with crisp white trim, the little house was in the middle of the block, with matching homes continuing all the way down the street. There was a very shallow porch, not nearly big enough for comfortable chairs, but Tracy had found a wooden bench that was the right size, and she'd wedged some colorful ceramic planters on either side of it, with spring flowers spilling over the tops.

Finally compelling herself to get out of the car, Dex knocked on the front door, waiting patiently. Tracy answered, cocking her head slightly. "Why didn't you just come on in?"

Dex shrugged, not thinking it wise to say she didn't know where she stood in the "make yourself at home" hierarchy. For all she knew, she was in the "don't even think about entering without an escort" group.

"Come in, come in."

Dex entered, then smiled reflexively. "It looks…pretty much the same. Really nice," she added. They'd had the parlor and the dining room walls skim-coated, and the whole place painted an elegant sidewalk grey. Surprisingly, the walls and the white woodwork still looked sharp.

"It's held up remarkably well," Tracy admitted. "Paying top-dollar for a quality painter really was a good choice."

"Really good." Dex turned her head, seeing that just about nothing had been changed, save for some nicer throw pillows and area rugs. "Kendall's mentioned some projects…"

"Want to see? My splurge was the master bathroom. Finished that about three years ago."

"Yeah. Sure. Mind if I go peek?"

"Let me take you. Then I can preen while you compliment me on my good taste."

Dex followed her up the stairs, amazed that Tracy would take time out from the party just to lead a tour. They arrived upstairs and Tracy walked into the bath, with Dex following. "Very nice job. Modernized but still looking like it belongs in a house from this era. Great tile work. Handmade?"

"Made to look like it," she admitted, smirking. "I saved thirty percent by going with a fake."

"Very good choice. Big question. Can you count on the toilet flushing?"

"Every time," she said, chuckling. "Replacing the pipes cranked up the cost much more than I saved on the tile, but it's been worth it."

"It looks great," Dex said. She noticed a door that shouldn't have been there. Curiously, she turned the knob, with the master bedroom revealing itself. "Why'd you do this?"

Tracy shrugged. "People want en suites now. I figured it might increase the resale value."

"Smart," Dex said, kind of mesmerized. Tracy had upgraded the bedroom at least as much as she'd done the bath. Now it looked like a tranquil oasis, with nice lighting, a big bed, expensive-looking bedside tables and a padded headboard. "Looks like a five-star hotel," Dex said, then realized that might sound a little familiar. "I mean…"

"I know what you mean," Tracy said, standing so close her volume had dropped significantly. "People want that hotel experience."

"Are you selling?" Dex asked, really, really hoping she wasn't.

"That's a definite possibility. With Kendall leaving, we might choose to live at Yardley's condo over in The Fan. It might be nice to let someone else worry about maintenance."

"Yeah. It might." Before she could stop herself, she said, "If you decide to sell, let me know."

"You? What would you do with a house in Richmond?"

"Nothing—now," she admitted. "But I love this house, and I wouldn't mind having a rental property to hold onto for a while. I've always thought I'd move back here when LA drove me stark-raving mad, and it would be nice to have a house just waiting—"

"Honey?" A voice that sounded like fingernails on a blackboard called out.

"Coming." Tracy rushed over to the door. "Gotta go," she said, disappearing in an instant.

Dex couldn't help herself. She walked into their former bedroom, envisioning it as it used to be—with cracked plaster and peeling paint. The windowsills had been so swollen from moisture that there was a gap that let in the cold and the wind on chilly nights. She recalled jamming a couple of hand towels into the cavity, even though they didn't help much. But there was no doubt they'd been happy in that space. Very happy. They'd planned on having the room painted as soon as they got the money together, assuming their bedroom had lead paint just like the baby's room had. But they weren't in a hurry once they'd made every other place Kendall might crawl or toddle safe. Keeping their door closed made it an adults-only zone, which had been kind of nice.

She walked across the hall to the baby's room, half expecting a crib tucked into the corner next to the rocking chair her grandparents had given them. But that was an odd memory. The crib had already been stored away by the time she'd been banished, replaced with a big-girl bed, as Kendall called it. That bed was now gone, along with all of the toys and stuffies. A full-sized one mostly filled the space now, with just a few mementos from Kendall's late-teenaged years decorating the walls and the bedside table.

Dex sat on the bed, thinking of all of the nights they'd paced the floor with the fussy baby. All of the crying they'd suffered through when Kendall started to teethe. The many, many nights she and Tracy had tag-teamed the infant, passing her off like a wailing football just so they didn't lose their minds. But those difficult nights meant nothing compared to reading to a sweet little thing who didn't even know how to follow your voice at first, watching in awe as she slowly learned about the world and how she was the center of it. That period faded as Kendall got some perspective, but Dex had to admit her world still revolved around her daughter. She was just about to burst into tears when she stood and forced herself to go into the bath and splash some cold water onto her face. She couldn't afford to get stuck on memory lane. She'd abandoned her family, and wanting to change history was truly a waste of psychic energy. It was time to make an appearance at the party, certain she'd be able to convince every stranger she met that she'd purposefully chosen to move to the City of Angels, and was enjoying the hell out of her spot in the heavens.

⬦⬦⬦

The minute Dex stepped out onto the patio, she was transported once again—this time into the dreams she and Tracy had once shared.

When they'd bought the house, the back yard was a sad, nasty mess. Dex had never lived near people who threw everything into the yard once it stopped working or wasn't wanted—toilets, broken dishes, a fender from a Ford Escort, truck tires, venetian blinds. There hadn't been a single blade of grass that had been able to break through the hardpan that years of abuse and no care at all had created.

She and Tracy used to sit on lawn chairs on hot summer nights, fantasizing about the changes they would eventually make. But in the two years they'd lived there together, all they'd done was hire a dumpster and four strong men to clear out the trash. There were simply too many projects inside that they had to tend to first.

Clearly, Tracy's fortunes had changed pretty dramatically. Or maybe Dex's financial contributions, more generous than any court would have mandated, had helped her complete some significant projects.

The awful little shed in the back corner was gone, now sporting a brick pad that held an attractive fire pit, along with six comfortable-looking spring chairs, their lime and orange striped cushions seeming like a breath of summer.

The small lawn was green and healthy, and an attractive wooden fence was decorated by climbing vines that were already showing some blooms. Perennials filled every spot that wasn't covered by a vine, with Dex almost crying at the beauty of the camellias, the one plant she'd gone to great lengths to grow in her relatively inhospitable ocean-front micro-climate.

But the deck, entirely covered by a sand-colored canvas awning, was the highlight. Built-in benches topped with cushions surrounded the space, and two rockers faced out, allowing Dex's grandparents to sit there looking like they owned the place. It took just a second for Dex to recognize one of the rockers as the one they'd soothed Kendall to sleep in, and she had to force her voice to sound cheery when she said, "Well, look at mammy and pappy holding court."

"Give me a kiss, you little rascal," her grandmother said, extending her arms.

There was nothing in this world better than having your grandmother make it abundantly clear how much she loved you, and Dex let the hug go on until her back ached. "I wish I could see you sitting out here every day," she whispered.

Her grammy wasn't nearly as sentimental as she was, which was for the best. "My yard's three times bigger, and my deck has misters, sweetheart. Not to mention a pool. I'll be sitting out there tomorrow, by the way, so you just come on by." She patted Dex's cheek when she stood. "Why not drive us to church? You can get yourself together by nine forty-five, can't you?"

"I can, and I will," Dex said, figuring it wouldn't hurt to have a little organized religion in her life. One day a year seemed like the right amount.

"Are you leaving on Monday?" her grandfather asked.

"No, sir. My plans are open-ended at this point. I don't have anything scheduled, work-wise, so we'll see what comes up."

"You have no plans at all?" Grammy asked, clearly surprised.

"I have one very important engagement. Kendall asked me to stay for her birthday."

"My, oh, my! You'll be here for weeks. How many times will you take me to lunch?"

"Many," Dex promised, really looking forward to that.

Kendall bounded up the stairs and grabbed Dex by the hand. "I've got some people to introduce you to. Fans," she added, with her impish smile making Dex laugh.

"Go be a celebrity," Grammy said. "No one I know has any idea who you are, or what you do, but Kendall insists you're famous."

"Only with a certain subset of people. Mostly kids, of course." She started to let Kendall lead her away. "Don't toss off my fame so easily, though. You have to have at least one acquaintance who listens to cozy mysteries, so you're in one of my demographics."

⚬⚬⚬

The house was air conditioned, but with people going in and out so frequently, the temperature kept rising in the narrow kitchen. Tracy was sweating freely by the time she took a look at the baked beans bubbling away in the oven. Fanning herself, she started to make the batter for cornbread muffins.

It would be at least an hour and a half before the brisket would be finished, but the tasks she had to complete might take more than that. How did women cook three meals a day for ten or more people in the good old days? They must have dreaded every dawn.

Yardley was helping, but she needed to be not only instructed, but lightly supervised. Libby had offered to help, but the main part of the kitchen was too narrow for more than two, and it was crowded at that. So she and Yardley bumped into each other frequently, which wasn't so bad, but it was starting to wear on her. How could the woman manage to be in precisely the wrong spot so damned often? Of course, it didn't help that every guest had to move through the kitchen to visit the bathroom. Each of them believed they were being polite by stopping and chatting for a while, but that just slowed production.

With mild guidance, Yardley finished making a light, lemony salad dressing, then got all of the vegetables washed and dried off. Tracy was about to expire from the heat, and she excused herself to go stand on the deck for a minute to cool off.

She felt a little guilty complaining about the heat when she caught sight of Randy working like a pit-master, with the sweet smoke billowing into his eyes, the hot afternoon sun baking down on him. He was a fairly formal guy, so it was never a tank top and cutoffs for him. Today he wore a colorful, short-sleeved button down, and a pair of once-crisp khakis. She wouldn't have been surprised if his deck shoes had been filled with sweat.

Tracy loved barbecue as much as nearly anyone, but she was perfectly happy to buy it from a local joint, not having the patience to spend the whole day minding the smoker. Actually, she never used the thing, a Christmas gift from Randy a few years ago. But having it there gave him something to do when he and Libby visited, and it was preferable to have him cook than tamper with her garden, something she was fairly proprietary about.

Kendall and her close friends were in the left corner of the yard, gathered around the unlit fire pit, with Dex right in the middle of the group. It looked a little odd to see her sipping on a glass of lemonade, looking cool as a cucumber, with the girls seemingly hanging on her every word. Sabrina, in particular, appeared transfixed, with her head leaning toward Dex as she gazed intently at her face.

Granted, it was a very nice face, but Sabrina was looking at her like she was Moses delivering the damn commandments. Dex was clearly being her usual self—charming and affable. Even though Tracy obviously couldn't hear her, she could nearly see the Haven charm oozing from her. The coy smile, the sharp intelligence that emanated from her eyes, the soothing, sexy voice that Tracy used to teasingly call her panty dropper. No one could defend against it. She knew that better than anyone.

Sabrina was a couple of years older than Tracy had been when she'd fallen for that delicious combination of traits, but age and experience weren't barriers. She'd personally witnessed women from two to ninety come under Dex's spell, all of them falling hard and fast.

A hand on her back made her start. "What's she up to?" Yardley asked, her voice dripping with suspicion.

"Talking, I suppose."

"Those girls are a little young for her, aren't they?"

Tracy hadn't been thinking anything suspicious was happening, but just having Yardley mention it let a comment float right out of her mouth. "I don't think youth is a barrier for Dex."

"Mmm. That was definitely true at Virtus, but she could also talk a sixty-year-old man into whatever she wanted. She's absolutely shameless," Yardley said, her voice as cold and hard as stone.

"You saw her hitting on women at Virtus?" Tracy faced her and snapped her fingers, trying to get her attention.

"She hits on everyone she meets," Yardley said, not really answering the question.

"Focus," Tracy demanded. "Did you see Dex trying to hook up with anyone when you worked together?"

"Well…" Her gaze slowly slid back to Dex, with her expression darkening. "I'm not exactly saying that. But if you'd told me she was trying to bed anyone from the maintenance staff to the CEO, I wouldn't have been surprised."

Peevishly, Tracy said, "I'm not asking if she had the *ability* to pull a woman into her clutches. She does. I'm asking if you know she was fooling around behind my back when you worked together."

Now Yardley gave Tracy her full attention. She didn't look happy at all when she conceded, "No, I don't. But if she had been, I wouldn't have been even a little bit surprised."

"I would have been," Tracy said softly. "Actually, I wouldn't have believed my eyes if I'd caught her in bed with another woman. Dex was loyal to a fault."

❈❈❈

Tracy had changed her diet up over the past few years, substituting beans, and green, leafy vegetables for meat when she could. But when you had a few slices of perfectly-smoked brisket and some almost-too-sweet pork and beans on your plate, she gave herself points for being able to resist this kind of deliciousness on a daily basis.

Randy didn't do anything halfway, and he'd thrown himself into the barbecue movement about ten years earlier. Libby was pretty sick of the whole thing, often inviting Tracy out for lunch to a vegan restaurant she liked, but Tracy was almost sure she wouldn't be able to resist having just about any style of barbecue just about any time.

Yardley wasn't exactly a vegetarian, but she was close. Tonight she'd had to skip both the brisket and the pork and beans, due to her allergy. Tracy had purchased a couple of chicken breasts, but Yardley hadn't bothered to put them out for Randy, who would have happily cooked them. She seemed satisfied with a massive helping of the green salad, along with a bagel she'd obviously hunted around in the kitchen for. Watching her eat a lightly buttered bagel while that addictive pork and beans rested on her plate irritated Tracy for no good reason at all, and her fork swooped over to her plate to relieve her of it. "Why did you take this, since you know you can't eat it?"

"I didn't realize there was pork in it until I examined it. But even if there hadn't been, I like beans made with just a little bourbon and maple syrup. Then you can really taste them."

"True. I guess." She took another bite, really savoring it. "I was raised on beans made just like this. Can't have enough ham hocks or blackstrap molasses for me."

Yardley smiled at her. "When your mom trains dietitians for a living, you don't develop a lot of bad habits." She hurriedly added, "Not that your habits are bad…"

"My habits are good enough. But if this kind of thing was in front of me every day, I'd eat it every day. Gotta be honest."

"Well, you'll have healthy baked beans if you move in with me. I'll wean you off that ham hock craving in no time."

Tracy nodded just to be polite. That not only wouldn't happen, she didn't want it to. She liked to practice moderation, and in her view, a moderate amount of even the unhealthiest foods made her a happier person. Too much virtue was just as doctrinaire as too much vice.

※

Dex sat by her grandparents on the deck, fetching them anything they needed. They were both in good health, and quite spry for their ages, but she liked to dote on them, and neither of them seemed to mind.

Her grandfather wanted just a tiny splash of bourbon to wash down his dinner, and she got up to go into the kitchen to see if she could rustle some up.

Tracy and Yardley were inside, with Tracy moving around putting things away, and Yardley starting to work on cleaning the enamel-coated Dutch oven the beans had been cooked in.

"Well, doesn't this look like fun," Dex said. "Once I get my grandparents set up, I'll gladly help."

"Nice timing," Tracy said, slightly coldly. "Yardley's on the last pot."

Dex wasn't sure what she'd done, but she'd clearly done something. But asking for details didn't sound like fun, so she moved on. "Uhm...do you happen to have any bourbon? You know my grandfather likes a little palate-cleanser before dessert."

"Hold on." Tracy went into the pantry, and Dex could hear her rooting around.

Kendall entered from the deck, and she put her arm around Dex's waist. "What are we doing here?" she whispered near her ear, clearly trying to tickle Dex and make her squirm.

"Waiting for the hooch."

From behind the wall, Tracy said, "I've only got Irish whiskey. I'd ask if your young admirer wants some, but Sabrina isn't twenty-one yet." She emerged from the pantry and stopped abruptly when she saw Kendall.

That comment was like a kick to the teeth. A very undeserved one. But Dex wasn't about to lob one back, even though she wanted to. When she'd agreed to come she'd firmly decided she would not be pulled into the smallest disagreement with Tracy, and she was going to stick to that plan.

Dex extended her hand and took the pint bottle, not commenting on the dig. "I'll go see if Gramps is willing to branch out from his bourbon. Be right back."

❈

By ten, nearly everyone had left, and after Dex helped police the yard for stray napkins or beer bottles, she started for the deck. If it hadn't been so dark she might have felt her way around the fence, to see if Tracy had put a gate in. Then she could escape without saying goodbye. But that would have been rude. If they were going to maintain any kind of relationship, she was going to have to eat some crow. It sucked to be forced to take a bite of something awful, especially when she didn't know why she was being punished, but they could work things out over time. For now, she was willing to do whatever was required to make Kendall happy. And that meant putting up with any amount of snark—for an evening.

CHAPTER FIVE

DEX WAS WELL PAST READY TO take off, but she didn't want to leave before her grandparents did. After her grandfather had sipped the last of his whiskey, he stood and straightened his slacks, then made sure his belt buckle was right where it belonged. "Well, Mother, I do believe we've worn out our welcome once again."

Dex stood and extended a hand to help her grandmother to her feet. She kind of loved hearing her grandfather use the term "mother," only because it was so unlike him. Odd little terms long-married couples used always made her smile. "I think you'd have to throw a few punches or break a window or two to wear out your welcome here," Dex said. "But if you're thinking of creating a scene, I'll go make some popcorn. I love to watch a good fight."

"Maybe next time," he said, leaning over slightly to give her a hug. "We'll see you in the morning?"

She blinked at him, then recalled she'd agreed to take them to church. "Yes, sir. You definitely will."

"Good night, sweetheart," Grammy said, kissing both of her cheeks twice. "Wear something nice, won't you? *Everyone* will judge you."

"Nice to know."

Kendall had been inside, and she poked her head out. "Leaving already? You know there's still liquor in the house, right?"

"We'll leave some for you," Grammy said. "You sit out here with Dexie. We'll see ourselves out after we thank your mother and…*Yardley*," she said, drawing the name out like it was three syllables long.

"Love you both," Kendall said, kissing them. She flopped down on the closest rocker. "How about going for a walk around the neighborhood?"

"A walk? Really?"

"Yeah. My buzz just kicked in, and I don't want to waste it."

Dex got to her feet, shaking her head. "Oh, to be young again."

She pushed open the door, finding Tracy and Yardley looking like they were about to exit. "Thanks for hosting such a nice party," Dex said, edging her way through the room. "I'm sure everyone had a great time."

"I suppose we won't be seeing you again, Dex," Yardley said. "It's been —"

"Why? Are you going out of town?" she asked, trying not to sound as hopeful as she truly was.

"You are."

"I am?"

"Aren't you leaving tomorrow?" Tracy asked. "You never stay longer than a weekend."

"Ahh… Well, since I don't have any work lined up at the moment, I'm going to stay for Kendall's birthday."

"Kendall's *birthday?*" That was possibly the least enthusiastic response she could fashion.

"Isn't that weeks from now?" Yardley glared at her hotly.

"I do believe it is."

"But what will you do?" Tracy asked. "Don't you need to get home to work?"

"I have nothing pressing right now, so I can play it by ear." Dex was rapidly growing uncomfortable with the building tension in the room, partially because she didn't understand its source.

Tracy was still staring at her, obviously annoyed. "You're not going to want to monopolize Kendall's time, are you? If she's only going to be home for a short while, I'd like to see her, too."

"I can set my own schedule, Mom," Kendall said, getting involved in exactly the way that made Dex sweat.

"Don't worry about it," Dex said. "I'll make sure to stay in the background." She swallowed the bile that rose in her throat, feeling as unwelcome as an ant colony at a picnic. "Thanks again for having me."

Kendall put her hand on Dex's back and gently pushed her from the room. They hadn't even reached the parlor when she hotly asked, "Why did you let her treat you like that?"

"Like what?"

This time the push wasn't so gentle. The ref would have called a foul if they'd been on a football field. "Are you seriously saying it didn't bother you that Mom and Yardley clearly wanted to load you into the car, drive you to the airport, and hurl you to the curb?"

Dex didn't reply until they were outside. After stepping over a couple of guys who were sitting on the steps, she waited for Kendall to bid her goodbyes, then they started to walk.

"Look," Dex said. "You can't expect two people who parted on such bad terms to be best friends right away. We've got a long, sordid history between us, honey, and it's not going to evaporate quickly, if ever. You have to be patient."

"Oh, god, that's so like you." Kendall looked to the sky, like she was at her wits end. "You *never* rise to the bait. You're so fucking zen it's infuriating."

"That's why I do it," Dex said, adding a pinch to her cheek.

A reluctant smile settled on Kendall's face. "I wouldn't put it past you. But the question remains. Why take her bullshit?"

"Uhm… One, I don't think it is bullshit. Once your mom has had the chance to get some of her anger out, I think things will get better."

"Jesus," Kendall grumbled. "There's no reason to believe that." She took in a breath, clearly trying to calm herself. "Sorry," she said after a minute. "I shouldn't jump on you. Especially after you went out of your way to be nice to my friends all afternoon. I truly do appreciate that, you know."

"I can't refuse my fans," Dex teased. "Seeing most of your buddies only when they came over to use the pool never gave me time to entrance them with lines from my seminal scripts."

"Ugh. It's beyond me that they act like *Dobie* was one of the most important touchstones in their lives, but I guess I should be used to that."

"You still haven't seen it, have you," Dex asked gently. She put her arm around Kendall and tugged her close so she could place a kiss on her temple.

"No," she admitted. "It's so *weird*. Half of the people I know love that movie way, way too much, but I can't even consider watching it."

"Have you tried?"

She nodded soberly. "Nana took me when it first came out. I was just…five, I think. Maybe six. As soon as I heard your voice—the whole damn point of going—I started to cry so much we had to leave."

How had they never talked about this? Why had Libby not mentioned it at the time? "Was it just my voice?"

"No," she said, sounding very glum. "The little boy was wandering around that damn forest, trying to find his mom after the storm. As soon as he heard the voice, I knew she was dead." She met Dex's eyes. "I wasn't even clear on what dead was, but I knew that kid's mom wasn't coming back. He'd only get to hear her voice." She rolled her eyes dramatically. "You don't have to be a psychiatrist to guess why I didn't want to hear your voice on a movie screen. I wanted you *here*."

"I'm so sorry, baby," Dex soothed. "If I could have possibly stayed in Richmond, I would have. But after two rehab failures…"

"I know you didn't want to leave. Nana has implied that you needed to get away from the people who didn't support your sobriety." She turned slightly, with her eyes hooded. "But I've always wondered why you didn't come back when you were confident you had everything under control."

Kendall looked so damn vulnerable, so deeply hurt. It was like a spike in Dex's heart. She took her hand and held it tenderly. "I can see that you'd wonder about that. I guess…" She thought for a few seconds, wanting to make sure she told the whole truth. "It took quite a while to get my act together. A few years, for sure. And by that time I'd gotten comfortable in California. I had a good support system, not to mention a job that fit me so much better than Virtus ever had." She let out a sigh, knowing her choices had always been better for her than they'd been for

Kendall. "I thought things were going well enough for you, and I was kind of terrified I'd relapse here."

"Did all of your friends party constantly?"

She almost took the easy way out, but if they were going to be honest with each other, she had to reveal some of the less positive things. "Uhm…no. By the time you were around ten, I was confident enough in my sobriety, and if that had been my only trigger, I would have been fine. But if I'd moved back to Richmond, your mom and I would have had to interact on a regular basis. It would have been impossible not to."

"That could have helped—"

"I don't think so. Your mom was so angry that I don't think I could have maintained my self-esteem. And it's that self-esteem that keeps me sober." She gazed at her for a few seconds, seeing the understanding in her eyes. "My friends in LA knew me as a mature, thoughtful woman who was always trying to be a better human. Your mom didn't feel that way, and I worried that I was still too fragile to be able to keep my head above water."

"Especially when she was actively trying to push you under," Kendall said, her tone far too bitter for Dex to let it slide. "Watching Mom imply you were hitting on Sabrina made me crazy! Where does she get off?"

"Oh, baby, don't let other people's issues affect you. We have a complicated history that you know nothing about. But your mom had good reasons for not trusting me. Believe me. It was better for all of us to have me gone."

"No," she said, slowing down. When she came to a stop she said, "I'm *not* going to believe you."

"You're not—?"

"I've been walking on thin ice since the day you left. I'm sick of that, and I'm sick of having both of you tell me I don't understand. I *want* to understand. I deserve to."

"I'm not sure that's true, Kendall. It's awfully painful to talk about that time. I'm ashamed of myself, and I don't like to revisit that part of my life."

"Fine," Kendall said, glaring at her. "Go ahead and have your secrets. Just know that I've spent my whole fucking life filling in the gaps, and believe me, the reality better not be as bad as my imagination."

Dex stared at her, dumbfounded. "You…do that?"

"Since I was little. And the more I learn about how horrible people can be, the more things I add to the list. So if you weren't caught molesting a child—you'll tell me what the fuck went on!"

"Shit," Dex grumbled. "I really don't want to do this. I'd feel much better if you talked to your mother."

"She's never told me a thing—which made me *certain* you did something so horrible that I had to keep an eye on you, too," she added quietly. "I don't feel that way now, but it was a nightmare when I started to understand what people were capable of." She stared at Dex for a minute. "Didn't you notice I started to make you leave the room when I changed clothes? Did you honestly not pick up on the fact that I stopped letting you read to me in bed? That took me *years* to get past."

If Dex had been standing near a cliff, she might have thrown herself off. How had she missed that? She'd just assumed Kendall was being more private—like many pre-teens. Dread filled her to the brim, but she could hardly go back to Tracy's and demand she clue Kendall in about their breakup. Not with Yardley hovering over her every second. "All right," she said. "Just promise that you'll try not to judge me too harshly. If you couldn't forgive me—"

"Dex," Kendall said softly. "You're my mom. No matter what you did, if you have remorse, and you don't do it any more—we're good."

"Then we're good," she said, her mouth so dry she could barely speak. "Uhm… Mind if we head to the park? I'd like to have a seat."

"You look a little shaky," Kendall said, clearly worried. "If you can't do this—"

"No, no, of course I can. I'm just sure your mom isn't going to like it, and I don't want to cause any more trouble."

"Fuck her," Kendall snapped. "I mean, seriously. Fuck her. If she caught you trying to go down on me, she's got a right to still be furious. If not…"

"Jesus," Dex moaned. "Give me a minute to think about what I'm able to share." She gripped Kendall's arm, pulling her to a stop. "It's nothing like you're imagining. It's…bad in a different way."

⁂

They reached the park sooner than Dex wished they had. But Kendall looked awfully spooked, so she got right to it as soon as they sat on a bench. "All right," she said, taking a cleansing breath. "Tell me what you know."

"Almost nothing." She faced Dex, speaking like she was offering directions to a stranger. "You were an alcoholic, and you did some stuff that made mom stop trusting you. That's kind of it."

"Got it." She tried to decide how deep she had to go. Given not much made sense if she didn't go all the way back, she got to the source of the problem. "Just after graduation, right after we'd moved to Richmond, I had to have surgery to remove my wisdom teeth."

"What the fuck?" Kendall's eyebrows hiked up.

"I'm starting at the beginning, honey. Stick with me. I had some post-surgical pain, so my dentist gave me a prescription for Oxycodone. I needed the pills for a day or maybe two, but I took the whole week's worth." She took in a long breath, thinking of how easy it had been to succumb to the drug's lure. "I was sure I was still in pain, and my doctor didn't blink when I asked for a refill. I wanted those capsules so badly I set the alarm so I wouldn't miss a dose."

Kendall looked totally confused. Maybe even frightened. "Why are you telling me about your dentist…"

Dex could see Kendall was having second thoughts about learning the whole story, but it was too late to turn back. She was a very curious child, and she'd quickly crave all of the details. "Bear with me, sweetheart. I'm giving you the background." She took a breath, and continued. "By the time those pills were gone, I would have done just about anything to get more. When I called for another refill, the dentist wouldn't even take my call, even though he was a family friend. He had someone in the

85

office turn me down, and I could hear something in her voice…suspicion, judgement. Something that shamed me. But I didn't let myself linger on that, even though it wasn't like me to brush something like that off. Instead of spending a minute trying to figure out what was going on, I quickly narrowed down my choices to doctor-shopping or trying to find someone on the street to buy them from."

"You aren't an alcoholic?" Kendall asked, her shaking voice nearly a whisper.

"Not at all, sweetheart. I drank like most college kids did. Too much sometimes, but it never held any power over me. Narcotics did."

"But how did you even know to doctor shop? I wouldn't have…"

"A whole lot of people found themselves addicted at the same time, and we all started snooping around online, trying to find a legal way to get more." She paused for a second, almost certain she didn't have to add the obvious, but she did anyway. "I quickly found a whole lot of illegal ways to get it, and I started to devote most of my free time to searching for pills."

Kendall nodded robotically. "You're saying you started to abuse drugs —just like that."

"Just like that," she admitted. "I think part of it was the drug, since Oxycodone is so powerfully addictive. And part of it might have been genetic. In retrospect, I was in the perfect mindset for addiction: I'd begun to take on the role of a competent adult, even though I was still pretty immature, we were trying to learn to parent, I was adjusting to my first full-time job, and I had the burden of supporting my family on a pretty modest salary. The drug gave me this false sense of calm that made it seem like everything would be fine—so long as I could get a steady supply, of course. But you can't keep that scam going for long. Someone always catches you."

"Mom?"

"Oh, yes. I was making withdrawals from our checking account every other day, not thinking she ever looked at the balance. I found out the hard way that she did."

"And that made her kick you out? Jesus! A little support would have been—"

"Kendall, stop. Your mom was very, very supportive. So were your grandparents. They got me into a good rehab facility. And Virtus had an excellent employee assistance plan. After I was in rehab for twenty-eight days, I thought I'd put it behind me. But I hadn't," she added quietly.

"You relapsed?"

"I sure did. It took me a while, but when my dad's mom dropped dead with no warning..." She had to take a breath to even finish her thought. "Less than a year after my grandpa died, I simply didn't know how to deal with the grief. I felt like I couldn't ask for support from my parents, since they were going through it, too..." She stopped and took Kendall's hand. "First massive mistake. When you're in trouble, your family *wants* to help you. But I was still pretty full of myself back then. I was super busy at work, and I stopped making my recovery a priority..."

"So you started using again."

"I did. I hid my habit pretty effectively for quite a while—maybe six months. But my tolerance kept increasing, which made me spend more time and more money chasing a steady supply. Your mom caught me again."

"Rehab?" Kendall looked a little ill.

"Indeed. Same facility. Same result. I was confident I was fine, and everyone wanted to believe that. My boss still trusted me, and I was on track for a promotion. Then I pulled your carseat out of the car one day and I found two pills stuffed under the seatbelt. I'm still not sure if I hid them there or if they'd fallen out of my pocket, but they were in my mouth—dry—in two seconds."

"Oh, shit..."

"Right. I knew I was out of options. Being found out this time would be the third strike at work, as well as with your mom, so I hid it every way I could. I shouldn't be proud of this, but I was pretty successful at lying my ass off to everyone I cared about. I made everyone believe I cared about you and your mom and my job, when all I truly cared about was scoring."

"How...?"

"The same way all junkies get drugs. I sold stuff at pawnshops, I stole Grammy's rainy day fund she had hidden up in her closet... I would have sold my blood, but you had to pass a drug test, and I knew I'd fail."

"And that put Mom over the edge."

"She didn't know, so she was still right by my side. Honestly, I don't think her faith in me ever wavered. She even threw me a party." She gave Kendall a warning glance. "Don't think you can hold onto your self esteem when your little girl gives you a cupcake and wishes you a happy sober anniversary—when you're as high as a fucking kite."

Kendall took her hand and brought it to her chest. "I've never heard you say 'fuck.'" She placed a hand on Dex's cheek, gazing deeply into her eyes. "You can stop. Really. If this is too hard..."

"I can't stop now. Not this close to the edge." She honestly thought she'd vomit, but she had to keep going. "I'd been buying from a guy who kind of had his act together, relatively speaking. He lived not far from here, in his mom's house. One day, I was running errands. With you," she added, hearing her voice start to shake. "I had fifty bucks on me that I'd gotten by padding my expense account. I was really shaky, and knew I'd go into withdrawal if I didn't score, so I went to his house. It was late fall, and it got dark early. You were sound asleep, like you usually were when we'd been in the car for a while. I knew it would only take a few minutes to conduct my business, and I didn't want his massive guard dog anywhere near you." She took in a breath, and finished. "So I left you in the car."

"You left me in the car? For like a long time? In the cold?"

The pain in her expression could not have made Dex feel a bit worse. She had so much self-recrimination still lodged deep inside that no one could effectively add to it. "It wasn't very cold out. And you were only alone for five or ten minutes. But yes, I left you in the car. Alone. Asleep." She took in a breath, trying not to cry. "The most important person in my life. A child I would have given my life for. My primary source of delight, of joy…" She couldn't keep herself together, bending over at the waist, sobbing pitifully.

"I'm so sorry," Kendall whispered, with her gentle voice right next to Dex's ear. "I think I know the rest. Mom caught you, and…here we are."

"Worse," she gasped, making herself sit up and finish. "There was another car about thirty feet behind mine. By the time I was halfway down the sidewalk, a pair of cops jumped out and arrested me for child endangerment."

"Child endangerment?"

"And possession. But it was the child endangerment that got me thrown out of the house—justifiably," she added, making sure Kendall understood that she had no excuses.

"Jesus," Kendall murmured. "And *that's* when Mom lost her faith."

"That did it. After your grandfather got me out on bail, and your mom claimed you from the social workers at Child Protection, she and I spent about an hour together. She was throwing my things into a suitcase most of that time, and I was squeezing you tight while both of us howled. And *that* was the last time I saw your mother—until Thursday."

"Okay," Kendall said, sounding kind of businesslike. "I'm very, very glad you told me. For years, I've believed that Mom was being a real hard-ass for no good reason. So it's good to know that's just not true."

"Not true at all."

"Right. I can understand, since if I had a boyfriend who lied to me repeatedly, I'd toss him."

"As you should."

"But you weren't just girlfriends, Dex. You had a child together. Mom should have worked harder to make things more comfortable for us as a group. I can see watching you like a hawk for a while, but after that?"

"Kendall, I was a total screw-up who blew a great opportunity to be a success. That's a lot to forgive. But when you add in that I risked our child's life…"

"You didn't do that," Kendall said, hugging her tightly. "The cops were trying to arrest a dealer and you got swept up in it, right?"

Stunned, Dex gawped at her. "How do you know that?"

"I watch TV."

"That's exactly what happened. They were staking out my dealer's house, and they obviously saw the car seat. Arresting me let them catch him in the act. But even though I didn't leave you there for an hour or two, I was risking your life, sweetheart. I truly was."

"By walking fifty feet? At worst, I would have woken up and cried, but I assume I did that all the time, right?"

"I left you alone, and out of my view, in front of a drug dealer's house!"

"For a couple of minutes. That's no different from running into the dry cleaners."

"You shouldn't do that either!"

"Oh, everybody does that."

"No, they don't. Your mom never did."

Kendall scoffed. "You have no idea what she did once you were gone. When you're a single mother, you get stuck and have to do things you wouldn't normally do. I can remember lots of times when she left me in the car alone."

"Not when you were four. No way. You can't claim that's true, since you wouldn't remember anything from that early."

"What difference does it make if I was four or six? Mom would run into the pharmacy, or the mini-mart, or to pick up carryouts. She did that all the time, Dex. *All* the time."

"I'm not buying that it's the same thing. But even if it was, it's too late to argue about it now. We did what we did, and time passed. Now I'm simply trying to have a better relationship with her. You've asked me to do that, and it's wholly within my power, so I'm determined to get it done."

Kendall looked at her for a second. "Is that the only reason you're doing this? For me?"

"Well, no. I'd like the chance to prove that I'm not the same woman who abandoned her child in a car. I'd like to earn back some of your mom's respect."

"Okay," Kendall said, not seeming very bothered by the story. She draped her arm around Dex's shoulders. "That wasn't a death penalty offense, Dex. I mean, I can understand that mom was furious that you were using drugs again, and that you'd been lying so much, but you didn't put my life in danger. You just didn't."

"But I could have. And I'm sure I *would* have if I'd gotten just a little deeper into my illness. I'm incredibly grateful to those officers for arresting me that night. They probably saved your life."

"Not buying it. But we'll never have to prove which one of us is right." She kissed Dex on the cheek, with a playful smile lighting up her eyes. "You *have* stopped using, right?"

"Of course I have, but all addicts lie, so..."

"Stop beating yourself up! It's been forever."

"I realize that. And all of those years have given me a lot of time to reflect and let my regret build. The statute of limitations on guilt is very, very long for child endangerment."

⸎

When they got back to the house, Kendall lingered on the front porch for a minute. "I think I'll go home with you tonight."

"Only if you clear it with your mom first." She took Kendall by the shoulders and turned her toward the door. "Go be polite to both her and Yardley."

Grumbling, Kendall said, "If she wasn't here, I'd be able to sleep in my own bed."

Dex watched her go, then sat down on the steps to wait. There was a little chill in the air now, but it was a pleasant one. It made everything smell fresh and clean and spring-like. Of course, the blooming plants on the porch helped with that. When did Tracy become such an avid gardener? Sighing heavily, Dex had to admit Tracy could have become a grandmaster in chess, or won prizes for origami. Her life was a near-total mystery. Maybe they could work on being more open with each other on this visit. Things would have to change for that to happen, but if she stayed long enough…

The door opened, and Dex started to stand. But a hand settled on her shoulder, holding her in place. "Tracy's talking to Kendall," Yardley said. "Just thought I'd let you know."

She started to go back in, but Dex called out, "Got a minute?"

"Uhm…sure." She leaned against the porch railing, not looking very casual even when she tried to. "What's on your mind?"

"Not a lot. I don't know what Tracy's planning for Kendall's birthday, but I'd like to celebrate with a dinner at my…my parents' house. Maybe the day before or the day after. Just the four of us."

"Why—" Yardley must have been about to say something rude, since she stopped abruptly and paused for quite a while before she finished her sentence. "What's the goal?"

"Glasnost," Dex said, then elaborated when Yardley looked blank. "Sorry. I was a European history major. That's the term the Russians used to refer to openness and transparency. I'd like a little more openness among us, if possible."

"Mmm. I'm not sure that's what Tracy wants, but if she does, I'm willing to go along."

That wasn't the most glowing reaction, but it wasn't a firm "no." "Check with Tracy. I didn't mention it to Kendall, since I didn't want to put you two on the spot."

"Thank you," Yardley said, showing what was probably a genuine smile. "My life would be easier if everyone in the family respected our relationship."

Dex felt her hackles rise in an instant. "Please try to give Kendall a break. It's been hard for her trying to negotiate the gulf between Tracy and me."

"I meant your entire family. Even your grandparents act like I'm a stray cat they wish would stop coming to the door."

Dex nodded. "They're all crazy about Tracy. Once you've convinced the group you truly care for her, they'll welcome you with open arms."

The door opened again and Kendall stepped onto the porch. "We're heading out," she said to Yardley, then started down the stairs. "See you." She continued to the sidewalk, having never made eye contact.

"I see what you mean," Dex said quietly, standing to shake Yardley's hand. The last thing she wanted was to be the force that drew the family closer to a person who clearly considered her a nemesis, but that might be a way to show Tracy she cared. That *was* the goal, right?

⁂

Later that night, Dex and Kendall sat on opposite ends of the sectional, with Kendall repeatedly nodding off. They were watching a travel show—in Chinese—about Cambodia. Given Dex didn't speak a word of Chinese, all she could do was watch the hosts, two young women, run around Phnom Penh. They looked like they were having a ball, but Dex preferred shows where she could understand the dialogue.

When Kendall's head fell back against the sofa, Dex tried to rouse her to send her into the main house to sleep, but she was not to be moved. "Blanket?" she asked, her sleepy voice too cute to resist.

Dex went to the closet and got both a pillow and a blanket, then tucked it around Kendall's feet after she'd spread it along her loosely. "Sleep well, baby."

Kendall stuck an arm out and wrapped it around Dex's legs, holding her tightly for a minute. "Thanks for treating me like an adult tonight. I know it was hard for you to talk about your arrest, but I'm very, very glad you did."

"I'm glad, too."

"And I'm going to try to get over being angry with Mom for keeping you at such a distance. I see that might have been the only way—at first."

"Hey," Dex soothed, reaching down to stroke along her back. "By the time you were in school, I was allowed to have you over here during my visits. That was very generous of your mom. *Very* generous."

"I guess. But I had to sleep in the house with Nana and Papa. I assume that was a requirement, right?"

"Uhm…my memory isn't great about the details. Let me just make it clear that I was thrilled your mom let us spend those weekends together,

Kendall. There was nothing in my life I looked forward to more than those trips."

"Me, too. But it sucked that I wasn't allowed to visit you in LA until I was in sixth grade. And I'm certain that having Nana take me was the only way that came about at all."

"It worked out great, sweetheart. I got to see you and my mom at the same time, and I could run off to do a quick job when I needed to. That was much better than having to hire a babysitter." She gave her another pat. "It worked."

"I guess," Kendall said, with her voice growing softer.

Dex stood there for a minute, watching her face relax as she nodded off. It actually *had* worked out fine. The shame of not being allowed to drive Kendall anywhere until she was old enough to drive them both had faded, and she had to admit that she might have had Tracy drug tested every other day if the situation had been reversed. Tracy had been very, very careful, but when you were dealing with something as precious as a child, who could blame her?

CHAPTER SIX

KENDALL WOKE UP EARLY, THEN walked over to the bedroom door. It was partially closed, and when she poked her head in she saw that Dex was sound asleep.

For a second, she surveyed her options. Dex wasn't an early riser, and Kendall hated to wake her for something so minor. Going into the house to pee was the obvious solution. But she didn't want to hang out today, and if her grandparents were up they'd all start talking, or run some errands together, and the day would be gone.

She put her shoes on, then quietly exited, deciding to go right home. Yardley would undoubtedly be there, but if Kendall could get into her room without being spotted, she could wait her out. Yardley seemed like the kind of person who'd have a list of things she had to do, and when she left to do them, Kendall would have her house back.

Even though she really had to pee, she went out of her way to stop by her favorite bakery and buy some cinnamon rolls—ordering three to provide a breakfast treat—if Yardley wasn't allergic to deliciousness.

Entering the house at seven, she stood quietly in the entryway for a minute, thrilled to not hear a sound. After finally racing to the bathroom, she turned on the coffeemaker, found her laptop, and went outside to sit on the deck. It wouldn't actually kill her to spend a few minutes with Yardley while having breakfast, and it might make her mom happy.

It was a beautiful morning, and after she checked all of her socials, she began to have second thoughts about her plan—which was to talk to her mom about everything she'd learned the night before.

They *had* to talk, but actually starting the conversation made her kind of edgy. So she pulled up a new blank page and started to write— usually a good way to work through her feelings, which were still pretty fucked-up.

By the time Kendall had gotten everything out, it was almost eight. Either her mom had been exhausted, or she and Yardley were going at it. They'd *probably* been exhausted, but on the off chance they were having wake-up sex, Kendall attached the document to an email, put her laptop back on the counter, and snuck out of the house again.

Hiding out at Nana's on a Sunday wasn't ever really a bad idea, and Dex's checkered history would still be there when Yardley eventually took off. There was no reason to rush.

By the time she got to her car, she realized she'd left the cinnamon rolls. Rather than risk waking up the happy couple, she drove right back to the bakery, this time buying five. Dex probably wouldn't want one, but she and Papa could easily handle two.

❈

Tracy had only been awake for a couple of minutes when she read her email, and one minute after that she sent Yardley packing. For the next hour, she worked in her garden frantically, stopping only occasionally to go take a few bites of those remarkably good cinnamon rolls. Why Kendall had brought breakfast over, then disappeared, was a question she'd have to wait to have answered, but wolfing down all three of the damn things gave her something to do while she went over and over the important parts of the letter.

She and Dex, but mostly she, had let the kid down in *so* many ways. Learning that Kendall had worried Dex might be inappropriate with her was the worst, of course, but all of it was bad. Really bad. And almost entirely her fault.

By ten, it was too humid to do any more weeding, so she went back inside and composed a text to Kendall.

I'm home—alone. Nothing on my agenda for today except sincerely apologizing to my beautiful girl for all of the ways I've let her down. Let me know if you're in the mood to listen. XO

Just a minute later, her phone rang. Like a normal old-fashioned ring. When she answered, Kendall said, "Come over here and hang out. Dex is at church, Papa's playing golf, and Nana's going to leave in a couple of minutes to meet some friends for brunch."

"You'd rather talk there, baby?"

"Not necessarily, but we don't have a pool. Do you mind?"

"Be there in twenty. Need me to stop for anything?"

"No need. I'm kind of sick to my stomach after eating two cinnamon rolls…"

"Amateur. I had three. I might sink, but I'll be right over."

❧

Tracy had faced some tough tests in her professional life, with her entire career resting on her ability to pull everything together to convince a teacher, or a board, that she knew her stuff. But having to look into a pair of trusting, warm brown eyes that a girl barely old enough to order a drink aimed at her felt like the biggest test of all.

They'd been light and breezy while getting ready to swim, and now Tracy had to get the ball rolling. They were each on a float, the kind that let you sit upright and dangle your feet into the water, and she took a deep breath, steeling herself.

"It's okay," Kendall said, pushing Tracy's float with her foot. "Actually, we don't have to talk about this at all if you don't want to. I think I know how it was for Dex, at least as much as she's willing to give up, so I basically just wanted you to know that I knew the dirty details."

"It's not okay," Tracy said. "It's not okay at all." She paddled back over so she and Kendall were close. The UVA baseball cap Kendall now wore was tugged down low, and she was wearing mirrored sunglasses, so her face was almost completely obscured. But Tracy still needed to face her, if only to watch her mouth twitch. She had a terrible poker-face, making it easy to guess what emotions she was feeling.

"Here's the biggest thing," Tracy said. "I've been a terrible role model, and that's something I'm never going to forgive myself for."

"Thanks," Kendall said quietly. "You have been pretty awful—but just in one area."

"Maybe. But it's a big area. I've always *told* you that talking about your feelings is important, that keeping secrets is corrosive, and that even when you've made a big mistake, you'll always be forgiven. But I made it clear, through my actions, that I thought all of that was bullshit. But it's not, Kendall. It's really not."

"I know, Mom. I got decent role modeling from Dex about some of that stuff, but Nana's been the star. She wouldn't like it if I did something truly awful, but I'm certain she'd give me a path to forgiveness." She must've been gazing right at Tracy, since her head didn't move for quite a few seconds. "I'm sorry you didn't have a Nana in your life. You didn't, right?"

"No," she said quietly. "I didn't have a Nana, or a Dex, or even a me. Every day was a surprise at my house. No consistency, no deep affection, no second-chances—for me, at least. My daddy started with a perfectly clean slate about once a week."

"He was…"

"An alcoholic," Tracy said. "Bad one. Could be violent, but usually only toward authority figures. He could also be so depressed he couldn't get out of bed for the entire weekend. He liked to keep everyone on their toes by being the most charismatic guy you'd ever met. His charm was mesmerizing when he wanted to win you over. But you never knew which version was going to show up, making it impossible to prepare yourself."

Kendall grasped her foot and pulled her close, then let it rest on her lap as she tenderly ran her fingernails over it. "I'm interested," she said quietly. "I've never asked, since I assumed that was one more topic that might make the world explode if we talked about it, but…if you want to talk about how it was for you growing up, I'd love to hear anything you want to share."

"Maybe later?" Tracy said, kind of astounded at how much Kendall seemed like current-day Dex. How did a girl so young and often so flighty come to be so kind, so empathic? "Let's just say that my daddy was a handful, my mama was completely under his spell, and my siblings were kind of a combination of both. Those two were only truly united in resentment toward me. When I did well in school, and made it clear I was going to college, they got even meaner."

"Your siblings didn't want you to go to college? Why would they care?"

"Well, neither one finished high school. My sister dropped out when she got pregnant at sixteen, and my brother dropped out on his seventeenth birthday. To avoid going to jail for car theft, my parents gave him permission to join the Army."

"I still don't see why that made them…" She stopped herself. "Sorry. You said you didn't want to talk."

"It's all right, baby. I don't want to get into it all, but I can summarize. I'm not sure why, but my daddy favored me. That caused a lot of resentment that built and built when it became clear I was going to leave home." She shrugged, still not able to figure out all of their screwed-up interactions.

"Then I'm glad you cut them off, Mom. That was brave."

"But I didn't," she admitted. "They cut *me* off, and it's only been in the last couple of years that I stopped longing for them to take me back." She gave her a wry smile. "Not very brave—about anything."

"I'm not buying that. You tossed Dex. Making yourself an unemployed, single mom at twenty-three sounds pretty brave to me."

"I'd already turned twenty-four," she said, smirking. "Much older."

Kendall shook her foot. "I mean it. You were a brave woman, and you made yourself do tough stuff—for me."

"I couldn't risk your safety, sweetheart. I would have stayed with Dex for the rest of my life if we hadn't had you. But we did, and your welfare had to come first."

"Understood. My only complaint, and it's a big one, is that you both —but primarily you—should have worked to stay in touch. It makes sense to keep your child away from a drug abuser. It doesn't make sense to stop talking to your co-parent."

"One hundred percent," Tracy said. "In just four days, I've seen the light. Now I have to try to make up for the harm I've caused through my rigidity—a well-known Lord trait."

"You're a Haven-Lord," Kendall said, with her grin making Tracy's heart swell. "We're all about being flexible. You just need a little more practice."

⣿

Tracy left before Dex returned, and when she got home she sat down at her desk and composed a note. It wasn't long, but she hoped this could be the first step on a path toward normalizing their relationship.

> *Dex,*
>
> *Kendall and I spoke about last night. I'm truly sorry you had to be the one to have that conversation. Actually, I'm sorry the situation existed in the first place. I'm sorry for so much—so very, very much.*
>
> *I'd love to get to a good place with you. I sense that you're willing to work toward that, too. I'm sure I'll be the stumbling block, but I hope you'll have some patience with me. Changing who I am is going to be difficult, but I truly want to be more Haven than Lord.*
>
> *With regret tempered by hope,*
>
> *Tracy*
>
> *PS-I'm truly glad you're staying for a longer visit.*

⣿

When Dex got home, it was almost two o'clock in the afternoon. No one was home, but a couple of floats were in the pool, and they hadn't been there when she'd left.

After going into the pool house to change out of her church-clothes, which she was pretty sure hadn't truly reached Grammy's standard, she got on what Kendall called the "dubya, dubya, dubya, dot" to do a little research.

When in Richmond, she usually went to a NA meeting at a church not too far away, but that was a Saturday morning thing. She *needed* a meeting, preferably right now, but nothing seemed to be happening in the middle of the afternoon on a Sunday.

The pandemic had been awful in every way, but one tiny benefit was that a lot of groups had flourished online. Thankfully, some helpful people put together an amazingly up-to-date listing of virtual meetings. After finding one in British Columbia that started in just five minutes, she went to log-in, assured that she'd have an hour to talk and listen to people just like her—people who couldn't afford to let stressful times get the better of them.

⁌⁍

The sun was still fairly high in the sky when Dex opened her door to go to the main house to help with dinner. Something fluttered to the ground, making a soft sound when it landed in the bristles of the welcome mat.

Bending, she picked up the envelope, seeing that her name was hand-written across the front. She would have recognized that handwriting anywhere, but seeing it made her wary. The interactions between her and Tracy had been all over the place, and she was afraid the envelope might contain anything from a diatribe to a cease and desist order. She walked over to a chaise to read it, wanting to give herself a minute to calm down if the contents agitated her. But when she opened it and glanced across the text, she could see it was an apology. That very pleasant surprise let her take a breath and read it carefully, then go over it one more time, enjoying the image of Tracy laboring over it—which she was certain she'd done.

Tracy was a good writer when she took the time to reflect, but reflection often wasn't her first instinct. She tended to react quickly, sometimes harshly, then apologize after a day or two. Some things clearly hadn't changed. But Dex had—in many ways. Twenty years ago she wouldn't have let this drop until they'd beaten it to death. She'd want to know all of Tracy's motivations for jumping on her, what her plans were to avoid doing it in the future, etcetera. But she'd learned that you couldn't truly change anyone, and making someone you cared for justify every action was punitive, not to mention futile.

Instead of dragging this out another moment, she took her phone out and found the website for the florist her family used. Given how Tracy loved gardening, another houseplant would probably be welcome. Especially when it silently signaled that Dex wanted a respectful, peaceful relationship with all of her heart.

∞

On Monday morning, Dex went into the kitchen after she'd gotten herself in visiting shape. Her mom was at the sink, washing up after breakfast. "My shift's over," Libby said, leaning toward Dex for a kiss, "but feel free to make yourself anything you'd like."

"I'm going to wait a bit. I'd like to have dinner with you and dad, and I only eat two meals a day, so breakfast is going to need to shift to a later time."

"Were you always such a planner?" Libby gave her a curious look.

"Not in the least. I'm sure I was over thirty before I realized my life got easier when I was better organized. Which brings me to my purpose in wandering over here. Is this a good time to talk?"

"The best." Libby dried off her hands, then sat at the kitchen table. "What's on your mind."

"The length of my visit. I bought a one-way ticket, but I didn't think to check with you before I did that." She laughed. "I'm not suggesting you'll evict me if I'm here for a while, but I don't like to presume anything…"

"Dexter, that's beyond silly. If you wanted to relocate, you know we'd pay for the movers. Then the problem would be that your grandparents would beg to have you move in with them, and that might get ugly. You're beloved, sweetheart. By all of us."

"Thanks, Mom. I assumed you wouldn't mind, but I like to be thoughtful."

"How long are you thinking of staying? Any idea?"

"Definitely until Kendall's birthday. Then…I'm not sure. I've got one job scheduled for August, but it's only supposed to be for a day or two. Just some ADR work for that animated feature I did in March."

"One or two days? Over two months?"

"I'm normally much busier, Mom. But I've been turning some offers down. If Kendall's going to China for a year, I'm going to spend as much time as possible with her." She looked up, seeing the concern in her mom's eyes.

"You're all right—financially, aren't you, honey?"

"There's not a thing to worry about, Mom. I'm certainly not able to retire and maintain my current lifestyle, but I can be off work for a while with no problem."

Libby looked unusually concerned. "You're leveling with me, right?"

"I went to church yesterday," Dex teased. "I heard all of the commandments, and I paid special attention to the one about lying. I promise I'm doing very well financially."

"We just worry about you, sweetheart..."

"Have you been listening to Grammy? She thinks I depend on the kindness of strangers to get by. I honestly can't figure out why she doesn't understand I have a real career, but..."

"Did she hurt your feelings with the teasing, honey?"

"Not really, but we were chatting with one of her church friends yesterday, and she told the woman that I didn't have a steady job. She said I just helped friends out with little things. She made it sound like I was a handy-woman!"

Libby laughed. "I've tried. God knows I've tried. I think it's possible she's trying to drive us slightly mad..."

"Mmm. Very possible. That *is* her thing."

"Always has been. My high school years were a *trial*," she stressed. "I was a grown woman before I realized I should relish her silliness."

"I relish her a whole lot," Dex said. "I'm going over on Wednesday to take her to lunch. She's allowed me to invite one guest. Want to be our third?"

"I'd love to. But see if Kendall would rather go. Grammy will miss her something fierce when and if she leaves for China."

"Don't remind me," Dex said, standing to go back to the pool house to plan not just her day, but her week.

✖✖✖

As soon as she was back in the pool house, Dex picked up her phone and called her house-sitter, who was her agent's assistant. "Good morning, Aja. It's Dexter. How are things?"

"Fantastic, as usual. The grass has been cut, I've thrown out buckets of unimportant mail, and you now have six new streaming services on your cable bill. I'm paying for them, of course, but I didn't want you to call the cable company and demand a refund when I'm diving into a new series."

"Six? I already pay for three…"

"I know," she said, like that was kind of sad.

"Well, I don't have anything pressing. You might mention to Margaux that I'm going to try to push that ADR work I have scheduled for August back a little, but she's probably not interested in such minor details."

"She's *always* interested in the details. I'll tell her. Does that mean you're not coming back soon?"

"I think it might mean that. But don't feel obligated to stay in the house if you've got plans—"

"I've got plans to stay here until you throw me out. I've never been to Richmond, but if it's nicer than Manhattan Beach, it must be stratospherically fantastic."

"The people are," Dex said, certain of that. "And I get more pleasure from people than I do weather."

"Yeah, well…you do you, Dex. I'm going to hit that beachfront bike path the minute I get home from work. It's ten times more fun than my usual yoga class, and there's a good cocktail bar at the end. Perfection."

✖✖✖

The following Thursday morning, Tracy got into her car and drove to the Haven house. She didn't have to be at work for two hours, and wanted to use her free time well.

The house was quiet when she arrived, but the front door was open. Libby liked to have some fresh morning air when possible, and Tracy loved that she could easily tell they were up and at 'em just with that signal.

She rapped on the wooden frame of the screen door, calling out, "Book delivery for Libby Dexter Haven."

"Come in!" Libby called, probably from the kitchen.

Tracy entered, letting her nose guide her to the coffee she could clearly smell. "I've got two good ones for you," she said, approaching Libby from the back and giving her a kiss on the cheek as she started to step away from the sink.

"We should start texting each other when we buy a book. Then we won't do duplicates like we did with that one by Elizabeth Strout. It was a good book, but we didn't need two copies." She took the books while reaching for her reading glasses. A big smile settled on her face. "I've read the reviews for this one," she said, lifting one of the books. "It sounded promising."

"They're both good," Tracy said. "The other one is a little challenging, but once you get used to the style, it will carry you right along."

"Thank you, sweetheart. Have you had breakfast?"

Tracy gave her a smile. "I thought we could have a cup of coffee together." She turned her head enough to be able to see the pool area. No sign of Dex, which was just what she'd hoped for.

"Pour two cups, then sit down while I make you some yogurt and berries."

"Why don't you sit down, and I'll make my own. I'm certain you've already worked the breakfast shift."

Libby laughed. "If I die first, Randy would get along just fine if he hired a short-order cook who did laundry."

Tracy took her by the shoulders and guided her over to the table. "I'm punching in. Coffee's coming right up."

"This is such a nice surprise. I thought you usually slept in on Thursdays."

"Oh, I suppose I usually do, but my neighbor started cutting his grass at seven thirty. Once I got myself all het up about how insensitive he was, I couldn't go back to sleep." She laughed a little. "My own fault." She poured a cup of coffee for Libby, and delivered it with the small Mason jar of cream they got from a local dairy farm.

"Thank you, sweetheart," Libby said, removing the top of the jar to add a spoonful to her coffee. "It tastes better when someone brings it to you. That's probably why Randy loves to be waited on."

"Or that's simply how he was raised. I didn't know her for many years, but his mother seemed very dedicated to taking care of the men in her life."

"You're right on the money with that observation. I'm sure she loved Randy's sister dearly, but I've always thought there were quite a few reasons Clarissa went to school in New England and never came back."

"There always are," Tracy agreed. She got her yogurt made the way she liked, then poured some coffee for herself. When she sat down, Libby placed a gentle hand on her arm.

"I think this is the first time we've had a minute alone since my prodigal daughter returned. How are you feeling about…everything."

"Oh, you know," Tracy said, not at all sure where to start, or even how much to reveal. "I'm over the shock now."

"Mmm." Libby took a sip of her coffee, and Tracy could tell she was waiting her out—a common tactic. But she wasn't ready to say too much, so she just let the silence continue.

"That's really it?" Libby finally asked.

"Well, no, there's a lot going on in my head. But I'm getting used to Dex being in town. Things feel less fraught than I thought they would."

"I can see that…"

"One thing," Tracy said, realizing she couldn't keep her mouth shut when Libby really wanted to know how she felt. "I've been going over things in my head, and I can't honestly recall why I kept everything just as it was for so long. I know that hurt Dex, but it also hurt Kendall. The wall of silence I put up was childish, and I truly regret it."

"You hurt yourself, too, honey. Sharing the burden of child-raising with a very willing partner would have made your life easier."

"Undoubtedly," she agreed, with her mood continuing to drop. "The Lord Curse strikes again. I cut Dex off just like my family did me—despite knowing how much it hurt." She met Libby's empathic gaze. "The shame's going to last for that one."

"Oh, honey, shame is such an unhelpful emotion. You can't change what you did, just like Dex can't. Let it go and try to be kind to one another now—the only time you have any control over."

She took a bite of her breakfast, nodding her head as she swallowed. "Good advice. As usual," she added, smiling at the only mother-figure who'd ever truly loved her.

❈❈❈

Two nights before Kendall's birthday, Dex sent her parents to a restaurant she'd found that she thought would appeal to them both. It would have been fine if they'd been in the house, but she truly wanted some alone time with Tracy and Yardley, neither of whom she'd seen since Kendall's graduation party.

She'd taken Yardley's red-meat allergy into account, and grilled a couple of whole red snapper, along with all sorts of side dishes, one or two with some heat for Kendall's very adventurous palate.

They were able to sit outside by the pool, and she'd arranged a pair of quiet fans to keep the mosquitos at bay. It had taken her all day to prepare the meal, but she'd gotten it right. Even Yardley seemed to enjoy the grilled vegetables, and Tracy ate like she'd skipped both breakfast and lunch.

"When did you learn to cook?" Tracy asked.

"I could always cook," Dex said, a trifle defensively. "I just didn't do anything adventurous until I...was on my own. Actually," she added, trying to keep the record straight. "I only started to really get into it when I started taking better care of my body."

"And that was when?"

"Mmm. Ten or eleven years ago. I wasn't going to be one of those people who ate food so bland it felt like punishment, so I had to learn how to make healthy things taste good."

"With lots of spice," Kendall said, cleaning the plate that held the remnants of the dish made with eggplant, tomato and Korean hot chili paste. "This makes my tongue tingle."

"Far too hot for me," Yardley said. "But I might like it without the sauce."

"Eggplant without sauce is…not my thing," Kendall said, with Dex cheering her on for taking a moment to censor what would probably have come out as a jibe.

Yardley hadn't touched the buttermilk biscuits, so Dex picked up the last one and put a little butter on it. What kind of creature would refuse a homemade biscuit?

"So Dex," Yardley said. "You'd just barely started your marketing career when it was…interrupted. How does an entry-level corporate job lead to voice-over work? Was that just luck, or did your family have connections in Hollywood, too?"

She'd paused before she added the "too," making a point of Dex's father getting her on at Virtus.

"No family connections west of Virginia," she said, not bothering to defend herself against the Virtus snark. "I suppose I have to credit luck for my first feature, but I'm certain I'm in a career that's a better fit for me than the corporate world ever was. Actually, I wouldn't have considered joining Virtus originally, but…" She gave Kendall a grin. "Babies like to be fed nearly every day."

"Mmm," she said, those sad, basset-hound eyes regarding her closely. "I'm sure all of the business majors and MBAs who worked their butts off in college appreciated your taking a spot they'd actually trained for."

Dex took a bite of her biscuit, chewing slowly, making Yardley wait for a response. Kendall reached under the table and patted her leg, obviously making it clear she was ready to step in if Dex needed her to. "I fully acknowledge how much help I had in getting on at Virtus. Actually, I had the job handed to me." She took another slow bite, spending a moment adding some spicy honey to the rest of the biscuit. Tracy was starting to give her a pointed stare, so she picked up the pace. "But Chuck didn't promote me because I was my father's daughter. I *earned* that job."

"How do you figure? Your dad was the head of governmental affairs," Yardley snapped, barely-controlled anger coloring her voice. "That would have pulled you all the way up the ladder—if you hadn't screwed up."

"Yardley," Tracy said, using the tone of voice you'd use for a dog who was about to bite. It was nice to see that she wasn't afraid of tugging on Yardley's leash.

"It's all right," Dex said. "Yardley's speaking the truth. It's no secret I screwed up. Repeatedly. It's also no secret that various connections have launched me in both of my careers. While I'm proud of my work, and really try to do my best, I've also been blessed with luck." She shifted her gaze to Tracy. "Of all of us, you're the only one who's had to get by exclusively on your talent and hard work."

"Thank you," she said, softening her voice as she gazed down at the table. "That's true when it comes to school and my profession, but... without your parents, Kendall would have been in day care for twelve hours a day. That wouldn't have been fatal, of course, but having your mom step in improved our lives dramatically. I don't even think I need to mention how helpful it's been to be able to build equity with our house."

"And I wouldn't have gotten into UVA if I hadn't gone to a good prep school," Kendall said. "The SAT tutor didn't hurt, either." She gazed at Yardley. "Were you the first in your family to go to college?"

"Of course not—"

"Did you go to a public high school in an underperforming district?"

"No, but—"

"Have you had mentors at Virtus? People who brought you with them when they were promoted?"

"Of course, but—"

"We're all privileged, Yardley. There's no shame in that—unless you try to make the case for being a completely self-made woman." Kendall playfully snatched the last bite of the biscuit from Dex's hand and popped it into her mouth. "Now *that's* shameful."

⚬⚭⚬

Much later, Dex was sitting out by the pool, doing absolutely nothing. She was sure it was close to midnight, but she wasn't in a rush to sleep. Having time alone refreshed her, and listening to the night sounds just added to her enjoyment.

Her phone rang, startling her. She was about to refuse the call, but it was a Richmond number, so she answered. "Hello?"

"Hi," Tracy said. "I wasn't sure you'd recognize this number…"

"I didn't. But when I saw it was from Richmond, I didn't hesitate. Is…everything okay?"

"Sure. I'm not calling too late, am I? I know you used to be a night-owl…"

"I'm wide awake and sitting out by the pool. I annoy Muffin by being out here, but if I let her out she'd be begging to go back inside in five seconds."

"Begging is her life's work. So…I wanted to call and thank you for tonight. It was very kind of you to invite us."

"My pleasure. I'd sincerely like to make things easier between all of us, Tracy. Yardley's going to be part of the family," she said, almost choking on the words, "so we'll be spending a decent amount of time together. I'd like to get past whatever little issues occurred in the past."

"Thanks, Dex. Really. You're being so mature about this, I'd think you were doing it to show me up. But that's never been you."

"Thanks right back. Are you a night-owl now?"

"Not usually. I'm anxious about the party, I guess. I couldn't sleep, so I snuck out of bed and went outside. I'm on the deck now, listening to a bullfrog that's got a whole lot to say."

If she had to sneak out, that meant that Yardley was upstairs. She was always close—leach-like. "No frogs here tonight. Lots of crickets, though."

"Hey," Tracy said, sounding a little unsure of herself. "I was thinking about Yardley's rude question."

"Oh, don't worry about that. She's got some—"

"Oh, I'm not apologizing for her. She can do that for herself. I was honestly wondering how you got into your career. Back when your mom told me you'd gotten a job voicing a character in an animated movie, I just about swallowed my teeth, but I never asked her how that happened. I…should have, of course, but—"

Dex didn't want to hear another apology, so she cut in. "Do you really want to know?"

"I do. Very much."

"All right. Well, I'm sure you knew I was in rehab for an extended period."

"Of course I did," she said quietly. "Three long months."

"Right. So once I got my bearings, I liked to spend time with the newbies, the ones who were really having a tough time adjusting."

"That's because you've got a kind heart. You always have."

"I'm kind enough," she said, sloughing off the compliment. "Anyway, I was worried about this one guy…" She stopped herself, realizing she couldn't possibly reveal what had happened. "Hmm. I can't say more without breaching someone else's privacy."

"Uhm… Can I guess?"

Dex laughed. "That's not really how it works. I'll just say that someone heard my voice quite a few times, and this person had some clout in the biz. I didn't give much thought to it when they made a vague promise about getting me some work, but after I'd been in sober-living for a couple of months, they hooked me up. I auditioned, the producers and the director liked me, and I got hired to voice the mother in *Dobie*. That got me into the union, and I got an agent…all of the stuff."

"I have a feeling there's a lot more to the story. But that will satisfy my curiosity. If I have more questions, I'll ask Grammy. She's a font of knowledge when it comes to your career."

"Don't get me started on her! I took her to lunch yesterday, and she asked the server if they had any openings. She made it clear I wasn't competent to wait tables, but she thought I could handle clearing them..."

"You'll never get too big for your britches with Grammy around, Dex. I'll let you go now. Thanks for chatting."

"Any time. When you're bored in the middle of the night, I'm your woman." That hadn't come out quite right, but Dex guessed Tracy knew what she meant. Her cheery sign-off make that even more clear. They were getting somewhere now. By the end of the summer, they were going to be friends—or at least friendly.

CHAPTER SEVEN

KENDALL'S BIRTHDAY PARTY HAD A very different vibe from her graduation bash. Dex wasn't sure why she'd wanted to keep it so small, but she'd invited a grand total of seven people she wasn't related to—plus Yardley, of course. All friends from high school.

Yardley and all of the relatives were on the deck, with all of the girls by the fire pit—unlit, of course. It was awfully hot, but the humidity wasn't too bad.

The girls were all drinking, but Dex wasn't going to be the one to warn them about day-drinking and the resultant hangover. If they hadn't learned that lesson yet, that was probably good news.

Kendall walked up to the deck, waving at Dex. "We're out of vodka. Any chance of you finding us just a little more?"

Dex took a pointed look at the stairs. "Have you sprained something?"

"No, Mumsie. But Lexie wants to meet you, and she keeps telling me not to call you over. But if you just *happened* to refresh our drinks…"

"All right." Dex took a look at Grammy, who was probably just about to comment that she couldn't understand why strangers wanted to meet her. Heading her off, Dex said, "It's like this, Grammy. If you got to meet Bambi's mother when you were a young adult, wouldn't you have jumped at the chance?"

"Well, no," she said, blinking up at Dex. "That was a cartoon, honey. That deer wasn't real, and even if it had been, it would have been dead many times over. Can you imagine a twenty-five year old deer?" she said, turning to her husband. "That's madness."

"Be right down with your vodka," Dex told Kendall, who was laughing. "I'm available for autographs, by the way." She gave her grandmother a narrow-eyed look. "My ego needs stroking. Badly."

※※※

Lexie actually wasn't a fan. She merely wanted career advice. Sadly, she had the worst combination of attributes for a fledgling actress: a burning desire, along with almost no nerve. Dex was sure she wouldn't last a month in LA, but she wasn't about to tell her that. Instead, she offered some practical advice about trying to get some work locally or even regionally before putting herself up against thousands of other talented actors, all champing at the bit for any kind of part.

The other girls quickly tired of eavesdropping on the conversation, and Dex couldn't blame them. So she took Lexie's offered phone and put her number into her contacts. This certainly wasn't the first time she'd tried to convince a young person not to move to Hollywood, but she hoped it was the last. If you *could* be talked out of it, you should be.

※※※

Kendall looked up when her mom approached the group, noting a decided glower.

"What's up?"

"I need some help." Her gaze was fixed on Dex. "I left some heavy things in the back of my car. Will you help me carry them in?"

"Uhm…" Dex gave her a puzzled look, but got up quickly. "Sure."

Kendall watched them walk away, seeing that something wasn't right. She gave them a little lead time, then stealthily went into the house to spy. By the time she reached the living room, she could hear her mom's voice, strained and angry.

"I *saw* you, Dexter. You were exchanging phone numbers with Lexie right in front of Kendall!"

"She wanted some advice," Dex said, her voice calm, but revealing her hurt.

"Advice? That's a load of bull, and you know it. When are you going to stick to women your own age? It's unseemly, and it sets a very bad image for Kendall."

"I don't—"

"Oh, I know you don't feel a responsibility to model a mature relationship for your daughter. You've made that crystal clear through the years."

Kendall pushed the door open and stood next to them on the porch, fuming. "You're being an asshole, Mom. You'd better shut up before you really dig a hole for yourself."

"Kendall," Dex said sharply. "I can take care of myself. This doesn't concern you."

"Yes, it does. I was right there when Lexie was begging for advice on how to break into the business. You took the time to sit there in the hot sun, just to be kind to one of my friends. I appreciated it."

She faced her mother, whose cheeks were flushed with anger. "I don't know what in the hell has gotten into you, but Dex doesn't deserve to be picked on."

"And I don't deserve to be called an asshole, Kendall. Just because it's your birthday doesn't mean you have free reign to—"

"You *were* being an asshole."

"Does an asshole throw two parties for you in the space of a month? I'd like an apology—"

"So would Dex," she snapped, turning to go back inside. "We're going over to Hannah's pool. It's too hot to sit outside."

On the way to the backyard, she stopped to kiss every cheek—except Yardley's. "You've been released," she announced to one and all. "I truly appreciate that you came, but you can return to your air-conditioned homes now. We're going to go jump into Hannah's pool to avoid melting."

She could see the puzzlement settle on nearly every face, but she didn't want to deal with a long explanation. "Sorry. Really. Love you all!" Then she was off, gathering up her friends to exit via the alley. There was no way she was going to walk past her mothers. If there was any justice, Dex was delivering a well-deserved tongue-lashing. And if there wasn't, Kendall didn't want to witness her voluntary humiliation.

❈

Tracy felt like she'd had the wind kicked right out of her. Never had Kendall been so insolent! So harsh!

She finally let her focus shift to Dex, who seemed thoroughly chagrined. Her gaze was cast downward, and she looked like she wanted some pockets to shove her hands into. But the style of clothing she wore didn't allow for them.

Dex had always been a little stylish, and now she'd adopted the flowing, loosely structured, monochromatic look of linen, silk, crepe and charmeuse many fashionable women wore. So far, Tracy had only seen her in cocoa, steel grey, black, or white.

Her sleeveless black top extended past her hips, with the Mandarin collar making it look crisp and polished. Her slacks were bright white, and very snug. Strangely, there wasn't a line showing anywhere, not even a wrinkle. She still looked as cool and carefree as she had when she'd walked in—except for her expression.

If Tracy had happened upon her, not knowing her a lick, she'd have wondered what this woman had done that she was so deeply ashamed of. But what sense did that make? Tracy had been a jerk to her...unless Dex really *had* been hitting on Lexie, which wasn't beyond the realm of possibility.

"What's going on here?" she finally asked. "I know you have a penchant for substantially younger women. Asking you to keep your paws off Kendall's friends does *not* make me an asshole."

"I didn't say you were. I have dated young women." Her gaze tentatively slid up to land on Tracy. "But I'd never, ever try to date one of Kendall's friends. Or anyone else as young as she is. Thirty's my lowest number, and it's got to be a very mature thirty-year-old to make me dip that low."

"Bullshit," Tracy said, furious at Dex for lying right to her face. "I've seen the photos."

"Photos?"

"Sometimes Kendall shows me pictures from her trips to LA. You're never in the frame, but at least half of the time there's a very young woman somewhere in the background. Given that Kendall has no friends out there…"

"*I* have friends," Dex said, still very quiet. "Friends I don't sleep with."

"Why would you hang around with twenty-something girls?" Tracy demanded, knowing she sounded peevish. "For their deep insights? Their worldly perspective?"

"I…" She shut her mouth, looking very uncomfortable. "I don't want to be too specific, but I have non-sexual relationships with a couple of women who are pretty young. I can relate to them, since I was around their age when I got into the same kinds of trouble they're having."

"You're saying you bring people from AA and NA over to meet Kendall?"

"I didn't say that," she said, finally showing a little backbone as her gaze met Tracy's. "I said what I said, and I'm not going to divulge anything else. I'll just add that someone I know is Chinese-American, and still has family in Chengdai Province. The last time Kendall visited, I asked her to come by, just to offer some tips about travel. I'm sure Kendall took some pictures with her."

"There was more than one woman," Tracy insisted. "This goes back years."

"Are you talking about the tutors I hired? I wanted Kendall to stay academically sharp during her summers… Jesus," she muttered. "Do you think I sleep with every woman who walks into my house?"

"I don't know what to think! I never ask Kendall about who's in a picture, and she never volunteers. I assumed…"

"Those assumptions are really unfair, Tracy. They're part of the reason Kendall feels caught in the middle, by the way." She closed her eyes, taking in a visible breath. "I thought we were going to stop making things uncomfortable for her."

Tracy took in a few deep breaths, really trying to get her brain to work properly. "You swear you didn't ever have your dates around when Kendall was staying with you?"

"Kendall has never met anyone I've dated. *Ever*," she stressed, meeting Tracy's gaze head-on.

"Why?" She really didn't want to know, but she had to. All of a sudden she was desperate to find out whatever she could about Dex's life.

"Our situation was confusing enough for her. I didn't want her to get the wrong idea."

"Which was…?"

Dex broke eye contact again. "I've gone out a lot, but I've never been involved with anyone I thought would last." Her voice lowered a little when she added, "There have been some women I wanted to make long-term, but they weren't still around by summer." She shrugged. "Bad choices on my part. Bad timing. All sorts of things can derail a new relationship."

"Oh, fuck," Tracy muttered, covering her face with her hands. "So I've been accusing you of…"

"I don't blame you," Dex said, her voice soft and gentle. "I have gone out with women a lot younger than I am. And I haven't been a great role model. I don't think it's good for Kendall to see that I can't stick with anyone for long. So I've kept my dating habits to myself."

Tracy felt like they'd been in a fight, even though that wasn't true in the least. If anything, she'd been the aggressor, with Dex just trying to cover up so she wasn't hurt too badly. "I've got to sit down. Join me?"

She plunked herself down on the steps, and Dex did the same, after carefully brushing off the wood to keep those white slacks spotless.

"It was a mistake to keep Kendall in the dark," Tracy said. "Once she was in high school I should have been more forthright. Much more."

"I should have been, too, but I didn't want to overstep."

"You never have," Tracy said, ashamed to admit that. "You've always treated me like I was in complete charge."

"You have been." A sad, half-smile covered her face. "I didn't have any legal standing, so I've always been careful. I knew Kendall's visits hinged on staying on your good side."

"She knew that too," Tracy admitted, sick over that fact. "She told me not long ago that she prayed every night that I didn't stop you from seeing her." She looked over at Dex, easily able to see the pain in her eyes. "I never would have done that. She's your child as much as she is mine."

"Of course you would have done that," Dex said, very calm and self-possessed. "If I'd started using again, that would have been it."

"But you didn't. Your mom told me how hard you worked to stay sober."

"I had a lot on the line," she said, with a very faint smile showing. "Not that I didn't originally, but it took me a while to understand what true sobriety was. It's a job I'm always thinking of. It could take me down tomorrow if I make a single mistake."

"God," she sighed. "If it's genetic, I hope Kendall hasn't inherited it."

"Uhm…she and I aren't genetically related."

"I meant from my family, Dex. I know how genetics works."

"Right. Right. I forget that your father…" She gave Tracy a curious look. "No contact?"

"None. When the Lords tell you to get out and stay out, they damn-well mean it."

"Sorry," Dex whispered.

"It's for the best. If it was just my parents, that would have been one thing. But if my brother or sister had the slightest influence on Kendall, I'd never forgive myself. Both of them were…awful," she added quietly.

"I know. There must have been a lot of pain in that house to screw up two out of three kids." She clapped Tracy on the leg. "But the chaos didn't get to you."

"Not entirely. But I've clearly got my issues. Thankfully, your family has been so supportive Kendall hasn't needed any more relatives."

"I was gifted with a very good family. God knows they've kept me going."

"And if I know them as well as I think I do, at least one of them has tip-toed up to the door to see if they can make their escape."

"My mom," Dex said, extending a hand to pull Tracy to her feet.

"Yardley," Tracy said, really dreading having to explain all of this. But since Yardley was the one who'd initially whipped her into a frenzy…

"You don't mind if I just skedaddle, do you?" Dex asked.

"Of course not. But how will you get home?"

"Do you have a set of Kendall's car keys around? I've never grounded her, but…she really shouldn't have spoken to you like she did."

"I've grounded her plenty. Once more won't hurt. Be right back."

⁕⁕⁕

The Havens were so well-mannered that they all acted like it was perfectly normal to be left on the deck while the guest of honor escaped through the alley, with the hostess out on the front porch, lobbing unfounded accusations at her ex.

Moments after Tracy reached the deck, Randy stood up, pointedly looked at his watch, and actually exclaimed, "Well, will you look at the time?"

It took only another minute for all four of the remaining guests to be up and out, leaving Tracy with one doe-eyed woman gazing at her. "Are you going to clue me in?"

"Of course." Tracy sat next to Yardley, trying to decide how to discuss this. There were two issues—Tracy's vow to never pick on Dex again, and Yardley's penchant for stirring up trouble.

There were Diet Cokes lying in a galvanized tub in the backyard, and the block of ice she'd put into it a few hours earlier was about the size of a softball now. That meant the soda was still icy cold. Unable to resist, she got up and jogged down the steps, calling out, "Be right back. Thirsty!"

Once that little delaying tactic was over, she sat down again and took a long drink. She didn't like Diet Coke much, but Yardley might not know that.

Yardley was gazing at her carefully, and Tracy finally got to it. "When you kept commenting on how involved Dex was with the girls, I started to watch her. At one point, I saw her take Lexie's phone and type something. I assumed it was her number—"

"She did what?" Yardley looked like she was going to blow a fuse.

"I jumped to a conclusion, and asked her to go out front with me so I

120

could tell her off. Kendall appeared just as I was winding up, and she and I got into it." She took the cold can and rolled it across her forehead, finding it cooled her down much more than drinking the stuff did.

"Your family is so damned odd. Kendall came out here, told everyone to leave, then she and her friends snuck out through the back gate. Everyone kept on chatting like that hadn't just happened!"

"They like to act like they don't notice little fights. Personally, I appreciate that," Tracy added. "They never get involved if there's any possible way to ignore an issue."

"Well, that's probably best," Yardley said, nodding soberly. "So you're saying that Dexter *wasn't* being inappropriate?"

"That's exactly what I'm saying. I felt like a fool for jumping on her, but she took it well. She barely defended herself."

"Probably because she's committed bigger sins that you haven't discovered yet."

Tracy almost snapped at her, but she got hold of herself quickly. "Or she just doesn't like strife. She'd rather be yelled at than fight."

"I can't disagree with that, either. You must be attracted to peaceable women."

"Mmm. Here's a big difference between you two," she said, almost certain she should shut her mouth and keep it shut. "Dex would never whisper in my ear if she saw you doing something that was possibly out-of-line. While she'd confront *you*," she insisted, certain of that, "she wouldn't lob idle bits of conjecture about you—or anyone else, for that matter."

"I—!"

"I'm asking you to stop doing that, Yardley. I don't blame you for today, since I took your speculation and ran with it. But I don't want to keep this up." She took her hand, with it feeling sizzling hot after the cold Coke can. "We need to concentrate on us. Our little universe is plenty to tend to. It shouldn't matter to either of us what Dex is up to."

"Of course it does! She's got a lot of influence over Kendall. Mostly bad, from what I've been able to see—"

"And what if that's true? It would be one thing if Kendall was a baby, and we were going to co-parent. Then you'd have a vested interest in how other people in her life behaved. But she's an adult. Your influence over her will be no greater than your influence over Grammy."

"Well, as long as we're talking about her, I think someone should have her evaluated for cognitive decline. She asked me if I was the person who'd parked her car!"

Tracy laughed, with the expression on Yardley's face so puzzled it really tickled her funny-bone. "That's just her sense of humor. What she was really saying is that she doesn't know you well. That was an invitation to sit down and talk."

"Some invitation!"

"You're going to have to get used to the family, Yardley. Seriously. I spend a lot of time with them, and that's going to continue."

"I make small talk with people I don't know well for a living," she grumbled, clearly unhappy.

Tracy gazed at her for another little bit. Given the scope of Yardley's job, she probably was called upon to talk to strangers and make them feel comfortable. Maybe that's why she hadn't been promoted for ten years.

⚬⚬⚬

Kendall didn't come home that night, texting from Hannah's that they were going to have a campout in the backyard. That actually sounded like fun, but Tracy was definitely not invited, and she wouldn't have gone if she had been. Acting like one of Kendall's friends wasn't her thing. She liked to behave like a mom—with all of the lack of coolness that entailed.

She was concerned about Kendall, not sure whether to ask her to come home, or just let this blow over. The kid usually exploded like a cherry bomb, then stomped away before things got too heated. Her norm was to keep her distance for a day or two, then wake up like nothing had happened. Tracy wasn't sure that was the best way to deal with conflict, but it had worked well enough.

But when Kendall texted on the second day to say she was heading over to her grandparents', it seemed like a little more intervention might be necessary.

"I was hoping you'd be home for dinner," Tracy texted back. "Yardley's in New York through the weekend, and I hate to eat alone when my baby girl's in town…"

A minute later, another text showed up. "We're on for dinner. Want me to go to the store?"

Tracy smiled as she made up a shopping list. The chill was over.

※※※

Even though they generally didn't tackle upsetting topics head on, it had become crystal clear that Kendall didn't like being in the house when Yardley was there. Something that divisive couldn't be ignored—as much as Tracy wished it could.

The heat wave had disappeared as quickly as it had come, and they sat out on the deck to enjoy their meal. Kendall had opened a bottle of white wine, and even though Tracy hadn't adjusted to drinking with her child, she forced herself to refrain from commenting. Did any kid like to continually hear how stunned a parent was that they were now an adult?

Kendall filled their glasses, then put the bottle in an ice bucket. Actually, it was a plastic pail she used to play with in her sandbox, but Tracy loved to repurpose things rather than add single use items to her pantry.

Tracy took a sip, and nodded her approval. "Nice choice. This goes well with salmon."

"It is good," she said, looking very thoughtful. "I think wine's going to be my drink. If Dex heads home before I leave for China, I'll go to LA for a visit. She promised to take me to Napa or Sonoma for my birthday present, and I'd like to get that done. I think wine snobbery is in my future." Her playful smile showed she was exaggerating, but knowing Kendall, she would learn all she could, then develop strong opinions.

Ignoring the additional California trip, along with the casual reference about the much bigger trip that Tracy was certain was still not nailed down, she got to the heart of the matter. "So…as you know, I've been dating Yardley for over a year now. Even though I've tried to take it slow, I get the feeling you'd like me to take it slower. Or push her off a cliff."

Kendall actually gasped. "I don't hate her, Mom. I'm just…not used to her," she finished, failing to make eye contact.

"Until this summer, I never invited her to stay overnight when you were home, wanting to give you time to get used to the idea. But you haven't been in the house more than three nights—total—when Yardley's been here."

"Like I said, I'm not used to her. Having someone new around upsets our dynamic."

"Mmm. How would you feel if I left the house every time the person you fell in love with appeared on my doorstep?"

"Uhm…" She took a bite of her broccoli, then dipped it in the hot sauce she'd pooled onto the side of her plate. "That would probably…not be great." She looked up and gazed at Tracy for a minute. "Let's face it. If you weren't comfortable with a guy I brought home, you wouldn't say anything. You're a lot nicer than I am."

"No, I'm not, sweetheart. But I feel like you haven't given Yardley a chance. You take off every time she comes over, and that makes her try harder—which is probably annoying."

"A little," she allowed. "I like people who are more like cats."

That wasn't true at all, given every boyfriend had been like a Golden Retriever. But Tracy wasn't going to make that point. "I'm afraid that's not Yardley's style. She just tries harder."

"So…What do we do? I like staying home, but it feels less like home when Yardley's here."

"And it will feel *much* less like home if I sell the house and move into her condo."

Kendall paled. "You'd do that?"

"I might. Yardley has a very nice place in The Fan. Three big bedrooms, three baths. You'd have your own space."

"No, no, no," she said quickly. "If you move, which I *don't* want you to do, I'll stay with Nana and Papa when I visit. I'm…" She looked away again. "I don't think I'll ever be comfortable staying at Yardley's. Don't count on me, Mom. Seriously," she added, as if Tracy might just toss this off as inconsequential.

"Honey, I see that you're not a fan, but you're acting like she's toxic! If you have something to say, please say it."

"Like…?"

"Has she made you feel uncomfortable?"

Kendall looked so blissfully confused that Tracy's blood pressure began to fall.

"I guess I'm uncomfortable, but I don't have any good reason for feeling that way. I…" She looked so serious as she thought. "Have you ever had a good friend who hooked up with someone new?"

"Of course."

"Things between you and your friend had to kind of readjust, right? They were less available, at the very least."

"Sure. I know just what you mean."

"It's like that, but a little worse, since she's not who I'd pick for you. At all," she stressed.

"Well, I wish that wasn't true, but I can't let your opinion of her influence my choice."

"She's so bland," Kendall moaned. "How can you go from Dex to Yardley? You can do so much better, Mom. Really."

That was going a little too far. "One, it's awfully rude of you to impugn my choices like that. And two, you don't know Yardley well enough to call her bland."

"I'm sorry," she said, seemingly sincere. "I should keep my mouth shut, since I really *don't* know her. But you've got to admit she doesn't have any of Dex's spark."

"Kendall," she said, keeping her voice level. "I was with Dex for five years. At this point, we've been broken up more than three times longer than we were together. You've got to let go, baby."

"I'm not saying I want you to get back with her," Kendall said, looking so earnest Tracy almost believed her. "I just want you to find someone who's half as good."

"Look. The woman you know is markedly different from the woman I fell in love with. While I'll admit that Dex was charming, and ingratiating, and persuasive, she was also very glib. She and the truth were not always close friends."

Kendall blinked at her for a moment, obviously confused. "I've never met anyone more honest. I'm not exaggerating, Mom. Dex is doing some kind of personal inventory of her failings every damn minute."

"I'm glad for that, honey. But she wasn't doing that when she was abusing drugs. When the woman you love lies to you repeatedly you begin to lose your trust. And once that's gone..."

"I get that your trust was damaged. I really do—"

"I didn't say damaged. I said destroyed. And when you can't trust a woman, you can't raise a child with her. It would have been like leaving a four-year-old to watch your two-year-old. Guaranteed mayhem."

"But didn't you miss her?" Kendall asked, with her warm eyes misting over.

That hit Tracy like a punch. She'd obviously been better at hiding her heartbreak than she'd thought. "Of course I missed her. I missed the woman I fell for more than I could ever say. But...she'd changed."

"I know that addiction changes you—"

"Yes, but that's not what I mean. Dex had been a star at everything. Sports, academics, her career. Developing a drug habit really knocked her off her perch, and when she relapsed that first time..." Tracy shook her head, unable to even put into words how dramatic the change had been.

"Is that what Nana means when she talks about Dex losing her self-esteem?"

"She does that?"

"Just since Dex has been here. Like the other day Dex gave her a cocky smile after she made some comment, and when she walked away, Nana said something about how glad she was that Dex seemed as full of herself as she had been when she was young."

"Mmm. Yes. That's exactly what I'm talking about. That first relapse definitely took a chunk out of her, but the second pretty much destroyed the things that made Dex who she was. When you're with someone who constantly tells you what a sorry excuse for a human she is..." She swallowed around the knot in her throat, thinking of the confident, brash young woman who'd been reduced to wearing sackcloth and ashes. "You start to agree with her, even when you really, really don't want to."

"Not to be a jerk, but don't you think kicking her out of the house and refusing to let her see me made that even worse?"

"It certainly couldn't have helped, but I didn't have to witness the results of my actions. But trust me, I have a long list of regrets too, honey."

"Family therapy? All of my friends have gone..."

"I think our family dynamic is going to be functional—thanks to your pushing us. Besides, we've done most of the parenting we need to do."

❧

A couple of days later, Kendall rolled up to her grandparents' house just as Dex was leaving in Nana's car. Kendall got out and walked over to the driver's side. "Where are you off to?"

"DC. Want to ride along?"

"Not so much. But I will if you need company."

Dex smiled up at her. "Did I tell you I was going?"

"You did not."

"Then I must not *need* company. I've got a bunch of podcasts I can listen to. I was just offering."

"What are you going for?"

"Work. There's a recording studio that I hope to be able to use to do a commercial I was just offered. We're only going to do some testing today, so it shouldn't take too long. If I can do little jobs in DC, I can stick around for as long as I want."

"Cool! But don't think I'm going to let you off the hook for that Napa trip."

"I'm not trying to get off the hook. If you come up with a firm date for your big adventure, we'll make plans."

"It's a deal. Have fun today. Break a leg, or whatever they say to voice actors."

"Thanks, baby. Will you be here for dinner? Big barbecue night…"

"Can I invite some people over?"

"Fine with me. Check with Nana."

Kendall leaned in and kissed her cheek. "Love you."

"Love you just as much." Dex gazed up at her, sometimes stunning Kendall with how truly pretty she was. But they looked nothing alike, and sometimes Kendall longed to share more than just eye color. "Maybe even a tiny bit more."

⸙

After spending a few minutes with her grandparents, Kendall went to the pool house to do a little research. Since she'd had such poor luck with convincing a fellow student into traveling with her, she spent some time posting queries on various message boards, asking for info on how to hook up with a travel buddy. She got a few responses, but nothing very helpful.

After a while, she grew tired of using her phone to read the long threads, so she picked up Dex's laptop to continue her search. After about an hour, she gave up, certain there was a better way to do this. She just hadn't found it yet.

She was about to close the laptop when her gaze landed on the photos icon. As a child, she and Dex had spent hours watching videos they made during her monthly visits home. It seemed silly now, but Kendall had loved learning some skill, like a cartwheel, or a handstand, then forcing Dex to film her making twenty attempts to get it right. Then they had to watch her massive accomplishment again and again and again. Now that she thought about it, a parent's main duty might have been watching your kid do really boring stuff for hours on end.

Paging through the list of videos, Kendall was a little surprised to see that Dex had a real treasure trove, predating Kendall's birth.

She opened the oldest one, taken by Nana, with Dex giving her a lot of unasked-for advice about how to use the brand new video camera. It seemed silly that they didn't just use their phones, but if a legit video camera provided a slightly better picture, Kendall could easily see her papa racing out to buy one.

The video had been taken on the day her parents had moved into an apartment in Charlottesville. Dex looked kind of beefy, like she weighed at least twenty pounds more. But when she took off her jacket, her snug t-shirt made it clear she was as lean as a greyhound. All of that added bulk must have been pure muscle. But even though Dex was bigger than she was now, both she and Tracy looked like children, with plump cheeks and bright eyes.

Dex was narrating a walk-through of the apartment, and Kendall could easily see what her mom was referring to when she spoke about Dex's swagger. It was there—in full color—with Kendall able to really see it for the first time.

At that point in her life, Dex had just talked a previously straight girl into having a baby. Kendall only knew that her mom had been with men because of a minor crisis, but it had been a good one, in retrospect.

Way back when she was in pre-school or kindergarten, Kendall had realized she liked boys better than girls, and that troubled her, since she thought she'd be like her moms. But her mom had assured her that you could like anyone at all, and that you could change your mind at any time, like she had, which had been pretty perfect advice for a kid.

So here was old Dex, having just gotten Tracy to jump the fence, now having convinced her parents to support them financially, as well as emotionally. Those victories must have enhanced the confidence she was clearly already blessed with, and that bluster showed when she moved around the empty rooms, declaring the smaller bedroom would be where they'd set up the nursery.

Tracy was holding onto Dex's hand or arm during the tour, looking a little shell-shocked, as well as super shy. She couldn't have known her girlfriend's mom very well, so having this really nice, really generous woman show up to get them organized must have kind of overwhelmed her. The Havens could sometimes roll in like a benevolent hurricane.

Papa wasn't in the movie, probably because he was carrying all of their stuff up the stairs. He'd always been the guy you could rely on to shoulder the weight.

The next video was even cooler. It was Christmas, and they were all seated around the dining table. They went around the room, with everyone offering their hopes and prayers for the new baby. Having your relatives talk about you before they knew a single thing about you was kind of odd—but awesome. Everyone seemed so excited, even though nothing was guaranteed—gender, physical health, a full set of intact chromosomes. All Kendall had been at that point was a concept to stake their dreams on.

Her mom looked like she'd gained a little weight, mostly in her face. She looked truly adorable, and the way she and Dex interacted was fucking heartbreaking. They were so tender and sweet with each other, with Dex maintaining she didn't care if they had a boy or a girl, or what the baby looked like. She just wanted it to be like Tracy. The camera shakily zoomed in on Tracy then, gazing at Dex like she could walk on water.

It was like watching the first act of Romeo and Juliet. You knew they were going to off themselves in the end, but you still got carried away by how certain they were that the other was the only person in the world they would ever love. They didn't let their families, or their youth, or their inexperience stop them from throwing every dollar into the pot, hoping they held the cards. But they didn't. Or they'd bet on a hand that looked better than it turned out to be. No matter what had gone wrong, their luck hadn't held.

≋

Dex got home at four, a little disappointed to note that Kendall's car was absent. She would have followed the kid around like an annoying little sister if she could have gotten away with it, but she didn't want to make a pest out of herself. Kendall had the right to enjoy her last weeks at home, without having to structure her day to include Dex.

When she got out of the car, she heard music playing, so she walked along the side of the house to see Kendall lying in the pool, with a portable speaker on the deck, blasting a song by what sounded like an angsty young woman. Kendall was reading what looked like a heavy, hard-bound book, although her mirrored shades might have disguised firmly closed eyes.

Dex walked over to the deck, and was just about to toss some water onto her when Kendall looked up sharply. "I'll give you three minutes to get in here."

"How about giving me ten? I'll go make us a snack."

Kendall smiled at her. "Will it be your kind of snack or my kind of snack?"

"I assume there's a bag of corn chips in the pantry. Salsa?"

"Please. A soda would make the whole thing pop." Her grin grew. "Get it? Some people call soda pop."

"You're treading into dad joke territory, but I definitely get it."

"Hurry up! I know you're going to have some kind of fruit or vegetable, and that takes longer to make than just grabbing a bag of chips. We've got sun to soak up."

"Can't wait." Dex nearly ran for the house, thrilled to have her little cookie all to herself for the rest of the afternoon.

⬦⬦⬦

They were both set up with snacks, hats, sunglasses, and a liberal application of sun block. As always, Dex had carefully covered Kendall's shoulders. That skin was too precious to let the sun scorch it.

"Hey," Kendall said. "Do you mind if I use your computer?"

"No. Want me to go get it?"

"I mean in general. Like do you have lots of stuff on it that you don't want me to see?"

"Not really. My email's private, but other than that…"

"Good. 'Cause I looked at some of the videos you had on there from the early, early years."

"Today?"

"Uh-huh. Sorry I didn't ask, but I had a real need…"

Dex tucked her container of cherries up against her lap and paddled over to Kendall. "What's going on, baby?"

"Mmm. Nothing bad. I just have so many questions about my origin story. It's important, Dex, more important all the time."

"Huh." She popped a cherry into her mouth, mostly to give herself a second to think. "I can see that you'd want to know some details. But I think your mom is the right person to talk to."

Kendall gave her a long look, clearly on the verge of asking Dex if she was joking.

"Okay. I understand your mom's been kind of closed-off. But that should be getting better, isn't it?"

"Not a lot." Kendall gave her a poke. "Ideally, I'd talk to both of you at once. Are you game?"

"Uhm…yeah, I guess I am. But how are you going to arrange that? Yardley's certainly not going to be interested, and she's around… constantly."

"All I need is permission," Kendall said, grinning slyly. "I can handle the rest."

❈❈❈

The day caught up with her, and Dex needed a nap before Kendall's friends came over for the barbecue.

When she went inside, she saw her laptop lying on the sectional. It came to life when she picked it up, with an image of Tracy, wearing a Christmasy sweater decorated with reindeer.

Dex didn't have a great memory for details about clothing, but she remembered that sweater—partly because she'd been given a matching one.

Grammy had been struggling a little to get used to the idea of Dex raising a baby with a woman the family didn't know. Actually, Tracy was the only woman Dex had ever brought home, and Grammy had obviously been trying to come up with Christmas gifts that a lesbian

132

couple would enjoy. She went with matching clothing, which was kind of adorable.

Dex took a look at the videos on the list, arranged in date order. The next one was also taken on Christmas, a few hours after the first, and she clicked on it.

They were up in her bedroom, and Tracy was lying on the bed, fully clothed, dozing. They usually ate Christmas dinner around two, so Tracy was probably napping between the big dinner and the subsequent sandwiches they'd have for an evening snack.

The camera focused on her face, so peaceful and serene as she slept. She was *such* a pretty woman, then and now. But back then she'd been so…soft. That was a funny word for how Tracy had seemed, but it seemed apt. Everything about her was soothing and gentle. Slow to anger, desperate to please, so remarkably grateful for the smallest kindness. Dex could cry just thinking about the looks Tracy used to give her—like she was the mast she was tethered to, and that they'd sail through life by tacking together.

Dex's hand touched the hem of the sweater, and she pulled it up slightly. Her voice, which was a little higher than it was now, said, "There's a baby right there." She touched Tracy's slightly rounded belly, laughing when she woke up enough to push her hand away and tug her sweater back down.

"Are you talking to the baby again? He or she needs a nap, too. They're probably overwhelmed by the number of calories flying through my blood."

"We do tend to go a little crazy on holidays," Dex said, now holding the camera steadier. "You'll get used to the drill and learn to pace yourself."

Tracy gave her a very uncertain smile. "Do you swear they liked me? I can't tell if everyone is just being polite or if—"

"They love you!" The camera swung around wildly, then bounced for a few seconds as Dex lay next to Tracy and tucked an arm under her head. "My family will always love you, sweetheart. Just like I will." She held the camera up, with the framing off a little bit.

"I'm not saying your family's not an upgrade, since it definitely is, but they're wearing me out." She patted her belly lightly. "Or maybe it's just that I'm pregnant, huh?"

"That could be part of it. Next time, I'll have the baby. You still want to have two, don't you?"

"Or three." She looked at Dex again, with that limitless faith that had developed so quickly shining brightly in her lovely eyes. "Who knows? We might have so much fun with this one that we decide to have six more." She leaned as far as she could reach to place a kiss on Dex's cheek. "Whatever happens, we'll be great. Now lie down next to me and let me sleep for another fifteen minutes." She made a very cute, not very fierce face while looking right into the lens. "No more movies. You're going to wear the camera out before the baby even gets here."

Dex turned the camera around, with a silly grin plastered across her face. "To be continued," she said, before stopping the recording.

With her heart racing, Dex pushed the laptop away. Where did that girl go? Tracy hadn't exactly hardened, but the sweetness, the optimism, the courage had all been tamped down—severely.

Maybe raising Kendall mostly on her own had sucked the lightness right out of her. Or maybe she just didn't show it to Dex any more. She sincerely hoped it was only that, because the trust that used to beam from those blue eyes had been the most precious thing in Dex's world. Before, or since.

CHAPTER EIGHT

ON SATURDAY MORNING, DEX WAS not truly awake, but she wasn't truly asleep, either. She liked to have the windows open at night, but that might have been a mistake. While she wasn't sure what time it was, it was definitely morning, and when the room was so hot and humid that she'd kicked even the sheet off, it was going to be a scorcher.

A key scratched around on her lock, waking her further. "Mom?"

"Child," Kendall said, standing in the bedroom doorway. She approached and slapped Dex on the butt. "Who sleeps in something like this?" she demanded, tugging on her silky camisole.

"I do," Dex sniffed. She wanted to pull the sheet up, but Kendall was now sitting atop it. "I became a mild hedonist when I got clean." She finally pried her eyes open. "I try to encase myself in the softest clothing possible. Lots of little physical pleasures give me small doses of serotonin. Those add up to make me happy."

"Well, it's time to get your little hedonistic butt out of bed. By the time you have your swimsuit on, I'll have made you coffee. Then we'll hit the road."

Kendall got up and started for the kitchenette, but Dex called her back. "Road? What road?"

"The road to Sandbridge Beach. Make it snappy!"

"Beach? We're going to the beach? On a steaming hot Saturday?"

"Have to. Mom's going with us, and she's only off on the weekends."

"Your mom...?" She felt like she was dreaming. Why was Tracy going to the beach with them?

"Yeah. She's waiting. Come *on*," she urged dramatically.

"But I haven't meditated. I haven't done my yoga..."

"Bring your mat. You can amaze all of the beachgoers with your ridiculous flexibility."

"Kendall," she whined. "I like to get up slowly. I need to ease into my day…"

Kendall marched right over to her and held up her phone. "Look at my lock screen."

Dex's mouth slid into a smile when she looked at the photo. "You know I have that same one, framed, on my desk at home."

"This was our last time at Sandbridge Beach as a family. I know it won't be the same, but it's truly important to me to go back with you and mom while you're being friendly. Please?" she asked, her voice dropping in volume.

"Can we stop for something to eat?"

"Mom's making you breakfast right now. Don't worry," she continued when Dex opened her mouth. "It'll be healthy."

"I was just going to say that I'll skip the coffee if you're in a hurry."

Kendall kissed each of her cheeks. "There's always time for coffee."

❈❈❈

Kendall had been so insistent about the outing that Tracy hadn't been able to refuse. She didn't have to work, Yardley was out of town, she had no other plans, and it was going to be too hot to work in the yard for long. But being in the car with Dex and Kendall was still a very odd thing. Kind of like deja vu, but with the players in the image having aged significantly.

Dex was sitting in the passenger seat, dressed in shorts and a top that barely covered her. Her clothing continued to perplex, as well as enthrall. Everything she wore was oversized or super-slim—total extremes. Today's coral-colored top was square cut, roomy, sleeveless, and very soft-looking. But her khaki green shorts were skin-tight and very brief. They also looked soft, maybe a washable silk. Where did you even find clothing like that? Every article she wore made Tracy want to rub her face against it. There was no doubt the fabric would feel divine, and when it was draped across such long, smoothly muscled legs, it was hard to concentrate on driving.

She tried not to look, but when she let her gaze slide over for a quick peek, Dex was smiling at her as she eased another spoonful of yogurt into her mouth. "I love the combination of raspberries and blackberries you put in here. The sunflower seeds liven it up, too. Thanks."

"You're welcome. I know breakfast is a big part of your day." At Dex's puzzled look she added, "After Kendall returned home from a summer with you, she'd go a week or two where she wanted fresh fruit and chia or flax seeds in some plain yogurt." She looked into the rearview mirror, catching her daughter's gaze. "Then it was back to arguments about how much Peanut Butter Toast Crunch I'd let her snarf down."

"That stuff is totally delicious," Kendall maintained. "But I don't eat it for breakfast anymore. Now it's my preferred snack for when I'm zoned out."

Tracy rolled her eyes, seeing Dex do the same. It was kind of nice to have a little support. Eye-rolling when Kendall intentionally tried to get their goats was a lot more fun in tandem.

❧

They'd had to walk quite a distance to find a spot that was uncrowded. Dex would have stopped much earlier, but she was carrying the lunch her mother had packed for them, so it made sense she'd give out first. For some reason, Kendall seemed to want to walk to North Carolina, and Dex was about to ask for help when both Kendall and Tracy agreed they'd found the perfect spot. It didn't look much better than the area a quarter mile back had, but Dex wasn't going to argue. She was going to drop to the sand and catch her breath. She had no earthly idea why their lunch basket was so remarkably heavy, but she'd worked up such an appetite she was in danger of eating all of it by herself.

❧

While hating the fact that years of living alone with a pretty flexible schedule had made her *less* flexible about every bit of her routine, Dex truly couldn't get into the spirit of the day without a reset. If she didn't have at least ten minutes to meditate and another twenty minutes to do just a few poses to loosen up and center herself physically, she wouldn't get the most out of the day.

Years of trial and error had convinced her that situations even slightly stressful demanded a clear head, and revisiting a place where they shared such fond memories was definitely in the stressful category. Even a good memory could be fraught.

While Kendall and Tracy were still shucking their sandals, Dex picked up her mat. "I'm going to go a little further down for a few minutes. Don't you two dare eat all of that food."

Kendall stared at her. "You're leaving one minute after we've gotten here?"

"I'm just going to get my head on straight. My routine was disrupted —even though I'm glad it was," she added when Kendall looked perplexed. "Just a few minutes will get me where I need to be."

"You need to be in the water with us, so shake a leg."

"Leg-shaking is part of my practice," she said, laughing when Kendall scowled at her. Dad jokes ruled.

⚛

"How long has the yoga thing been going on?" Tracy asked as she watched Dex walk toward a deserted part of the long beach.

"Long time. I think it, and meditation, are big keys to her staying sober. Can't argue with success."

"No, you certainly can't. I keep thinking I should start with some yoga, just to keep my joints flexible. God knows running isn't doing them any favors."

"But you love running, Mom. Doing what makes you happy's not a bad practice, either."

"How about you?" Tracy said, gazing at her daughter's enviable body. She was shaped just like Tracy's older sister had been at the same age. Tall and slim, with broad shoulders. She looked like she might have played volleyball, or even basketball. But she hadn't. Organized sports had never been her thing. "You haven't done much since you ran cross country in prep school."

"I've got time," she said, grinning while she lay on her side, with her bikini bottoms leaving a gap where her flat belly didn't shift to fill it. "When things start to go off the rails, I'll probably start getting serious about yoga or Pilates. Until then, I'm going to enjoy the fact that I can go on a long hike or even a run if I want to, and not be sore the next day."

Smiling at her logic, Tracy said, "If you got into doing something now, you might stay on the rails a little longer."

"That might be true, but I'm not motivated. I've got stuff to do, Mom." She reached into her bag and pulled out a book. Her language skills had increased to the point where she could read difficult novels in Mandarin, this one recently sent to her by a girl who'd graduated a year earlier and was now living in Beijing. Why she'd paid what must have been a fortune in postage to send a real book was a question Tracy pondered, but Kendall and her buddies were always doing things that seemed illogical from her perspective. Why should this be any different?

❧

Tracy hadn't looked at her phone, so she wasn't sure what time it was. But her stomach knew it was time to eat. The moment she took her focus off her e-reader, a pair of dark eyes were gazing at her.

"If Dex isn't back in three minutes, I'm going to get her."

Tracy sat up and held her hand over her eyes to cut down on the glare. "I can't even see her. Did you notice how far she went?"

"Nope. But there's a big break way down there," she said, pointing. "That's my guess. She's probably up against the sea grass or whatever that is. She likes to be alone."

Tracy stood and extended a hand. "Let's get our blood moving. Some wind sprints before lunch will be a great appetizer."

"I'm already starving!"

Slapping her on the belly with the back of her hand, Tracy said, "You'll live. That big group of people way down there is about a quarter mile away. Let's do it."

"Damn! Why can't I have even one parent who likes to lie on the sand and do nothing?"

"Luck of the draw, kid. Let's put it in gear."

The spot she'd targeted wasn't a quarter mile, but if it had been, Tracy's times were getting faster. She was still able to beat Kendall at anything over a hundred yards, which made her happy, but the kid would always dust her at short distances. Her quick-twitch muscle fibers had given her a genetic advantage Tracy would never be able to match.

Kendall crossed the imaginary finish line a few seconds later, with her cheeks flushed. "It's too hot for this nonsense!"

"I think you meant to congratulate me on leaving you in the dust, but I'll turn your poor sportsmanship into the compliment I deserve."

Kendall draped an arm around her shoulders, her skin hot and damp. But Tracy didn't mind. When your adult daughter still liked to be physical with you, you were a fool to complain about her sweat.

"I'm sure you'd qualify for the Olympics if you had a little more time to train. Now can we please find Dex? Going back alone is also fine with me. I've *got* to eat!"

"We passed her about a hundred yards back. She was standing on one foot at the time. I believe her other leg was way behind her, but I was too busy dusting you to be certain."

"She could have been doing almost anything. Her balance astounds me. She's a great teacher, too. If her voice ever gives out, she could always make a living teaching yoga."

"Oh, she'd have competition. I bet they've got as many yoga teachers in LA as we have lobbyists."

"Oh, not that many," Kendall said, with a rueful smirk on her face. The girl hated politics with her whole soul, believing all sides were self-serving narcissists who were attracted to the profession only for power and fortune. Tracy didn't have a great argument against that belief, but she pointed out every legislator who seemed to actually care about the under-represented. It wasn't a long list, but it was still a list.

She easily found Dex again, located right where Kendall predicted she'd be—close to a stand of beach grass. When they'd run by, Dex had been upright, but now she was resting her entire body on her hands.

Tracy's mouth opened as they got closer. From the side, she could see that Dex wasn't *wholly* balancing on her hands. Her knees were pressed against the backs of her arms, which must have helped—a little. Still, it was an impressive display of strength, balance, and flexibility. Not to mention concentration. She was certain Dex wasn't aware they were just twenty feet away. Kendall also respected her focus, and didn't say a word until Dex moved her legs back slightly to lower them to the ground in a slow, controlled motion.

"Such a showoff!" Kendall called out.

Tracy let her go alone to pull Dex to her feet. She stayed just where she was, trying to convince her eyes not to linger on Dex's flushed skin, or the healthy glow her cheeks held. And definitely not the damp spot between her breasts. The more her eyes resisted focusing on her breasts, the better.

≈≈≈

Throughout lunch, Tracy observed with interest as Kendall manipulated Dex into trying to recreate a photo. Tracy didn't recall the original, but Kendall and Dex must have been very familiar with it, since they argued about the details for a half hour. Tracy recalled the day in question, though, certain they'd gone to the beach on a hot Sunday, just after Kendall's fourth birthday.

Kendall finally convinced Dex that she'd been in shin-deep water, holding Kendall's hands while she dipped her. Since Kendall was now Dex's height, that couldn't work. Dex was clearly game, though, and Tracy took on the photography task. Dex grasped Kendall by the waist and lifted her until just her tootsies touched the water. That was awfully impressive all on its own, especially since Dex looked less muscular than she'd been in her twenties.

Kendall was doing her part, laughing like a four-year-old, so that element was nailed. But Dex had to struggle to hold her for more than a second or two, and she kept looking like she was in pain rather than sporting the big grin they'd agreed she'd had in the original.

Kendall kept racing back to Tracy to check the picture quality, and she eventually came up with a new idea. "I'll get on my knees. Then you can hold my hands up. I think that will let you look like you're not about to burst something."

"This was so much easier when you weighed thirty pounds."

"Play along. We've almost got it." She turned and smiled at Dex. "Just try to look happy this time."

Even from five feet away, Tracy could see Dex's eyes start to fill with tears. Kendall didn't catch it, though. For about the thousandth time in the last month, Tracy was tempted to cry, too. *Dex has missed so much.* It was incalculable how many small developmental milestones, how many silly faces, how many sweet kisses their little girl had bestowed only upon Tracy. And each one of those missed opportunities had been because of Tracy's unjust, unkind grip on the power she held to keep Dex away. How was she any less blameless than the Virginia legislature, who'd worked so hard to make sure they couldn't be recognized as a family under the law?

Her duties distracted her, but she was still feeling guilty when Kendall got down on her knees in the fairly calm water. Now Dex was able to grasp her hands and hold them at full extension. A wave undercut them a little bit, but when they checked out the photo, the effect had been kind of perfect. Kendall looked almost like she was still four—shocked by the cold water, but blissfully happy. Amazingly, Dex looked exactly as Tracy remembered her—totally over-the-moon with their perfect little girl.

❈❈❈

They stayed in the water for a long time, playing around and riding the mild waves. Dex had taken a halfhearted interest in surfing when she'd been much younger, but she'd never truly gotten into it. Body surfing was more her style. Being able to let a wave carry you, and giving into it to deliver you safely, was pretty thrilling. If Kendall had lived in LA, she would have been a surfer, for sure. She was exactly the type who'd want to ride on top of the waves, rather than give herself over to them. She'd always been bolder than Dex was. But she did pretty well at body

142

surfing, with her tenacity keeping her in the water until she could catch a wave and really get a thrill from it.

They'd been out for so long they all needed a snack. Knowing there was a whole Pyrex dish full of fudge brownies certainly hadn't made them easy to ignore. Even though the containers had been tough to carry, Dex certainly couldn't argue about the contents.

Once they'd playfully fought each other for the dish, Kendall took over and placed it on her legs, still glistening with saltwater. She held the knife in her hand and started to cut. "Who wants the first one?" A devilish grin settled on her expressive mouth. They both raised their hands, and as Kendall freed the first big square she said, "Whoever volunteers to tell me about how you fell in love gets it."

Dex immediately lowered her hand. "That's not a fair question, sweetheart. If your mom hasn't talked about that in private, she's certainly not going to want to talk about it in front of me. Come on now."

"That makes it sound like *you've* been willing to tell me anything," Kendall said, narrowing her eyes. "You both act like you were underage or unable to consent for some mysterious reason." Her voice softened when she placed the brownie back atop the dish. "I'm an adult woman with two living parents, and I know less about the circumstances of my birth than my friend Dziko, who was adopted from an orphanage in Malawi."

"There's nothing shameful or illegal about our getting together," Dex said. "The relationship was fine. Great, actually. It's the breakup we hate to talk about, and it's all mixed in together."

"It doesn't have to be," Kendall said. "I'm not asking about your breakup. I just want to know if…" She pursed her lips together, clearly on the verge of crying. "I want to know if you chose to have me because you loved each other." She held her hand up for a moment. "I've seen the videos. I've seen the pictures. But I don't know if you truly *wanted* to be together. I know Dex isn't comfortable with abortion, so I thought she might've talked you into having me when she realized you were on the fence. Like…I thought you might have both made the best of a bad situation."

"Not true," Tracy said, the strength of her voice carrying over the lapping waves and the brisk wind. "We loved each other, Kendall. Very much. We chose to have you, and we were both very glad we did."

Like tempting a stray dog, Kendall held the brownie out. "Tell me why. Come on. You can do it."

Tracy looked to Dex, lifting an eyebrow. Assuming she was asking for permission, Dex nodded. "Go right ahead."

"Okay." She made Dex smile when she gave into temptation, grasped the brownie and took a big bite. "We were roommates…"

"Freshman year?"

"Uh-huh. I was a very shy girl from a tiny town in Appalachia, worried college was going to be too much for me. On that first day, I looked up from my little single bed to see this one walk into the room." She laughed, but Dex could see she was nervous. "Libby and Randy and all four grandparents started bringing in trunks—literally *trunks* full of clothes and electronics and sports equipment. If she'd been followed by paparazzi, I could not have been more surprised."

"Oh, it wasn't that bad," Dex insisted. "And I didn't have trunks. I had suitcases… Okay, trunk-like suitcases." She shrugged. "I had a lot of stuff."

"Everything I owned fit into a backpack, a big suitcase with a broken latch, and a grocery bag full of food. My mama didn't want me to go hungry," Tracy added, laughing. "She wasn't willing to drive me, but she made sure I had food."

"That would make a good sitcom," Kendall said thoughtfully. "Even the part about the jerky mom who won't take her kid to college."

"Wouldn't watch that one," Tracy said, brushing by her mother's lack of interest. "So Libby and the grandmothers insisted I join them to have lunch. Randy and the grandfathers got busy putting some sturdy storage cubes on the floor, which lifted Dex's bed up, and gave her some much needed storage space. Then they painted the walls," she added, giving Dex a look, "and put up curtain rods. They checked to make sure I didn't mind the butter-yellow color on the walls, or the cheery green and yellow floral curtains, but I'm sure I wouldn't have said anything if yellow made me ill. I was stunned into silence."

"That's definitely a meet-cute scenario," Kendall said, looking so delighted Dex was unable to stop chiding herself for hiding all of this from the kid. "So…? Were you in love by like the end of the first week?"

"No, no," Dex said, unable to keep quiet. "It took until winter term for your mom to even get used to having a real, live lesbian in her room. You've never seen an eighteen-year-old girl cover up more than she did. I don't think I saw her ankles until spring."

"I'd never, *ever* met a lesbian," Tracy said, giving her a chiding look. "Everything I'd heard was hair-raising, so it took me a while to let my guard down."

"But you liked mom right away," Kendall said, pointing her finger at Dex. "Tell me I'm wrong."

"You're not wrong," Dex admitted. "I loved how shy she was, and how tentative. Smart as a whip, but never one to push her opinions."

"That's changed," Kendall snickered.

"It changed between us, too. But it took quite a while. I don't think your mom was used to people asking her opinion on many things," she said, trying to keep it brief.

Kendall gazed at her for a minute, clearly curious. "I'm tempted to delve into that, but I don't want to lose my focus. So when did you give into temptation, Mom?"

"It wasn't quick. We got to be good friends, and by the time spring term was almost over we'd started being a little physical with each other."

"A little," Dex said, unable to stop herself from laughing. "I'd toss my stuff onto my bed when I got back from class, and your mom would say, 'Want to come over here to study for that history test?'"

"What do you mean…?"

"It seemed like an awful lot of work to take that book bag off the bed, honey," Tracy said. "I thought it would be so much simpler if we shared a textbook while we jammed against one another on my single bed."

"Oh, my god!" Kendall let her head tilt up as she laughed hard and long. "Were you really that clueless, Mom?"

"One hundred percent. I spent my whole day thinking of ways to have even five extra minutes with Dex, who was always running around playing field hockey or lifting weights, but it never dawned on me that I was desperately infatuated with her."

"Wait." She turned to Dex. "You played field hockey?"

"She played everything," Tracy insisted. "She could have played any number of varsity sports—"

"Not true," Dex interrupted. "I was good enough to make the club team, but I never had the discipline to give all of my attention to one sport." She smiled at Tracy. "Or one girl. Until you made me want to race back to our room and act like we were studying."

"Ooo…" Kendall reached out and grasped both of their hands. "That's so sweet!" Her smile fell quickly when she held onto Tracy's hand for a moment. "But it breaks my heart to think of how naive you were."

"I was as naive an eighteen-year-old as you've ever met. One night, when we were lying on the floor, wrestling…" She slapped her hand over her eyes. "Yes, we used to wrestle. It seemed…athletic," she said, holding her head up high.

"You wrestled?" Kendall scowled at Dex. "You knew she was into you. Why didn't you just put it out there?"

"No way! I'd already tried to hook up with three girls who didn't know they were lesbians. Each time was horrific. Thrice burned…"

"Chicken," Kendall grumbled. "So… You were wrestling…like one does."

"Right. We must've been making a lot of noise, and the girls in the next room came over and told us to keep it down. When they left, one of them said something snarky. I don't recall exactly—"

"I do," Dex said. "And if I ever run into her, I'll give her a lecture she won't ever forget."

"What did she say?" Kendall asked, clearly enthralled.

"Melinda Hart, Grade-A troublemaker, said 'Don't ask, don't tell only works if you don't make so damn much noise.'" Dex reached over and caught Tracy's hand, holding it gently when she saw the shame coloring her cheeks, so many years later.

"Something like that," Tracy agreed. "That was our last wrestling match."

"Oh, Mom," Kendall sighed. "You were embarrassed?"

"Ashamed. I was mortified that it was obvious how close we were. I still thought about Dex all day, but by the time the term was over, I was relieved. I needed to get home and settle my thoughts."

"And you let her go?" Kendall demanded, glaring at Dex.

"What was I supposed to do? My parents were living in Switzerland for the year while my dad was babysitting the European office."

"He was what?"

"Long story. But he had to be in Switzerland for the whole year. They'd made firm plans to travel around Europe with me, so I didn't have many options. But I really tried to stay in touch." She let go of Tracy's hand when she could feel her start to pull away. "It was hard. The time difference, your mom's lack of interest…"

"I was interested, Dex. You knew that. I just didn't know how, or if, I could show it."

Dex shrugged. "It was a tough summer. But when classes started again, I could see that something had changed. Something had clicked into place." She gazed at Tracy, unable to keep the pleasure from her voice. "In a very good way." Tracy smiled back, looking an awful lot like the girl who'd returned from summer vacation with a whole new attitude.

"That first day, I was putting some books on a shelf and had to stand on a chair. Dex held onto my legs, and when I looked down, she was smiling up at me."

"I went for it," Dex said, laughing when Tracy elbowed her. "Well, I did. I started to hug her legs, then rub my face against them…"

"Then Dex was sitting down and I was on her lap." Tracy laughed. "It was *quite* a day."

"Go on," Kendall said, clearly mesmerized.

"I think you've got enough experience, not to mention imagination, to guess what happened next," Tracy said, giving her a slap on the knee. "We had a fantastic fall term, even though we nearly went on academic probation." She stopped, then quietly added, "The problem was that I didn't spend the summer in Switzerland. I spent it working at a tiny restaurant in Bland, Virginia. Just me, a busboy, and two cooks. One of them was named Clayton, and we started to get together at the end of our shifts. I think he was more into me than I was him…"

"Anyone would have been into you," Dex said, then caught herself. She had to be more circumspect!

"Thanks," Tracy said softly. "Anyway, Clayton and I got a little drunk on my last night in town. He convinced me, without much trouble, to have sex. Intercourse," she added. "We'd been doing everything but, and I'd convinced myself only a truly straight girl could enjoy intercourse. So I was up for giving it a try, even though I honestly didn't want to."

"Oh, Mama," Kendall sighed, using a term Dex hadn't heard her pull out in years. "You were *so* innocent."

"And frightened, and certain my life would be very, very hard if I was a lesbian."

"And you got pregnant." She nodded. "I could never convince myself that you two had it together enough to go to a sperm bank…"

"I wish that's how you'd entered the world, sweetheart. It's a lot less romantic to admit the condom broke. But I was certain I wasn't ovulating, so I honestly didn't worry about it. I was so relieved that I hadn't enjoyed intercourse that all I thought about was leaping into Dex's arms—which I did."

"So when did you find out about me?"

"Just before Thanksgiving break. My periods were kind of unpredictable, but Dex got hers in September, and October… We went together to have the test."

"I was thrilled," Dex said, telling the full truth. "I'd always wanted to raise a child, but I didn't have any great need to give birth. It truly seemed like a blessing."

"Not to me," Tracy said. She took Kendall's hand and held it tenderly. "I would have been elated to have gotten pregnant once I'd graduated from medical school, but we were so young…"

"It's all right, Mom," Kendall said, getting up on her knees to hug Tracy tightly. "I would have definitely had an abortion if I'd gotten pregnant after my freshman year." She smiled when she sat down. "I'd have an abortion if I got pregnant now, as a matter of fact."

"Kind of harsh," Dex said, flinching. "You make it sound like it's just birth control."

"It *is* a form of birth control, but it's not the form I choose. I'm simply saying that I don't expect Mom to be happy she got pregnant by a guy she didn't care for. I wasn't *me*," she insisted. "I was the possibility of life at that point."

"You were you from the start for me," Dex said. "Obviously, I would have supported your mom if she'd chosen to terminate, but I argued my butt off to convince her to keep you."

Tracy gave her a very fond look, then shifted her gaze to Kendall. "She brought out the whole Haven army. Libby drove Dex back to school after Thanksgiving break. She sat me down and convinced me that she and Randy would help us in every way possible if we chose to have you, and after thinking about it for a week, we decided to." She put her hand on Dex's shoulder. "You owe your life to Dex, and I'm not exaggerating in any way when I say that."

"I loved you," Dex said softly. "The thought of having a little Tracy was a dream come true."

"It was wonderful to have your support. Not to mention your family's. How many parents would offer to help nineteen-year-old girls have a baby?"

"I can't think of any," Kendall said. "My friends' parents don't even want them to drive."

Dex smiled at Tracy. "I had to do a little salesmanship," she admitted. "My parents didn't know you and I had fallen in love. So I had to convince them of that, then make it clear that I wanted this baby desperately. I added that I was certain you'd be a wonderful mom—which you have been."

"I didn't know you'd done that," Tracy said, looking like she was holding back tears. "I thought they just jumped right in."

"Close. But they tried to make me realize how having a baby so young would change every part of my life." She poked Kendall on the leg. "Which you definitely did. All for the better."

"I wish…" Kendall began, but shook her head briskly for a few seconds before starting again. "I'm very glad you decided to keep me. I couldn't have asked for better parents." She made a funny face. "By the way, I'm not ever going to ask a single question about this Clayton joker. I've got two awesome parents, and that's all I'll ever need."

⸎

Dex needed another application of sunblock, so she sat close to the water and watched as Tracy and Kendall played.

Water had always been Tracy's thing, and Dex was very glad to see it still was. She acted a little like she had the first time they'd been to the beach together, back when they were freshmen—absolutely joyful.

Even back then, Tracy had been a very serious student. She had plans —big plans—and a towering GPA was the only way to achieve them. But if Dex worked on her, she could get her to pack her books away on a Saturday. They'd leave Charlottesville at dawn, and be one of the first to claim a patch of sand. Back then, Dex spent every day mooning over Tracy, and watching her play in the water in a tiny bikini was one of the highlights of her young life. Then, like now, Tracy appealed to her on *such* a deep level.

In a way, it made no sense at all, especially now. Even though Dex was a youngish woman in the real world, she was a little long in the tooth in LA. But even though she was late middle-aged in Hollywood years, she didn't have any trouble finding women. Young, vibrant, beautiful women who spent most of their days trying to look even better. She was still puzzled by thirty-year-olds who spent an hour caring for their skin every night, exercising like mad, and eating like every calorie was a threat to their survival. But the system had convinced them that their worth was one hundred percent dependent on how they looked. That was criminal. And also true, in Hollywood, at least. Dex unjustly benefitted from that, by being able to bed some gorgeous, energetic, vivacious women. But not a single one of them had appealed to her like Tracy had.

To an impartial bystander, Tracy would definitely be considered cute. She was in very good shape for a forty-something woman, and she'd avoided damaging her skin as much as possible. But no one would claim she was as hot as the most recent woman Dex had bedded. Actually, Miranda Simon was objectively the hottest woman Dex had ever touched.

But the outermost layer of a person wasn't the important part, and even though it had taken Dex a while to learn that, she now believed it fully. Tracy blew Miranda out of the water in every area that counted. Tracy was *very* bright, had a strong social conscience, was well-read, and had well-thought-out opinions on nearly everything. Even more important, she loved their daughter with her whole heart. Having developed such a strong relationship with Dex's family had only made Tracy more attractive, since family was the keystone to Dex's happiness.

Tracy's only fault had been her inability to get over emotional wounds, and Dex had unquestionably delivered a deep one. But she seemed open now, at least partially, to developing a friendship. More precisely, to rediscovering the deep connection they would always have. When you shared a child, you were bound together for life. And if Dex could have her way, they'd work to build that connection. That goal was so strong she was willing to witness Yardley Simpkins putting her damp hands on Tracy's scrumptious body—and nothing could underscore her determination to fix things more than that.

⚬⚬⚬

When they finally got too tired and too cold to stay out any longer, Tracy and Kendall returned to the blanket. They'd brought Kendall's plastic sand pail and had filled it with clean water, then used it to wash the sand off their feet. In no time at all, Kendall was setting up a napping station, using Dex's yoga mat to stretch out. Once she'd gotten comfortable, she put her hat over her face and stuck her leg out, poking Dex until she moved around to be able to rub the foot. It was a sin how easily Kendall could manipulate Dex into doing nearly anything she wanted, but Tracy had to give the kid credit for not abusing her absolute power. Even with Tracy, Kendall generally only asked for some physical contact and a sympathetic ear. If she could get those two things, her needs were pretty much fulfilled.

That wasn't a huge change from how she'd been as a child. Dex had always been "fun Mommy," even though that was a role Tracy longed for. It's not that Kendall hadn't wanted to be close to her—she did. But being the custodial mom had made Tracy more of the boss, leaving the fun parts of parenthood for Dex to enjoy.

Tracy could still recall being jealous when she'd hear Kendall on the phone in her room, laughing it up for an hour or two when she talked to Dex, then being nothing but cranky when Tracy had to force her to finish her homework before bed, or do her household chores. It had hurt them all to have Dex live over twenty-five hundred miles away, but it had made Tracy's job significantly harder. Being the enforcer was never fun, and having to break Kendall of the bad habits she'd get into over the summers with Dex was always trying. But now that Kendall was an adult, Tracy realized how good it had been for the child to have someone she could regard as a friend more than a parent. Dex had gotten off kind of scot-free, but you couldn't really argue with success, and no one could argue that Kendall wasn't very well-adjusted, despite being from a fractured family.

After Dex rubbed Kendall's foot for a few minutes, she seemed to fall asleep. Tracy tried to take a peek under her hat, but it covered her face completely. "I feel like I did when she was a baby," she whispered. "Do I have time to do a load of laundry? Can I prep something for dinner?"

"Maybe a nap?" Dex said, grinning. "I was always in favor of a nap."

"You've always needed your sleep," Tracy said. "I could get by with less."

"Only because you were more of an adult."

She had a point, but Tracy didn't want to belabor it. "So… We've got a little time. Why don't you bring me up to date. I honestly would like to be friends, but there are so many gaps in what I know about your life that…well, it's odd."

"It is odd. Given that I tell my story to strangers all the time, it's really strange that you don't know it."

Tracy laughed. "We've got a kid who really knows how to keep secrets. When she'd come home from LA, I only got the most vague descriptions of what was going on with you."

"Same here. Kendall acted like everything was top secret."

Tracy took a look at Kendall, noting that she hadn't moved. "I think it's made her feel safer to keep us separate. I'm sure that wasn't great for her emotionally, but I don't think we've screwed her up too badly." She met Dex's gaze. "At least I hope not."

"Parenting's hard. I don't know how you managed for nine or ten months out of every year. I only had to rearrange my life for the summers and even *that* was tough."

"I didn't rearrange much. I used my summers to catch up on sleep, read some good books, and pick up carryouts on the way home. I acted like a single, childless woman when she was gone." She smiled. "It was a nice break, once I got used to it."

Dex's smile was a little shy when she said, "I haven't had to rearrange much in recent years, but the first time you allowed Kendall to come for a month I really missed having dates."

"A month?" Tracy raised an eyebrow. "You're complaining about a month? I didn't have sex for years, and what I had the first time wasn't worth the damn trouble." She reached over and slapped Dex on her long, lean leg. "You've got a lot of nerve."

"I'm not complaining. It's more that I'm owning how immature I was. For years I simply substituted women for drugs. I was still reveling in my addictive behaviors, which isn't the way to achieve any kind of lasting sobriety."

Tracy smiled at her, finding it kind of charming that Dex looked so sincere. "I'm sure it was hard for you to stay sober, but you'll never convince me it was hard to find women."

"Well..." She shrugged, revealing that sweet smile that made her look like an adolescent. "I didn't have a line of women snaking down the street, but..."

Tracy poked her in the knee. "Probably close to that. "You're a natural-born charmer."

The smile disappeared and Dex gazed at her for a few seconds, almost stone-faced. "I'm ashamed of myself for the way I used women, Tracy. I had no intention of being in a relationship, but I craved the high I got from sex. The women stayed the same age—early twenties—as I grew older. That's unseemly, and I hate that I lived that way for far too long."

"How long is long?" Dex obviously had some real discomfort about this part of her life.

"I started trying to grow up when I was around thirty. I pledged I was only going to date women my own age, and that I'd work to find a partner—no more hookups."

"And have you kept your word?"

Dex looked away, seeming very uncomfortable. "I've sincerely tried. But it's been hard to find a nice woman my age who isn't already involved. I know it's a joke to say all of the good ones are taken, but people who are good partners tend to seek out another one when they're single. And I had so many requirements that a lot of potential partners gave me a pass."

"Requirements? What are these big requirements?"

"Big one." She nodded soberly. "They have to not mind that I have my daughter with me all summer, and that I spend a long weekend—at a minimum—in Virginia every other month. That's been a problem."

"Tell me about it. Yardley's the first who hasn't minded being number two, and I'm now sure that was solely because Kendall was gone most of the year. Finding someone who wants to be a stepparent, and doesn't mind your taking a strong lead with parenting is very, very tough."

"Right. And I had the added requirement that while I didn't mind dating someone who drinks or smokes weed, I didn't want to be with anyone who did it to excess. Like I said, it hasn't been hard to find women to sleep with, but I haven't even gotten close to finding a partner." She laughed a little. "In recent years, I've narrowed my focus. I'm not even trying to find a partner. I just want someone nice to have sex with. When I'm upfront about my intentions, it makes life easier."

Kendall lifted the brim of her hat and blinked her eyes a few times. "Where were these women when I visited? I thought you and Mom had the same monk-like life."

"Were you sleeping at all?" Dex demanded.

"Uh-huh," she said, with her voice having the slow, hazy sound it always did when she had just woken. "I woke up to hear you say you liked to love 'em and leave 'em."

"I didn't say that," Dex said, giving her a scowl.

"Close enough. So why didn't I ever meet any of them?"

"If I wasn't sure I was serious about someone, I kept her at arm's length until you went back to school."

"Huh. Just like Mom."

"You did that, too?" Dex asked, clearly interested.

"Yes, but I'm sure I didn't have your luck. I met someone when Kendall was a freshman in high school, and I thought she had promise, but I wouldn't let them meet until we were solid. The problem was that she wouldn't commit until she knew she and Kendall would get along. We reached an impasse, and eventually ended things."

"Grr..." Kendall grumbled. "And you wonder why I say I'd have an abortion if I got pregnant without a partner. Being a single mom is detrimental to your sexual health."

"It can be," Dex said. "But there hasn't been a day I would have traded you for the best relationship in the world. You're my number one," she said, leaning way over and crawling a few feet to place noisy kisses on Kendall's forehead. Tracy just wished she hadn't used those few seconds to check out Dex's ass. Doing that made her feel like a prized jerk, and that wasn't how she saw herself. She'd had her bite of that apple, and it was time to close her eyes to the temptation. Even when it was right in her face, and so scrumptious-looking it made her shiver.

⚬⚬⚬

The crowds were starting to pack up, but they had enough leftovers from lunch to make a nice afternoon snack, which gave them the energy to hit the water again. At around five, they went back in to play around in the surf, which was a little stronger now at high tide.

Mostly they stayed out by a sand bar and ducked under the waves as they started to break. The water was cool, but not cold. Kind of invigorating.

Kendall's head popped up just after Dex's did, and she sputtered to get the water out of her mouth. "I'd do better if I wasn't always talking," she said, spitting with a look of distaste.

"You're not always talking," Dex said. "I feel like I'm the one who hasn't shut up. I've revealed more today than I have in a heck of a long time."

"It's good for you," Kendall said, swimming around to climb onto Dex's back and wrap her legs around her waist. "I appreciate that you've tried to shield me from your wild life, even though I have my doubts that it was very wild." She put her arms around her neck snugly and added, "I know you're kind of famous, especially with people who've memorized your animated movies, but…"

Dex tried to reach behind herself and give Kendall a slap on the butt, but it was hard to do when they were riding low in the water. "I'm not very famous, and you know it. The problem is that you don't have to be famous to attract impressionable young women. That's what I'm ashamed of. I used them, and that just wasn't right."

Kendall hugged her tightly, squealing when a wave hit them right in the back. But she held on, and they stayed upright. When Dex cleared her eyes, Tracy was still close. "Are you two all right?"

"Fine," Dex said, even though she'd had a half second of panic when she realized how Kendall's weight inhibited her ability to swim.

Kendall slid off, then took Dex's hand before reaching out to grasp one of Tracy's. The next wave lifted them all up, and they bounced around like three buoys, all well above water.

"Better," Kendall said. "Just one last thing before I forget. Don't feel bad about using young women. They're using you, too."

"Maybe," Dex said, "but that doesn't make it right. I'm older and more experienced. The burden's on me to make sure I'm with people who are mature enough to guard their hearts."

"Not buying it," Kendall said, missing the break by a few inches and getting a strong face-full of water. She sputtered loudly. "I have a friend who was a sugar-baby for a guy she chased like crazy. Believe me, she knew exactly what she was doing."

"No way," Tracy said. "Someone your age doesn't have the ability to know what she's doing when it comes to navigating something like that." She wrinkled her nose, gazing at Kendall carefully. "Being a sugar-baby is sex work, right?"

"Uh-huh. This rich guy paid her rent and bought her nearly anything she asked for."

"Who is this girl?" Tracy asked. "Someone from school?"

"Like I'd tell? Sorry, Mom. I promise I haven't done it, and that's all you get."

"It's someone I know?" Tracy looked like she was about to burst, so Dex jumped in.

"It's not right," she agreed. "The guy has all the power."

"Wrong! She has the power most of the time." Kendall looked thoughtful for a moment. "Like when she wants something expensive, like *crazy* expensive, she'll do some of the sexual stuff she hates. To me, that's totally using him."

Dex stared at Tracy for a second, and as a wave hit them from the side they both slid under the water, shouting in unison, "No, it's not!"

⣟⣟

Kendall drove home, with Dex sitting in the rear. They'd stopped for dinner, even though they truly didn't need another meal. But going to the beach and not having some crab claws or shrimp was a wasted opportunity.

On the ride home, Dex could easily have fallen asleep. She actually might have been asleep when Tracy said, "You haven't mentioned your plans, Dex. Have you booked a flight?"

"No," she said, trying not to yawn. "I haven't even thought about going home."

"What do you mean?" Tracy's voice had a pretty big note of surprise to it. "I thought you were only staying until Kendall's birthday."

"Since I've got no projects for the rest of the summer, I thought I'd enjoy Kendall's company until she leaves for China. *If* she leaves for China," she added, sticking her hand out to pat the kid on the head.

"Don't be in such a rush to get rid of me. I'll go as soon as I'm set."

"That might be months," Tracy said, now truly sounding alarmed. "You're honestly going to just stay in the pool house for…however long?"

"I think so. I've got enough money saved that I can be selective. Actually, I've turned down the few offers I've gotten in the last couple of weeks. I'm having more fun seeing Kendall than I would from the money I'd earn."

"Did I tell you Dex went to DC to do a commercial, Mom?"

"No, you didn't." She was quiet for another moment. "It must be great to have that kind of flexibility."

Dex was certain that what she was hearing was *not* enthusiasm. But given how open and friendly Tracy seemed when just the three of them were together, Yardley's anticipated reaction had to account for at least a part of her grimace.

⚭

Tracy didn't get into bed until eleven, but even though she was exhausted, she didn't drop off to sleep like she'd thought she would. Her phone made a faint buzz and she took it from her night stand to see a text from Yardley, who was still in New York.

"Just got back to the hotel from my final client dinner. Still up?"

It was cheating, but Tracy closed her eyes, as if that was the same as actually being asleep. She kept them closed, trying to recall the calm of being in the water, body surfing in the sun, with the clean, salty waves gently pushing her along.

But her mind kept returning to Yardley. Having Dex in town for much longer was possibly the very worst thing for Tracy's relationship. Even if Dex didn't make trouble, Yardley would believe she was actively trying to. And that was worse than if Dex had been intent on breaking them up. Jealousy was a very, very insidious emotion, and learning that Yardley was bedeviled by it had been the worst part of Tracy's summer. By far.

CHAPTER NINE

KENDALL DROVE OVER TO HER grandparents' house around eleven the next morning, hoping Dex was in the pool house, doing whatever it was she did in there. Knowing her, she might have been levitating.

After a quick knock on the front door, Kendall went inside. "Anybody home?"

"Just me," Nana said. She walked into the entry, holding the front section of the *Washington Post*. "I didn't know you were coming over. I'm afraid Dex is with Grammy and Gramps this morning, honey. They're trying to make her into a church-goer."

"I came to see you, Nana. Got a minute?"

"I've got until I have to whip up another batch of barbecue sauce." She put her arm around Kendall's shoulders and led her into the kitchen. "I'm not sure when I was pulled into this barbecue game, but my duties continue to increase."

"Were you outside?"

"Not quite. But I was heading there. Need anything to drink?"

"No, thanks. I had a cold brew on my way over. I've got so much caffeine in me I think I could run to DC."

"You do look a little agitated..." They went outside to sit under the large, buff-colored umbrellas that shaded the dining table. "What's on your mind, sweetheart?"

"Big news. Big, big news, as a matter of fact. I finally got my very secretive mothers to tell me at least part of my origin story."

"You did?" Nana looked stunned enough to make it clear Dex hadn't said anything.

"I had to beg, but I now know they didn't find a sperm bank crazy enough to load a couple of goofy nineteen-year-olds up with a few vials."

"I wish that's what had happened," Nana said, looking very sober. "It would have been better for everyone if they'd waited until they'd finished school, and your mom had gotten her medical degree."

"Didn't happen. Clearly. So…I don't know your drug history, Nana, but what were you and Papa smoking to go along with that plan? They were sophomores!"

Her expression morphed into a smile, clearly not offended. "You know Dex. What would have happened if we'd refused to help?"

"Mmm…" She thought for just a second. "They would have had me anyway. But…they probably would have had to quit school and get crappy jobs to be able to afford an apartment."

"That was the threat," Nana admitted. "Obviously, we could have let them struggle, but how would that have helped? And god knows I didn't want to force your mom into getting an abortion only because of money…"

"No, I can't see you doing that, but…nineteen! I don't think I was mature enough to get a cat."

"Oh, you would have grown up fast if you'd had to. You just didn't have to. Dex and your mom did—or had convinced themselves they did." She patted Kendall's shoulder. "I was going to try to persuade Tracy to give birth, then find a couple to adopt the child. But they were *so* much in love," she sighed. "I would have preferred they were closer to thirty than twenty, but we got you in the bargain, so I'd say we hit the jackpot."

Kendall gazed at her for a moment. "What would you have done if *I'd* wound up pregnant after my freshman year?"

"With Kevin?"

"Sure. Why not?"

"Hmm. I'm not sure exactly what means of persuasion I would have used, but I would have done almost anything to make sure you weren't stuck with that waste of oxygen for the rest of your life. What were you *thinking* when you dated that boy?"

Kendall shrugged. "I was in my himbo phase. He had an awesome body."

"And all of the manners of a goat. Good lord, Kendall, you'd have a three-year-old now, and you'd be spending most of your time trying to get *Kevin* to appear when he promised to. Can you imagine getting a cent of child support from him?"

Kendall laughed. "He didn't even graduate. I saw a mutual friend not long ago, and he told me Kevin's almost a full year behind. He parties so hard with his AEPi brothers that he doesn't have time to go to class."

"I'm glad your mother made sure you had access to birth control. *Very* glad."

"I guess Mom didn't, huh? Want to spill some tea about my other grandparents?"

Nana smile enigmatically. "Who wants to hop into the pool? Feel free to have some of your friends come over, sweetheart." She stood and kissed Kendall's head. "I'm so glad I'm not a great-grandmother—yet."

∞∞∞

Tracy didn't get a chance to actually speak to Yardley during the day on Sunday, but a couple of texts alerted her that she was coming directly to the house from the airport. That made sense, of course. They hadn't seen each other for five days. But there was something about Yardley's assumption that Tracy would be not only available, but waiting for her when she arrived that was a little annoying.

As Tracy moved around the house, neatening it up, she spent some time examining her thoughts. It wasn't a good sign that she wasn't thrilled about Yardley's imminent arrival. Actually, there was no way to look at her reaction and see it as a positive. But things had been tense—almost continually—since the day Dex had arrived.

Tracy knew she and Yardley had to get back to their peaceful, easy ways. But she wasn't sure how. It was like seeing a very attractive bubbling brook just fifty feet away, with no discernible path to reach it. The only thing she could think of that might help was if they moved in together. Then they could work on adjusting to being true partners, each of whom had the right to occupy the same space. It wouldn't feel like Yardley was coming over without checking, since she wouldn't need to

163

check. The house would be her home. That made sense, but Tracy was pretty sure she wouldn't offer that up as a solution—yet. She wasn't even sure why she was hesitating, but it felt too soon. It truly wasn't. She knew that. The fact remained, though, that she usually made better choices when she was certain about something. The offer would have to wait.

❈❈❈

Yardley had enjoyed a good conference, and had met up with some state regulators who were receptive to having Virtus sponsor some "alternative nicotine delivery system" programs in their junior colleges, as a way to guide their students away from smoking leaf tobacco.

Tonight wasn't the night to discuss this again, so Tracy did her very best to keep her mouth shut. The ANDS was, almost certainly, a better choice than smoking tobacco. But Yardley was a true believer, firmly convinced Virtus was trying to keep young people from becoming addicted to all of the carcinogens leaf tobacco contained. How she could honestly believe that was hard to fathom. What corporation tried to get people *not* to use its main product? But even if Virtus had nothing but pure motives, there was no way electronic cigarettes would fail to attract kids who'd never smoked leaf tobacco. And once those kids needed nicotine, they'd invariably flip back and forth between the ANDS and cigarettes, depending on availability and cost. That was just human nature. But mulling that over while they were getting ready for bed wasn't smart. They needed to get close again, not start another fight.

They were in the bedroom, working together to take off and fold the comforter. Yardley was wearing her pajamas, a nice pair of lightweight cotton ones that she must have sent to the laundry—unless she ironed them herself, which was too persnickety to even contemplate. Once Tracy got her out of her clothes, they could start repairing some of the damage the last weeks had done to their relationship. Physical closeness always helped.

Yardley pulled back the sheet and got into bed, sighing heavily while Tracy draped the comforter over a chair.

"Feels great," she said. "I've been lonely in my hotel bed." She smiled at Tracy, clearly waiting for an equally enthusiastic response.

"I have too," she said, giving her a smile that bore even more brightness. She got in on her side, pleased to have Yardley start to scoot over, but she beat her to the punch.

"I missed you," Tracy said, snuggling up to Yardley's body. She was built like a swimmer, long and lean, with breasts that barely showed when she was wearing a T-shirt. While Tracy hadn't been overwhelmingly attracted to her at first, she'd been pleasantly surprised when they'd started to be intimate. Of course, she'd only had sex with three people prior to that, and one of them was Clayton, who definitely did *not* know what he was doing. So Yardley didn't have to clear a very high bar to make her the second most thrilling lover Tracy had ever been with.

Okay, so thrilling wasn't the best term. But there were so many other attributes that combined to make someone a good partner. And Yardley had a lot of them. Even if they didn't set the bed on fire, they were both committed to giving each other pleasure. Maybe it was sedate pleasure, but that was a hell of a lot better than no pleasure at all. Tracy had nearly two decades of celibacy to cement that belief in her mind.

She tucked her arm around Yardley and pulled her close for a kiss, pleased when Yardley picked up the baton and started to run with it. They played around for a minute or two, almost wrestling. Then Yardley got her onto her back and started to slide over.

But she stopped, abruptly, jumping out of bed to hurl the sheet away.

Tracy gasped, even though she didn't know what she was gasping at. "What's wrong?"

"There's...sand all over the place." She ran her hand across the foot of the bed, then gave Tracy a sharp look. "Why is there sand in the bed?"

"There shouldn't be," she said, hearing how dumb that sounded. She got up and hustled over to Yardley's side, seeing about ten grains lying there. "Aren't you just the princess and the pea," she said, thinking of all of the toys, bits of cereal, and crumbs of all kinds Kendall had deposited into the bed through the years. It would have taken an ounce of sand for her to even notice it. "I'll get the cordless vacuum. Hold tight."

She'd only gone a step when Yardley's hand landed on her wrist. "I didn't ask you to clean it up. I asked why it's there." Her voice had a coldness to it that made Tracy's stomach flip. Where was the soft, almost tentative tone Yardley had shown on a pretty consistent basis since they'd met?

Purposefully pulling her arm away, Tracy continued to walk toward the closet. "I went to the beach with Kendall yesterday." Of course there was more, but Yardley was certainly not creating an environment that fostered full honesty.

The sand was whisked away in fewer than five seconds, but there was no question that Yardley wasn't through. She stood right where Tracy had left her, arms crossed over the chest of her stiffly ironed pajamas. "We texted back and forth at least three times yesterday. You didn't once mention you were at the beach."

"I didn't mention I had two brownies, either," Tracy said, glaring at her. "Or that the fried shrimp I had for dinner forced me to take an anti-diarrheal to get to sleep." She stepped closer to Yardley, gazing into her dark eyes. "I don't include every moment of my day in texts. If we'd talked in general about what we'd done, I would have mentioned the beach. But every one of our texts was about something *you'd* done or someone *you'd* met. I was trying to let you get some things off your chest, and show that I was interested." Her voice grew louder. "Speaking of that, I just spent the last hour listening to you talk about how great it was to convince some state legislators to push nicotine on kids." She grasped the pressed collar of her top and tugged on it sharply. "I *had* been in the mood to show you how much I missed you, but that's past tense. Now, I'm planning on sleeping in Kendall's room."

"Dexter was with you," Yardley said, her anger seething out of her.

"She certainly was. It means a lot to Kendall to have us get along better, and she thought we could have a day where we just talked and goofed around in the water." She got even closer now, with Yardley's eyes almost crossing to keep her in focus. "Kendall was right, by the way. Going to the beach was a very low-stress way of diffusing some of the tension between us."

"And you're equating going to the beach with Dexter to having diarrhea, right? Both inconsequential events that don't deserve a mention?"

"I didn't tell you about my intestinal problems because I know you're squeamish about the digestive tract. I didn't tell you about Dex because I know you're squeamish about her mere existence."

"I'm not squeamish!"

"All right," Tracy said, going over to her side of the bed to pick up her watch from the charging station. "Then you're priggish about her. Either way, it's exhausting."

Yardley grasped her as she tried to leave the room, catching her around the waist and holding on tightly. "Do *not* run away from me."

"I have to be at work at seven. We can talk about this tomorrow night."

"Why is she still here? She was supposed to be here for a damn weekend! That turned into weeks, which still seem to be dragging on."

"She's..." Tracy peeled Yardley's hands off her body and stepped back. "She's going to be here for a while. I can't say how long, since she doesn't seem to know."

"The woman needs to go home and let us get on with our lives!" Her entire face had turned pink, and Tracy could see that her body was trembling.

"I'm not in charge of her, Yardley. Dex will do what she wants—as she pretty much always has."

"She's here to cause trouble. There's no doubt in my mind. She's alienating Kendall from both of us—"

"That's ridiculous. Utterly ridiculous. She assumes Kendall is leaving for at least a year, and she wants to spend time with her before she goes."

"If she wants to spend time with Kendall, she would have bought a round-trip ticket for herself, and a nice, matching one for Kendall. They could have left the day after Kendall's birthday, then Dexter could get back to work, and Kendall could lie by *her* pool all day."

They were *not* going to get into Yardley's very hard-line beliefs about Kendall's lack of enterprise. "Stay in your lane," Tracy said firmly. "Dex chose to spend her summer here, and her relationship with Kendall is truly none of your business."

"It definitely *is* my business. Dexter has clearly lured her over into the Havens' lair. She's essentially moved in over there, and I don't like it. Kendall is going to be my step-daughter in just a few months, and she should be spending her time trying to fit into *our* family."

Tracy would have bet every dollar she'd ever earned that Kendall would never think of or refer to herself as Yardley's step-daughter, but this wasn't the time to make a point of that. "Kendall's an adult. If she wants to stay at her grandparents' home, it doesn't affect you at all."

"It certainly does. She's going to be leaving for China soon— allegedly. This summer was my only time to get to know her better. To win her *over*," she stressed. "This is important."

Softening because of the sincere expression she wore, Tracy said, "You can't force Kendall to feel comfortable with you. It will happen when it happens."

"But it would happen faster if you forced her to stay home. Put your foot down!"

Tracy shook her head slowly. "I don't treat her that way. I stopped telling her what to do once I felt she could take care of herself. I'm not going to change, by the way." She put her hand on Yardley's waist and looked into her eyes. "I barely recognize the woman I consented to marry this spring. You'd never displayed the slightest bit of jealousy, but now it seeps out of every pore. What in the hell has caused all of this?"

"It's Dexter!" She was so angry she looked like she might scream. "Since the day I started at Virtus, she's been a thorn in my side."

"Yardley, she hasn't worked there for nearly two decades! You've got to get over your animosity. Truly. It's not good for you to be so focused on old slights."

"I can't," she growled. "She undercut me and ingratiated herself to our boss. She got every plum assignment, every possible leg-up. Gordon

Kincaid treated her like she was the second-coming—all because he thought her father would eventually reward him." Her voice grew even more strident. "Do you have any idea how important Randy was…and still is? He's pulled Gordon along with him every step of the way. Now Gordon's got the job I'd been aiming for since I started at the company, and I'm effectively blocked from moving up. All because of Dexter and Randy!"

"Listen," Tracy said, feeling like she was having a conversation with a woman whose screws had very recently come loose. "If Gordon favored Dex, there's every chance that she was just damn good at her job."

"That could not have been the real reason. When she left, he talked about her like he'd lost a child! He knew his path to the top depended on staying in her good graces."

"Then why did he keep getting promoted once Dex was gone? Listen to yourself! You're unnaturally jealous of her, and you'd better learn to deal with that or we've got big, big trouble."

"We already do," she said, gripping Tracy by the wrist again and holding on firmly. "If we don't get into couples counseling immediately, we're going to crash." She rushed to get back into her clothing, leaving her pajamas lying on the floor as she stepped over them. The worst part was that Tracy didn't say a word to stop her. In fact, if Yardley hadn't left, Tracy might have—and she was in her own damn house.

❧

Tracy stumbled down to the kitchen the next morning, so distracted and hazy she didn't notice the scent of coffee brewing. She started when she saw Yardley sitting at the table, dressed in a business suit, looking up at her with those sad-puppy eyes.

Tracy's heart went out to her when she saw how drained she looked. Walking over to her, she put her hand on her head and pulled it to rest against her belly. "You didn't sleep at all, did you?"

"No." She stayed right where she was, which was slightly reassuring. At least she hadn't pulled away.

"Let me get a cup of coffee. I've got to be out of here in twenty minutes, but we need to reconnect."

She didn't even bother putting milk in her cup. After getting down a mouthful of the strong, bitter brew, she sat down and moved her chair over so they were shoulder-to-shoulder. "Talk to me," she said gently.

Yardley looked at her for a moment, then nodded. "In April, things were great. Really great," she stressed. "Didn't you think so?"

"Of course, I did. I didn't hesitate for a second when you asked me to marry you. Actually, I was going to ask you if you hadn't asked me."

That brought a small smile to her lips. "There's only one thing that's different. And you know what that is. Dexter is trying to drive a wedge between us, and she's been very successful—as always."

"Why on earth would she—?"

"Look at the facts. In all of the time you've been apart, you've never gotten this close with anyone. Dex had to know that."

"She claims she didn't know anything about my life…"

"With Libby and Kendall both in constant contact? Come on. Why would both of them hide that from her?"

"I'm not sure, but Kendall certainly doesn't tell me much about Dex…"

"You're telling me that Libby let Dex be blindsided by our engagement? I'm not buying it. Doing that would be cruel."

"I guess that would have been pretty cruel…" She thought for a second. "She's always given Dex every kind of emotional support possible. So letting her be surprised by our engagement was kind of—"

"Libby talks about Dex like she's made out of glass. There's no way she'd let her be blindsided by our engagement."

"Fine. Let's say you're right. That still doesn't mean Dex is here to cause trouble. It just doesn't. She came for Kendall, and she's staying for Kendall."

"I'm not buying it. She's had every opportunity to come back for a long visit, but she hasn't. In the year we've known each other, Dex has never been here for more than three days. Isn't it suspicious that she waited until you were engaged to plop herself down in her mother's pool house? There's no reason for her to be here this long. None!"

"Mmm. She did admit that she'd been turning down work…"

Yardley's expression grew even more grim. "She's turning down work in LA to be in Richmond in the summer, even though she could have easily had Kendall spend the summer with her—as she has for the last ten years. Look at the facts!"

"It's puzzling, now that you put it like that."

"Think about this objectively," Yardley said earnestly. "Who would choose a summer in Richmond over Manhattan Beach?"

"I *am* trying to be objective. While I agree it's odd that Dex and Kendall didn't do what they've done since Kendall was in sixth grade and spend the summer in LA, I still can't see why Dex would want to cause trouble."

"Because she's so competitive! She's been a failure at finding a relationship, and she can't stand to have you beat her to the altar. It might not even be conscious, but I swear that she's jealous of you. I'm certain she doesn't want you to be better than she is at anything. Think about it," she insisted, with her voice echoing in Tracy's head as she slugged down another gulp of coffee, kissed Yardley on the head, and hurried upstairs to get ready for work.

⁂

A few years earlier, Dex had tweaked her system to be satisfied with two meals a day. That let her, for the most part, ignore calories. At home, she ate around ten or eleven, and again at four or five. Unless she was meeting up with friends, or had a date, of course. The early bird special at a diner wasn't prime first date territory.

Even though her system worked well at home, she hadn't been able to make it work in Richmond. Her parents ate at eight, a time that would have been perfect if she'd been able to stay on LA time. But she'd adapted to eastern time much faster than she'd thought she would.

Her late breakfast did not stick to her ribs until eight pm, so she'd started going to her room in the late afternoon to nap, or read, or take a long bath. Anything to take her mind off dinner, which seemed like it was days away.

Her mom was such a fan of baths that she'd insisted even the pool house have one, a luxury that Dex was getting to enjoy during this long trip. Soaking while listening to a podcast relaxed her thoroughly, and she was feeling great when she got out of the tub. But she'd read the clock wrong, thinking it was seven when it was barely six.

With two more hours to kill, she lay down to take a power-nap. But the bath had made her feel more sensual than sleepy, and she decided to give herself a little loving.

Over the years, she'd come to strongly prefer sex to masturbation. This trip had recalibrated her system, though, and she'd gotten into the habit of touching herself a couple of times a week. Given she had exactly zero interest in bringing a woman to the pool house, and she didn't want to have to explain any overnight absences to her mom, she hadn't even tried to hook up.

She liked a long build-up, with a whole lot of touching. Starting to tease herself, she got into it pretty quickly, gliding along in her fantasies while she ran her free hand over her legs, then up her belly. A rigid nipple caught her attention, and she tugged on it firmly, always surprised that she treated her own breasts more aggressively than she allowed a lover to.

Both feet lay flat on the bed, legs spread wide apart, fingers delving into her wetness, a sated smile on her face. Until a sharp knock on the door jerked her out of a very erotic fantasy.

Growling to herself, she tossed her feet to the floor and slid into a thin, seersucker robe, barely covering up before she threw open the door, ready to give Kendall another reminder that texting was the preferable way to communicate when the door was locked.

"Tracy," she said, feeling very underdressed, and a little guilty at having been caught touching herself. But she wasn't twelve any more, and she knew that was a silly reaction. "Was I expecting you?"

"No," she said, breezing in to drop her bag on the counter.

Dex watched her pace across the small kitchen, still clad in her work clothes. She wasn't wearing a white coat, but Dex guessed she normally did. Now some wine-colored scrubs and a pair of clogs made her look like she could have been anything from a cafeteria worker to a surgeon. But the way she commanded the room tilted the odds toward a job where she was in charge.

Whirling to face Dex, she slapped her hands on the counter and leaned forward, like she was calling an important meeting together and wanted to get everyone's attention immediately. But that was overkill. She had Dex's full attention.

"I'd like to know what's going on here," she said, making it sound very little like a true question.

"Here?" Dex said, entirely puzzled as her gaze traveled around her small living space.

"Here," Tracy said, twirling her arm over her head, indicating…who knew what.

"I have no idea what you're getting at." Dex looked longingly at her bedroom. "Do you mind if I get dressed? I wasn't expecting company."

"I won't be here long."

"Okay…" Dex tightened up her robe, and made the tie a little more snug. She sat on one of the stools by the counter, trying to look dignified, but certain she wasn't selling it.

Tracy moved over to stand right next to her. "I want to know why you're here. I want to know why you're passing up jobs. I want to know why you didn't take Kendall back to LA with you—like a day or two after her graduation or her birthday."

"Uhm…" Dex could not for the life of her figure out what she'd done, but Tracy clearly believed she'd done something. Something bad. "I don't have a great reason, to be honest. I was just in the mood…"

"Of course you were," she snapped. "Just like always. When C. K. Dexter Haven wants to do something, she just does it. Everything will magically fall into place." Her words were laden with sarcasm, but Dex had no idea why.

"Why do you care about my motivations? How am I hurting you by staying?"

"You're hurting my relationship! As if you didn't know that."

"How or why would I do that?" She felt like they were having two completely different conversations. Like Tracy had confused her with someone else.

"Don't give me that innocent look. I've seen it enough times to know it's total bullshit."

That hurt. Dex couldn't even begin to argue that she hadn't spent the better part of their relationship lying her ass off, but she'd rehabilitated herself—thoroughly. "I'm not bullshitting you, Tracy. I have no idea what you're talking about."

She started to poke Dex in the chest, punctuating her words. "You're lying to me. I know the signs. Your mouth is moving," she added, really hitting below the belt.

"What in the hell has gotten into you? I was trying to be thoughtful by staying in Virginia to spend time with Kendall. I didn't want to gobble up all of her remaining weeks if she's actually leaving soon."

"Oh, please! You've been trying to get more time with her since the day you left. I don't believe you've suddenly gotten a conscience about that."

"So unfair," Dex gasped, feeling like Tracy had slapped the air right out of her lungs.

Tracy's face was so flushed she looked feverish, and her eyes were sparking with anger. "I've devoted my entire adult life to raising our daughter, Dexter. My sex life has been next to nonexistent, and my love life even worse. And the first time I've got someone…" She was panting with anger, gasping for breath. "And you just happen to breeze into town, stirring up shit." She poked her again, harder this time. "You're here to ruin things for me. Admit it!"

"Why would I *want* to ruin things for you?"

"You're…" She seemed to be stuck, with her face growing redder by the second. "I think you're jealous. This is the first time in your life you haven't bested me. You can't stand to have me succeed at something you haven't been able to get for yourself."

"With Yardley Simpkins?" Dex knew she had a look of supreme distaste on her face, but she couldn't help it. Yardley had been a whining baby when they'd worked together, and from what Dex had seen, she hadn't grown up a bit. "Is that what you're implying? That I'm jealous you're with Yardley Simpkins?"

"That's exactly what I'm implying," she snapped.

Taking just a second to try and figure out what the real issue was, Dex was still at a loss. None of this made sense—unless Yardley was behind it. This sounded more like her kind of paranoia than Tracy's. Lowering her voice, and trying very much to sound like one of her caring, maternal, animated characters, she said, "I'm glad you've found love, Tracy. Truly."

"You are *not* glad for me. You're over here luring Kendall away when she should be home with me!"

"Then ask her to do that," Dex said, even more perplexed. "You know she'll do exactly what she wants, but if you've got a strong preference, tell her."

"I can't compete! I never have been able to. You've always been the fun option, and that hasn't changed. Kendall's craved time with you since the minute you left. It's not fair to me. It's never been fair to me. I've been cheated out of so much!"

Dex could take a lot—a whole lot. But claiming that Tracy had gotten the raw end of the deal was such a lie she couldn't let it go unchecked. "Fair? Do you want to talk about fair?" She could feel her blood pressure rise, with many years of working to control her feelings no help at all. "Was it fair that I wasn't allowed to see, to speak with, or to communicate in any way with my daughter for seven months? After I got out of sober living, I came back to Richmond to find a completely different kid! A kid who was so tentative around me it took months to pull her out of her shell!"

"I didn't keep you in rehab for so long, Dexter. Your parents and your doctors were behind that decision."

"I needed that long. I'm not arguing about that. But I was hanging on by a thread, with the promise of being reunited with my little girl the only thing keeping me going. Yet, when I was finally able to call her on the ride to my sober living placement, I found out you'd changed your number. I had no way of even talking to Kendall before I went into lockdown again."

"You left our child in the car to buy drugs! You're lucky I ever let you see her again—which I would *not* have done if your parents hadn't spent months pleading your case."

"Oh, that was hugely magnanimous of you. You were a fucking beacon of care and concern. Four months in sober living without a single letter. You abandoned me when I was at my lowest, with not even a drawing to give me hope. I sat by the door every afternoon, just waiting for the mail to come. But nothing, nothing ever came from the person I was desperate to hear from. That was merciless," she growled. "So heartlessly cruel."

"Kendall was too young to understand why you'd left or why you couldn't talk to her on the phone. So I distracted her as much as possible while I tried to get my life together. Sorry I didn't have time to make sure *you* were doing well. Trying to pay the fucking mortgage with what was left of our savings after you'd squandered it buying drugs took up a good bit of my free time."

"I'm not saying I didn't screw up. I've never claimed that. But if you'd ever truly loved me, you would have tried to make my re-entry into society just a little easier. Instead, you made it so, so much tougher."

"I had to focus! Kendall came first, then my education. Given that I had to shoulder the whole financial load, it was vital that I earn as much as I could. Do you think it was easy to throw myself into a tough masters program as a single parent? I simply didn't have the excess capacity to look after you."

"Excess capacity," Dex murmured, stunned by her cavalier attitude. "For someone you'd pledged to love forever."

"We had nothing in writing," she insisted, as if that mattered at all.

"You're lucky I was as generous as I was."

"Oh, that's a great way to put it. I was Kendall's mom until I screwed up. Then I was a stranger—allowed to see my daughter only under supervision."

"You were a drug addict!" Tracy screamed.

"I was a *recovering* drug addict! I haven't had anything stronger than acetaminophen since the day I was arrested. Didn't the humiliating drug tests you made me take have any impact? Years of sobriety weren't enough to convince you to let her visit alone?"

"Not with the most precious person in my life," she said coldly. "Not even close."

"How about now? Is eighteen years of sobriety good enough?"

"Kendall's an adult now. If she trusts you, that's all that matters."

Dex got to her feet and tucked her robe closed again. Getting right into Tracy's face, she leaned over slightly, so their noses almost touched. "I jumped through every hoop you held up. I followed every single rule you set. Still, there wasn't a day that went by that I wasn't worried sick you'd yank her away from me." She sucked in a lungful of air. "You should be ashamed of yourself for the way you treated me. My deeply held wish is that Kendall *doesn't* take after you. You've got a big dose of Lord vindictiveness hiding right under that seemingly-kind veneer, and believe me, it's a very unattractive trait." She started for her bedroom, adding, "Maybe that's the real reason you've been alone all these years. Once a woman gets a taste of your self-righteousness, she heads for the hills."

Tracy jumped to her feet and pushed open the door that Dex had just closed. "You knew I was engaged. Don't try to convince me that Libby didn't tell you."

"I knew *nothing*. Feel free to march right up to the house to check on that. Although given how little you believe the people you've promised your eternal love to..." She went into her bathroom and dropped her robe to the floor, staring at Tracy via the mirror. "Isn't it time you went home? Or are there any other old scars you're desperate to rip open?"

❈❈❈

Tracy reached in and slammed the door, then stormed out of the pool house, covered with sweat. She hadn't unleashed on Dex like that since the night she was arrested. And even then she hadn't been so harsh. It was like all of the years of slights and hurts had burst out of her like lava from a volcano that had been quietly rumbling. She would have to apologize. Soon. But she couldn't bear to do it now. She simply didn't have the guts.

⚛

Tracy hadn't specifically invited Yardley to have dinner, but she was in the kitchen, stirring something on the stove when Tracy entered the house.

"Hi, honey," Yardley called out. "Have a good day?"

"No. Can you open some wine?" She started up the stairs, not even taking the time to offer a proper greeting.

"Sure."

"Do we have a magnum?"

"Are you okay?" Yardley had clearly moved over to the stairs so she could be heard, but Tracy truly hoped whatever she was cooking needed constant attention.

She stripped off her clothing when she got to her bedroom, then got into the shower, trying to cool down. As she washed her body, her fingers encountered an embarrassing amount of lubrication between her legs. *No!* She cried out to any gods who were listening. It wasn't fair. It wasn't right. She was in love with Yardley. Period. Getting turned on by a massive fight with Dex wasn't the way this was supposed to go. But she *was* turned on, damn it. She'd known it during the fight. If she could have thrown Dex to the bed and had her right then she would have. Every single time they were together she felt—more. That was it in a nutshell. Everything was heightened when she was near Dex. Her happiness, her unease, her anger, her longing, her memories, her regrets. Every emotion, every feeling zoomed to the top of the scale.

If she'd acted on her instinct—if she'd grabbed Dex and torn that thin robe from her ridiculously toned body, she would have destroyed her life and regretted it forever. Like that wasn't the gist of the Lord family life-plan. Blow everything up, while insisting you were the hapless victim.

∞∞∞

After dinner, Tracy cleaned the kitchen, allowing Yardley to catch up on a few work-related items.

Once the kitchen was tidy, she went into the living room and sat next to Yardley on the sofa. After a few minutes, she scooted around and poked her gently with a foot. "Mind if I rest my legs on your lap?"

"I'd love it," she said, giving her a fond smile. Tracy was working on a book on her reader, and she shifted about until she was comfortable, still able to see the screen clearly. Yardley was using her phone to do some emails, and the soft tapping was kind of soothing. Familiar. Tracy began to feel a little more settled, with her affection for Yardley feeling like it had in the spring. Reassuring. Calming.

She wasn't sure how much time had passed, but a jangling sound from the front door made her look up like a watchdog. The door opened, and Kendall stepped in, then stopped on a dime to give Tracy what seemed like a guilty look.

"Sorry I didn't call," she said, her gaze shifting to the floor.

"You don't need to call." She immediately removed her legs from Yardley's lap. "This is your house, sweetheart."

"Still…" She headed for the kitchen, and Tracy could hear her open the refrigerator. Then a pop-top opened, and the sound of effervescence made its distinctive noise. When the back door opened and closed, Tracy got up and gave Yardley a pat on the shoulder as she moved past her. "I'm going to go see what she's up to."

Yardley grasped her hand and held on. "She just came home, honey. She's not a visitor. If she needed something, she would have said so."

"You're right," Tracy said, leaning over to give her a quick kiss. "I still want to talk to her. Back in a few."

Yardley opened her mouth to add something, but Tracy intentionally moved quickly and was out of earshot in just a second or two. She opened the back door and sat next to Kendall on one of the spring chairs.

"Why have I spent the evening inside?" she asked. "The weather's perfect."

"Yeah, it is." Kendall leaned forward, reached into her back pocket, and pulled out a folded envelope. "For you," she said, handing it over.

Tracy took a look, seeing Dex's familiar handwriting. Cocking her head, she said, "What's this?"

"A note. No, I don't know what it says. But given how Dex was acting at dinner, and the fact that she forced me to come over here, I got the impression something's gone down between you two."

Tracy tapped her leg with the envelope. "Dex honestly didn't say anything?"

"Nothing at all. She took me aside after dinner, said she thought it was a good idea if I went home, then handed me that. I couldn't get another word out of her."

Tracy really hadn't wanted to get into this, but she was kind of stuck. "Uhm…we had…words, I guess." She leaned forward, not able to see very clearly in the dim evening light. "Did you tell Dex about my engagement? Before she got here, I mean."

"Of course not," she said immediately, like that was a crazy question to even propose.

"Why?" Tracy was not at all sure she knew the answer.

"Why?" Kendall's voice rose slightly. "One of the bedrock foundations of my existence was that I was never supposed to mention Dex to you, or you to Dex. Nana does the same, in case you hadn't noticed. We talk to each other about both of you, but I'm certain neither of us has ever volunteered anything truly personal to either of you." She took a breath, with Tracy finding herself a little back on her heels. "I can't speak for Nana, but I'm opting out of that unspoken rule. From now on, when something's troubling me about one of you, I'm going to talk to the other if I think it'll clear things up."

"That's fine," Tracy said, with her stomach flipping at the implications of Kendall's decision. "I don't blame you for not wanting to maintain the news blackout." She reached over and rested her hand on

Kendall's knee. "I'm sure I never told you not to talk about me to Dex, but I'm certainly not surprised you didn't feel comfortable."

"Don't you want to read the note? Maybe she needs a pint of blood or something."

The envelope wasn't sealed, and Tracy easily lifted the tucked-in flap.

Tracy,

For years, I've worked on having greater control over my emotions. I usually do a pretty good job of that, but I failed miserably today.

You were obviously angry, even though I still can't figure out why, but that doesn't give me carte blanche to unload on you. I apologize for losing my temper, for shouting at you, for storming away, and for starting to get dressed while you were still in my room. That was unconscionably rude of me, and not in keeping with how I like to treat others.

We clearly have a lot of long-repressed anger toward each other, and I think it's a good idea to express some of it. Not while we're angry, of course. But if you're willing, I'd like to talk, in depth, about all of the ways we've hurt, disappointed, and betrayed each other. I'm sure I've got the longer list of failures, but people can't be in a significant relationship and not have some issues that linger.

Again, I'm sorry for today, but I hope that blowing our tops will lead us to a place where we can truly clear the air. In my opinion, it's time.

Dex

She placed the note, writing down, on her leg, feeling that once again Dex had bested her. The apology she'd been composing in her head wasn't nearly as comprehensive as Dex's had been. And hers had come together much faster, too. Infuriating.

"No comment?" Kendall asked.

Tracy gazed at her for a few seconds. "I have a lot of comments, but

I'm not sure many of them are coherent." She blew out a frustrated breath. "I feel like the ground has shifted in the last month. Things don't feel stable." Reaching over, she grasped Kendall's hand. "Part of that is because you've been gone so much. Having you in town, yet seeing you so infrequently has made everything seem…off. I feel like the minute Dex showed up, she lured you over to your grandparents', and she's not giving you back."

"Wrong," Kendall said sharply. "At least every other day she tries to get me to come here for dinner or to sleep."

"And you don't want to," Tracy said, feeling like Kendall had taken a chunk out of her heart.

"I wouldn't have come tonight, but Dex was insistent. When I left, she said she wants me to spend at least half of my time here from now on."

"Are you going to?"

"Doubtful," Kendall said, her voice having grown soft. "This past winter, I mentioned that I was planning on spending the summer in LA, as usual, then leaving from there to go to China. But Dex absolutely refused. She thought that would be unfair to you, even though it would have made her life easier."

"You…believe that?"

Kendall gazed at her for a minute, clearly puzzled. "You're asking if I believe it would be easier for her to live in her own home: a nice, big, modern one with everything set up perfectly for her needs? You're asking if it would be easier for her if she could attend her favorite meetings, see her sponsor, see the people *she* sponsors, see her friends, do her job…" She gripped Tracy's hand firmly. "What kind of question is that? She's jammed into three hundred square feet here so she can spend time with me, while letting me see you, too."

"I had no idea that was her plan, honey. I didn't think—"

"I'm sure you didn't," she said, giving her a chiding look. "She thinks of you and your needs a lot, Mom. From my perspective, she goes out of her way to make things as fair as they can be. And you *don't*."

"I don't try to take advantage of—"

"I'm not saying you try to screw around with her. But she keeps you and your needs in mind. I don't always see that from you."

"You're truly the one who wanted to spend the summer in California? You swear that's true?"

"Of course," she said, looking up to face her squarely. "I knew it would drive me crazy to have to spend the summer with Yardley." She held up a hand. "I know I don't know her well. I know there's every chance I'll come to like her. But I'm not there now. I thought it was better for you two to have time to get used to living together. Plus, I wanted to hang out with a girl Dex knows who grew up in China. I thought she could help me make plans."

"I owe Dex a huge apology," Tracy sighed. "I need to do it in person. When's the best time to catch her alone?"

"Your schedules don't overlap a lot. You're at work for an hour or two before she even gets up."

"Before dinner?"

"That would work, but she's usually in the pool house by then. She doesn't really like to be disturbed…"

"Are you going over there tomorrow?"

"Uh-huh."

"If I write something tonight, will you take it over?"

Even in the dark, Tracy could see the wry smile on Kendall's face. "Sure. Am I the official go-between now? That's a new role."

"If you don't mind, I'd appreciate it."

"I don't mind, Mom," she said, standing to place a kiss on Tracy's head. "I'm going up to bed."

Tracy gripped her hand and held it. "I'm glad you're here."

"I am, too. G'night."

Tracy watched her leave, then tried to recall where she'd put the note cards Libby had given her a few years earlier. She wasn't much of a writer, but she was going to have to work on her game. There had to be something she could do as well as C. K. Dexter Haven, even though the odds of that weren't fantastic.

❦

The next day, Tracy was swamped, with a surprising number of parents bringing kids in for vaccines for school. There must have been some district-wide deadline that was looming.

After finishing her notes on her last patient, she grabbed her things and stepped out the back door of the office to her car. While walking the short distance, her phone rang and she pulled it from her back pocket.

She leaned against her car and read the text from Dex. It made her smile to consider that she'd chosen to text rather than call. Maybe she was a little nervous about this, too.

Thanx for the apology. It's fully accepted. Let's agree we were in weird moods and put it to rest. I think we need to clear the air, but there's no rush. We'll get to that when we're both in a good place. CKDH-L (I can never decide if I need the hyphen. Opinion? It's totally clear that I have too many initials, but I'm very happy with them.)

That was so Dex-like. She never wanted to have a fight last one second longer than it had to. Tracy got into her car and started it up. Oddly, she had a vision of Dex's soul. It was blindingly white, truly pure. She was a regular human, of course, and had her share of flaws and deficiencies, but her essence was pure.

Of course, acknowledging that just made Tracy feel like an even bigger jerk for doubting her. Dex would never, ever cause trouble just because she could. She hadn't been like that as a nineteen-year-old, and she certainly wasn't going to start behaving that way now. The fact that Tracy had let Yardley push her into believing such nonsense showed just how off-base she'd let herself get. She needed to get her feet back under herself—pronto.

❦

By the time Tracy got home the next night, Yardley was getting out of her car. She had a nice one, of course. It was a unique color, kind of a deep emerald green, and it was washed and polished often. Her car matched her in a lot of ways. She worked on looking good, wanting to show she had excellent taste and could afford the nicer things in life. She also needed everything to be tidy—polished. But life wasn't always like that, and they were going to have to face some of the issues that had been stirred up.

"Going my way?" Tracy asked as she stopped next to her and presented her cheek for a kiss.

"I thought I would." She raised a brown bag with handles. "I picked up dinner so neither of us had to cook."

Tracy leaned over the bag and sniffed. "Smells delicious. The little bit of rain we had cut the humidity. Want to eat outside?"

"Love to. I brought a change of clothes for tomorrow."

They walked in together, then Tracy went upstairs to change. When she got back downstairs, Yardley was putting their dinner on plates.

"Mmm. I love a good gazpacho," Tracy said. "The salads look excellent, by the way."

"Vivacious Veggies is so overpriced it's not funny, but I always find myself going there when I want to bring something home. Their things are always fresh and tasty."

"I'll bring the utensils and some napkins. Wine?"

"Sure. Just a couple of ounces, though."

After gathering everything, Tracy struggled with the screen door for a second. Yardley jumped to her feet to hold it open for her. Good manners and thoughtfulness really did help keep a relationship calm and even-keeled.

After they ate a few bites, Tracy said, "Dex and I cleared the air a little bit."

"How did you do that?"

"I went over there yesterday after work." Yardley opened her mouth to speak, but Tracy kept going. "I'm just guessing that we cleared the air, if I'm being honest. But I assume that screaming at each other for a while might have done that."

"You were—" Yardley sat up straighter in her chair. "Why didn't you mention this last night?"

Tracy gazed at her for a minute, pretty sure Yardley was open to a discussion. "I didn't want to go from one fight to another. Given there was every possibility that you were still angry, I wasn't willing to risk it. I needed to relax and think about things."

"Did you?" Now *that* was the old Yardley. Calm, open, and interested.

"I hope so. The big issue is that I believe Dex is sticking around only so she can see Kendall frequently. By the way, Kendall assured me that she proposed spending the summer in LA, but Dex wouldn't bite." She put her soup spoon down and gazed at Yardley until she looked up. "I say we give all of that a rest, and focus on us."

Warily, Yardley said, "What do we need to focus on?"

"A few things. I've noticed that every time we have a disagreement, let alone a fight, you go back to your condo."

She nodded emphatically. "A cooling-off period works best for me. Words said in haste can cause a lot of trouble."

"Mmm. I suppose that's true, but we're not learning how to fight." She waited until Yardley looked up. "We need to."

"I'd prefer not to—fight or learn how to. Fights aren't productive. Discussions are."

Tracy thought about that for a few seconds. "Do you plan on living together?"

"Of course," she said quickly. "Now would be fine, but I'm willing to wait until we're married."

"I think we need a stress-test. Since we're considering living in your condo after we marry, why don't we give it a trial run. Like right now? After a couple of months, we'd know if living there suits us."

"How would that change anything? We're basically living together now."

"It's the basic part I'm worried about, Yardley. Having an escape option lets us gloss over everything. While I agree that it's better to have calm, rational discussions about major issues, sometimes a volatile one can't be avoided. When that happens, we have to have the skills and the practice to weather those storms—while they're happening."

"I don't know… I prefer to take shelter during a storm, and hunker down until it's passed."

"I have a tendency to do that too. But that can be disastrous over the long term. Things can build up when you never vent your feelings."

The smile she showed when she was trying to talk Tracy into something was awfully cute. "But if you're not venting them, they must not need to be vented, right?"

"That's not true in the least for me. I let things slide rather than face them. Then I blow up. Not good," she added. "I threw an awful lot of old resentments into Dex's face yesterday afternoon. Having those hurts resolved when they were fresh would have been a heck of a lot better for me."

"But Kendall will never stay at my condo," Yardley said, pouting. "If you move out, she'll use that as an excuse to stay here alone."

"That could happen. But she needs to get used to our being together, and she can't do that if we're not actually together." She nodded, with her certainty growing. "Kendall has to decide how much effort she's willing to put into getting used to us as a couple. Of course, I'd be devastated if she drifted away, but even if she does, I'm sure she'll come back fairly quickly."

"I…" Yardley paused and let out a breath. "I'm willing to try. Let's pack up your work clothes and take them over this weekend." She picked up her phone and made a note. "Would you mind stopping by Gentle Cycle for me? It's close to your office."

"Gentle Cycle?"

"That's my laundry."

"Sure."

"I've got the ticket in my purse. Let me give you some money."

"I can afford to pay for your laundry. How much could you have?"

She started to tick off her list. "I send out all of my blouses, my casual shirts, my jeans, and my pajamas."

"What's left?"

"Just underwear and socks. I wash those myself. Unscented detergent. Delicate. Extra rinse."

"Mmm. I throw everything in together and hope for the best…"

"Then we'd better each wash our own things. Sometimes I get a rash…"

"Good idea. I'll pick up your stuff tomorrow." She held out her hand. "Do you have a blank check? I think I'll need it."

CHAPTER TEN

ON SATURDAY MORNING, DEX SLIPPED out of bed and spent a minute making herself look presentable. There was no question that her mother was truly happy to have her home for such a long time, but Dex knew the welcome would chill slightly if she didn't comb her hair and put on a fresh shirt before heading over to the house. Her mom was a deeply conservative woman who clung to the old ways, with her manners and her formality coming from the fifties—the decade she was born in. Thankfully, she was socially liberal, which made a long stay pretty stress-free. Not having to step lightly around politics, sexuality, and gender kept things on an even keel.

When Dex opened her door, something fell inside with a thump. A rectangular box, wrapped in brown paper, nearly whacked her on the shin.

After picking it up, she went into the kitchenette to get a knife. The package certainly hadn't come through the mail, since there wasn't a word of writing on it. When she cut the string, the paper fell open, and she sighed with pleasure to find a framed version of the photo of her and Kendall at the beach. Some process had been applied to make it look like a water color, which set it off beautifully. And the frame itself looked like driftwood, a perfect choice. Enormously pleased, and a little surprised, she went back outside, seeing that Kendall had already staked her claim by the pool. She was lying on a chaise, with her phone propped up on one leg. Even though it was early, she was already in her swimsuit, covered by a man's dress shirt—undoubtedly one of Randy's.

"You made my day," Dex said, ruffling her hair.

"I did? Just by lying here?" Her eyes twinkled. "I can make every one of your days until you go back home, since I'm planning on doing nothing more than lying here reading."

"I'd be happy to have you parked here for the duration. But you made my day by having that photo framed so nicely. I didn't know you did that kind of thing."

"I didn't either," she said, sitting up a little taller, "since I don't know what you're talking about."

"You didn't…"

"I didn't do a thing."

"Interesting."

"Interesting…what?"

"Your mom had our beach photo framed. Go look if you want. It's really nice. I'm going to go inside and see if there's any coffee. Want anything?"

"No, thanks. I'm perfectly happy."

As Dex walked toward the house, she stopped to pick some spent blossoms from the azaleas, spending a minute thinking.

She should have guessed that Tracy had been the one to have the photo framed. She'd always been into little gestures like that, and was very good about following up on things. Dex often had good intentions, but she wasn't a pro at bringing them to life. Tracy was kind of the opposite—at least she had been when they'd been together. She wasn't awash in big plans, but when she had an idea that meant something to her—she took it to completion. The fact that their outing meant something to her was awfully touching. Knowing Tracy, the gift was also an addendum to her apology. She was good about that, too.

After placing the blooms in a little pile for disposal, she went inside, kind of pleased to find everyone gone. She'd really wanted to sit by the pool to meditate, but even if Kendall respected her need for quiet, she'd still be clicking away on her phone, or laughing at something one of her friends sent her. She could be quiet, but she simply couldn't be silent.

After gulping down a cup of coffee, Dex went up to her old room, which had only been lightly curated since she'd left for UVA. She always stayed in the pool house, much preferring the privacy. But having her old room largely intact was kind of nice. She sat on the bed and got into a good position, trying to blur her mind to all of the little things lying around that could have easily distracted her.

It took quite a while to settle down, since her mind was continually buffeted by thoughts and noises, some of them surprising. Why would the theme song for a TV show she'd loved as a small child pop up? Then an image of a girl from her kindergarten class got stuck in her head. That made no sense at all, but then the original photo of her and Kendall took up some space and stayed there.

Normally, she tried to think of random thoughts, images, and sensations as pretty little clouds suspended in a perfectly clear blue sky. Each one came about for no real reason, and it floated away when it was ready. She could observe the cloud for a while, but she didn't need to. It had its own timeline.

But when thoughts of that old photo filled her head, refusing to float away or dissipate, she lay down on the bed to give it the attention it deserved.

She hadn't told Kendall, or Tracy, that she kept the original on her desk for two reasons. One was that it was the last good photo of her and Kendall taken when they were still a family. Seeing her child's gleeful face always made her smile. But her own expression, which would have seemed perfectly normal to anyone else, reminded her of her mental state back then. Dex knew she looked normal only because she'd used at the right time. She wasn't very high, since her eyes were bright and clear. She didn't have even a glimmer of the haunted expression that would have been revealed if she'd been obsessed with where and how and when she'd score next, meaning she was quite a ways from craving the drug. The photo had caught her at a perfect moment. But she knew that if it had been taken an hour earlier, or a couple of hours later, she'd look like a different person. A person who should not have been driving a car, much less caring for a child.

Looking at that photo every time she sat at her desk had been a very good reminder of the darkness that had pervaded every minute of her life back then. But she decided right then that when she got home she was going to put the photo in a drawer. The new picture, the one where she was clean, the one where she was proud of how hard she'd worked to stay sober, the one where Kendall and Tracy both knew exactly who she was —that was the one she wanted to see. That was the one she wanted to be inspired by.

※※※

Once she'd worked through her thoughts on the photo, Dex was able to slide into a contemplative space with relative ease.

Eventually, time lost its meaning, and she found herself sinking deeper and deeper into her breath. Soon, the beat of her heart and her slow, steady pulse filled her brain. Nothing else mattered as she clung to the feeling like she was riding a smooth wave.

When she slowly became aware of her surroundings, she felt a thousand percent better. She wouldn't have believed how rejuvenating it could be to think of nothing but her breathing, but when she was able to get into a good head-space, she felt so peaceful, yet energetic, that it was almost impossible to explain to someone who hadn't experienced it. Her fondest hope was that Kendall got into some form of meditation or another type of spiritual practice during her time in China. Anything that would help her focus more deeply and have more control over her mind and body would be a helpful life skill.

When Dex went back outside, Kendall hadn't moved. After pulling a chaise close, Dex said, "Do you think you might actually be part snail?"

"It's a possibility. But I have devoted some energy to thinking about what I want to do today." She stretched out and yawned. "Of course, the odds are that I'll lie right here and try to get through this book."

"Big agenda." Dex wanted to get loosened up and do some yoga, but when she had Kendall's full attention she hated to pass up an opportunity to talk. "Why don't we spend a few minutes getting caught up."

"Okay," she said, looking a little wary.

"It's almost July, baby. Granted, you've only been out of school for a month, but…"

"I'm working on it," Kendall said, giving every indication she wasn't in the mood to talk about her plans.

"May I ask where you are in the process? Or is that top-secret?"

"Not top-secret," she said, giving her a sly glance. "Moderately-secret's more correct."

"Come on." Dex tried not to sound as frustrated as she really was. "You've got to have *some* plans firmed up by now."

"Nope. Every plan I thought was viable is falling apart." She took in a breath. "It's pissing me off."

"I'm guessing that means you still don't have anyone to travel with, right?"

"Right," she admitted glumly. "My last hope backed out a few days ago. I've got just one person left, but she's a year behind me. So she'll be ready to go *next* June, but that doesn't do me much good."

"This is someone you're certain will follow through?"

"Uh-huh. Yawen is a lock. She's already signed up to start her TESOL certification in the fall."

"That's promising. But how do you know she'll actually want to go? I know from experience that people are better at talking about plans than completing them."

"True. But Yawen's a planner, not a talker. Her grandparents live in China, and even though she's visited every other year, she's never spent a whole lot of time with them. She wants to remedy that now that she has the time. Best of all is that she wants to be close to them, but not too close. So Nanning is on her short list."

"Mmm. They don't get along?"

"No, they do, but they live in Shijiazhuang, and the air quality is horrible. Yawen would like to teach somewhere that she can breathe, hopefully making enough money to pay for her grandparents to visit for a week or two at a time."

"Ahh. So she wants to see her grandparents on her own turf."

"Right. Like I said, she's a planner."

"She sounds like a good kid, too. But if you lived together, you might have extra roommates for weeks at a time."

"Don't care," Kendall said blithely. "Stuff like that doesn't bother me."

Dex had her doubts about that, since the mere sight of Yardley set her scampering from the house. "So Yawen's planning on moving to China permanently?"

"Oh, no. Not at all. She wants to teach Mandarin here, hopefully at a public high school, then teach English in the summer in China. She's got this nailed down, Dex. Actually, she's the only person I know who has a life-plan that could actually work."

"It sounds like a good one. You two get along?"

"Everyone gets along with Yawen," Kendall said, laughing a little. "She's calm, and agreeable, and always up for going out for something good to eat. Also, she's a big reader, like me. She's neater than I am, but I could step up my game if we lived together."

"Hmm…" Dex wasn't sure Kendall was in a receptive mood, but she tried anyway. "I know your schedule prevented you from getting certified to teach English as a second language while you were at UVA. But you've got to get the credential at some point, right? Why not look at this setback as part of *your* life plan? Get certified now, then leave next year—with someone you're sure you'd get along with."

She shook her head immediately. "Can't do it. I couldn't afford to rent an apartment, and I'm not going to live with Yardley. Even if I liked her a lot more, I don't want to be the third wheel."

"You know you could move into the pool house, baby. Your grandparents would be thrilled to have you so close."

She shrugged. "I love them to death, but I don't want to live with them. They aren't overbearing or anything, but I want to be on my own. Kind of," she added, with that cute smile showing again.

"You know you could talk me into paying your rent, but I appreciate that you haven't asked."

She seemed very sober when she said, "I don't want to be that person —the one who gets everything handed to her. I mean, it's not really being on my own to live with Mom, but I don't add to her expenses—much."

She held up her hand, as if she could stop Dex from speaking if she made the gesture dramatic enough. "If I *could* stay with mom, I'd get some kind of job and pay rent."

"But you can't because Yardley will either be at the house, or the house will be sold."

"Ruins everything," she sighed.

Dex continued to work this over in her head, thrilled to have Kendall actually considering her suggestions. These opportunities couldn't be wasted! "How about going back to Charlottesville? A masters in teaching, with a concentration in English as a Second Language would set you up to teach here or abroad. That's a life plan if I've ever heard one."

"Solid," she said, nodding thoughtfully. "But the thought of more school isn't great…"

"It's one more little year, and it will pay off for your entire teaching career. You'll qualify for better jobs in both China and America. Isn't that worth another year in Charlottesville?"

"I wouldn't *have* to be there," she admitted. "I already checked out the program. They have an on-campus version and an online version."

"Then do it! I'll happily pay your tuition."

Kendall looked at her speculatively. "Can you? I mean, can you pay for a masters without digging into your savings? I don't want to put you into a bad—"

"Uhm, I'm not sure why no one in this family thinks I make a good living, but I do!"

Kendall reached over and patted her gently on the head. "Don't lose your shit. I'm just trying to be considerate."

"Sorry. I can normally take a lot of teasing, but Nana and Papa are now in on the 'Won't you starve if you stay here much longer' thing. I'm about to show them copies of my investment account statements."

"You can show me, and I'll pass on the info…"

"No, thanks. Just believe me when I tell you I can pay your tuition without having to sell my blood."

"All right," she said, squinting her eyes as she thought. "So where would I live? If I went back on campus I might be able to find a spot in Shea House. Living with people in my major was kind of great, since a lot of them were already pretty fluent in Mandarin."

If it was possible to keep her in Richmond, Dex was sure going to try. "Uhm… What if I bought your house from your mom? Would you live with me?"

Kendall sat up like a shot. "You'd buy my house? You'd live in Richmond?"

"I've been thinking about it."

"Seriously?" She stared at her, open-mouthed. "Why?"

"LA's been wearing on me. I've been considering coming home—permanently."

Clearly puzzled, Kendall said, "Let's say I believe you've got money. Don't you have to work to keep it coming in?"

"Sure. That's why I've been thinking of putting together a professional-quality recording studio. I could continue to narrate audio books from home."

"That would be enough to live on?"

"Maybe not. But I could easily go to LA for a week or two if I booked a feature. I've got friends I could stay with…"

"We'd be roommates?" She was grinning so broadly it was crystal clear she was fully in favor of the idea.

"Well, I'd still mother the hell out of you, but yes. Are you in?"

"*So* in," she said, jumping to her feet and bending over to hug Dex soundly. "Does Mom know you're buying the house right out from under her?"

"We've discussed it. Briefly. When we spoke she seemed to be leaning toward moving to Yardley's condo."

"Mmm." She didn't look happy about that. "Such a bad idea. Mom's just not a condo person. It might sound nice not to have to do yard work, but she loves it, Dex. She really does."

"Obviously, your mom has to *want* to move. But if she does, I'll buy the house." She gave Kendall a tap on the head. "Oh, what the hell? If your mom doesn't want to move, I'll buy something else. Get your application in for that online master's program, buddy. We're going to be roommates."

CHAPTER ELEVEN

ON A HOT, STICKY SATURDAY MORNING, Libby drove over to Tracy's to pick her up. They'd been taking little day trips for years, trying to find every ancestor of hers or Randy's who was buried in a marked grave anywhere in Virginia. Maybe they should have taken the summer off, but Libby hated having the weather control her plans.

After she gave the horn a quick toot, Tracy exited the house, dressed in a summery, pale blue shift. When she opened the car door, Libby said, "Don't you look cool and breezy? Is that a new dress?"

"Not so new, but you might not have seen it. I thought it was just the thing for a hot summer day." She latched her seatbelt and adjusted the angle of her seat-back. "Do you need me to put an address into the GPS?"

"I'm all set. Randy's finally convinced me that doing it before I leave the driveway is best. But *please* don't tell him I listened to his advice. If he knows I pay attention every once in a while, he'll never stop."

"Your secret's safe with me. We're going to Culpeper?"

"We are, indeed. The Dexter line has a long history in the area, and I'd like to find my four times great grandmother's plot."

"Sounds like a plan. Do you need coffee?"

"I've been up since seven, so I'm fully caffeinated. But I'll be hungry by ten, so maybe we can stop and get a glass of tea or something around then."

"I approve of your plan. As always."

They'd barely gone a block when Tracy said, "You know, in all the time we've known each other, I've never asked why Dex has so many names. Were you trying to make everyone happy?"

"Seems that way, doesn't it?" She laughed, thinking of the hours of discussions she and Randy had slogged through, with neither of them truly believing the choice was theirs alone. "We chose to name her Cordelia, after Randy's mother. I liked the name, and thought we could tinker with it if it wasn't quite right—like shortening it to Delia or something like that if the full name wasn't perfect."

"That didn't work out," Tracy said, giving her a grin.

"It certainly did not. The day after we brought her home, I told Randy we'd made a mistake. That baby didn't have a bit of Cordelia in her. But Randy's mom was quite alive, so I could hardly change it at that point."

"Kendall didn't work?"

"I think that's where we would have landed, but we called Dex pet names for years. We rotated among Sunny, Sassy, Sugar, Peach… We were still undecided when she was ready for kindergarten."

"Kindergarten? You didn't have a consistent name for her when she was five?"

"We don't like to rush important decisions," Libby said, enjoying the look of shock on Tracy's face. "But Dex had clearly gotten tired of the game. On her first day of kindergarten, she marched up to her teacher and said her name was C. K. *Dexter* Haven. Strong emphasis on the Dexter. That's what her teacher called her, and we eventually went along with the program."

"Ooo. I can just see her," Tracy sighed. "But how did she know to use initials?"

"Oh, simple. Her paternal grandfather was D. D. Stuart Haven, and everyone in the family called him Double D. She knew his full name was Davis Derby, and I think she figured out how to do generally the same thing with her own name. For a while, it felt odd calling my little girl such a masculine-sounding name, but my mother was happy to have her maiden name featured." She shrugged. "Once Dex and Mama were on the same side, the battle was over."

"So even with three names, Dex doesn't have a single one that wasn't handed down from a relative."

Libby gazed across the car for a second. "Why would we make something up when we have dozens upon dozens of ancestors to honor?"

Tracy nodded. "Dex said the same thing when we were naming Kendall. I voted for Lauren, but I'm glad she won that argument."

"Is there a Lauren in your family?"

"Not a one."

Libby reached over and patted her gently. "Then I'm very glad you lost that argument. A child needs to know she's part of a tradition that stretches way back."

"I'm truly glad Kendall has those family ties. All from your side of the family, that is. It wouldn't hurt a thing if the Lords went extinct."

∞∞∞

They reached Culpeper close to ten, and Libby started keeping an eye out for a Starbucks. They, and every other kind of chain, filled the town, and she considered how her ancestors would feel if they could see the place now.

The population had exploded in the last twenty years, with Culpeper becoming a bedroom community of DC. When you got out of the center of town, it looked like every other suburb, but it had retained a charming business district that let it hold onto a little bit of its past. Of course, now there were ice cream shops, modest jewelry stores, and cafes, rather than the kinds of workaday businesses that had kept towns vital a hundred and fifty years ago.

Deciding to buy local, Libby slowed down and nabbed a parking space, certain they'd be able to find something that would suit them.

"Will you look at a review site to find us a place where we can have a cool glass of tea and some kind of baked good, honey? You're much better at that than I am."

"I've been looking," she said, her focus locked onto her phone. "Here's something promising. It's two blocks away, and people say their mini-donuts are fantastic."

"Mini-donuts?" Libby laughed. "You know that's just a way to get you to buy two or three, since they're small. I bet each is as expensive as a full-sized one from Dunkin' Donuts."

"Of course it will be. But I've memorized the menu at Dunkin'. Let's branch out."

"Prepare yourself," Libby said as she threw her door open. "Good, lord, this heat might kill us both."

"Oh, it is nasty," Tracy agreed, already fanning herself. "The last thing Virginia needs is global *warming*. I haven't been able to go running once in the last week."

"Come swim. Drop by on your way home from work. You swim well enough to get in a workout."

"I might," she said, not sounding convinced. "I just don't want Dex to feel like I'm taking up her space."

"She's usually inside in the afternoons, chatting away on her phone." She laughed. "I'm used to Kendall and her crowd only texting. It's odd to see Dex using hers the old-fashioned way."

After making the mistake of walking down the sunny side of the street, they approached the coffee shop, which was decorated to appeal to upper-middle-class urbanites who didn't mind paying close to five dollars for an iced tea.

Libby was pleased when Tracy went, laser-like, for a table that a pair of women was just about to vacate. She said a few words to them, then started to clear the table before an employee could beat her to it. By the time Libby reached the spot, Tracy had pulled out a chair. "Table for two," she said, waiting for Libby to sit before she scooted the chair close. "I'll get in line." She leaned over to whisper, "The lobbyists are out in force today."

Libby laughed a little, and started to speak, but Tracy just pressed her shoulder and took off. She was a very thoughtful girl, always offering to wait in line, race into a store during a storm, or park the car on a cold day. She'd also grown confident, a trait Libby was thrilled to see. Back when they'd first met, Tracy reminded her of a child who'd recently aged out of a foundling home—almost Dickensian in her meager wishes. She would no more have ordered without asking for Libby's choice than she would have flapped her wings and flown. Not now. Tracy had developed a real backbone. At least when it came to interacting with society in general. She obviously had some work to do on her love life. Choosing Yardley Simpkins over every other woman on earth showed she was still terrified when it came to dreaming big.

A few minutes later, Tracy appeared with a tray, competently balancing large glasses of iced tea, along with an assortment of mini donuts, as well as a scone that looked positively delicious.

"If that's fresh peach, I will fight you for it," Libby said.

"It is, indeed, fresh peach. The guy at the register said it was their best-seller. I snagged the last one, and it is for you," she said, placing the plate in front of Libby with a flourish. "I'm going to sit right here and eat more of these donuts than I should." She picked one up and held it close, examining it. "This one's hibiscus." She took a bite, then smiled, always looking a little devilish when she treated herself with just about anything. "I will consume this with pleasure."

Libby took a bite of her scone, nodding her head dramatically. "Such a lovely use of a ripe peach. You've done a wonderful job of finding us a good snack."

"If we don't perish from the heat, there's a new brewery close by. Not to mention a place that makes their own chocolate."

"I'll drink to that," Libby said. "And if we do perish, they can bury us nearby, with the Dexters. Full circle."

"I would not mind spending eternity with Grammy's people."

"Actually, if we had our choice, we should go with Grammy's mother's folks. The Kendalls were a significantly more prominent family than the Dexters, but none of my ancestors were as renowned as Randy's people. The Randolphs are quite high up in the ranks of the First Families of Virginia."

"I'm sure mine were high up in the families who fought to stay with Virginia during the Civil War. Joining a free state would not have been our style." She laughed ruefully. "I'm almost certain we never had the capital to actually own human beings, but I'm *sure* we wanted to."

Libby reflected on that for a moment, as she'd done many, many times through the years. "It will always be difficult to be a southerner and have much to be proud of when it comes to slavery, honey." She lowered her voice to add, "Randy's people were British loyalists, so his folks were not only opposed to independence, they jumped onto the secession bandwagon *early*. My people fought Britain for independence, which I'm proud of, but their deeply held belief that Black people weren't human beings will always prevent me from having true respect for them."

"History's tough, isn't it? If you go back far enough, all of us come from people who've done some awful, awful things."

"True. All we can do is try not to continue along that line. We're doomed to repeat history if we refuse to learn from it." She tapped Tracy on the hand. "Speaking of learning, Grammy's church book club is reading a book on anti-racism. Want to participate? It starts in September."

"I'd love to. Maybe we can get Dex to join in…if she's still here then."

Libby smiled. "I see no sign of her leaving, and I say that with a great deal of pleasure, along with a little consternation. How can she afford not to work?"

"I have no idea. There are so many things about her that are completely opaque to me."

"As always. Even as a child, she kept us guessing. That has continued to this day."

∞∞∞

Even wearing hats, the sun beat down on them hard as they made their way through the cemetery. They had a plot map that Libby had found online, and it didn't take too long to find the grave. It was a simple one, with Libby's ancestor's name carved into a stone slab, right below a faded cherub. "Fidelia Lee Dexter," she murmured. "We have no Lees in our lineage, so that might have been plucked out of the ether." She gazed at the stone for a minute. "Could she have been named after General Lee? Oh, of course not. She was born in 1840."

"Mmm. Well, she lived to a ripe old age," Tracy said. "Making it to seventy was a feat."

"Yes, but the children she outlived must have weighed on her for every one of those years." She clucked her tongue. "Imagine burying three babies."

"I can't. I don't *want* to," Tracy added. "Life is frightening enough without thinking of losing children. It says Fidelia was the wife of Elijah, but he's not here."

"Mmm. He fought and died during the war, but the records I have for him aren't complete. He's likely over in the cemetery across town for the war dead."

"A whole cemetery built just for…"

"They had to, Tracy. Churchyard cemeteries weren't large enough for all of the bodies. I think there are around a thousand *unidentified* men buried there, not to mention the ones with proper markers. They say Culpeper was one of the most fought over parts of the entire south. That's what happens when you're on the main road between Washington and Richmond."

"Do you think Elijah was killed in battle?"

"I don't yet know. Obviously, a lot of soldiers died from what would be minor infections today. Or contagious illnesses. Or heat stroke. I'm going to keep looking, of course. I think I'll come up here in the fall and look through the public library's records. I'll find something," she said, always dogged.

The churchyard was nearly silent as the hot wind wafted across the parched grass. They were the only people around, with most sane folks staying indoors. Even the streets were deserted, with no one wanting to venture out even in an air conditioned car. It seemed like she, Libby, and some crickets in the distance were the only living beings in Culpeper. Besides the gnats, of course. They swarmed around their faces, with Libby barely bothering to shoo them away.

Tracy got down on her knees to sweep away some recently cut trimmings, exposing the names of the children. "Cornelius, Chester, and Coraline. None of them made it to their third birthday." Wincing to herself, Tracy said, "Coraline died in 1865. Her father had to be gone by then. So much loss…"

"Coraline," Libby said thoughtfully. "Not too far from Cordelia." She gave Tracy a hand up. "Dex never mentioned any negative feelings about being named after her paternal grandmother, did she?"

"Oh, no. She was crazy about Randy's mom, and I never heard her say a negative word about the name. But even if she'd hated it, she wouldn't have admitted it. She's very good at keeping her feelings to herself if she thinks they'll hurt anyone."

"How about you?" Libby asked, sounding nonchalant as she bent down to take some closeup photos of the graves. "Just for the sake of argument, let's say you were angry that I participated in the scheme to lock you and Dex in the pool house…"

"Oh, Libby, I'm not angry about that. Not at all." Tracy waited until she was finished with her photo duties, then she took off her sunglasses so Libby could see her eyes. "I'm thankful. I just wish I'd listened to you eighteen, or seventeen, or sixteen years ago."

"Did I honestly bother you that often? I tried not to be a pest."

"You've never been a pest. You were very gentle—but persistent. But no matter how persistent you were, I just couldn't let Dex back into my life. I didn't trust her enough." She gazed at Libby for a second. "You stopped asking by the time Kendall was seven or eight. Did my stubbornness finally exhaust you?"

"No, no, I stopped because Dex asked me to."

"She did?" Tracy put her glasses back on just to cut the glare and give the gnats less access to her eyes.

"She did. I think she was afraid of upsetting the apple cart. Having me be the go-between was working, and I think she was worried that things might get dicey if you started to speak directly." She shrugged. "It's hard to know with Dex. Especially back then. Those first years were…"

"I'm sorry I wasn't able to be more supportive to Dex and to you," Tracy said, feeling so self-involved that it made her stomach ache. "I'm sure you were worried about her every minute."

"That's just about right." Libby took Tracy's hand, then made a face, quickly wiping her own hand on her skirt. "I'm not sure which of us is sweating more, but I'm certain it's time to go find that brewery."

"But you don't like beer."

"No, but you do. They'll have cider or something. Come on now. I'm not ready to be planted next to Fidelia just yet, which I will be if we don't get out of this heat."

⚬⚬⚬

They'd settled close to an air conditioning vent in the tasting room of the little brewery, and Tracy was diligently trying not to drink her pilsner too quickly.

Libby had found a rosé cider she seemed fond of, and Tracy was sure they'd stay for quite a while. At least until they weren't sweaty and dehydrated, which wouldn't be soon.

"So…while we're talking about Dex and secrets," Libby said, even though they hadn't really been talking about that specifically. "I have one for you."

"A secret?"

"Um-huh," she said, taking a sip of her drink and settling back into her chair, giving Tracy an enigmatic look.

"Do I want to know?"

Her smile grew. "I don't know. Do you?"

"Of course I do!" They were sitting just close enough for Tracy to be able to elbow her playfully. "Out with it, woman!"

"It's nothing major. Actually, it's just a comment Dex tossed off a few years ago."

"And that comment was…"

Libby took another sip, playing it out just like Dex sometimes did. "Well, I asked her if communicating through me was still working for her, and she said she didn't have many options, as she didn't trust herself to speak to you directly."

"Didn't trust herself? What could she have meant by that?"

Libby took Tracy's hand, recently washed and sweat-free. "She said she didn't need the temptation. She'd gotten very good at avoiding any issue that might frustrate her, and she thought talking to you might fall into that category."

Tracy nodded, with that making perfect sense. "Understood. I can't say I blame her. I can be intensely frustrating."

Libby cocked her head. "That's how you took the comment? I assumed she meant that she didn't want to remind herself of how much she missed you. But maybe you're right…"

"This was a couple of years after we split?"

"No, honey. A couple of years—ago. I know Kendall was in college."

"Are you serious?" Her heart started to race. It wasn't possible that Dex had feelings for her just a couple of years ago. That made no sense at all.

"Of course I am. But maybe I misunderstood. As you say, you *can* be frustrating." She ran her hand across Tracy's shoulders. "As can we all. It's part of the human condition."

Tracy was certain confusion was also part of the human condition, and she was now bedeviled by it. It didn't seem possible that Dex had missed her just a couple of years ago. She'd had to have known Tracy was one hundred percent single, and there was no reason to miss someone who you could have just called… Or maybe she *hadn't* known that Tracy had been unhappily single. *Damn!* With everyone keeping so many secrets, and being so damned discrete, she wasn't sure what Dex knew or when she knew it. She also wasn't sure Libby wasn't just speculating. But one thing was certain. If Dex currently had feelings for her, she'd done a very good job of keeping them hidden, and she'd had more than a few opportunities to let them slip. *That* was indisputable.

Chapter Twelve

A FEW DAYS AFTER HER TRIP to Culpeper, Tracy's phone buzzed when she was leaving the office. She took a quick peek at the screen, seeing Dex's name. "Got some time to talk about my buying your house right out from under you?"

Tracy wrote back immediately. "Why don't you meet me at Soft Serve Sally's? I've been craving ice cream all afternoon, but I hate to go alone."

"So late on a school nite?!?"

"I'm living wild. 9:30?"

"You're on. I'll even buy."

"Get moving!"

⊗⊗⊗

Dex was smiling to herself as she got into her mom's car for the fairly short drive. The name of the place was just Soft Serve. But the super-friendly woman who'd worked there the first time they went, back when Tracy was pregnant, was named Sally, and the name had stuck. Actually, Dex hadn't known Tracy had kept the name going, but it made her happy that she had.

She pulled up to the small drive-in, going slowly to avoid the ruts in the unpaved parking lot. By the time she'd parked, Tracy was standing by her door, grinning at her. She was wearing a set of sage green scrubs, and looked dog-tired.

"Hey, there," Dex said as she exited. "You're just home from work?"

"Yeah," she said, putting her hand over her mouth to cover a yawn. "I work late one night every week. I should have been out of there by eight-thirty, but I got involved in counseling a kid whose diabetes has been tough to get under control. I'm beat," she said. "But I don't have to be in until ten tomorrow, so I thought this was the perfect night for a sundae."

"A sundae, huh? You're going all out."

"When it's dinner, you can do that." She smiled. "Well, the kid with diabetes shouldn't, but…"

"Where's Yardley?"

"Business dinner. Second one this week."

"Got it. Why don't you go grab us a table? I'll wait in line."

"Sure you don't mind?" She held her phone up and moved it back and forth. "I've got some emails I could reply to…"

"I insist. Chocolate ice cream, doused in marshmallow, right?"

Tracy gave her a very sunny smile. "Good memory." She waved her index finger sternly. "But no cherry on top."

Dex flashed her a smile. "You might have changed, but you haven't changed that much. I've never met a woman who hated maraschino cherries as much as you do."

"Thanks," Tracy said, gripping her around the elbow. "I'll be right over there."

"I'll be quick." After waiting in the longish line for her cone and Tracy's sundae, Dex rushed over to the table to avoid having it melt in the warm night. "Delivery," she said, setting the dish on the wobbly metal table with the even more wobbly metal chairs.

"Mmm. Come to mama," Tracy said, taking the spoon Dex had tucked between her thumb and forefinger. "Damn, I love ice cream." Her gaze fell onto Dex's tiny cone. "What's that? It's so small it's hardly visible."

"Orange sherbet," she said, shrugging. "Child's size."

"A disgrace to true ice cream eaters everywhere." She smiled warmly. "I'm glad you agreed to meet. I always feel kind of lonely when I come here by myself."

"No need for that. I'll accompany you on a moment's notice."

She took another bite, seeming to enjoy it so much that Dex got kind of a contact high from her pleasure.

"So…you're serious about buying the house, huh?"

"Very. If you're ready to sell, let's get on it."

"Mmm. Yardley and I have decided to live in her condo for a while. Just to test it out. But I've never lived in a condo, and I'm worried I'll miss my yard…"

"Well, I'll have to sell my place to have the cash to buy yours, so that will take a while. Why don't I just put it on the market right now and see what happens. I can hold out for a king's ransom."

Tracy gripped her arm, staring. "You're seriously thinking of relocating? I thought this was going to be a second house. An investment property."

"I only need one home, so if I buy here, I'll sell there."

"Amazing. I'm really surprised, Dex. I've always pictured you as the prototypical LA woman."

"Not really. I fit in all right, but I'm a Virginian at heart. I'm ready to come home."

"If you're sure… But I'm reticent to sell before I know I can be happy in a condo." She took in a breath, then let it out slowly. "I want you to be happy, of course, but Kendall's going to miss her summers in LA."

"I think those are close to over anyway," Dex said, feeling a stab of loss from the mere thought. "She's hinting about getting a job. Where they pay you."

"A job? Kendall's thinking of getting a job? Now? When she's supposed to be leaving…?"

"Actually," Dex said, drawing out the word. "She's planning on going back to our dear Alma Mater to get her masters. When she gets to China, no sooner than a year from now, having a masters will qualify her for a much better job."

Tracy playfully slapped at her arm. "You talked her into that?"

"Kind of," she said, nodding. "I've been told I can be quite persuasive."

"Oh, you sweet-talker, you! I'm so glad you used your impressive talents for a good cause. I've been so worried about her fumbling around in a foreign country with no real plans. Thank you, Dex. Really. Thank you."

"I'm very glad she was persuadable. I'm actually feeling great about it. I'm ready to set up a recording studio and get back to work."

"So many plans!"

"All I need is a house. What do you say?"

Tracy concentrated on her sundae for a moment, clearly thinking this over. "What if we agreed to a three-month trial period? That will give me time to make sure I can be happy without a yard."

"I can be patient. If you choose not to sell, I think I'll go the condo route. It would be nice to not have any unexpected costs drop into my lap..."

Tracy gazed at her for a few seconds, clearly on the verge of saying something.

"You look... I'm not sure what."

Tracy smiled and shrugged her shoulders. "I was going to ask a probing question, but I'm not sure if I should."

"Probe away. I'm not shy about declining to answer."

"Okay." She placed her hands on the tiny table and squared her shoulders. "Are you in trouble?"

"Trouble?"

"Financially. I know you must have a lot of bills. Has it gotten to be too much...?"

Dex laughed. "I'm solvent. Honestly," she said, speaking slowly. "I'm working class for my zip code, but I do just fine for any normal city. I'm simply tired of LA. I want to come home."

She held up her hands. "I'll back off. I wouldn't have even asked, but Kendall's a little worried, and your mom's mentioned it..."

Dex blew out a breath. "I generally don't talk about this, but I think I can—since he has."

"He has..."

"Orion Delgado." Tracy looked blank, so Dex continued. "The main creative guy behind the highest grossing Pixel Pictures?"

"Oh! I haven't paid any attention to the humans involved. I've seen most Pixel films, many of them fifty times, but all I know is that Kendall was addicted to them." She gave Dex a very sweet smile. "And I know that the best ones always had a loving, soft-voiced mom who holds the family together."

Dex rolled her eyes. "I just read my lines. It's the creative team that comes up with the stories. That's where Orion shines. He's a masterful storyteller, screenwriter, animator, director. The guy's an absolute genius."

"And what does this have to do with your finances?"

Dex found it hard to start, even though she knew it was allowed. Holding onto confidences so tenaciously was a hard habit to break. "Uhm…Orion gave an interview to the *L. A. Times* not long ago, where he talked about his recovery journey…"

"Ooo. He's an addict?"

"Um-hmm. Heroin for him. He got addicted at CalArts. Film school," she added when it was clear Tracy didn't get the reference. "Just like me, he thought he could stay on top of it, but…you can't."

"I feel like I'm pulling teeth, Dex. We don't have to talk about this if you don't want to. Really."

"No, I'd like to clear this up, and now that Orion's talked about the details of his struggle, I feel okay sharing how we overlap."

"If you're sure."

"I am. He wanted to name me in the article, but I didn't want to have that out there. So…we're good." She took in a breath and tried to get her facts straight. "So I was just about to leave rehab when Orion arrived. He'd gotten very successful, very fast. He was riding this big wave after his first Pixel film, *Triad*, broke all kinds of box office records. But when you're a junkie, that's what you have to devote your life to. As the stresses of his job built, he went from snorting to shooting-up, and he got caught. Pixel sent him to rehab, but they made it clear that he had to get clean and stay clean. His wife echoed that sentiment, giving him one chance."

"Did he make it? I don't know a thing about him, so…"

Dex smiled. "He made it, but those first few weeks were really tough. He was detoxing, which is awful even if you're weaned off the drug slowly. He was terrified he'd lose everything—which he would have—if he didn't get clean. But his confidence had been destroyed."

"And you helped him," Tracy said, the belief she used to have in Dex still shining brightly in her pale eyes.

Dex shrugged, knowing that every addict saved himself, but Orion definitely hadn't seen it that way. "He couldn't concentrate enough to read, or watch TV, or even think clearly. So I sat by him in one of the lounge areas and read to him from the Big Book every night. For hours. Most of the time he fell asleep," she said, chuckling at the memory of this big guy snoring on the sofa. "But he stuck with it, and by the time my three months there were up, he was better. Not well, but better."

"You're a very generous person," Tracy said softly. "You're kind, and patient, and very empathetic."

"It was easy to be empathetic, since I felt just like Orion had a couple of months earlier. Anyway," she continued, just so she didn't have to dwell on how much harder Tracy's lack of faith had made her journey, "Orion followed me to sober living. We got to be true friends there, and we talked about his ideas for *Dobie* for hours and hours…"

"I still haven't seen it," Tracy said, making a funny face. "Kendall won't watch it, so I haven't—"

"It's fine. Anyway, Orion credits me with helping him get through those first few weeks. He claims my voice reminded him of his mother reading to him when he was a child."

Tracy started to sniffle, wiping her eyes with the tiny paper napkin Dex had given her. "Kendall was truly transfixed by your voice when she was a baby. I can just picture her little face relaxing when you'd start reading, even if she'd been wailing her head off just a moment earlier. You were magic."

"Good memories," Dex murmured, sure she'd lose it if she lingered there for too long. "So… After Orion demanded the studio audition me, I was still justifiably surprised to land the role. Not many former junior marketing associates wind up with lead roles in animated features." She paused a second, waiting for Tracy to look up. "But I was much, much more surprised when Orion gave me a piece of his compensation. He insisted I'd helped him develop the plot for the movie, and he was going to make sure I got paid."

"A piece of his compensation?"

"Uh-huh. He had a very complex deal, which I understood nothing of at the time." She smiled, knowing she looked like the cat who ate the canary. "When I started getting royalty checks, I realized how generous Orion had been. It's been seventeen years, and I'm still pulling in enough to make a difference." Laughing, she added, "I can't afford a spread on the top of a hill in Malibu like Orion has, but I was able to put twenty-five percent down on my house—which is a pretty nice one, if I do say so myself. It's not on the beach, but I've got a great water view..."

"Enough!" Tracy said, laughing. "The first time Kendall and your mom visited, they both went silent when I asked if you had room for both of them. I'm sure Libby cautioned her not to go on and on and on..."

"It's just a house, Tracy. I bought it when I thought possessions would make me happy. Now I'm trying not to let material goods have such a hold over me. That's why I'd really like to scale back. Just because I *can* buy expensive things doesn't mean I should."

"The Zenmeister." She chuckled. "One of the many names Kendall has bestowed upon you." Sobering up quickly, Tracy reached across the table to place her hand over Dex's. "Just like Orion, I owe a lot of my success to a few people. If I sell my house, I'm going to pay your parents back for the downpayment—plus interest."

"Ooo. That will be an interesting argument—that you will lose. But I'd love to watch."

"I'm not saying it's going to go over well. But I'm going to push to get them to take the money."

Dex thought it over for just a second, then made an offer. "I think we should split it down the middle and each pay half."

"Half? You lived there for two years!"

"Doesn't matter. If we hadn't had the house, I would have had to pay much more in child support to get you two into a nice place. It's a fair deal."

"All right." She shrugged. "By that I mean we'll take another look when we're ready to make a decision."

"Fair enough. So…? When do we do this?"

"Well, I'm moving into Yardley's on Saturday, so I guess you could move in on Sunday. I'm only taking my clothes and my toiletries. Do you mind having to sleep in my bed?"

Ignoring the many responses she could have had to that, Dex popped the end of her tiny cone into her mouth. She extended her hand, and they shook. "I'm ready to begin my Virginia rebirth, surrounded by everything you aren't in the mood to take with you."

CHAPTER THIRTEEN

TRACY WAS DRAGGING A LITTLE on Sunday, having spent the entire previous day getting her scrubs, a few nice outfits, and most of her summer wardrobe moved over to Yardley's. Kendall had helped get her packed up, and Yardley had hired someone to carry all of the suitcases and boxes into the apartment. That wasn't quite the same as actually carrying a box or two herself, but Tracy felt childish grumbling about that, since the result was identical.

The hired hand hadn't helped unpack, of course, and that had taken hours. To her credit, Yardley had really jumped in to help with that.

They'd had only one minor glitch. Yardley had unpacked all of the scrubs onto the bed, neatly placing them on hangers while Tracy arranged her current stack of hardcover books in front of her bedside table.

Yardley hadn't even said anything, but she glared at the stack of books like they were an invading army. Tracy decided not to mention the glare. Normally, she would have gotten into it a little bit, but she was trying to be more accommodating, and much less argumentative than she sometimes was. Living peacefully with another adult was going to take work, not to mention patience. Every minor issue didn't have to be adjudicated.

On Sunday afternoon, they sat together in the unfamiliar living room, with Yardley doing some work-related tasks on her computer. Tracy's phone buzzed every few minutes, which made Yardley twitch. She was going to have to get used to that, since Kendall often sent ten or more unimportant texts a day: usually just silly memes or funny little videos. But Tracy had to look at them all, since Kendall also would have texted to announce she was leaving for China that afternoon. Tracy read the latest, seeing it was a little more important than your garden-variety meme.

"How about dinner here tonight? Dex is at the store right now, so she could add entrees for you guys. Are you in?"

"Won't you be too tired to have company?"

"Tired? If Dex had a bike, she could have carried everything over on her back. She travels like a spy. It took her fifteen minutes to unpack her two little suitcases. Come on! We're having steak, but she can add fish for you two."

"I'm in," Tracy typed. *"Just add another steak. Yardley's going to a benefit dinner for a charity she supports, so it'll just be me."*

"Great! Come any time. Now's perfect."

"I shouldn't go until Yardley takes off. Maybe an hour?"

"Hurry! Starving!"

Tracy laughed at her histrionics. Kendall had been just like that as a baby. The minute she got hungry, she needed to eat. Actually, Dex was like that, too. They'd make good roommates, if that was the proper term for a woman who moved in with her adult daughter—with just two suitcases.

◌◌◌

Once Tracy kissed Yardley goodbye, she went upstairs to change clothes. She didn't want to expend a huge effort, but she'd grown tired of wearing scrubs nearly everywhere. So she ironed a colorful print blouse, and put a crease into a pair of sage green shorts. A little lipstick and some mascara had her looking like she hadn't just rushed out of work, which gave her an emotional boost. She felt better about herself when she dressed with some level of care.

When she arrived, Kendall guided her into the kitchen, where Dex was grinding a pepper shaker over a steak big enough for an offensive lineman—or maybe two. "Are you trying to make it up to the beef industry for Yardley's not eating meat for the last five years?"

Dex barely looked up, but she'd obviously taken in a lot with a brief glance. "Nice shade of lipstick. Goes well with your skin tone. Pretty."

"Thank you. You look nice, too."

"Oh, everything's a repeat for me. Once someone has seen me three times, they've taken in my whole wardrobe." She turned the steak over and added more pepper. "I decided it's easier to cook one big steak that we can share. I loaded up on veggies, by the way. Blanched Swiss chard, roasted beets, and smashed sunchokes drizzled with thyme-butter. And… a green salad with lots of snap peas. Good?"

"Much better than good. How can I help?"

"No help." Dex met her eyes and smiled. "You're a guest today. For the next three months, this is *my* kitchen." She shifted her gaze. "Kendall, take our guest's drink order, then you two go sit on the deck and enjoy some appetizers."

"Oh, my, I get appetizers, too?"

"You're in a first-class establishment, Tracy. The Haven-Lords don't do anything by half-measure."

⊗⊗⊗

It had turned into a gorgeous night, with a light breeze keeping the mosquitos away, and dozens of lightning bugs beginning to hover over the lawn as dusk closed in.

She and Kendall had just about polished off a bottle of white wine, but Tracy didn't feel even a little tipsy. Actually, she felt very clear-headed. And comfortable. Easy. Dex had gone so far out of her way to make it that way. She'd been light, jovial, always teasing. Of course she was a wonderful host. You couldn't grow up with the good examples Libby and Randy had set and not learn a thing or two about making your guests feel welcome. But it was more than that. Dex was clearly trying—hard—to make their ongoing relationship stress-free for their daughter. Was there anything more comforting than having your child's other parent be so concerned with her happiness and her security? No. There simply was not.

It was funny. Once again, Tracy felt like the volume had been turned up slightly. But she was starting to get used to that. From the day they'd met, Dex had made her feel like she'd taken a hit of nitrous whenever they were together. Everything was funnier, her observations were sharper, her legs were longer, lips a little more kissable. It felt like they were still in college, with each day making her feel a little out-of-control. While that had been great when they had been romantic partners, it was a little disconcerting now. But with time, she thought it would fade—or maybe it wouldn't. There were worse things than feeling a little high.

⊗⊗⊗

After walking her mom to her car, Kendall started to clean up, beginning with the yard. It didn't take long to get the grill closed up, raise the awning, and rearrange the chairs. Being neat wasn't truly part of her DNA, but she was going to make an effort, given that Dex was so orderly.

As she went to fill up the bird-feeders, Kendall mused over why tonight felt so…emotional. She and Dex had spent hundreds of nights together: first in an apartment in Charlottesville that she had no memory of, then this house, then at Nana's, and finally at Dex's, starting the summer Kendall had turned twelve. So this should be no big deal. But she'd seen a mournful expression on Dex's face more than once during dinner, each time seeming like she was on the verge of tears. That wasn't common for her, so Kendall had paid attention.

Once she had everything neatened up, she put her hand on the screen door and started to push. But Dex was holding onto the sink, looking like she'd been frozen.

Quietly, Kendall entered, then walked over to her, seeing that her face was streaked with tears.

"Hey, what's wrong?"

"Nothing," she said, her voice choked with emotion. "Everything's perfect."

Kendall stepped forward as Dex reached for her. The air was nearly squeezed from her lungs as Dex held on tenaciously. Kendall was kind of sure Dex had never hugged her with such…desperation. But that didn't make sense. They were finally in the house they should have shared for many years. Everything was great!

"Hey, hey," Kendall soothed, feeling Dex tremble in her arms. "Tell me what's going on."

220

"I'm so happy. And so sad."

"Why are you sad? Everything's finally clicking."

Her voice was shaking, but she got it out. "I should have been right here every night of your life, Kendall. I'd do anything to go back and fix my stupid, selfish mistakes. I swear I would."

"Hey…" She pulled away so she could get a good look at her. "You're here now, right? We'll get it right this time."

She took in a deep breath, her body shaking. "It's not that easy, baby. No matter how much you apologize, there are some mistakes you can't truly fix." She hit the big, old, farmhouse sink with her fist, banging into it a few times. "Everything's reminding me of what I lost. Just washing dishes made me think of how much you loved it when we gave you a bath in this sink." A tiny smile start to build. "You splashed so much, there was water at the top of the window."

"Dex," Kendall soothed, leaning against her to rub her shoulder and arm. "Even if you'd been here every day, you'd still feel sad about some of that stuff. What matters is enjoying today. That's your thing!"

"I know," she sighed. "I'm just feeling weird. Maybe it's the thought of sleeping in a bed your mom shared with Yardley. I know that shouldn't bother me, but…"

"Come sleep with me. I've got plenty of room." Kendall grasped Dex's hand and started to pull her away from the sink. "I owe you a few hundred nights as payback for all of the times I crawled into your bed." She laughed a little. "I didn't stop that until I was in high school."

"I'm a big girl, I can sleep alone." She hugged her again, very tenderly. "But thanks for trying to take care of me. It's nice."

"I will always try to take care of you. Just like you do me. We'll switch back and forth for whomever needs more support." She gripped Dex's hand again. "Sure you don't want to sleep with me? I'm told I'm very well behaved in bed."

That made her smile. "There's no way I'm going to ask who said that, or what they meant. I might be shaky tonight, but I'm sharp enough to know when you're messing with me." She made her hands into pinchers and chased Kendall upstairs, with her unable to stop herself from squealing. She jumped into bed and pulled the sheet up tight so Dex couldn't easily get to her.

"Cover up tight so those bed bugs don't get you," she teased, just like she did when Kendall had been a little kid.

"I love you," Kendall said, reaching up to pull Dex down for a kiss. "And I'm so happy you're here."

"You'll never know how I've dreamed of this, Cookie." She ruffled her hair, placed another kiss atop her head, then went to the door, where she now looked more like her normal self. "I'll get these old feelings out soon. They're just a little sticky, and not as easy to whisk away as I wish they were."

Chapter Fourteen

Just two days after her mom moved to Yardley's, Kendall suggested they have dinner together. Her mom sounded so damn thrilled by the suggestion that Kendall felt a little guilty for having been so unwilling to extend herself. Maybe her mom's new location would give them the chance for another try—on more neutral ground.

As Kendall drove the fairly short distance, she basked in the glow of her generosity for actually having suggested the meal. The fact that Dex had been bugging her to do so for the last 48 hours hadn't even been her primary motivation. The truth was that her mom had been so deeply generous in so many ways that Kendall couldn't have even begun to add them up. The very least she owed her was an earnest attempt to find some common ground with Yardley.

Thinking about the woman, she could *almost* see why Yardley had appealed to her mom. She had a very good job, she was as reliable as an atomic clock, trustworthy, thoughtful, mature, and apparently quite generous. She supposedly had a good relationship with her family, who were currently living in Wyoming, the place the happy couple were planning to visit for Thanksgiving. That would work out just fine. Kendall and Dex could deep-fry a turkey. Actually, they could have done that with Yardley, too, since she was able to eat poultry. But not having to deal with her was a much nicer prospect.

Kendall wasn't happy that her mom had chosen certainty over spark, but she had the right to make that choice. For all Kendall knew, Yardley was a different person when they were alone. Maybe she was relaxed, and clever, and a real charmer. That was unlikely, of course, but Kendall really hoped they had, at a minimum, fun together. That was the very least her mom deserved.

Yardley's condo was in the fan-shaped neighborhood just east of their place in the Museum District. VCU took up a big chunk of the neighborhood, but it was also filled with some pretty nice homes.

Kendall would have chosen Carytown if she was going to buy a place, since there was a lot of pedestrian traffic, and some restaurants she liked, but she could see her mom liking The Fan's location, a bit closer to her office, as well as its quiet streets.

Her phone told her she'd arrived, but the big, blocky warehouse she'd stopped in front of didn't look right at all. After finding a parking spot, she walked down the side street to see that someone had tricked out an old building into fancy lofts. This was *not* a place she could see her mom. She wasn't a wheeler-dealer/stockbroker from an 80s movie. Neither was Yardley, for that matter, but this was obviously the place. There couldn't be too many "Y. Simpkins" in town.

The elevator wasn't fast, but it was quiet. When the doors opened on three, her mom was there, giving her a huge grin. "I'm so glad you suggested this," she said, throwing her arms around Kendall. "I thought I'd have to drag you over here by your ear."

"I'm not that big a jerk," Kendall said, bumping her with her shoulder. "Now that I'm living with the Dali Lama, I'm getting lots of examples on opening my heart to the concerns of others." She pressed her hands together, then bowed her head.

Her mom took her arm and led her away from the elevator. "Dex certainly does seem like a different person since she's gotten into meditation. When she was your age she was *very* driven. Actually, I think she could have gone all the way to the top at Virtus. She honestly fit in there like a hand in a glove, even though she'd previously expressed distain at the thought of working for a big company."

"She definitely wouldn't fit in now," Kendall said, chuckling. "She sleeps until nine or ten if I let her, needs utter silence to meditate, then has to do some yoga right afterward or she's cranky. Plus, she can't eat at normal times. She'd be a mess if she had to go to big dinners with clients, and that kind of thing seems like the majority of Papa's job."

"Dex loved entertaining clients, just like your papa does. According to Randy, every state regulator is looking for an expensive steak dinner, and an even more expensive bottle of wine." She laughed. "Randy says he's grateful for every dinner where the client doesn't suggest they find some women to hire—on Randy's dime, of course. He says he's perfected the art of convincing people he's so deeply religious he doesn't even know what they're talking about." She paused for a second. "I wonder what Yardley does…"

The door opened and Yardley stood there, looking excited, as well as stiff as a board. "Welcome!" she said, her voice kind of booming in the long, high-ceilinged hallway.

Her attempt at a hug was super-rigid, like she thought Kendall was either really fragile or might bite. Given that the whole point of this exercise was to be a team-player, Kendall put her arms around Yardley and gave her a squeeze. Proud of herself for having taken the lead, she let go and smiled with as much warmth as she could. "Thanks so much for having me. I've been looking forward to seeing your place."

"Great! Dinner's nearly ready, but we can take a minute for a tour, can't we?" she asked, looking to Tracy.

"Of course." Tracy took Kendall's hand and pulled her into the space, which was big, and tall, and very bright. A pair of huge, curved windows took up the majority of the far wall, flooding the place with light.

"The building used to house a thread manufacturer," Tracy said. "I assume those windows were the main light source back in the day."

"Oh, I'm nearly certain they would have had other sources of light," Yardley said, looking very thoughtful, "but oil was quite expensive. Keeping costs low has been a constant of manufacturing, so they would have tried to stick to natural light."

"And when your employees go blind, you can just toss them away and get new ones," Kendall said, trying to joke. But Yardley didn't seem to get it, or maybe she just didn't find it funny.

"If you go into business, you'll learn that companies have to walk a fine line between profit and concern for the individual. Sometimes it's not possible to stay afloat and provide optimal working conditions." She shook her head slowly. "Of course, some of the burden falls on the employee. If they would simply refuse to work under unsafe conditions, employers would *have* to change, wouldn't they."

Kendall stared at her, trying to figure out if she was joking. When Yardley continued to look sober, Kendall let it slide. Anyone who believed employees could have a meaningful impact on safety and working conditions had her head so far up her butt it was a waste of time to even make the argument.

"The room is really nice," she said, acting like the previous minute hadn't occurred. "I've never seen ceilings this high in a home."

"I love it. I feel like I can really breathe."

She was right about that, but the place felt like it could be a factory again in less than a day. Everything was grey or cream-colored, and the fabrics looked stiff and a little rough. It was definitely more industrial than homey. But everything was undoubtedly expensive, and that must have been the look she was going for.

"Let me show you the room we'll set up for you," Yardley said, leading the way like a puppy showing you where she'd buried a bone.

"Wow," Kendall said, kind of overwhelmed by the big room, covered with wainscoting painted a pale gray, the walls above it bone white. The room currently had a sleek desk and a modern black desk chair facing another massive window, and it could have easily been where Ebenezer Scrooge sat to tote up the day's receipts. Soulless, but providing a dramatic reflection of his wealth. "I appreciate that, Yardley, but don't bother with that until I'm home from China. I'd hate to have you lose your office before it's necessary."

"I'd give it up in a minute if you'd stay over—frequently," she said, her expression so eager Kendall was afraid she'd lick her face.

"There's no rush. Really," she stressed. "Who knows what the situation might be when I get back? Dex might find she misses California by then, and I'll..." Her mom had discretely stepped behind Yardley and was giving Kendall a "shut up!" look.

Yardley cocked her head, curious puppy-style. "What do you mean? You're not implying that Dexter is going to stay in Richmond long-term, are you?"

Kendall's voice came out high when she said, "Oh, who knows what she'll do? God knows she has a lot of options. She seems to take things as they come."

"Nice work if you can get it," Yardley said, scowling. "Some of us have to work at jobs that require regular attendance."

"I assume I'll have to get one of those," Kendall said, even though she would have much preferred to mimic Dex and do exactly what she felt like. She reached over and took her mom's hand, pulling her close. "I had a very good role model for seeing how hard work and perseverance can provide for a good home and a stable life."

"You could hardly have done better on that front," Yardley agreed. "I think Tracy's work ethic is her most attractive trait."

Kendall nodded, thinking she'd vomit if the man she loved said that. That was the kind of thing you thought after you'd been together for a long time and no longer got hot when you looked at each other. She supposed there was a chance that Yardley was just being discreet. But Kendall would have much preferred her lover to be so mesmerized by her body that he didn't even notice if she *had* a work ethic.

⊗⊗⊗

At ten minutes after ten, Kendall walked into her house and dropped to the cushion right next to the one Dex was occupying. "Mission accomplished," she said, sighing dramatically. "Can I have at least a week to recover before I have to go again?"

"Ooo. The poor little thing had to suffer through a home-cooked meal that her loving mother provided. My heart breaks for you," she teased, pouncing on Kendall to tickle her until she was breathless.

"I swear," she panted, "if you ever tell anyone I date that I'm horribly ticklish…"

"Anyone worth his salt will figure that out all on his own," Dex joked. "I can't see you with a guy who wasn't adventurous enough to learn all of your weaknesses."

"True," she admitted. "But don't help out, just in case."

Dex slapped her firmly on the leg. "So? Did you have a good meal?"

"Meh," she said. "Vegetarian, which I'm fine with, but Yardley didn't have any kind of pepper sauce in the house. I'm going to have to start carrying a bottle in my purse. Hillary Clinton does that, you know."

"I did not know that. But I applaud her for it." This time her touch was lighter and more loving when she rested her hand on Kendall's leg. "How did it go? Seriously."

"Okay," she said, unable to muster much enthusiasm. "I want more for Mom, but if Yardley is her dream lover, I'll be able to spend an evening with them every couple of weeks."

"That's all you can promise? Two evenings a month?"

"Well, a whole day is more of a commitment than I'm comfortable with at this point, but I'll be able to work up to that. I assume that Yardley will calm down eventually, which will help. If she'd stop trying so hard, she'd be tolerable."

Dex nodded soberly. "It's kind of a shame. She's a very bright woman, and she could have gone far at Virtus. But she's overly eager to please, and that turns people off as much as being a bitch does." She rolled her eyes. "A woman has a very narrow window of opportunity to fit into a corporate culture. You can't seem like a pushover, but woe to the woman who's seen as being strident."

"I've seen some strident peeking out…"

"Maybe. But I think Yardley's bigger issue is her inability to stop herself from trying to win people over. That makes everyone assume they can roll over her, so they all try. It must be a struggle…"

Kendall sat up a little taller. "Are you saying she hasn't *already* gone far at Virtus? I thought she was a big deal."

Dex shook her head. "I'm not sure she knows this, but she topped out at least five years ago."

"Isn't she like a vice president?"

"Uh-huh. But there are an awful lot of them. Yardley won't get to the next level—the one where the real decisions are made. Gordon Kinkaid got the job she wanted, and if he gets the next promotion he's gunning for, he'll put one of his favorites into his current job. That won't be Yardley."

"That's Papa's old job, right?"

"Right. But you see that Papa is still consulting for them. That wouldn't be true if they thought Yardley could slip in and maintain the relationships he fostered."

"You know that for a fact?" She paused a second. "Does Mom?"

"I can't know anything for a fact, honey, but Yardley doesn't have anyone at the C-level who loves her…"

"C-level?"

"The top rung. CEO, CFO, CIO… All of the big guns."

"But Papa wasn't on that level, and he did just fine, right?"

"Oh, sure. You don't have to run the place to be a success. But Yardley wants to go all the way. Papa didn't. He loved his job, mostly because he was very independent, and didn't have to manage people. He made a great salary, while doing things he enjoyed. Does Yardley seem like she'd love entertaining relative strangers?"

Kendall rolled her eyes. "Do you think Mom knows?"

"Why are you fixated on that?"

Kendall shrugged. "Maybe she likes her partly because she thinks she's a big shot."

"No way. If your mom loves someone, she wouldn't care what they did for a living. If Yardley's happy, that's all that would matter." She paused for a second. "But if Yardley's miserable…"

"Ugh. I'm staying single as long as I can stand it. Relationships are so damn hard"

"Not if you're with the right person, Kendall. Loving someone makes life better, easier, and much more fun. Trust me on that."

"I'll trust you until I prove you wrong," she said, knowing she was driving Dex crazy. "Uhm… Isn't it weird that when Papa's around Yardley he never really talks to her? I mean, he's polite and everything, but I would have never guessed they worked together."

"It's definitely weird, and I'm going to talk to him about it. I know Yardley's not his cup of tea, but he's crazy about Tracy, so he's got to step up. Everyone in my family does," she added, really looking unhappy. "Your mom deserves our full support, and I'm going to do my best to make sure she gets it."

CHAPTER FIFTEEN

DEX HAD FINALLY GOTTEN INTO a groove. With lots of advice from some of her LA friends and associates, she'd bought everything needed to record pro-quality audio at home. The very small third bedroom was kind of perfect for that, and now that she had temporarily attached foam baffles to the walls, and put down a big area rug, the sound was clear with just a little vibrancy to it. It had taken a week's worth of tweaks, but a friendly recording engineer had walked her through everything she had to adjust. Now she had to remember to send her a nice gift. She'd installed a small white board next to her desk, and she made a note, having to rely on physical reminders, since her memory wasn't great for things like that.

Work-wise, things were picking up. Recently, Clarissa Everett Sprague had informed her publisher that she wanted Dex to voice all of her audio books. Clarissa even had enough clout to insist that Dex do new narrations for her backlist of mysteries, which was a pretty big coup.

Audio books had come a long way in the last twenty years, and Clarissa was very unhappy with her publisher's early efforts—much to Dex's benefit. They'd been done by a guy who read them so ponderously that they were guaranteed to put you to sleep. His weighty, stentorian tones now gave Dex fifteen books to cover, and she was certain Clarissa would have a new title out before she could get close to finishing the backlog. The woman could write nearly as fast as Dex could narrate, which was astounding when you thought about it.

After a few misses, she'd also hit on some good AA meetings: one that met every weekday morning, another that was women-only on Thursday nights, and a third on Saturday mornings.

In LA, her preference was for NA, but she honestly could have even gone to Gamblers Anonymous and gotten something out of it. Being with other people who struggled with compulsive behavior was what worked for her, and everyone who struggled shared a common bond, no matter their substance.

She was still working her way through greater Richmond's yoga practices, though, not having found one that clicked. Just that week, she'd found a teacher she liked, but their schedules didn't sync very well. But she was confident she'd find a home if she kept plugging away.

Through happenstance, she'd run into a woman she'd gone to high school with, and found that she and a few other old classmates had a monthly dinner club. They always went someplace special—with no boyfriends, no husbands, and no kids. They also had a firm rule that politics could not be discussed. That was the kicker, so Dex had agreed to join them, and was really looking forward to it.

She still didn't like getting up early, but she needed a regular AA meeting more than she needed sleep, so she'd started going on Tuesday mornings to give her a couple of days between meetings. She'd only gone to one a week in LA, but she was still getting her feet under her in Richmond, so she was erring on the side of caution.

That morning, she'd followed her routine, then got to work, plugging away at recording a fairly interesting "who done it" that only had four primary characters. That was nice. Even nicer was that none of them had an accent. Well, Clarissa's lead character was a private detective in Savannah, but it wasn't hard for Dex to sound like an authentic southerner.

She took breaks during the day, mostly to rest her voice. By four, she was toast, and she was just about to take a quick nap. But her phone rang, and seeing a familiar name on the screen made her hit the button. "Hello, Miranda. How's every little thing?"

"Things are good," she said, her warm alto voice sounding even better on the phone than it did in person. "And I bet they'd be even better if you came by my apartment tonight. I'd like to run my tongue over every inch of you."

That was a slightly bold, not unwelcome thought. "Is your apartment still in Marina del Rey?"

"Uh-huh. Why wouldn't it be?"

"No reason. But that's a bit of a stretch for me. I'm spending the summer with my family in Richmond."

"North Carolina?"

Dex smiled to herself. Half of the people she'd met in LA couldn't place Richmond on a map, if they'd even heard of it. "Richmond's in Virginia," she said. "I'm spending time with my daughter who's going to China next year to teach."

"She's old enough for that? I thought she was in high school."

"College. Actually, she graduated this spring, and is going to start working on her masters in August. Time flies."

"Hmm... So you're not coming home soon, huh?"

"Not very soon at all," Dex said, starting to feel a gentle tug in Miranda's direction. That voice could make you overlook her inability to recall anything that was truly important to you. Her sinfully beautiful body didn't hurt, either. And the fact that she had almost no boundaries in bed... While Dex's tastes were pretty vanilla, Miranda had made her want to get a little wild—something masturbation couldn't replicate.

"Do you have a computer nearby?"

"I've got a tablet right here. Do you want me to look something up for you?"

Miranda rarely got any of Dex's silly responses, and today was no exception. "I can look up anything I want. But I can't see your sweet, sweet ass without some help. Why don't you get naked and call me right back. Video," she stressed.

"Two minutes," Dex said, glad she'd shaved her legs that morning. No one wanted to have phone sex with someone who hadn't taken the time to look sharp. She locked her door, turned on some music, stripped down to her underwear, and started to dial, certain that masturbation would be much improved with the addition of a partner.

⬧⬧⬧

Dex had not only had a sexy afternoon, she'd wrapped things up to be able to eat dinner at four, her favorite time. Kendall entered the house at six, and made herself some pasta, quite able to take care of herself.

When she brought her bowl into the living room, Dex said, "Where were you all day? Did you sneak over to the pool to work on your tan?"

"I don't tan," she said, as if that was below her. "I want to look as good as you do when I'm forty, so I cover myself with sunblock before I leave the house." She took a bite of her dinner. "You'll be pleased to learn that I've found a tutoring client. I've got cash money in my pocket, Mumsie."

"Are you serious? I had no idea you were going to do that. Are you tutoring people from UVA?"

"Kind of. This is a recent high school grad, who's trying to test out of Mandarin I. Her skills are easily good enough for her to ace the test, but she's an anxious test-taker. I hope I can help her confidence, since she really belongs in a more advanced class." She held up her thumbs. "She's got friends from school who are trying to do the same thing. I hope to have a full roster soon."

"I'm so glad you're doing that!"

"Me, too. If I'm going to teach, I might as well start now. Better to find out now if I hate it, huh?"

"A damn sight better, I'd say. Nice job, Kendall. Really."

After Kendall finished her meal, she got up and put her dish in the sink. Then she plopped down next to Dex, and they found a movie to watch on her laptop.

"You know what this does?" Kendall asked.

"What?"

"Sucks," she said, pouting. "This is the only house in the western world without the ability to stream a movie."

"Maybe that's a slight exaggeration," Dex said, picking up a napkin to dab at the tomato sauce still staining the side of Kendall's mouth. "But we can remedy that. Get online and buy a stick that we can use on the TV. You know my sign-in."

"But wouldn't it be worlds better to watch a movie on the big screen?" she said, batting her eyes. "From the comfort of your yard?"

"What do you want, and where do I buy it?" Dex asked, knowing she was the world's biggest sucker. That might have also been an exaggeration, but not a very big one.

Kendall's face lit up in a childlike grin. "Lacey's gear-head dad just set one up. I'll ask him for the details." She leaned over and kissed Dex's cheek. "You do spoil me terribly, Mumsie," she said, letting her voice drop down to a deep register as she adopted a posh British accent.

"I'm well aware of that. But you don't act spoiled most of the time, so I'm not motivated to change."

❈❈❈

It had been a busy day, what with hours of recording, a spirited bout of phone sex, and being played for an outdoor movie experience. But knowing Kendall, she'd do her best to buy the least expensive system that would give her the experience she wanted. She definitely wasn't a spendthrift—compared to her peers, at least.

The phone sex was actually the thing that Dex was feeling a little odd about. While it had been a lot of fun when she was in the middle of it, she wasn't sure she'd do it again. Not with Miranda, at least.

Dex pulled her pillow out from underneath her head and fluffed it. Sleeping in Tracy's bed was taking some getting used to, but that only made sense. She'd undoubtedly had sex with Yardley right where Dex was lying, and that truly made her woozy. But she didn't want to make it clear what a baby she was, so she hadn't purchased a bed of her own. When and if Tracy agreed to sell the house, Dex would get right on that. But she was, essentially, house-sitting. And no sane house-sitter spent a couple of thousand bucks on a bed when she was guaranteed just a few months of use.

She had, of course, bought new sheets and pillows, and that helped a little. But rolling around on the bed this afternoon, with Miranda directing her as carefully as Spielberg would have, made her feel a little… creepy. It had been fun, and exciting, and physically satisfying, but puzzlingly creepy.

Pulling her phone from the night stand, she saw that it was after midnight. How long had she been ruminating about a single act of phone sex? Over an hour, for sure. But she really couldn't get off the topic. It wasn't even that she didn't like Miranda. She did. But she didn't like her enough to even entertain the possibility of being in a relationship with her—if Miranda would have her, which she doubted.

Miranda had made it pretty clear that she wanted sex—only. They'd seen each other five or six times, and after their first dinner together she'd rebuffed Dex's suggestion to have a meal or even a cup of coffee. She wanted to drop by Dex's house, have sex until they were both satisfied, then take off. While that had seemed kind of ideal at the time, it felt less so now. Today had made Dex feel entirely disconnected, which made the act feel even less intimate than masturbation.

Lying in Tracy's bed, the bed where she and Yardley had developed a connection deep enough to compel them to marry, made her feel like she was using Miranda, even though she knew that was silly. If anything, Miranda was using her. But Dex was now certain she wasn't going to do it again—not with a woman she didn't care for.

Decision made, she rolled over and felt a little more comfortable—at least emotionally. The bed was still too soft for her.

She started to relax, and as she did she reminded herself that one of the reasons she'd wanted to return to Richmond had been to meet a nice woman. Someone who didn't spend her whole day trying to be prettier and thinner and more shapely. She wanted a woman with a real job, real friends, and close family ties. And if she worked hard enough—she was sure she'd find her.

CHAPTER SIXTEEN

ON WEDNESDAY EVENING, TRACY HAD only been in her car for five minutes when a text came in. Her car was smart enough to read texts aloud, and she asked it to as she headed for home.

"Message from Kendall Haven-Lord." The voice always did something funny with the pronunciation, putting the stress on the wrong syllable. "Dinner and a movie. Six o'clock. We're grilling, but we've got veggies for Yardley. RSVP ASAP."

Smirking to herself, Tracy replied at the prompt. "I am responding to your shockingly late invitation. One person. Veggies appreciated, but optional. I'll be there in ten minutes. I'm willing to stop and pick up anything you've forgotten."

The reply took several minutes, but it came through as Tracy had expected. "Can you ever really have enough ice cream? We're expecting six, so don't be stingy."

Six? Kendall and Dex had convinced three other people to come with no notice at all? Knowing Dex, she had access to some blockbuster that hadn't been shown in theaters yet, but still.

As Tracy pulled into her favorite mini-mart, she paused to consider the logistics. Were six people going to crowd into the living room to watch the screen Kendall had been insisting was Lilliputian? That should be interesting. The food had better be great.

⁂

No one answered when Tracy rang the bell, so she went around to the alley, where voices rang out, one feminine tone climbing over another as she got closer. Pushing open the back gate, she smiled at the image of Dex, clad in faded red shorts and one of her roomy crop tops, this one navy blue. Bold color choices tonight. An apron covered a lot of her, but even the sauce-stained garment didn't take away from her very casual, yet polished look.

"Welcome," she said, beaming. "Yardley couldn't make it?"

"Business dinner." Tracy moved over to stand next to her and take a peek at the grill. It looked like she was cooking for four different parties. A single chicken breast, two burgers, a few huge Portobello mushrooms, and a big block of tofu. "What's going on here?"

Dex twitched her head to the left. "Our daughter's friends are a very picky bunch," she added, sotto voce.

Tracy turned to see three of Kendall's long-time buddies: Morgan, Lacey, and Sophia. "Hi, girls," she said, waving.

"Hi, Ms. Haven-Lord," Morgan, the nearest one, said. "I was charged when Dex told us you were coming."

"You know, Dex is two months older than I am. If you're on a first-name basis with her, why should you have to refer to me like one of your teachers?"

"No reason at all," Morgan said. "It's Dex and Tracy from now on."

She wanted to suggest that "Tracy and Yardley," might be a better pairing, but the girls were adults now, and they were all sensible. They'd surely pair her with Yardley when appropriate.

"Mom!" Kendall called out as she came down the stairs, dressed in what had become her summer attire: one of her grandfather's oxford-cloth shirts and black Lycra shorts that barely breached the hem of the shirt. It was a very casual look, both modest and revealing—especially since she didn't wear a bra under the huge shirt. Her outfit wasn't easily categorized, but Kendall had obviously begun to favor Dex's habit of having a good portion of her clothing barely touch her skin.

Kendall gave her a kiss to the cheek and took the bag. "I'll go put this in the freezer. Have Lacey show you the set-up."

Tracy turned again, now seeing that Lacey was sitting by a small table on the deck, fussing with a piece of machinery.

As Tracy got closer, she saw that it was a projector, then a bright light hit her in the face and she covered her eyes to walk the last few feet.

"Sorry Ms. Haven-Lord," the girl said. "I'm checking the focus and didn't see you come in."

"That's all right, honey. I just suggested to Morgan that you all call me by my first name—if you're comfortable with that."

"Sure," she said, glancing up. "Among my friends' parents, you're the only holdout."

"I am? It never occurred to me…"

"It's not a big deal. A lot of them asked me to call them by their first names when we were still in grade school, which was a little weird."

"I guess I'd rather be the last holdout than a little weird…"

"You're cool," Lacey said, giving her a grin. "You never get sloppy drunk, or expect us to give you free weed. It's nice being around parents who don't mind actually being parents."

"I don't mind a bit," Tracy said, bending over to kiss Lacey on the head. She'd been doing that for at least fifteen years now, but could only currently manage it when the kid was sitting down. When did girls get so damn tall?

Sophia emerged from the kitchen and gave Tracy a bright smile. "I'm taking drink orders. What can I get you, Ms.—"

"Switch to Tracy," Lacey said, not looking up from her work. "The last holdout has fallen."

"Awesome. Drink?"

"What are you making?"

"Gin and tonic, vodka and soda, and sparkling water so far, but I can make anything. I'm working as a bartender at The Piedmont Grill this summer."

"Ooo. We'll have to come by some night."

"I can give you one free drink," she said, frowning slightly. "That's all I can get away with."

"We can pay," Tracy said. "I'd just like to see you at work."

"Closed Mondays. Kendall swears we're going to keep this up all summer, so block off your Monday nights."

Tracy finally turned to see a screen, at least fifteen feet wide, tucked behind the fire pit. "I think I might just do that," she said, kind of thrilled at the prospect of spending the rest of the summer enjoying the bounty of her hard work—a very good relationship with her daughter and her friends, and a burgeoning one with her ex. Dinner and a movie wasn't a bad throw-in, especially if Dex could grill anywhere near as well as her dad.

⁂

Dex proved to be a good cook. Not quite in her father's league, but nothing was over or underdone. After being allowed to pick her entree, Tracy had chosen Italian sausage, made even better with the addition of grilled red peppers, which had a nice char to them. She leaned over and whispered to Dex, "Has your dad been giving you grilling lessons? You've got some talent."

"Little bit," she admitted. "This is the first time in ages that we've had much free time together. When I can get him to stop talking about work, we talk about barbecue."

"How long before he has a movie setup like this? A week?"

Dex smiled. "I think he'll be happy to use mine, since he doesn't have a lot of patience with technology. They were busy tonight, so they're coming on Wednesday. Good thing I don't have outside friends, huh?"

Tracy liked very much that Dex didn't have other friends…or lovers…pulling her away. She wouldn't admit to that, of course. "You could have a bus full of friends if you wanted to. You're just concentrating on your nearest and dearest right now."

"Happily," she said, touching the rim of her glass of sparkling water to Tracy's gin and tonic.

They both turned their attention to the movie again, some kind of superhero thing that Tracy couldn't begin to understand. It surprised her that Kendall's friends liked this genre, but when the very hunky leading man finally whipped off his shirt and flashed his prodigious pecs and abs, she reminded herself that girls were just as shallow as boys when it came to appreciating hotties.

All four of the girls were lying on the lawn. Kendall had put down a drop-cloth, and had brought out every throw pillow from the living room. The girls were splayed out in every kind of position, with Morgan lying on her side, Kendall using her body as a bolster. They were all, as far as Tracy knew, straight, but they seemed much less doctrinaire about it than girls had been when she'd been in school.

She let out a sigh as she rocked slightly in her chair, feeling a deep sense of not only contentment, but true pleasure. This was exactly what her dream had been when she and Dex had decided to create a family. She'd jumped in—certain she'd found an open-hearted, caring, doting partner who'd be an excellent parent. And she'd gotten exactly that—but only for a short time. Then she got pieces of it. Good pieces, but never again the most important one—the enduring love of the woman who'd set it all in motion.

※※

Dex wasn't crazy about superhero movies, but she watched many of them. She loved to actually go to a theater, and sometimes the only new movie on the bill was a superhero epic.

Since she wasn't truly involved in the plot, she was able to sit back and reflect, certain she'd get the gist of the film if she just assumed there would be three lengthy battles, with the superhero seeming to lose the penultimate one, only to reemerge, battered, but determined, to kill, capture, or vanquish every adversary.

The night was warm and fairly humid, with the mosquitos descending upon them as soon as the sun began to set. But Tracy hopped up to get the industrial-strength mosquito repellent.

Watching her move amongst the girls, carefully spraying each of them made Dex as happy as a clam. This was all she'd ever wanted. Quiet nights with people she cared for deeply, enjoying each other's company, while doing something even mildly interesting.

Now that she'd been home for a while, she was both relieved and deeply pleased to confirm that she truly didn't revel in the "if you get some, I'll get less" Hollywood ethic that made enemies out of people who were natural allies. Nor did she miss spending an hour and a half in her car only to cough up three hundred bucks for dinner with a promising date. She'd been able to survive in LA, then she'd started to thrive. But she'd never loved it. Never even liked it much.

It struck her that she was happier than she'd been in years, doing something so mundane with her daughter and her ex. But this was her happy place—watching Kendall laugh with her friends while she and Tracy just sat quietly in the darkening night. The jasmine was filling the air with its sweet scent, with the lingering hint of the barbecue still lightly in the air. If there was a way to encase this night in amber, she'd jump at the chance.

Kendall got up to go inside, with Dex watching to see if she might be getting some dessert ready. Dex wasn't a big ice cream person, but the movie held her attention so poorly she was more than happy to get up and help. But Kendall must have just been going to use the bathroom, leaving Dex to try to follow the anemic plot. The superhero had just been humiliated by his arch-nemesis, and as he skulked away he tripped and landed on his face. Tracy's laugh, an epic one, rang out, and Dex began to laugh right along with her. Even in the darkness, Dex could see the other girls turn to give them a "what's so funny?" glance, but she couldn't stop herself. The scene was only mildly funny on its own, but when Tracy threw her head back and really let it go, Dex was powerless. If Tracy had laughed for a half-hour, Dex would have stayed right with her. That's how it had always been. Each found the other's laugh contagious.

Kendall emerged, stopped, then put her hands on her hips as she stood over them. "Slapstick?" she asked, sighing.

"So funny," Tracy said, gasping for air. "He's a superhero, but he fell right on his face. When he lifted his head, his expression was priceless."

"It really was," Dex agreed, dabbing at her eyes with her dinner napkin. "Academy Award worthy. This guy's a better actor than I thought."

Shaking her head, Kendall went back to her friends. Dex could hear her say, "Don't ask. Nine-year-olds and those two have identical senses of humor."

Dex was about to defend their taste, but Tracy gave her such a fond look, one that struck her right in the heart, that she couldn't utter a word. If the damn projector had cost three times what it had, it would have been worth it just for that glance.

❦

The movie ended at ten, and Kendall reached into her shirt pocket to pull out the gummies she'd fetched when she'd used the bathroom. "I've got five left," she said, extending her hand.

"What are you offering?" Tracy called out. "Don't forget your mothers are right here."

"Gummies. Lightweight ones. Want one?"

"Is there THC in them?"

"There better be."

"How much?"

"I'm not a chemist." She dropped one into each of her friends' hands, then walked over to the deck. "These don't make me very high at all." She extended her hand. "Come on. Get wild. How long has it been since you smoked weed?"

"How old are you? Add six months."

"Six?"

"Sorry," she said, smirking. "I didn't know I was pregnant until almost three months in. Be glad I wasn't much of a drinker. Alcohol is much worse for a fetus than marijuana."

"My mom and my step-dad smoke more than I do," Sophia called out.

"My grandparents are high nearly every night," Lacey agreed.

Morgan sat up and started to gather their spent glasses. "My grandparents only use CBD—on everything. I don't think it does a thing, but they swear it helps with their aching joints." She shrugged as she moved past Kendall to put the glasses in the kitchen. "If they think it helps—it must."

"So…what's the routine?" Tracy asked. "You eat a gummy and then just hang out?"

"Sure. I like to lie on my back and watch the stars. It's not a big deal, Mom. It's just like having a couple of drinks."

Tracy turned toward Dex. "What do you think?"

She looked a little puzzled. "Are you asking for permission?"

"Well, no." She shrugged. "Yes, I guess I am. If you think it sets a bad example…"

"If Kendall was ten, I wouldn't like it," Dex said. "Now? Live your life, Tracy." She reached over the railing and grasped Kendall's hand, tugging on it until she went up the stairs. Dex grabbed her and held her tightly, wrangling her onto her lap. "We've screwed this poor child up so much there's no more damage to be done."

"Kind of true," Kendall said, giggling when Dex tickled the back of her neck. "Come on, Mom. We'll get slightly high while we lie on the grass. Everyone can practice calling you Tracy. This will be a right of passage now that we're all adults."

"Oh, what the hell. Will you drive me home if I'm having visions, Dex?"

"I certainly will." She blew a raspberry on Kendall's neck. "Because none of these little princesses is getting behind the wheel."

"We never do," Kendall pledged, finally squirming away from Dex's annoyingly tight embrace. Moms should just not be that strong!

⊗⊗⊗

Kendall had been absolutely right. The high was very, very mild. Actually, Tracy thought she might have been imagining it. But she was more relaxed than she'd been recently, and maybe more reflective.

They'd been lying on the tarp, looking up at the sky for a very long time, with Dex bustling around in the kitchen. Kendall's head rested on Tracy's hip, and she'd been running her fingers through her hair, so very much like her own, but shinier and a little thicker.

"Hey," Tracy said, tugging on a few strands. "Did we scare Dex away?"

"Hmm?" She turned her head to look at the empty deck. "No. She's on the phone a lot at night."

"Talking to…?"

"Don't really know. She'll get a text, then go into another room for a while. Sometimes the whole evening."

"I guess she's got a lot of LA friends."

"Yeah. I don't know. We try to give each other some room, you know?" She rolled over and sat up. "Thanks for getting high with me, Mom. I really like it when you're a little less…"

"Maternal?"

"Oh, no, I love that. But I also like it when you're less…supervisory maybe?"

"Ahh. Yeah. That makes sense. I never got to that point with my own mother, but I would imagine it might be a positive change."

"You're doing great," Kendall said. "We're changing a little, but not too much."

"That's how it feels to me, too. If you ever have extra gummies, I'd be happy to do this again. Of course, I'll pay you back, since I don't want to be thought of as a mooch. Just don't give me anything stronger than this. I *refuse* to act the fool around my baby girl."

⊗⊗⊗

Dex poked her head out a little after eleven, smiling when she saw five women avidly watching the clear, night sky. They must've been trying to pick out constellations, something she'd often wanted to do in LA—to no avail. A couple of times a year she convinced a woman to drive out to Joshua Tree to escape the light pollution and have a little romance under the stars, but being able to do that in your own back yard was awfully nice.

"Does anyone have a bedtime?" Dex called out. "I hate to be the adult here, but…"

"I do," Tracy said, lifting her hand. "I need to be at work at eight. Will I make it?"

The gummy must have been working, since she sounded a little hazy. Dex walked over and plunked down next to her on the tarp. Quietly, she said, "Why don't I drive you home?"

245

"Really?" Tracy's eyes were halfway closed as she squinted at Dex. "I wasn't high at all, but I think I might be now."

"I am," Kendall said, raising her hand. "I'm gonna go get the rest of the ice cream."

"Do it," Sophia said lazily. "Do it right now. Bring fudge if you've got it."

"Come on," Dex said, holding her hands out to give both Kendall and Tracy some assistance.

Both of them rose easily and steadily. "Say goodnight to your little friends," Dex said, watching Tracy tug her top into place and smooth her hair down.

"I had a great time, girls. See you Monday?"

"We'll be here," Lacey said, sounding like she was half-asleep.

"I'll be back in a half hour," Dex said. "Don't anyone leave."

"We all live within three blocks," Sophia said. "But don't worry. No one's leaving until all of the ice cream's gone."

"That might take you three minutes. I'll rush."

She put her arm around Tracy's shoulders, just in case she tripped going up the stairs. They stopped in the kitchen, and Tracy kissed Kendall goodnight as she juggled three containers of ice cream and four spoons. When they reached the front door, Tracy paused in the entryway for a second. "I wish I still lived here," she said, letting out a heavy sigh. She looked into Dex's eyes for a minute, holding the gaze so long Dex started to feel uncomfortable. "I wish *you* still lived here. I wish Kendall was just a baby," she said, starting to cry as she kind of fell into Dex.

Stunned, Dex wrapped her arms around her, holding her just the way she'd soothed her back when they were together. It hadn't happened all that often, even when Tracy had been pregnant and her hormones had been spiking all over the place. Having been raised in chaos clearly made her wary of revealing her insecurities, and it touched Dex that she was able to do so now.

"I wish you still had your god-damned wisdom teeth. Can you imagine how different our lives would be?"

"I try not to," Dex said quietly. "Wallowing in regret isn't good for me." She put her hands on Tracy's shoulders and held her a little bit away from her body. "We have the lives we have. But no matter how many mistakes we've made, we did something wonderful together. Kendall is such a gift," she sighed, near tears herself. "I didn't know it was possible to love someone as much as I do her."

"You're right," Tracy said, standing on her own and wiping her eyes. "I'm just feeling…a lot."

Dex gave her another hug. "That's because you're high." She opened the door and gripped Tracy's arm to guide her down the stairs. "Is Yardley going to mind?"

"I…" She closed her mouth quickly. "I don't know how she feels about marijuana. I guess I might find out." As they walked toward Tracy's car, she muttered, "She's all in favor of convincing kids to vape, so she doesn't really have any standing to complain about this…"

Dex just nodded, then patted her back pocket to make sure she had her phone. Her Lyft app hadn't gotten a workout in a while, but she was going to need it tonight. The funny part was that she was sure Tracy was oblivious about that necessity. Weed might be fun, but it made you awfully dumb.

⊗⊗⊗

Tracy entered the condo a few minutes before midnight, very late for her. She'd put on a sleep shirt, and was in the guest bathroom brushing her teeth when Yardley tapped on the door and cracked it open. "May I?"

"Sure."

Yardley walked in, so business-like in her dark suit and white top. She slipped her jacket off, showing her bare arms. The top was actually kind of sexy, fitting her closely, highlighting Tracy's favorite body part, her broad shoulders. "I'm as full as a tick," she sighed, "and I've had too much to drink. I had to take a car home." She gave Tracy a pouty look. "Any chance of you taking me by Manelli's Italian Steakhouse in the morning?"

"No problem," Tracy said, going to hug her, but having second thoughts when the scent of garlic and wine and…maybe Scotch hit her. "Why don't you put on your pajamas and watch TV for a while. You know you get indigestion when you lie down too soon after dinner."

"I might," she agreed, turning to leave. "Did you do anything tonight?" She looked at her watch, clearly puzzled. "It's so late."

"I saw a movie. Feel free to skip *General Galactica.*"

Yardley gazed at her for a long moment. "That's what you chose? Every time I've asked you to see a superhero movie with me, you say you don't like them."

"That's what was starting when I got there," she said, not *technically* lying. "But if you want to see it, I'll go again. I'll wear my ear buds and listen to a podcast."

"You're a good egg," Yardley said, giving her a sweet smile that Tracy truly hoped wasn't a prelude to her making a pass. Some people could easily metabolize garlic, and some couldn't. Regrettably, Yardley couldn't, and it would stick with her for at least twenty-four hours. But that alone wasn't what put Tracy off. It was the fact that she'd tossed off a lie instead of telling a harmless truth. Of course, it didn't help that she'd basically told Dex she wished they were still together. No matter how busy Tracy was the next day, she was going to start searching for a counselor. They needed to get into couples therapy—stat.

CHAPTER SEVENTEEN

ON WEDNESDAY EVENING, DEX'S MOVIE night was even less work than her previous one had been. But once again she didn't get to watch something she would have chosen. Her mom was in charge of all Haven family entertainment, and she preferred period pieces, light comedies with actors close to her own age, and non-violent thrillers. Dex searched the hell out of Netflix, and let her mom make the final choice while her dad was out by the grill, cooking up some fish.

While they watched him work, Dex and Libby sat on the deck, enjoying cool drinks. "I should make him wear a mask," Libby said thoughtfully. "Your father inhales so much smoke it can't be good for him."

"You're probably right. I bet Tracy has a box or two of them lying around. There hasn't been one thing I've needed that I couldn't find— along with a spare. She's the epitome of preparedness."

"Tracy says Yardley's got her beat in that area." She met Dex's eyes. "They might as well turn that third bedroom into a storage area for their duplicate supplies, since Kendall's never going to use it."

"No, Kendall's not going to stay there," Dex agreed. "Maybe not even for a night."

Libby waved a hand in front of her face, wafting away a stray bit of smoke. "If you're serious about settling down here, that won't be an issue. Kendall will continue to have her home."

"I am serious, Mom. Very serious. I've already had a conversation with the real estate agent who sold me my house. I'm going to put it on the market."

"But this is just a trial run—"

"Being in *this* house is a trial run. If Tracy kicks me out, I'll buy something else."

"But surely you have things to do to get your house ready to sell, Dex. You can't just leave for a short trip and never go back!"

"I can have someone else handle everything. My agent's assistant has been staying there, and she's always looking for ways to earn some cash. Since she charges by the hour I never feel like I'm taking advantage of her."

"That's… How can you possibly think you can move without going back?" She peered at her closely. "Are you trying to avoid being served in a lawsuit? You seem to think going to LA is an awful lot of trouble, but you've done it every month or two for two decades…"

"I've made the trip often enough, Mom. If I can pay Aja to pack up and ship all of my jewelry and keepsakes, she'll just need to supervise a moving company to do everything else."

"You'll pay a moving company to pack for you? That would cost you thousands of dollars, honey."

"Maybe I'll sell the house furnished. I had a lot of custom pieces made, and they wouldn't fit here—or any other small house I'd buy."

"But your furniture was so nice," Libby said, looking truly upset. "That sectional in the media room was the most comfortable thing I've ever sat on."

"It was. But there's no sense in moving it if I don't have room for it." She reached across to grip Libby's hand for a second. "It will work out fine. Even paying Tracy's mortgage, I'm saving thousands. If she agrees to sell, I'll be able to pay cash. And it will *thrill* me not to have a mortgage."

"She's going to want it back," Libby said, making what sounded like a statement rather than mere opinion.

Randy walked quickly across the small lawn, with a platter of fish in hand. "Incoming!"

Dex jumped to her feet, held the kitchen door open, and took the platter from him. "Go ahead and wash your hands, Dad. I'm all set here." She plated the fish next to generous servings of a Moroccan beet salad and some spicy cauliflower, then handed a pair of plates to her father, who took them to the table. Dex followed along, and took her seat. "This would be perfect if Kendall was here," she said. "She's crazy for this cauliflower."

"She's been home more this summer than any time I can recall since she was twelve years old," Libby said, giving Dex a fond gaze. "She's so happy you're here."

Dex took a bite, nodding at her father. "Great job, Dad. Just cooked through." She laughed a little when she thought of her mom's comment. "I guess I can reassure myself that Kendall truly loves me. When your kid gives up a summer at the beach to hang out with you in her hot, humid home town, she's nuts about you."

"Always has been," Randy said. "I remember how she looked at you the first time you held her. Love at first sight." Randy actually looked like he might cry, not a common occurrence for him.

"Best day of my life," Dex said. "I wish we could have had another baby or two, but I'm not going to complain. Having one pretty perfect kid's more than anyone deserves."

"Where *is* my favorite grandchild?" Randy asked.

"She went to a concert with a couple of her buddies. I assume she's currently high as a kite, but her friend Josh is going, and he doesn't smoke or drink." She let out a soft laugh. "I don't think anyone's crazy about poor old Josh, but he's figured out a good scheme. People buy him a ticket to whatever they're going to, and he drives. He's busy enough that Kendall has to make arrangements well in advance to get on his schedule."

"Does Yardley drink much?" Randy asked. "I've been to many client dinners with her, but I've never noticed."

"I try not to keep track of how much other people consume. Why do you ask?"

He looked slightly perplexed. "I've been trying to think of what could have compelled Tracy to pair up with her. I thought having a built-in designated driver might have done the trick. Tracy always sticks to one cocktail, but maybe she's always craved a few…"

"Randy," Libby said, her scolding tone definitely not impacting him much.

"What? The woman's a damp squib, Libby. If she wasn't willing to prepare every presentation, labor over every budget, and slog through every mundane task that requires a high level of acumen, she would never have gotten promoted to her current slot."

"Dad," Dex said, giving him a chiding look. "I know you don't like her, but Tracy's going to marry her."

"I didn't say I didn't like her." He paused for a second. "But I don't. Even if I did, though, she's a bad choice—"

"I agree with you. But it's not our choice to make. I know how much you love Tracy, so you've got to step it up. Seriously."

"*I* have to step it up? What does that mean? I'm always polite."

"When Yardley was sitting out here during Kendall's graduation party, I don't think a single member of the family tried to engage her in conversation. That's rude. Plain and simple." She fixed each of her parents with a disappointed gaze. "I thought you'd do better than that."

"What in the hell am I supposed to talk to her about?"

"You *ran* the department she's in, and you currently consult on the exact same product. Doesn't that give you a tiny bit of common ground?"

"Not really," he said, and Dex realized this wasn't going to go her way. Once Randy felt trapped, he invariably dug his heels in. Only after he'd had time to reflect and feel like he'd come to the decision on his own did he start to see the logic of any point.

"One, I don't want to talk about work at my granddaughter's graduation party. Two, Yardley's my least favorite kind of person. She's always trying to show you how smart she is, while simultaneously trying to ingratiate herself. I agree she's smart, but who wants to be around someone so desperate to impress you?"

"I agree she's challenging. So talk about…Tracy. Talk about Kendall—"

Her mom was giving her the "turn back!" signal, but Dex didn't get it in time.

"I'm *never* going to talk to her about Kendall," Randy said, his face turning red as he slammed his hand down on the table. "She had the gall to tell Lucy that she only asked Tracy to marry her after she learned Kendall was going to China. She said Kendall was a spoiled brat who hadn't been taught any limits."

"Who on earth is Lucy?"

"Your father's former administrative assistant. She's well known for being able to get people to reveal their deepest secrets, then spilling the beans to anyone who will listen. I'm *so* glad your father doesn't have her whispering into his ear every day." Libby gave Randy a surprisingly stern look. "For the five years they worked together, he was always upset about something or other."

"Lucy's reliable," Randy said flatly. "If she said that Yardley called Kendall a brat, then she called Kendall a brat." He was really worked up now, a fairly infrequent event. "Imagine her strutting around Virtus, acting like she's doing Tracy a favor by proposing. The damn nerve of that woman."

"Oh, boy," Dex sighed. "Now you've got me upset. What in the heck has gotten into Tracy? Why's she willing to settle for so little?"

Libby reached out with both hands and gripped her husband's and daughter's ears, giving them a tug. "Listen, you two."

Dex pried Libby's fingers away at the same time Randy did. "You don't have to manhandle me," he said. "We're obviously listening."

"You might be listening, but you're certainly not understanding. Yardley's what Tracy has been wanting for years now. She's stable, usually agreeable, not very demanding, and she dotes on her."

"You don't dote on someone you cut down behind their back," Dex grumbled.

"She wasn't cutting Tracy down." She smiled faintly. "She was cutting *you* down. Yardley attributes all of Kendall's faults to you, honey."

"And that makes it better?"

"Well, no, not for you. But I would think you could summon up some empathy for someone who's desperate to be liked, to be needed. Yes,

Yardley's a pill, but Tracy likes being taken care of. She got very little of that from her own family, and…" She trailed off, not adding that Tracy had been forced to spend the last three years of their relationship watching over Dex like a premature infant.

"That's it? Seriously?" Dex demanded. "You think she likes Yardley because she feels taken care of?"

"Definitely. She's never going to have to worry about Yardley sneaking around on her, or spending her money, or…well, anything. She'll be like a loyal gun-dog. Not exciting, but reliable."

Scowling at Dex, Randy muttered, "If the woman I was engaged to thought you were a brat, she'd be the woman I was *formerly* engaged to."

"I'm with you. But if Yardley makes Tracy happy, we've got to support her choice. Truly, Dad." She took his hand and pressed it against her cheek. "I know how much you love Kendall, but I can see that to someone like Yardley, someone with a stick up her…personality," she added, sparing a glance at Libby, "might think she was spoiled. I don't, but that's because I know how caring and loving and connected she is. But if all I saw was her independence and her single-mindedness…" She shrugged. "Yardley doesn't seem to regard Kendall as an adult—yet. Over time, I'm sure she will." She paused, thinking for a minute. "And if she doesn't, Tracy will convince her to change."

"And if that doesn't work?" Randy said, his eyebrow rising up.

"Then she'll divorce her. There isn't a woman in the world who could come between Tracy and Kendall. I'm positive of that." She finally took another bite of her fish, which was not quite as good at room temperature. "Now let's come up with topics we can resort to when we're trapped in a room with Yardley."

"I could talk about my genealogy work," Libby said without much enthusiasm.

Randy let out a sigh. "Tracy says Yardley likes cars. I don't know a lot about them, so I could let her lecture me…"

"That's a start," Dex said, certain she could find some common ground if she was willing to eat a little crow. With enough hot sauce, she could get just about anything down. Tracy deserved much more, but if Yardley was her choice, they had to make peace with her decision.

❄

Tracy had been recommending talk therapy to her patients for over fifteen years, but she'd never gone herself. She was certain it was helpful, but she'd always been quite private, and spilling her guts to a stranger just wasn't something she craved. But she and Yardley really needed to air out the things that were holding them back, and she was quite sure neither of them knew how to get past their own barriers.

She'd asked the doctors in her practice if they knew any good couples therapists, not admitting she was looking for herself, and had come up with a small list of names. After chatting with each of them on the phone, she'd picked a woman who seemed direct, yet friendly.

Finding a time they could meet was another hurdle, but Lila had early morning hours, and she had an opening on Thursday at eight a.m. Given that was the day Tracy went in late, it seemed like kismet, so she booked the session.

That morning, they drove separately, since Yardley had to attend a dinner after work. Waiting in the silent anteroom, with a clock that made Tracy flinch with each passing second, she began to regret the decision to come.

Then the door opened and a pleasant-looking, nicely dressed, Black woman about their age gave them a welcoming, friendly smile. "Good morning," she said, and Tracy knew she'd made a good choice. You could tell a whole lot by a woman's natural warmth.

They went in, and after the usual introductions, Lila said, "Why don't you tell me what brings you to therapy, Yardley?"

"Oh," she said, like that was a question she hadn't studied for. Tracy cringed, knowing Yardley wasn't the perfect candidate for therapy. Revealing herself did not come naturally in any way, and she truly hated to admit to any weaknesses. "Well, there's nothing pressing," she said, with her smile looking amazingly false. "We're planning on getting married in the next year, and I think we both want to make sure we're on firm footing. An ounce of prevention, you know."

"Ahh. Well, that's a very good instinct. It's hard for nearly every couple to get used to merging their lives, and knowing where your problem areas lie can be very helpful."

"Oh, there aren't any problems," Yardley said. "Everything's been pretty idyllic."

Lila opened her mouth to speak, but Yardley kept going, in fits and starts. She never quite seemed to recognize when it was her turn to speak. "We've just started to live together, and even though it's only been a couple of weeks, I think everything's gone very smoothly." The smile she beamed at Tracy was exactly what it would have been if someone had told her she'd be shot if she didn't look sincere. "I'm sure Tracy agrees with me on that. Smooth sailing."

"Do—"

"Of course, that's what I would have expected. Tracy's very even tempered. She's also very good at saying what's on her mind. Open communication," she stressed. "That's the key."

"Would—"

"I know some people have trouble when they're partnering with a woman who has a child, but that's been fantastic, too. All's right in our world, and—"

Lila seemed like a very polite person, but she clearly wasn't going to let Yardley run the session. In a very gentle way, she held her hand up. "I'm glad things are going so well. Why don't we let Tracy check in so we don't let the time get away from us. Tracy?"

Two sets of eyes were on her, but Tracy didn't let the near-pleading look from Yardley stop her. She told the truth. All of it. As she spoke, Yardley seemed to shrink, all of her false confidence seeping out.

"Like Yardley said, we've recently gotten engaged. My daughter was away at college when we first got together, but she's home now. At the start of the summer, Kendall invited her other mother to come to Richmond for a long visit. Dex, my ex, and Yardley used to work together."

She could see Yardley fighting the urge to jump in, but she kept talking.

"They didn't get along well then, and Yardley seems to harbor a lot of resentment toward her."

"I don't—"

"May I finish?" Tracy asked, then continued. "Since Dex arrived, Yardley and I are fighting about things that had never come up before. For the first time, Yardley has also been voicing complaints about my daughter. Those have *really* caught me by surprise. To me, that means trouble is brewing," Tracy stressed, "and we need to get in front of it."

Lila looked toward Yardley, and in the blink of an eye she started trying to repair the damage Tracy had done to the image she obviously needed to protect. "The conversations we've had about Dexter have been productive, honey. Now that I know more about your history, I've been able to get a new perspective. And Kendall and I are going to eventually become friends—good friends. In fact, I'd be surprised if she doesn't wind up loving staying with us once you sell your house." She let out a nervous laugh. "If your former in-laws would stop taking her in, she'd be more motivated to give that an honest try."

"They aren't my former in-laws," Tracy said, evenly. "They're Kendall's grandparents, and they will always take her in when she feels the need to stay there." She took a breath and delivered the kicker. "If I sell my house…" Giving Lila a quick look, she said, "That's still up in the air, but if I do, I'm going to sell it to my ex."

"She's buying it for Kendall?" Yardley asked, cocking her head like a puzzled German Shepard.

"Partially. But she's planning on living with Kendall, so it's as much for her."

"In Richmond?" Yardley asked, turning pale.

"Yes. In Richmond."

"But why would she want to do that? She's got an apartment at her parents' house."

"She wants more space, I suppose. Kendall's going to get her masters degree, and she and Dex plan on living together while she's doing that. Kendall's decided another credential will help her get a better job—wherever she winds up"

"Are you saying Kendall's not leaving for China soon?"

"Not soon, no. She and Dex are going to give living together a trial run."

"At your house," Yardley said, clearly stunned. "Dexter is going to live in your house."

"Yes, she is."

"She's letting some kind of mansion sit idle so she can live in your house."

"I think that's correct, but I didn't ask if her house was occupied. For all I know, she's renting it out while she's here."

"And when is this supposed to happen?"

Tracy had to make a choice. Look into Yardley's eyes and lie, or try to sidestep the question. But this particular question didn't leave much room for sidestepping. She cleared her throat and said, "It's already happened. Dex is there now."

"Now?" It was clear Yardley was trying to sound calm, but Tracy could see her knuckles whiten when she gripped her hands into fists.

"Yes, now."

"And this is supposed to go on for how long?"

"Unclear," Tracy said, even though Dex had indicated she might be giving LA up entirely. But she hadn't done that yet, so it wasn't technically a lie to not mention it…

"Unclear? A woman has moved into your house, and you don't know what her plans are? She could be there for a week, or twenty years? You're not the slightest bit curious?"

Tracy started to reply, but Lila jumped in. "Your expression indicates you've got an opinion about this, Yardley. Do you want to take a second and think about it before you share it with Tracy?"

"It's fine!" she said, nearly yelping. "If that's what Tracy and Kendall want, why would I have an objection? I'm not on the title."

"It's not a question of ownership," Lila said. "It's more a question of your comfort with Dexter being so close. Where does she live now?"

"Los Angeles. She moved there for her health." Lowering her voice, she added, "She's a drug addict."

"She's in recovery," Tracy said, giving her a lethal look. "I believe in giving a person credit for the hard work they do to stay sober."

"All right," Lila said, her voice having grown even more calm. "I think today has shown us that there are a few areas that we might take a closer look at. Smoothing things out before your marriage can be a very good idea."

"Things are perfectly smooth," Yardley said, her voice having risen a half octave. "Really. When Kendall eventually leaves and we don't have Dexter shoved into our faces—"

"Kendall might leave," Tracy said, with her voice full of warning, "but she'll return. And when she does, we'll spend time together. A lot of time," she added, making that clear. "I'd like for the two of you to form a good relationship, because she's going to be a big part of your life."

"That's great! I'm really looking forward to that." Her tone made it clear she was lying through her pearly whites, exactly the last thing it made *any* sense to do in therapy.

∞

It seemed like only ten minutes had passed, but Lila had them wrap it up, then they agreed on their next appointment. Yardley acted pretty normal when they were leaving the building—until they got to the street. Then she pulled her keys from her purse and started to walk—quickly—to her car. "Late," she said, not adding another word. But Tracy knew there would be more to come. She was willing to bet the farm on that.

∞

When Tracy checked her phone during her quick lunch break, there was a text from Yardley.

I'm very disappointed to learn all of the things you've been keeping from me. I'd appreciate having my apartment to myself tonight to let my feelings settle.

Reading the message twice, Tracy didn't bother to reply. She was going to be at the apartment when Yardley returned, whether she liked it or not. When you lived together, you had to take the bitter with the sweet.

Yardley walked into the apartment at ten, stopping abruptly at the door when she saw Tracy sitting in the living room. "Didn't you get my message?"

"I did." Tracy got up and moved over to stand in front of her. "We need to learn how to have differences of opinion, Yardley. Like I told you before, we need to learn how to fight."

"I don't want to fight," she said crisply, turning to head for the master bedroom. As she walked, she spoke under her breath. "If I had a fiancée who told me what was going on, there would be no need to fight."

"Please stop and talk to me. We can work through this."

Yardley started to take her thinnest pajamas from their hanger, then went into the bathroom to change, something she usually did in front of Tracy. "We can talk when I'm feeling better," she said, speaking loudly to be heard through the door. "That's not tonight. I've got a splitting headache from too much wine and too much stress."

"Let me help relieve some of the stress," Tracy said, leaning against the door. "We can discuss this calmly."

"I'm perfectly calm," she said as she emerged, all buttoned up. "But I have to face the fact that you hid something big from me. That's going to take some time. Betrayal lingers," she added, marching into the guest room, where she quietly closed the door and threw the lock.

Tracy leaned against the door for a few seconds, tempted to plead her case. But she wasn't going to be able to convince Yardley to see her point of view in the space of ten minutes. As she walked back to the bedroom, she was actually kind of glad they didn't have to fight so close to bedtime. While she knew that wasn't the best way to run a relationship, having the bed to herself was kind of nice. The chill of a partner who was furious with you could make you feel much lonelier than you did when you were truly alone.

❈

Tracy stopped at the wine shop on her way home the next night, determined to make a nice dinner and talk things out. She normally bought inexpensive wine, not truly able to taste the difference between a seven and a twenty-seven dollar bottle. But she splurged tonight. Yardley liked French reds, and they were three times more than Tracy liked to spend. But showing she was trying to make amends might go a long way. Yardley always seemed to appreciate it when Tracy made it clear she'd noticed her preferences.

After dropping thirty bucks on a French Bordeaux, she got back into her car and started to put her seatbelt on. Her buzzing phone distracted her, and she reached for it. The text was brief.

"Dinner plans. Home late."

Tracy gave the phone a narrow-eyed glance. Yardley had created a joint calendar for them, so Tracy could see all of her scheduled business dinners. While it wasn't beyond imagining that something had come up at the last minute, that wasn't the norm. Yardley liked a scheduled, predictable life. One that could be plotted on a calendar, with her appointments in green, and Tracy's in blue.

Almost certain that Yardley had made up the dinner, or was going alone to see *General Galactica,* Tracy started to head for home. But the apartment still didn't feel remotely like hers. It was big, and bright, and decorated much more expensively than her own home, but it wasn't homey. Not only didn't it appeal to her, it didn't really seem to appeal to Yardley, either. Everything had been purchased by an interior decorator, even the photos on the walls. They were artful, and attractive, but they didn't represent places Yardley had been, or scenes that had left an emotional mark on her. They were meant to show off, to make it clear that the woman who lived in that apartment had good taste, as well as a pretty big bank account.

While Tracy didn't think she'd have trouble getting used to it, the place didn't soothe her like her own home did, and on a hot summer night she longed to pull some weeds to keep her garden neat. Getting her hands in dirt was important to her, and she pondered what kind of spell she'd been under to willingly give that up so blithely.

She was wearing her scrubs, and they certainly wouldn't be hurt by digging around in her garden. In fact, her fledgling wine-snob daughter would definitely enjoy a quality French red. She checked her watch. Barely five thirty. Dex ate early, but Kendall liked to wait until around seven. If she was home, Tracy was sure she'd be happy to share cooking duties...

Her house was just about five minutes out of the way, and she found her car heading for the familiar neighborhood on auto-pilot. Seeing Kendall's car on the street made her smile, and she found a spot just a few cars further down.

Carrying the wine, Tracy walked to the front door, feeling a little funny to be ringing her own bell. No one answered, but she knew all too well that you couldn't hear the bell if you were in the yard. So she walked down to the end of the block to go in via the alley. She pushed open the back gate, spying Dex on the deck.

She was looking pretty fancy tonight. Actually, her clothing wasn't technically fancy, but it was a step up from her usual "I'm going to contort myself into a complex yoga pose in the next two seconds" look. Her top was still roomy, but it seemed silky, as did her slacks. Both pieces were dark, maybe grey, but she also wore a couple of silver necklaces, and some silver bangles that the late afternoon sun reflected off.

Tracy was about to call out when the back door opened and a very attractive, very fit woman emerged. She was older than Kendall, but not by a lot. Her clothing was on the same sophistication level as Dex's, but more brightly colored, and when she passed behind Dex's chair she let her hand trail across her shoulders.

When she sat down, she lifted her wine glass and touched Dex's, which probably contained water. This was a date! Standing there in her scrubs, her hair kind of a mess, made Tracy feel like a slob—an unfashionable slob.

As quietly as she could, she backed out of the yard, doing her best to avoid making a sound or moving in any way that would catch anyone's eye.

She made it, to her great relief, and stood there in the alley, perplexed and heartily disappointed. Where was Kendall? Who was this mystery woman? What was her place in Dex's life? Had they been out before? If so, why hadn't Kendall said anything?

Glumly, Tracy had to admit that Kendall wouldn't have told her if Dex was dating Tracy's own sister. There was no reason for Kendall to start revealing anything about Dex's life at this point. If Tracy wanted to know what was going on, she was going to have to ask. But how did you do that? Was questioning Dex about her social life a good idea? No! It was a truly awful idea. When you were engaged, your interest in your ex-lover's life should focus only on the parts that impacted your daughter. And if Dex was going to get it on with the pretty young woman she was dining with, the impact on Kendall would be a big, fat zero.

Tracy trudged down the alley again, glad she didn't have to pass right next to her house. To *Dex's* house. Dex was occupying the only home Tracy had ever felt emotionally connected to. The home she'd given away without really considering the consequences. What in the hell had she been thinking? She was living in a soulless, cold condo without the ability to vent some of her feelings by sticking her hands into dirt. And she really needed a place to work things out, since her roommate seemed just about ready to toss her.

∞∞∞

Yardley seemed a little wary when Tracy entered the condo the next night, but after presenting her with the bottle of Bordeaux, she perked up a little. It was *so* easy to make her feel appreciated. Or maybe the right term was validated. Noticed. Whatever the term, Yardley needed to feel needed, and Tracy truly wanted to give her what she craved.

"I have some things in the refrigerator," Tracy said. "I was going to make us a nice dinner. Interested?"

"If you want to," Yardley said, still looking skittish. "Or we could order in."

"You choose. I'm going to go change. Back in a minute."

She dressed more carefully than she usually did, putting on a cotton blouse that she'd ironed, along with her best shorts. After combing her hair and adding a little lipstick, she'd achieved the look she was going for —a woman who wanted to show her fiancée that she was worth some extra effort.

Yardley smiled at her when she came down the stairs. She'd poured wine into two glasses, and handed one to Tracy. "Dinner's on the way," she said. "I ordered from the Greek place you liked so much."

"Really? Were there enough vegetarian dishes for you?"

"With all of the dinners I've had to go to this week, I thought a salad was enough for me. Maybe I'll pick at your charred octopus."

"My favorite," Tracy said, smiling at her.

"And some sea bream. It sounded really good."

"Thanks so much," Tracy said, clinking her glass against Yardley's, then taking a sip. "Good stuff."

"Very good. I appreciate that you bought something special that you knew I'd like."

Tracy put her glass on the mantel. After wrapping her arms around Yardley, she gave her a hearty hug. "Let's get a few things out on the table, okay?"

"Like what?" She stepped away, looking spooked again.

"Come on," Tracy said, taking her hand to lead her to the sofa. When they sat, she continued to hold her hand just to stay connected. "I assume you feel like I dumped a lot of things on you at therapy yesterday, and I'm sorry for that."

"Well, you did—"

"I know. I really do know, Yardley. And while I wish I hadn't had to, I still feel like it made sense to hold onto a couple of upsetting things to discuss with Lila in the room. That's what she's there for."

"To have me look like a fool?"

"You didn't look like a fool. Not at all." She lifted her hand to cup

Yardley's cheek. "Lila's used to people airing all sorts of dirty laundry, honey. What we were talking about yesterday probably bored her to tears. It was all minor stuff."

"Then why didn't you tell me about any of it?"

"Well, it was minor to Lila. I knew it wouldn't be to you."

"It wasn't," she agreed, now looking very sober. "You made decisions without even running them past me. That's...bad."

"I can see why it seems that I did that. But the only true decision I made was in going along with a foregone conclusion. Kendall would have invited Dex to move in the moment I moved out."

"You admitted you talked to Dexter about buying the place! We agreed we were going to merge our finances when we marry. Striking some kind of financial arrangement without consulting me—"

"I didn't strike any kind of deal. But you're right about one important thing. I shouldn't have even hinted I'd sell without talking it over with you first." Grasping her hand again, she said, "I'm really sorry about that. It made sense when we discussed it—especially when she offered to take over my mortgage payment. But this is about more than money."

"A lot more." She still looked like a puppy who'd been nipped by a much bigger dog.

"I'll try not to hold onto things until we get to therapy, but I need for you to be more open to discussing issues that might be upsetting."

"I can't guarantee I'll be able to change much in that area. It's worked well for me to let things play out for a while. Sometimes issues go away if you ignore them until they're less charged."

"That might be true for a lot of things, but not for Kendall and Dex and—"

"I know," she sighed. "But I don't like telling a stranger my thoughts, and I really don't like having you talk about things that make it clear we've got problems."

"I really do understand," she said, acknowledging she was more like Yardley in this area than not. "I felt more comfortable talking to Lila than I thought I would, but it still wasn't easy. But I'm sure we've got to try, honey. Our relationship is worth the discomfort."

Yardley nodded. "I'll try. So... let's clear the decks before we have to go back. I'd like to know about anything you've agreed to or even discussed with Dexter or Kendall. No more secrets."

"I'll happily tell you about Kendall's plans, then you'll see how Dex fits in. I have nothing to hide."

Chapter Eighteen

KENDALL WANTED TO PLAN A LITTLE party for Dex's birthday, which was in just five days. The obvious thing was to have the family come over to the house for dinner on Saturday afternoon, but they got together for dinner all of the time. Expanding the roster made sense, but she wasn't sure who Dex was truly friendly with. She was so damn zen that she seemed to like just about everyone with the same level of enthusiasm.

Obviously, Kendall would have liked to invite her mom, but having Yardley tag along made that prospect less compelling. Maybe the high school friends that Dex had been out with once? Or the yoga teacher she'd had over for dinner not long ago? Dex had said she'd had a good night, but Kendall wasn't sure if she'd seen the woman again. Actually, she wouldn't have known she'd existed if she hadn't left a sweater on the deck. When she'd dropped by the next day to pick it up, Kendall had assumed the woman had resorted to the old trick of intentionally leaving something behind so you'd force another interaction. But Dex had been Sphinx-like about her. Actually, she was like that about nearly everything. It was impossible to know what she was thinking if you didn't specifically ask her.

Deciding that was the only way, Kendall knocked on Dex's door that night before bed.

"Hold on." She opened the door a moment later, with the phone pressed to her chest. "I'll come find you when I'm finished, okay?"

"Sure. I'm getting ready for bed, so..."

Dex put a hand on her head and gave it a scratch. "I won't be long."

Kendall had just finished flossing her teeth when Dex entered the room and kind of fell onto the bed. "Tired," she sighed.

"You're like a teenager," Kendall teased. "Hidden away in your room for hours a day. Do you play some kind of RPG?"

"Doubtful. What's an RPG?"

"Role playing game. I thought maybe you were a game-master and were building some fantasy empire…"

"Are you…?" Dex scooted around to sit up and lean against the headboard. "Does it bother you that I'm in my room kind of a lot?"

"No, of course not. You're in yours a lot more than I'm in mine, but I like that we've got kind of a *Freaky Friday* thing going on."

"Oh, my god." She started to laugh. "We watched that movie more times than I can count. For at least a year we saw it every time we were together."

"Loved it," Kendall said, shrugging.

"Uhm…you know I sponsor people, right?"

"Sure. Kind of."

"Well, I don't think I'm revealing anything confidential to mention that those people and I used to be in the same physical space. Now we're having to adapt to my being gone, and change isn't always easy…"

"Oh! You have to talk to the people you sponsor because they're losing it since you're not around."

Dex smiled at her. "That's a little extreme, but it's a period of adjustment. One or two people might eventually find they're better off with a local sponsor, but we're trying to see if this can work." She held up her hands. "I don't normally like to reveal even that much, but I also don't want you to think I'm just hiding out in my room." She lunged forward and grabbed Kendall to chuck her onto her back. Then she cuddled up next to her and tossed an arm and a leg over her. "I'd be with you every minute if I could."

"Too much!" Giggling, Kendal pulled away, fully acknowledging that Dex could have kept her right there if she'd wanted to. She was spookily strong. "So… Your birthday's this weekend, and I wanted to have a party for you. Guest list?"

"Ooo. You don't have to do anything special. I'm sure my dad would love to have an excuse to barbecue up a storm…"

"I'd like to do something here. Papa can sit on the deck and let me cook for him for a change. Guest list?" she repeated, thrilled by the delighted smile on Dex's face.

"Well, we could just invite the usual suspects…"

"Mom?"

Dex's smile got a little more playful. "Is Yardley out of town?" She stood up and arranged her top, which had gotten kind of twisted up.

"I don't know. I can't really invite Mom without inviting Yardley…" Kendall looked at her for a few moments. "Would you mind if I didn't invite either of them? I'll have Mom come over some night next week when I know Yardley's not available."

"Kendall, I was joking. It's not a good idea to shut Yardley out."

"I'm going to cook, Dex. That's enough pressure without worrying about Yardley taking little bites out of you."

"Fine. Just invite my relatives. That's easy."

"Not that yoga chick?"

"Vashti?"

"Yeah. Are you seeing each other?"

"Uh-huh. I'm committed to going to her Kundalini class every Friday morning."

Kendall gave her flat belly a poke. "You're intentionally avoiding the question."

Dex laughed as she bent to kiss Kendall, then turned to leave the room. "Paybacks, baby. Now you know how I felt from the time you were fourteen until about six months ago."

❈❈❈

Kendall texted Tracy on Thursday afternoon, as she had at around the same time every day that week. "What's up?"

"Work's a madhouse. Thankfully, Yardley's going to a client dinner tonight, so I don't have to think about what to cook. Want to take me out for ice cream to make up for the lousy day I'm having?"

"Better plan. I'll make an early birthday dinner for Dex. Be here by seven. No need to bring anything. XO"

Tracy stared at the text while she lingered outside an exam room. Dex's birthday was on Saturday, and either Libby or Grammy would plan something. Obviously, Tracy had been left off that invite list, which stung a little. But she couldn't blame a single member of the family for not including her. Yardley hadn't been herself since May, and not one member of the extended family had any appetite for conflict or even a hint of impoliteness. If Yardley didn't get her act together, Tracy's social life was going to take a major hit.

⚬⚬⚬

On the drive to her old home, Tracy stopped at a shop to buy a birthday card. She didn't have a single present for Dex, having not had time to pick anything up. The only bad thing about Dex's sobriety was that it prevented you from gifting her a nice bottle of wine, the easy present for all wine-drinkers.

She hadn't gone home to change, choosing to spend a little time finding a card that conveyed some of her feelings. After picking out kind of a sappy one, she got back into her car and thought for a minute. What could she possibly give Dex? The very expensive yoga-style clothing store wasn't close, and Tracy didn't even know of a local place that sold anything that looked like Dex's regular stuff. A wealthy suburb near DC would undoubtedly have the ultra-soft things she liked, but Tracy had missed the opportunity to do that.

So...no clothes, no liquor. Dex didn't read extensively, and she only used a streaming service for music. Tickets to something? A gift certificate to a nice restaurant? Nope. Too impersonal. She really wanted something special, even a token gesture, to make it clear they were on the road to peace.

Opening the card, she re-read the sentiment. "Happy birthday to someone I care for deeply, even though I don't always make that obvious. I'm going to try harder this year to let you know how special you are." Laughing, she pondered how many people must share that feeling for card-crafters to have picked up on it. Probably a lot.

An idea hit her in the blink of an eye. She dug into her purse to find a pen, and started to write…

⊗⊗⊗

Kendall didn't have a lot of experience with cooking, but she had good instincts. Dex watched her get all of her ingredients ready, ticking things off a checklist she'd made on a notepad. "Any limit to how spicy you'll go?" she asked absently.

"Well, yeah, I have a limit. It's not a high limit, but I'm not going to eat a handful of Scotch bonnet peppers."

"Got it. No limit."

A knock on the back door made Dex jump to her feet. "Your mother seems to like coming in via the alley. We'll stay out of your hair."

"Okay," she said, not looking up. Obviously, Kendall needed to concentrate to cook.

Dex went to the door and tossed it open. "Our daughter is cooking. I think we should lie low and stay out of harm's way. Glass of wine? Cocktail?"

"A tumbler of whatever you've got. Well, not rum, but anything else is fine."

"Have a seat. I'll bring you a Big Gulp."

There actually were some 32 ounce plastic cups in the pantry, and Dex loaded one up with ice, sparkling water, and a good slug of the white wine Kendall had chilling. She almost waved her hand in front of Kendall's face as she passed by, but she was holding a knife, so she thought better of it.

"Whew," she said, taking one of the rockers to sit next to Tracy. "To fight the heat, I made you a giant wine spritzer. Kendall's opened a nice Gavi that you can share with dinner, but you look like you could use some immediate cooling off."

"It's gotten more humid since I left work. Must be a storm coming in." She took the cup and knocked back a few gulps. "I'm glad you didn't give me straight wine. I'd be asking for a refill already."

"Well, even though you're hot and tired, you look nice. You know, your scrubs fit you very well. I'm used to seeing those cotton ones that

271

look like rumpled blue sheets."

"Oh, if the hospital or office provides them, those are what people still wear. But I switched to these a few years ago, since I have to buy my own. Fewer pockets, slim fit, a little bit of stretch."

"I like the navy blue. Makes your eyes look darker." She laughed. "I've always been jealous of your blue eyes. You and my mom have almost the same shade."

Tracy batted them, looking really cute when she acted silly. "Kendall loves that hers are brown—entirely because they're close to yours. From the time she was about five until…well, now, she's wanted to look more like you. Kids are horrible, aren't they?" She laughed, always looking so pretty when she revealed that sunny smile.

"She's never been *horrible*, but all kids take you on a roller coaster ride. Parenthood is not for people who get their feelings hurt easily."

"Too true." Tracy's smile disappeared just as quickly as it had formed. "You know, when she was born and we couldn't both be listed as her parents, I tried not to let it get to me. But it did."

"Me, too. It was a needlessly cruel act on the government's part. Having more people responsible for kids only helps the kid *and* the state."

"It's the kid and the parent I was concerned with," Tracy said softly. "Of all of the mistakes I've made in my life, and god knows I've made a bundle, the one I'm most ashamed of is making both you and Kendall worry that I'd cut your connection. I swear I wouldn't have, but—"

"It's okay," Dex said. "Water under the bridge."

"No way. It's many years too late to have any real bearing on anything, but it has symbolic meaning." She pulled out a card from her bag. "I have a little birthday gift for you. It will take some time to come to fruition…"

Smiling, Dex took the card and opened it. "Wow. How many people have tough histories with people they celebrate birthdays with?" She laughed. "This is sweet, Tracy. Thank you."

"Read the back."

Dex flipped it over, reading the neatly printed words.

I can't make up for not doing this the moment it was legal, so I'm going to do it now. When I find a good attorney, I'm going to have Kendall's birth certificate amended to have both of her parents listed. You've been a great mom to our daughter, Dex, and you two deserve to be legally recognized as parent and child.

Tracy

Dex just gazed at her for a minute, then made sure her voice would hold up. "Thank you. Even though she's an adult, this would mean so much to me." She held the card to her chest. "Does Kendall know?"

"It might take a while, and I didn't want to promise something I couldn't deliver. But there's no valid reason the state would prevent the change at this point, so I thought I'd tell you I was going to do it."

"You couldn't have gotten me a better present," Dex said, still struggling with her emotions. "Thanks for knowing how much this would mean."

"You've had a few rough parenting patches in the very distant past, but your love for Kendall has never been in question. You're her mom, and if I have to hire the best attorney in Virginia, we're going to make sure that's permanently noted. Years from now, when Kendall's great-grandchildren are adding to your mom's genealogical tomes, I don't want there to be any confusion about who her moms were."

Dex laughed. "Kendall's progeny will appreciate that. Now don't get too focused on hiring the *best* attorney in Virginia. You know he's busy getting billionaires hooked up with iron-clad non-disclosure agreements. I'm sure a relatively competent lawyer can get this done. I bet my dad has some recommendations."

"I've already texted him. He's going to check around tomorrow." Tracy rose a few inches and leaned over to kiss Dex's cheek, which tingled from the contact. "Happy birthday, Dex. I hope this is a fabulous year for you."

"The last half of the previous one has been awfully good. I'd be thrilled if I could continue to ride that wave."

❈

On the day before her birthday, Dex took her grandmother to her favorite restaurant for their weekly lunch. She wasn't sure why she was always left with the check, nor why they exclusively went to places her grandmother favored, but she didn't mind.

They all believed Grammy was very well-fixed, having inherited a good bit of land when her parents died. She'd sold bits and pieces to developers over the years, but had purposefully kept her financial picture entirely to herself. One thing was certain, though. No matter how much money she'd amassed, she never reached for her wallet—if she even owned one.

They were waiting for Grammy's bourbon shrub with apple and fennel, which sounded mighty odd to Dex. But she truly appreciated that Grammy would try nearly anything new, and then politely, yet thoroughly lecture the server if the concoction wasn't up to snuff.

"I got an early birthday present from Tracy," Dex said, having thought of the birth certificate a few hundred times in the last two days.

"Do tell?"

"She's going to hire an attorney to have Kendall's birth certificate updated to show that I'm one of her parents."

Grammy smiled, briefly, then a thoughtful look settled on her face. "That's as it should be, of course, but it seems like an awful lot of trouble, Dexter. Especially when there's an easier way to accomplish that."

"There is?"

"Of course. Win that girl back," she said, frowning slightly. "Then you can marry her like you should've been able to do originally."

"Marry her?" Dex was sure she was gawping.

"Of course. You can't argue that this isn't the perfect time."

"I think I can, Grammy—"

"There's *never* been a better time. I know you loved each other before, but you're both ready to marry now. You've grown a lot, sweetheart. Both of you have. There's no question that you're a mature, thoughtful woman. And you can't argue that your love for Kendall will always bind you. Given that you're both single—"

"Tracy's engaged, Grammy."

"In what?" she asked, obviously working to look blank.

"She's engaged to be married to Yardley. Don't act like you don't know that."

"Oh, honey. You've been out in the sun too long. Tracy's not going to marry that poor, unfortunate woman. What would she feed her? Did you know she can't eat a single mammal?"

Dex started to speak, but Grammy kept going.

"Come on now. You need to get moving on this. Tracy's got a very good job, and she'll be able to take care of you just fine."

"I have a job!"

"Shh! Don't make a scene, Dexter. Ladies don't speak loudly in public." Reaching over, she patted her hand. "Now, I know you like to pretend you've got something going on, but there's simply no shame in being poor. Don't be so snooty."

"I'm not poor!"

"Honey, you have to *work* to earn a living, but you've done nothing but sit by the pool since the middle of May." She poked at Dex's bare arm. "Now that we're on the topic, how have you not gotten a better tan?"

Dex took in a cleansing breath. "All right. If you really want to know how I've been spending my days, I'll tell you." She gazed at Grammy for a few seconds. "I sit in Tracy's office, all alone, and read books. Aloud."

Grammy patted her shoulder soothingly. "I'm so glad to hear that. If reading's difficult for you, I bet sounding the words out will help with your comprehension. It won't bring a cent into your coffers, of course, but at least you're trying to improve yourself."

"God knows I try," Dex sighed, certain she'd never learn exactly how much her grandmother was jerking her around—but it was undoubtedly a *lot*.

❈

Tracy got home late the following Wednesday night, pleased to see that Yardley had waited to have dinner together. They sat on stools in front of the counter, eating carry outs that Yardley had picked up on the way home from work.

"This is delicious," Tracy said. "I know you're not crazy about cooking, so it's really nice of you to launch a preemptive strike and pick up something so neither of us has to bother." She scratched along Yardley's back, usually a spot she loved to be tickled. "You possess a lot of really thoughtful traits, you know."

"I do try." She shrugged, looking kind of adolescent. "I'm not always successful, but that's not from lack of effort."

"I know you try. And that's really all either of us can do. We've got to work with the skills we have, while trying to pick up some new ones." Increasing the pressure of the scratch, she added, "Maybe we'll learn some tips at therapy tomorrow morning. You're not going to have trouble making it, are you?"

"Not in the least." She took a bite of polenta and chewed thoughtfully. "I'm going to try to be more transparent. Like I said, it's not instinctive for me, but I promise I'll try."

"That's all I ask, honey. I just want you to give it your best effort."

CHAPTER NINETEEN

AS THEY HAD THE WEEK BEFORE, they took separate cars to therapy. Lila was right on time, and Tracy spent her check-in revealing that Yardley had asked her to stay elsewhere after their last visit.

She could see that Yardley was quietly furious about that revelation, but they truly couldn't get anywhere if they didn't talk about their reality.

"What made you want alone time, Yardley?" Lila asked, her tone and expression pleasantly neutral.

"I felt betrayed after we met last time," she said, steadfastly not looking in Tracy's direction. "Hearing about Dex moving into the house just underscored that there's a Haven-Lord pod that I'm never going to be invited into."

"That's not true—"

"Let Yardley finish," Lila said softly. "Tell us how this pod feels to you."

"Well, I've never dated anyone who had a child, and it's…more difficult than I thought it would be. It's become more and more clear that Tracy values Kendall's opinions and feelings a lot more than mine." She gazed at Lila thoughtfully for a moment. "That might make sense if Kendall was ten, but she's a college graduate, who *should* be working…"

Yardley trailed off, possibly because of the laser-like glare Tracy was aiming at her skull.

Lila turned to Tracy. "You look like you're having trouble waiting to respond. Would you like Yardley to give you the floor?"

"Please." She turned her head slightly. "May I speak?"

"Sure. But I can already tell I'm not going to like what you've got to say. You're doing that…" She ran her finger over the space between her brows. "That thing where your eyebrows look like they might touch."

"That's a possibility," she said, trying to hide her annoyance as much as possible, and doing a poor job of it. "Yardley admittedly has little experience with children, but that hasn't stopped her from having strong opinions about mine. She doesn't seem to understand that Dex and I will always be co-parents, and we'll necessarily have to interact—"

Like the most disliked tattle-tale in junior-high, Yardley interrupted. "That's just not true. Before this summer, Tracy hadn't spoken one word to Dexter in nearly twenty years. They used Dexter's parents as go-betweens, a practice they could *easily* revert to on the very rare occasion they have to confer about child-raising decisions concerning an adult. A non-working adult who lives at home, contributing nothing financially as far as I know."

"Tracy?" Lila said. "Would you like to comment on that?"

"Love to," she grumbled through gritted teeth. "I made some very bad decisions when our daughter was growing up, one of them my refusal to speak to Dex. Kendall wants that nonsense to stop, and I can see why. She's suffered because of my choices, so I promised I'd work on reestablishing a relationship with Dex, and it's going remarkably well." Gazing at Yardley, she added, "My ability to have a good relationship with Dex will show that I'm not as judgmental and rigid as I used to be. That benefits you."

"Tracy has a valid point there," Lila said. "In my experience, people who get along well with their co-parents make better partners. There's much less tension in a marriage when everyone in both the inner and the outer circle is at least civil."

Yardley suddenly looked like she was about to explode. Tracy had no idea what had set her off, but something clearly had. "Dexter Haven doesn't *deserve* civility. She broke Tracy's heart, abandoned their child, and raced off to California to lie in the sun and make a lot of money repeating other people's words. Some skill," she groused. "You don't need a high school diploma to do her job, yet she apparently earns enough to afford a palace..."

Lila looked a little puzzled, so Tracy broke in. "Dex does voice work for animated movies."

"Ahh…"

"She's a user," Yardley said flatly. "A backbiting user who gets what she wants, precisely when she wants it. And she's influencing Kendall to be exactly the same."

"She is not!" Tracy stopped on a dime and backed up. "Dex isn't a user. She never has been. And if Kendall takes after her in any way, I'll be thrilled."

"You wouldn't say that if you'd worked with her. She snapped her fingers and got every assignment she ever wanted. She leapfrogged over people who'd been there longer, and had MBAs. She and I were treated like peers, even though she was a history major, and I had my MBA. From *Duke*," she stressed. "But my education didn't matter as much as her father's position in the company did. Her entire tenure was based on nepotism," she insisted. "And if Tracy doesn't step in and make some changes, Kendall's going to repeat that pattern. She'll be yet another Haven who's showered with benefits she hasn't earned."

"Are you honestly concerned for Kendall?" Lila asked, the question sitting there like a ticking bomb. "It sounds like Dexter might be the real issue here. Please, correct me if I'm wrong…"

"What exactly do you mean by that?" Yardley said, not looking as focused as she'd been a second earlier.

"She's asking if you were attracted to me for myself or my connection to Dex," Tracy said, feeling like the reality of their relationship was snapping into focus for the very first time.

"That's *not* what I asked," Lila said, speaking very clearly. "Actually, I don't think that's a good question to pose, Tracy. It's unnecessarily—"

Yardley finally faced Tracy, and spoke in a quiet, reflective tone, acting as though Lila wasn't in the room. "I hope that wasn't my prime motivation," she said, looking like she was really trying to figure this out. "But the thought of winning something Dex had lost was awfully pleasurable." She nodded, seemingly happy with her calculation. "I'm pretty sure that wasn't my prime motivation, though."

"Pretty sure? You're *pretty* sure?" Tracy's voice had risen to eardrum-damaging levels. She found herself standing, but wasn't sure when she'd gotten to her feet.

"Tracy," Lila said, her own voice growing firm. "Please sit down. Shouting isn't helpful."

She barely glanced at Lila. "This is important. Tell me what percentage of my attractiveness had to do with my being Dex's former lover."

"Actually, it's not that you were her lover," Yardley said, seemingly unaware of how deep a hole she was digging. "I'm sure she's had hundreds of those. But having the family she couldn't have… It's not insignificant. Maybe twenty percent."

"Tell me *exactly* why you love me," Tracy demanded.

Lila had gone silent, obviously realizing it was too late to erect a guardrail on the precipice of the cliff they were about to career off.

"I think…I *thought* we shared a lot of the same views, the same goals. But when I see how you treat Kendall, I'm not so sure."

"And what exactly do I do with Kendall that you disapprove of?"

Lila jumped back in. "You're both getting way off track. Let's take this one issue at a time. Yardley, if you'll consider how your feelings about Dexter have—"

"You let her run the show," Yardley said, showing some fire again. "I'm not saying children should be seen and not heard, but they should be much, much more respectful than Kendall is."

"Kendall has *always* been polite to you. You're imagining things if you don't believe that."

"Is it polite to walk right out of your own birthday party? You weren't on the deck at the time, so you didn't watch her behaving like a four-year-old. She announced that the party was over, then marched out the back gate with half of the guests. I swear she didn't even make eye contact with me. Not a word of thanks for the gift I gave her."

"Did she write you a thank you note?" Tracy knew her blood pressure had spiked to dangerous levels.

"Yes," she said, with her voice dropping slightly. "But she should have thanked me during the party. I carefully shopped for a gift, and that should have been acknowledged in public."

Tracy stared at her, astounded that Yardley could be so amazingly self-involved.

But she wasn't finished. Her list of complaints was clearly very long. "I've done my best, but Kendall hasn't done the same. At this point, I don't think I'd welcome her to stay at my condo. I'll admit I was upset about Dexter moving into your house, but that might have been a blessing in disguise. Now I won't have to deal with Kendall on a routine basis."

Tracy reached for her hand and wrenched her engagement ring off. Yardley's mouth dropped open as it landed in her lap.

"We're through," Tracy said, too angry to cry. "I will not marry a woman who thinks my perfectly imperfect girl is an imposition."

"You can't break up with me over that!"

Lila stood and moved so she hovered between them, still sounding awfully calm. "Tracy, please sit down and take a minute to gather your thoughts. Things you say when you're this angry can't be taken back."

Ignoring her, Tracy craned her neck to be able to see Yardley's face. "I can, and I *will* break up with you over this. This is the first time I believe you've been truly honest with me, and I'm glad for that. It's better to know how you feel now than after we're married. Divorce is *expensive*," she added, with the words coming out as if they'd been dunked in acid.

She went directly to the door, turning briefly to add, "If I were you, I'd stay in therapy. Just in case I haven't been clear, I'm not going to be around to find out if you took my advice." Unable to stop herself from adding one last word, she moved back to look down at Yardley. "Don't give yourself a pass in thinking *any* of this is because of Dex. It's not. I'm breaking up with you because of you. One *hundred* percent because of you."

⁂

In the fifteen years she'd been with her practice, Tracy hadn't called in sick at the last minute. That streak ended today. Along with the streak of her weddings dutifully following her engagements. That was out the window at zero.

She must have sounded as shaky as she felt, because Gretchen, the office manager, was not only solicitous, she insisted Tracy take as much time as she needed. Given she hadn't provided any details about why she wasn't coming in, her pain must have been glaringly obvious.

Tracy hadn't been able to wait even a second to think about where to go when she'd run out of Lila's office. She'd blindly gotten into her car and driven until she came across someplace green and tranquil looking. She'd lucked out, winding up at Deep Run Park, a spot she was sure she'd never been.

Not having the energy to actually walk around, she reclined her seat while staring blankly at the trees that surrounded her.

All of her stuff was at Yardley's. All of her scrubs, most of her casual clothes, many of her dressier things, her laptop, her backup glasses, all of her toiletries. Yardley didn't seem like a person who would burn everything out of spite, but she hadn't seemed like a person who'd find Kendall too obnoxious to have at her condo overnight, either.

So…she had to go get her stuff. Then what? She'd obviously have to tell Kendall about the breakup, but today was not the day for that. She'd act like everything was fine until she had some idea of what she was going to do—and where she was going to live.

Letting out a groan, she closed her eyes and tried not to cry. It wasn't fair to kick Dex out. She'd gone to a lot of work and expense to get the little office set up as a recording space, relying on an explicit commitment of at least three months. But Tracy couldn't possibly afford to stay in a hotel for that long. While she made a good salary, it wasn't good enough to spend a couple of thousand a month on housing.

She truly didn't want to impose, but Libby would be hurt if Tracy didn't rely on the family when she needed them. And this time she truly needed them. The thought of how kind the Havens had been to her for all of these years finally brought her to tears, and she stayed right there in her car, crying her eyes out until it was too hot and humid to even catch her breath. Eventually, she got herself together and raised her seat. Taking a look in the rearview mirror, she thanked the good lord that Libby loved her no matter what. Even when she was a swollen-eyed, blotchy-faced mess.

※※※

It didn't take long to get to the West End, and as Tracy drove along the tranquil, tree-lined streets that led to the Havens, she began to feel slightly better. Or a little more in control. She was still shaky, and knew that would last for quite a while, but she wasn't visibly trembling now.

When she pulled into the driveway, she was both relieved and dismayed to see Libby in the front yard, trimming the rose bushes that had been putting on quite a show. She liked to keep on top of them, certain she could get them to bloom again with proper care.

Libby looked up, clearly puzzled, then offered a wave that only lasted a second or two. She must have gotten a look at Tracy's face, since she dropped her shears and race-walked across the lawn.

"What's wrong?" she asked, her face turning pale in a matter of seconds.

"I need a hug," Tracy whimpered, surprised to find that Libby had the strength to physically pull her from the car. As soon as comforting arms wrapped around her, Tracy started to cry again. "I'm so stupid," she murmured.

"You've not had a single stupid day in your life," Libby soothed. "Now tell me what's got you so upset, sweetheart."

She drew in a long breath, and let it out all at once. "I broke up with Yardley this morning, and I have to get my things out of her condo before she comes home."

"You what?" Libby gasped, holding Tracy at arm's length as her gaze roved all over her face. "You ended things?"

"I did. It only took two sessions with a couples counselor for Yardley to make it clear she wasn't the partner I needed." She *so* wanted to drag her through the mud, to tell Libby exactly how unfeeling Yardley had been. But that wasn't fair. Randy worked with her, and would continue to, and Tracy couldn't allow her feelings to harm Yardley's professional prospects.

"Oh, sweetheart," Libby sighed. "I'm so sorry to see you in pain."

"I'm still stunned, even though I'm the one who called it quits. She said some things, and I said some things, and it got clear as day that we didn't have the same…goals," she finished, even though she wanted to say "values."

"Come inside," Libby said, guiding Tracy into the house. "You're overheated."

"I get like a sweaty baby when I cry."

They went inside, and when they got to the kitchen Tracy could see Randy outside by the pool.

"I should go tell Randy what happened, but I'm so confused." She sat down, barely noticing when Libby placed a glass of tea in front of her. "Thanks," she said, gulping it down quickly.

Libby took a chair and moved it so they were knee-to knee. "Now. How can we help?"

"Would it be asking too much to use the guest house for a little while?"

Frowning, Libby said, "I'm not going to chide you because you're so upset, but if you needed it, you could have the main house, and both of our cars. You know that."

"I do," she murmured, breaking into tears again. "You've always been right there for me when I needed you."

"And we will be now. Tell me what the issue is about getting your things. Do you need to do that today?"

"I think so." She looked into Libby's understanding gaze. "I just want to get it over with."

"Understood. Why don't we have Kendall meet us there. With three cars and four people…"

"Oh, please, please don't tell her about this. I'll do it, but not today. I have to get my head on straight first, Libby."

"All right." She patted her soothingly. "Why don't Randy and I take his big SUV over there. I'm sure we can figure out which things are yours…"

"I can't ask you to do that. It's too much."

"Nonsense. Are your things all mixed up together?"

"No," Tracy said, glad that Yardley was so obsessive about order and neatness. "All of my clothes are in the guest bedroom closet, and my toiletries are in the guest bath. Actually, only my things are there, so it's clear what's mine. The only other thing is my computer, and I'm almost certain I left it on the sofa in the living room. It's a Mac, and Yardley uses a PC, so it shouldn't be too confusing. But…"

"We'll go right now. When we get back, I want you in that guest house, lying in bed."

"But…"

"But nothing, young lady. Now, march!" She pulled her to her feet, set her shoulders to face the pool house, and gave her a gentle push. "I want you at the dinner table at eight. Having dinner with us will give you some structure, something I believe you need when you're hurting."

Tracy turned and gave Libby another tight hug. "You're a lifesaver."

"No, I'm not, but even if I were, you don't need your life saved. You just need some tender care while you lick your wounds. But trust me— you'll bounce back from this. I swear you will."

"I hope so. But I don't feel very bouncy today."

⁑

Randy was even more solicitous than Libby had been, but that didn't surprise Tracy. He'd always been the softer touch. The three of them sat at the round kitchen table that night, with Tracy having to force herself to eat the perfectly delicious barbecued chicken Randy had cooked. She'd spent the afternoon kicking herself for her poor choices, and her inability to see who Yardley really was. That had served to exhaust and depress her.

Randy wasn't being very talkative, but after a while he set his glass of rosé back on the table and said, "It's likely not a secret that I'm not Yardley's biggest fan, but I'm very sorry you're so broken up over this, honey. I'm sure I would have been able to form a good relationship with her, and I'm ashamed of myself for not trying harder."

"You did nothing wrong. I'm the one who's ashamed."

"Why should you be ashamed?" Libby asked. "It's easy to pick the wrong person. It takes a while for people to reveal their true selves."

"It's more than that," Tracy said, having gotten a little clarity while lying in bed. "I made a conscious choice to marry Yardley, thinking her reliability and predictability were great pluses. But those traits can be synonyms for unimaginative and rigid." She met Libby's eyes. "When did I become someone who settled for safe?"

"There's nothing wrong with wanting a safe, predictable life, sweetheart."

"Safe is one thing. I was looking for easy. I think I reasoned that Yardley would be my anchor. I was never someone who sought out the steady, pragmatic person. Where's the girl who had a baby with another woman when we were both too young to order a cocktail?" Both Libby and Randy gave her a fond smile at that memory.

"That's who I *am*. My impulsive, passionate side is the best part of me, but I chose to marry someone who appealed only to the more frightened part. The part that needs security over everything. The part that would rather be bored than risk…anything."

"That's not a bad thing," Randy insisted. "You've suffered through a lot of blows. Not wanting another isn't surprising. It's…self-protective."

"It's boring, Randy. I chose Yardley because I knew she'd never cheat on me, never develop any self-destructive habits, would never leave me, and would always be able to support me—monetarily, if not always emotionally. But that was crazy! I can support myself, but it's a heck of a lot harder to give myself emotional sustenance. Our life together would have been safe, secure, and arid. And I deserve a heck of a lot more than arid." She took in a big breath. "I've got to find the remnants of the bold, trusting young woman I once was, and construct a new persona for myself. One I can be proud of."

Libby beamed at her. "I have no doubt that you'll do exactly that."

"But first, I have to think this all through. I'm going to need some time to take this from insight to action."

"You'll have it," Randy said. "All of us will support you."

"Just us for now, okay? I need a few days before I tell Kendall. And once I do, I don't want her to have to keep another secret. So...will you be patient?"

"I won't say a word to Kendall or to Dex." He gave her an encouraging smile. "But I want you to remember that both of them will help you get back on your feet. Don't shut them out for long, honey."

"I won't. And I'll continue to text with Kendall. But I'd really rather not see her until I have a better handle on things."

"I'm not sure how long you can go without Kendall insisting on seeing you, but we won't get involved. Take as much time as you need."

CHAPTER TWENTY

ON A STICKY FRIDAY AFTERNOON, a full week after Tracy had arrived at their door, Libby stared at her phone, dismayed to see a text from Kendall. The phone had been in the kitchen, and she'd been outside for quite a while, so she couldn't even guess when the call had come in.

"I'm going to be saint-like and take my mother and her fiancée out to dinner. Heading over there now. How about a movie after? Let's think of something Yardley will hate. XO."

Libby was stuck. Uncomfortably so. She'd known at the time that it wasn't wise to aid Tracy in concealing her breakup, and she'd let it go on much, much longer than it should have. But she didn't want to be the one to tell Kendall about the split.

Tracy was out for a run, and hadn't taken her phone, which was lying on the counter. So Libby had to either let Kendall find out from Yardley, which was an abhorrent thought, or she had to do it.

Grimly, she dialed Kendall's number, but it went to voicemail immediately. She certainly wasn't going to deliver the news that way, so she simply said, "Call me back, honey. Right away."

Then she went to stand by the front door, hoping to see Tracy jogging down the street. This was truly her issue, and she should be the one to handle it.

⁂

Dex had spent the bulk of the afternoon in DC, recording a TV commercial. The money was worth the time she'd had to spend, as well as the cost of the rental car, but the jewelry store she was touting was one her parents believed was very overpriced. You really had no control over what you were paid to sell, but she always felt a little uncomfortable pushing something she didn't personally believe in.

She'd gone home, but it had been too hot to even sit on the deck. So she'd decided to make good use of her parents' pool. No sooner had she cracked open the door of the unfamiliar, small rental car than her mother was racing down the sidewalk. "I've done something unwise, honey. On many levels. Ideally I'd tell you all about it, and just take my medicine, but there's no time for that. Run over to Yardley's right this minute. If you rush, you might beat Kendall, who's somewhere between Charlottesville and Yardley's condo."

"Pardon?"

She started to open the door fully, but her mother pushed it closed.

"Please, honey. I don't want Kendall to find out what happened from Yardley."

Dex stared at her. "I don't know what you're talking about, Mom."

"You'll find out soon enough. Now, go! Go right now. Yardley's apartment's in the old thread factory. You know exactly what I mean."

"I know nothing!"

"Get going. Please." She sounded so insistent that Dex couldn't even think of refusing her.

"Fine. But call me the minute you get inside so I have some idea of what I'm doing."

"I can't right now." She started to back up toward the front door. "I'm going to jump into my car and find Tracy."

As she walked, Dex could hear her grumble loudly, "Why did I let her talk me into this—"

Flustered, Dex backed the car from the driveway, then called Kendall's phone, but it rang and rang. She probably had the ringer off since she didn't seem to understand you could use the phone for actual calls. Why didn't manufacturers just omit the damn feature? It had to take up a lot of space…

As she drove, supremely distracted, she thought about the old thread factory building. What an odd place for Yardley to wind up. She seemed more like the four thousand square foot home on three acres of land kind of woman. Lots of unnecessary space so she could throw an annual cocktail party for all of the work colleagues she wanted to impress. Actually, if it was possible, she'd rent a well-trained Golden Retriever for the day to add to her appeal.

Dex thumped her thumbs against the wheel as she anxiously waited for her mom's call. When it hadn't come by the time she was halfway across town, she called her. But as with Kendall, it just rang and rang. Her mom definitely used her phone for actual calls, but she often had the ringer volume turned way down. Not to mention how infrequently she carried it on her person. Could no one actually use a damn phone any more? Alexander Graham Bell must be turning over in his grave. His invention was in nearly every pocket, roundly ignored. Infuriating!

∞

Kendall had been almost certain she'd be able to get into UVA's masters program for teaching English as a second language. It wasn't that she was such an outstanding scholar that had convinced her of that, though. She just knew that they'd do their best to carve out a spot for a recent grad—especially one who didn't need tuition assistance.

She'd spent the day in Charlottesville, getting everything set for fall term, which was hurtling toward her like a meteor. How had she let Dex talk her into going back to school?

She wanted to share the good news with her mom, but they hadn't seen each other in over a week, which was really odd. Tracy had also refused two movie nights, and had come up with a thin excuse to decline Kendall's offer to take her and Yardley out to brunch last Sunday.

That was so unlike her that Kendall had decided to get more aggressive. She was simply going to drop in. It was Friday, barely six o'clock. Her mom would just be getting home, and she wouldn't have to get up early in the morning. They could all go out for dinner to celebrate, and she could bank some brownie points for including Yardley.

She'd only been to the condo once, which was also odd. She'd kind of expected her mom to invite her over for dinner—frequently. But that hadn't happened. It was possible that things weren't going well, but… No, she would have said something if there was trouble.

After finding a spot for her car, Kendall went to the entry and buzzed the apartment. The system had one of those big, fisheye cameras, and she assumed Tracy would see her clearly. She stepped super close, and stuck out her tongue and crossed her eyes, hoping to make her laugh.

She pushed against the entry door well before the buzzer sounded, but it opened with ease. Apparently, even expensive condos had glitches. She'd have to mention that to Yardley, who'd probably have a fit and have to scream at the property manager immediately. Maybe she'd make such an ass of herself Tracy would wake up from her spell and see her clearly. Her mom was engaged to a passive jerk who was ineptly trying to hide her anger—which wasn't insignificant. At some point, Tracy would catch on, so why not today?

When the elevator arrived at the proper floor, no one was there to meet her, so Kendall walked down the hall and got ready to knock, really pleased with herself for being so magnanimous.

⬡

Once she'd reached the proper street, Dex spotted Kendall's car and jammed her rental into the little spot right in front of it. After jumping out, she placed her hand on the hood of the sedan, finding it very warm. Great. Now she had *tons* of info. Kendall had recently parked her car. How did that help?

The look on her mom's face when she'd sent Dex on this mission had been really strange. A jolt of fear hit her as her mind raced in circles, landing on the possibility of Tracy being ill or hurt. But Libby had seemed…frustrated, or even annoyed. How in the hell were any of them involved in this—whatever it was?

As she jogged to the entry, she was anxious about even announcing herself. What was she supposed to say? Ask if anyone knew why she was there? Libby could poke fun at Grammy all she liked, but she came pretty close to starring in her own screwball comedy. That apple hadn't fallen far from the tree in the Dexter branch of the family.

⬡

Yardley threw open the door and stood before Kendall, wearing a pair of steel grey pajamas that looked like they'd been—starched?

"You have the nerve to come to my apartment and make faces at me?" she demanded, her voice much louder than Kendall had ever heard it.

"I—"

"What kind of sick person would find this funny?"

"Where's my mom?" she said, with her heart starting to race.

"How would I know? After she threw her engagement ring in my face, my interest in her whereabouts has dimmed a little."

"She what?"

"Don't play the innocent. I know you've never cared for me, but this is taking it too far."

"When did this happen?" Kendall demanded, pushing her way into the apartment, with Yardley backing up quickly. Kendall got right into her face, determined to knock her on her ass if Yardley tried to screw around with her.

"Last week. Thursday." She put her hand on Kendall's shoulder and squeezed it tightly. "You're saying you honestly don't know about any of this? Tracy hasn't been home?"

"I know nothing, but if anything's happened to her..." She was so angry she thought she might punch Yardley just for the hell of it, but as the seconds passed terror started to take over. Her mother was *not* the kind of person to disappear for over a week with no explanation. What if she was...hurt, or worse! Kendall forced herself to think for just a second. They'd been texting every day, but it was possible the texts hadn't actually come from her mom. They'd been brief, and infrequent, and kind of humorless. Maybe someone with no sense of humor had actually sent them...

"Did you take her phone?" Kendall demanded, glaring at Yardley with her fiercest look.

"Why would I take her phone?"

Just a second of looking into that clueless face made it clear. Yardley didn't have the guts to murder someone and try to hide her tracks.

"Forget it," Kendall said. "Sorry to disturb you."

"Oh, now you're sorry. Where was your sympathy a couple of months ago when I really could have used your help? If you hadn't been such a spoiled brat, everything would have been fine." She took in a deep breath and spit out her words like they were knives. "Actually, if you didn't *exist*, everything would have been fine."

"Jesus," she gasped, almost frightened by the fire that burst out of the normally wimpy woman.

From behind, Kendall felt the air in the room change, then footsteps clicked across the entryway tile. A second later, Dex was two inches from Yardley's face. "Don't you ever say something like that to my daughter," she growled, all of her zen having flown the coop. Her body was coiled, with Kendall able to see the muscles in her arms pop the way they did when she was doing a handstand.

Kendall gripped her arm and tugged on it, but she was barely able to move Dex. She whirled around, with her expression softening. "Go wait in the car, baby. I need to finish up here."

"No way," Kendall said. "I'm not leaving without you."

"Please?"

"No," Kendall said, steadfast. She was not going to let Dex go to jail for assault, and Yardley was exactly the kind of person to taunt you and then sue your ass off when you barely bloodied her nose.

"Get out of my house. Both of you! Actually, get out of my life!" Yardley was amped up again, looking as fierce as Dex had. "We never need to lay eyes on each other again, which will be a blessing."

"The hell you say!" Dex shouted. "If Tracy's living here, you'll necessarily be around Kendall—"

Kendall put her hand on Dex's arm again. "No living here. No running into each other." She pulled again, to no avail. "Let's go to the car and I'll tell you—"

Yardley started to yammer again—loudly. "Oh, sure! You're both innocent little lambs who just happened to show up at my door. I'm not stupid, you know. Just admit you thought it would be funny to rub salt in my wounds!"

"What in the holy fuck are you talking about?" Dex demanded, gripping the lapels of the pajamas with her fists. Kendall was astounded. Profanity and anger in tandem? Where had this element of Dex's personality been hiding?

"I'm talking about you," Yardley spat. "The heir apparent. The undereducated, underqualified little princess who marched into Virtus twenty years ago and derailed my rise to the top." Her expression grew harder, with her voice gaining volume. "If I didn't know it would cost me my job, I'd knock your damn block off."

"Try it," Dex seethed. "Your teeth will be so far down your throat you'll need an otolaryngologist to find them."

"Knock it off!" Kendall yelped.

"I'm so sick of her," Dex growled. "She doesn't deserve to be anywhere near your mom."

"Oh, I got very, very near her," Yardley smirked. "I put my hands and my fingers into every spot you've been shut out of all of these years. You were able to keep me out of the C-suite, but you couldn't keep me out of Tracy's sweet little—"

Dex slapped her hand over Yardley's mouth, holding onto the back of her head in what must have been a vise-grip, given Yardley was unable to wrest herself away. Her eyes were nearly bulging from her head, but Kendall was sure that was just rage, not suffocation—regrettably.

"Listen to me, you sniveling idiot. Yes, I got the job because my father gave it to me. But I kept it, and was promoted, because I was good at it. And, yes, I was much better liked at Virtus. But that was only because I'm more likable!" She shook her, with Yardley looking like a rag doll, even though they were roughly the same size.

"I was promoted over you because the job wasn't hard. In fact, your precious MBA was a waste. All you needed to succeed was to kiss plenty of ass, and make the clients like you. But you insisted on trying to make everyone think you were smarter than they were. You had no idea of how to kiss ass, and you've clearly not learned. *That's* why you're never going higher in Governmental Affairs. If you had any sense, you'd transfer to a department where your skills were an asset, you big dunce!"

Yardley was actively fighting her now, but Dex still had her hand clamped against her mouth, controlling her like she was a weak child. "You could be a good auditor. You could run rings around a lot of the people in finance." She gave her another shake, this one a little more gentle. "I know you work hard, and I know you're smart, but the job you're in was made for charmers." She let her go, immediately rubbing her hands on her shorts. "I hate to be unkind, but you're not now, and you never will be, charming."

Yardley wiped her mouth with her hands, eyes blazing. "I was charming enough to take something important right out from under you, you big bully. To be honest, it was a snap to snag Tracy. She was so hungry for a reliable, sober lover that on our second date I had her right on that sofa—"

Kendall barely saw the flash of color before her mom flew into the room and launched herself at Yardley. It happened so fast all she knew for sure was that Tracy's feet were off the floor as she reached out with her hands, aimed for Yardley's throat. How Dex got her arms around her in mid-air was a question Kendall didn't think she'd ever be able to answer, but they whirled around together for a half-second, then wound up on that sofa, with Tracy splayed across Dex's body, both of them gasping for air.

Kendall's heart was racing so fast a few heartbeats might have passed, but not much more than that. Then Tracy scrambled to her feet and stormed over to Yardley. Her hand reared back, and this time Kendall grabbed it. "Let's go," she said, using all of her strength to control the surprising power her mom had tried to unleash.

Dex got to her feet then, giving Yardley a look hot enough to singe her hair. "You'd better find yourself a transfer. Pronto. Once my dad learns about this…" She got close, and her voice lowered to an almost gentle purr. "You know, even after three trips to rehab, Virtus begged me to come back. Granted, that was mostly because of nepotism, since I'd proven I couldn't be trusted to stay sober." She filled her lungs, then let out one of her cleansing breaths. "Think about that for a second. If my dad convinced them to take me back when they thought I would fall off the wagon in a matter of weeks, how much trouble would it be to convince them to kick you all the way to the curb?" She straightened her top, then her hair, then wrapped one arm around Kendall's shoulders, and one around Tracy's. They marched out of the condo like a trio of low-stakes super heroes, with Dex politely closing the door quietly behind them.

Kendall pulled away once they were in the hallway, and got an arm around each of her mothers, pulling their heads toward hers. She placed a gentle kiss upon each of their foreheads, then said, "After I harangue Nana about aiding and abetting Mom for the last week, I'm going to find the gummies I've hidden in the pool house, take two, then float for a few hours. Tomorrow, I want you two jokers to tell me every damn detail that led us all here today. Adios."

As she walked down the hall, she waited for the elevator to open to toss off her final salvo. "Please get your shit together, okay? It's like twenty years past time."

❧

Every bit of calm energy she normally could access was way, way past Dex's grasp. Her body was still shaking, and she felt a little woozy, not having called on that much adrenaline in a very long time.

Tracy looked up at her, also seeming pretty hazy. "I do not think this is the ideal place to get our shit together. Where should we go?"

"Home," Dex said, not a question in her mind about that.

"I don't have a home. I've been staying in the pool house for the last week…"

Dex gazed at her for a few moments, seeing a spark of the exact same energy Tracy had shown the first time they'd made love. Deep interest, a little fear, and smoldering desire. She was still too shy to put words to her thoughts, but they were crystal clear. Letting out all of that pent-up energy had clearly snapped something open, and Dex was beyond ready to find out exactly what she meant.

"You'll always have a home," Dex murmured. "With me."

"Oh, god," she whispered. "Is that true? Do you swear it's true?" Her eyes closed briefly. "If I could cut this past year out of my life…"

"Let's do better than that." Dex leaned over so she could whisper into Tracy's ear, a sensation that had always given her chills. "Let's act like the last twenty years never happened. If I'd skipped my appointment to have my wisdom teeth taken out, I'd have the day off work, right? Kendall would be at pre-school, so we'd have the whole afternoon to ourselves…"

"Can we?" Tracy blinked slowly. "I mean, will that work? Can we just act like none of that happened?"

"No," Dex said, straightening up to laugh. "Not long term. But I bet we could use the fantasy to launch our second act."

Tracy turned to her, tilting her chin so their eyes met. "I've always preferred the second act of a great play. That's when the main characters realize they're meant for each other, no matter what obstacles stand in their way before the intermission. Can we do this, Dex?"

"We can definitely do it, and as soon as we get home, I'm going to pull the curtain up. Get ready for the start of a very happy ending."

CHAPTER TWENTY-ONE

THEY ARRIVED AT THE HOUSE just about simultaneously, and Dex carefully watched Tracy get out of her car. She expanded her focus to take in the little row-house, looking just like it had when they'd lived there together. Everything was totally different, and stunningly the same. Tracy was still the prettiest woman she'd ever known, and Dex couldn't wait to get into that house and make that crystal clear.

She jumped out of her car and bounded up the sidewalk, standing uncomfortably close to Tracy. Grinning shyly, she leaned against Dex as she took her keys from her purse and unlocked the door. They walked in and Dex centered herself, taking in a few deep breaths of a place that even smelled a little like it had twenty years earlier—minus the scent of baby powder.

They were going to have to move away from the front door, but she felt slightly stuck. But she wasn't going to let her fears stop her now. She was a fully-formed adult, and she could get past any trepidations.

Clearing her throat, she took Tracy's chilled hands and held them to her chest. "The past is past. Now we have to shape our future." She closed her eyes for a moment, sure she'd start to cry. "*Please* share your future with me."

"Are you sure?" Tracy's body was visibly trembling. "Are you positive, Dex? You know I couldn't take it if—"

"I've been sure since we were college freshmen. You're the only woman I've ever loved. The only woman I've ever *wanted* to love."

Tracy's eyes closed for a moment, and her voice was shaky when she said, "There hasn't been a day that's gone by that I haven't missed you." She took Dex by the shoulders and shook her slightly. "Do you know how hard it has been to look at that simulation of a woman I agreed to marry and try to do the right thing by her? Torture," she murmured. "It's been brutal."

Dex let out a soft laugh. "How do you think I felt knowing I was going to have to outlive Yardley Simpkins to have a second chance with you? Did you have to pick someone more moderate in her habits than I am? She might live to a hundred and ten."

"Poor you," Tracy sighed, with her hands settling on Dex's shoulders. A shy smile graced her lips, making her look exactly like the girl Dex had kissed on that warm, fall day. She moved even closer, filling her lungs with the scent of Tracy. The clean, fresh, scent that had tickled her senses back then, and had continued to mesmerize her ever since. "I need to kiss you," she whispered.

"I need to *be* kissed. Right now. By you."

Pulling her closer, Dex slowly slid her arms around Tracy's waist, with even that little bit of contact making her hands tingle. As their bodies grew closer, she let her eyes close, so much more able to experience every sensation when she relied on her other senses. Tracy's scent grew even more prominent when the gentle weight of her arms draped around Dex's shoulders.

Even Dex's ears got into the game, with the hairs on the back of her neck standing at attention when she could clearly hear Tracy's breathing get a little faster.

They held each other tenderly, almost shyly. It was so much like their first sensual embrace that it was like being hurled into the past while simultaneously standing on the brink of a very bright future. In fact, everything was brighter, more colorful, softer, and sweeter. "I love you with my whole heart," Dex whispered, enveloping her in her arms as their lips touched gently.

The kiss was achingly sweet, with Dex's head filled with a swirl of emotions, all of them compelling her to keep her arms wrapped around Tracy for the rest of her life. But a drop of salty liquid touched her lips and she pulled back to see tears tumbling over Tracy's lids.

Immediately, Dex started to catch them with her fingertips, desperate to whisk them away. Anything to take even a hint of sadness from her.

Tracy's arms compressed around Dex's body, holding on tenaciously. "I'm afraid," she whispered. "You're all I've ever wanted, Dexie, but I'm terrified to let you in again. If you break my heart now…"

Dex squeezed her tightly, realizing she felt exactly the same way. "I will never choose to leave you again. Never," she murmured. "You can trust me, sweetheart. I've been born again."

"You have?" Tracy pulled back slightly. "You've become…religious?"

"In a way. I think of my sobriety birthday as the day I was re-born. So I guess I'd say I'm faithful to my sobriety, and part of that is being honest—with myself and with others." She took in a breath. "I don't make promises I can't keep. So when I promise I'll be right by your side for the rest of my life—that's a guarantee."

"I believe you," Tracy said, with her beautiful eyes closing for a moment. "I'm still terrified, but I believe you." She put her hands on Dex's shoulders and moved her slightly so she could gaze directly into her eyes. "I keep flashing back to the day we made love for the first time." Her fingers slid through Dex's hair as a big grin settled on her face. "You were *so* much more experienced. You had a bluster about you that was ridiculously irresistible."

"I don't feel like that much anymore. I've had enough failures to know I can't just talk my way out of trouble. I can only show up, own my strengths and weaknesses, and hope that's enough. That's all I've got."

"That young Dex was awfully compelling," Tracy admitted, "but this new, mature Dex is the one I need now." She kissed her gently on the forehead. "You were so full of BS back then, so overconfident, that I don't think it even occurred to you that you didn't have all the answers."

"I'd lived a pretty charmed life," Dex admitted. "Everything had come easily up to that point." She laughed softly. "Talk a pregnant, straight girl into making a permanent commitment? Why not? Raise a baby when I'd never even held one? How hard could it be?" She started to laugh. "We were absolutely loony!"

Tracy held her tenderly once again. "And it would have all worked out just great if you hadn't had your damn wisdom teeth removed. We would have made it work. There's not a doubt in my mind."

Dex squeezed her tightly. "We've had a really long break, but I know we can get back to that place—the place where we have everything we need. We just have to put our trust in each other."

Tracy moved back slightly and put her hands on Dex's cheeks, gazing into her eyes for a few long moments. "You have my trust. You have my heart. Now and forever."

Now the tears came from Dex's eyes, with Tracy's watery image dancing before her. "I don't know if I deserve that, but I'm going to make sure I earn it."

Leaning forward, Tracy placed a gentle, lingering kiss on Dex's lips. "You know what we should do?"

Laughing softly, Dex said, "I was one hundred percent sure back in the day. Now? I feel kind of paralyzed."

Tracy's hands dropped to grip Dex's. "Are you saying I have to take over? I *will*…but shouldn't the one with more experience lead?"

"Given what you've told me about Yardley, it looks like we have exactly the same amount of experience." Dex felt those tears trying to get out once again. "We've each only truly made love to one person."

Tracy started to laugh, really getting into it. "You beat my number of sex partners when you were still in high school. As much as I love Kendall, she *killed* my sex life."

"She didn't kill it," Dex said, now feeling like her feet were on firmer ground. "She just…sent it on sabbatical. All of those urges you never got to express are just waiting for you to call on them." She put her hand on Tracy's cheek, with her heart skipping a beat at the thought of touching her again. "Now's good for me…"

Tracy grasped Dex by the forearms. "Show me what you've learned while I've been on sabbatical."

Dex wrapped her in another firm hug, murmuring, "All I've learned is that making love is so, so much better than just having sex. No comparison."

Tracy's face nuzzled against her neck for a few moments. "I'm nervous," she murmured. "I haven't spent the last ten years turning my body into a temple of awesomeness."

"I've seen you in a swimsuit," Dex whispered back. "You're selling yourself very, very short." Looking into Tracy's eyes, she added, "I've touched some pretty awesome bodies, and I definitely enjoyed some of those experiences. But none of those bodies did a thing for me—not where it truly counts." She placed her hands behind Tracy's head, running her thumbs across her cheeks. "I truly can't wait to touch every bit of your endlessly beautiful self."

"Then let's go take a peek at that renovated bedroom you paid for. Only seems fair…"

❦

Nearly twenty-three years earlier, Tracy had looked down from the chair she'd been standing on and almost involuntarily slid onto Dex's lap. In an instant, the cocky young woman had taken over. She'd been like a two-year-old filly, waiting for the starting gate to open. The second she saw daylight, she burst into action.

At their first kiss, Tracy was stunned by the sensation, so different from kissing a boy. But Dex raced ahead, not giving her time to process the differences and let her brain catch up to her body. After just a few frantic kisses, they were on the bed, yanking their clothes off like they were allergic to them.

In retrospect, it had been an awesome first time, but it had been rushed, slightly out of control. Now, so many years later, it felt like they were entirely different people. Measured, restrained, even a little tentative. It was odd, given they were much, much more mature, not to mention realistic, but Tracy was easily as nervous as she'd been then.

Dex had lost much of her brashness, and Tracy had lost *all* of her naivety. She knew who Dex was now, knew what was important to her, what she held dear. And she was certain Dex knew all of her faults, which sometimes seemed like a very long list. But they were choosing each other again. Purposefully. Carefully. And that was so touching, so stunningly improbable that it nearly knocked her off her feet.

C. K. Dexter Haven-Lord was gazing at her shyly, looking like a very excited woman who couldn't wait to rip the paper off a gift she was certain was exactly what she craved.

Tracy could count on one hand the number of times she'd taken the lead in bed, but this was a new beginning, so why not start some new habits? Carefully, she slid her hands up under Dex's cocoa brown crop top, tickling along her ribs.

"I like that," Dex said, smiling gently.

"I love the way your tops fit you. Just a hint of your flat belly shows, and when you bend over, or even twist, I can see your bra." She pulled her close and licked all along her ear. "I love to see your bra. I get just a little hint of what's hiding under there."

"Well, well," Dex said, grinning at her. "Who knew you were looking?"

"I didn't want to," she admitted, "but I did. Often." Her fingers slid around to the front, and she ran her thumbs over nipples hardening under the ultra-soft fabric. "This is the kind of thing you'd use to swaddle a baby," she said, chuckling. "I'm not even going to ask how much something this soft cost, but if you don't buy me one very soon, I'll be profoundly disappointed."

"One for every day of the week," Dex promised. "If a woman can't wear a comfortable sports bra, what's the point of exercising at all?"

"Having abs like yours might be the point. Off with the top." Dex lifted her arms, and Tracy whisked it from her, finally able to see everything that the roomy fabric didn't hide well at all.

"Sinfully sexy," she said, falling to her knees to kiss all along Dex's middle. Her abs were works of art, but there was so much more! Unable to resist, Tracy started to peel the shorts off. Now she could finally see what had always been one of her favorite parts of Dex's body. As the fabric fell to the floor, Tracy licked those very well-defined quads, now even more starkly etched than they'd been when they were girls.

"It's amazingly sexy to watch you lick my legs," Dex said, her tongue sounding like it was thick in her mouth. She let out a deep sigh, stretching her body as her hips began to twitch.

Tracy gripped her ass, also laden with hard-earned muscle, pulling her close as she rubbed her face all over Dex's soft skin.

Fingers glided through her hair, making little riots of sensation across her scalp and down her back. She kept kissing, licking, even taking gentle bites of the muscles, able to smell Dex's luscious scent. "I'm so turned on I could melt into a puddle," she sighed, her voice barely audible.

Dex bent slightly and began to tug on her tank top, getting it off with little trouble. Then gentle hands were on her arms, lifting her until they were face to face. "I can't wait another second," Dex said, her gaze fiery. "I need you on that bed. Naked."

Ahh, the old Dex was still in there. Still unafraid to state her needs. Still impatient. Even years of meditation hadn't been able to tamp all of that brashness down.

Tracy cuddled up to her, letting Dex push her shorts down and tug them off. Quickly, Dex pulled her own bra over her head, grasped Tracy firmly by the waist, and tumbled them to the bed, where they fell with a loud "thump."

"Now I'm happy," Dex said, truly looking it. "But I need an awful lot of kisses."

"Always," Tracy said, surprisingly not embarrassed at being naked with a woman who clearly spent a ton of time working on her body. Tracy knew she'd be a nervous wreck with a new partner who might be judgmental about bodies in general. But that wasn't Dex. She'd always seemed most concerned with playing her sports better, or running faster. Getting admiring looks from others didn't seem like it was part of the equation. But now Tracy was going to get the pleasure of nibbling on the results of Dex's hard work, which she was going to get to as soon as she kissed those beautiful lips, so pink and soft.

After just a few gentle touches, they were right back where they'd left off. Dex had always been the best kisser Tracy thought it was possible to be, and she'd only honed her skills. Her lips were firm, but very pliable.

Never sloppy or too wet. Absolutely perfect in every way. With the power of her feelings all wrapped up in the tender touches, Tracy's head spun, her love for this woman almost swamping her senses.

"I love you," Tracy murmured. "I've missed you, Dex. So often. So much." She held her tightly, murmuring into her ear, "I'm so sorry for shutting you out. So very sorry."

"No more apologies. We're together now. Better late than never is an adage that's one hundred percent true."

"Wait," Tracy said, sitting up to rest on an arm. "I want you to know something."

"Mmm?"

"I didn't put up a wall to punish you."

"I didn't think—"

"I put it up solely to keep myself from begging you to come back," she said, unable to stop herself from weeping. "I knew I couldn't trust you, but I still loved you so much. The only way I could stay strong was to never see you, or hear your beautiful voice. I'm so sorry," she whimpered. "I truly didn't trust myself to keep my distance."

Dex put her arm around her shoulders and murmured gently. "I'm going to allow that apology. But it was your last one, so you'd better savor it."

"I'm sor—" Tracy winced. "I can't stop myself. I've got such a long list of things I regret."

"Shh," Dex murmured. "We both have lists, but we have to let them go."

"I just wanted you to know about that one. I had to protect myself, and, at first, that meant hurting you. But that was never my goal."

"I had a feeling that might be true," Dex said, smiling sadly. "But I assumed part of it had to be because of your anger. You had every right to be angry."

"That didn't last," she insisted. "Maybe a year. Once I saw how determined you were to stay close to Kendall, I let it go. From then on, I was just trying to avoid falling into your aura." She placed her hand on

Dex's chest, feeling her heart thump away. "It's such a powerful one."

Dex's smile was so shyly sweet. How had it gotten so much cuter with age? "Obviously, I wish we'd gotten to this point many years ago, but maybe…" She nodded. "Maybe now's the perfect time."

"It's the only time we have. That makes it perfect."

Dex laughed. "That sounds like one of the motivational sayings that drop into my in box every day."

"I think I made that one up, but I'd love to have you motivate me to learn yoga. Running's too solitary. I need to spend my exercising time with my sweetheart."

"It would be a pleasure. We'll start after we've thoroughly satisfied each other in bed. Next week good for you?" she teased, the sparkle fully back in her warm eyes.

"Aim big," Tracy said, flipping her onto her back again to begin to kiss her with renewed passion. Just a few minutes of letting some of the old feelings out felt like it had freed her up to let her body speak. It had been so quiet for so long, and now it felt like it might never shut up. But there were definitely worse ways to exhaust yourself.

"God, this feels wonderful," Dex said after coming up for air. "If I could even count how many times I've fantasized about being with you again…"

"Really?" Tracy said, pushing her hair away from her face to get a good look at Dex. "You've done that?"

"Have I done that?" She laughed, clearly finding the question funny. "Many, many times." Her eyes narrowed as she appeared to think. "Last week? Uh-huh. Definitely last week. And for sure the week before." Her head nodded firmly. "Kendall was out with her friends, so I had the whole night to myself. I took a bath and soaked for a long time, and as soon as I got out…" She held up her hand and wiggled her fingers. "I know it's kind of counterproductive to touch myself as soon as I'm clean, but it's a thing. It's definitely a thing."

"It was a thing in college," Tracy said, giving her a poke. "On maybe the second or third day we were together we took a shower before class—

which we then skipped because you had me back in bed before I was completely dry."

"Get used to that," Dex said, grinning happily. "Tell your office you're going to be late. Like all the time."

"We'll shower at night. Problem solved." She laughed, thinking about the immediate future. "Think Kendall's going to regret getting us back together? She'll never see us."

"She's going to be so happy she'll burst something. So will my mom, my dad, my grandparents, my aunt, my cousins…" She pressed a quick kiss to Tracy's lips. "But most of all me. I'll be the happiest."

"You seem like a teenager again. A very spritely teenager."

"I think this might be another born-again experience. Is it okay to have two?"

"It's perfect to have two, since everything about you is perfect." She dipped her head and sucked a nipple into her mouth. "Especially these," she said, beginning to lick all around.

"I promise not to complain if you do that for a while—like an hour."

"I keep losing my focus. But having my mouth on you is bringing it right back."

Dex lay on her back and purred softly as Tracy loved her breasts with care. They seemed just as sensitive as they'd been when they were kids, but now she wasn't pushing Tracy to rush. Dex had definitely grown more patient with age, seeming less focused on popping off orgasms, and more on experiencing the sensuality of touch. Who said growing older had no upside?

⋙⋘

A half hour later, they'd touched each other everywhere, at length, and Tracy could tell that Dex was ready to get serious. She'd paced herself to go slow, becoming more focused as she moved down Tracy's body a couple of inches at a time. She'd had her hands dangerously close to all of the good spots more times than Tracy could count, but hadn't yet given her the slightest bit of relief.

The very minor problem was that Tracy got most aroused by

watching her partner's excitement grow. If Dex went for it, Tracy would definitely enjoy it, but she'd miss that extra burst, and she didn't want to miss a thing. As Dex's gentle hand started to finally slip between her legs, Tracy shook off the instinct to lie back and let the pleasure wash over her. Shifting her body slightly, she was able to grasp Dex's leg and tug on it until her foot was flat on the bed.

Their eyes met, with Dex's expression showing surprise.

"I can't wait." Tracy's fingers slid up that muscular leg to touch Dex just like she was being touched—gently, inquisitively.

Dex's eyes fluttered closed as Tracy slipped into her wetness. The sensations in her own body shot up when she could see the pleasure hit Dex like a wave.

"I'd tell you to hold off, but I'm not an idiot," Dex whispered, with her voice sounding so sweet, so slow, so sexy that Tracy got chills. Their eyes met for a second. "It's still hard for you to be the sole focus, huh?"

"It's not *hard* for me," she said, so much more aware of her needs now. "Watching your arousal grow just makes it hotter for me."

"Then you should be *very* turned on. I'm racing ahead here."

"I could tell." Tracy smirked, hardly able to keep her hand from sliding right off Dex's slippery skin. "If you could just reach my mouth, we'd really be getting somewhere."

Dex shifted around until they shared a pillow, now letting them easily reach each other's lips. "Perfect," Tracy sighed after Dex's tongue entered her mouth at the same time her fingers delved inside her body.

It was almost impossible to focus on her own pleasure while paying rapt attention to Dex's, but having to do both slowed Tracy down—her prime goal. Feeling how hot Dex was getting made her excitement climb fast, but having to be gentle with her was the perfect moderating force.

It truly felt like she was enveloped by a cloud of pleasure, with Dex kissing her so forcefully, nearly overwhelming her with her growing need, while gentle fingers probed inside her body, then slipped out to caress her clit. Back and forth those talented fingers moved, pulling her close to the edge, then gently guiding her away from the cliff.

Tracy was so distracted she was afraid she wasn't focusing enough on Dex, but the sounds she made gave a pretty clear indication that wasn't true in the least. Dex had always been more vocal, expressing her need, her frustration, and her satisfaction with just a slight difference in tone or pitch. Now she was purring, gently and slowly thrusting her hips every time Tracy got close to her always-sensitive clit.

With so many sensations flowing over her, Tracy was having a tough time keeping her eyes open. But when Dex pulled away from a deep kiss to arch her back languidly, Tracy stared at her boldly, her heart so filled with joy that she nearly burst into tears. For a split second, she began to fall into the very unproductive habit of chastising herself for keeping this woman out of her life for so long. But she fought that instinct. They both had to let go of their mistakes and weaknesses in order to grow. And no matter what it took, she was going to grow with Dex.

Speaking from her heart, she whispered, "You are the most beautiful woman I've ever known—inside and out."

Dex blinked a few times, like she was having trouble focusing. Then a sated smile transformed her expression into a joyous one. "I feel awfully pretty when you look at me that way. I can almost forget I'm ready to explode," she added with a tiny laugh. "If you could just kiss me again…"

Tracy inched closer, able to reach her sweet mouth for a long, sultry kiss. When her tongue entered Dex's warm mouth, she ignored the sensations buffeting her own body to pay rapt attention to the flesh that began to pulse around her fingers. Dex yanked her head away and sucked in a deep breath, with every part of her starting to shake. Everything seemed to happen at once, Dex's gasping cry, her hips flying from the bed, Tracy's own arousal skyrocketing. Only a few seconds after Dex's climax began, Tracy's body signaled it was past the point of no return.

It took a second to realize that Dex wasn't able to touch her with anything close to dexterity. Tracy continued to thrust her hips, chasing Dex's hand, which was almost limp. But she rallied quickly, turning completely onto her side to slide her fingers in to give Tracy something to push against. "So good," she moaned. "Stay right there…" She was sure she made some kinds of sound as sensations touched every nerve, but she would never know what they were.

Finally forcing her eyes open, the devilish expression Dex bore filled her vision. "I'm going to stay right here for the rest of the night," she murmured, her voice so tender and sweet. "I want to see that look on your face again and again and again…"

Tracy was nearly boneless, but she managed to roll onto her side. Needing Dex even closer, she draped her leg around her hip and drew her in. "If you'll give me thirty seconds to rest, your wish will be granted." She strained her neck to catch a glimpse of the clock on the bedside table. "It's only nine. I don't have to be at work for eleven hours, so we don't have to rush."

"It's Friday," Dex said, giving her a big grin. "You don't have to be at work until Monday." She kissed her hungrily, obviously ready to get right back to business. "I'm going to wear you out so thoroughly you're going to have to nap between patients."

"That's a small price to be here with you." She tickled under Dex's chin, loving to listen to her giggle. "You'll just have to be careful not to strain your voice. You're not the quietest girl in the world, you know."

"Can't help it. When I'm happy, I make noise." She pulled Tracy closer and rubbed their noses together. "And I'm damned happy." Her smile faded in an instant. "Wait. Did you say it's nine?"

"Uh-huh. Why? Do you think you're going somewhere? Because you're not."

"No, no, but my mom serves dinner at eight. Since you've been staying at the house, she might assume you're going to eat with them. Should we call…?"

"You want to tell your mom we missed the entree because we were making love?" Tracy began to laugh. "Sometimes you're too polite for your own damn good." She ruffled Dex's messy hair. "I'm sure Kendall has told your parents all of the gory details of the afternoon. Maybe we'll go over for breakfast tomorrow. We can let them torture us then."

"Disquieting thought," Dex said, shivering slightly. "But I talked them into supporting our love when we were nineteen. I think I can get them on our side once again without too much trouble."

"They're going to be thrilled. Not as thrilled as Kendall, but pretty darned thrilled." She laughed gently. "Maybe we should sleep in your recording studio. Those foam panels you put up might let Kendall have a good night's sleep."

"Nope," Dex said, shaking her head. "You put in a very nice master bedroom, and we're going to use it. Every night for the rest of our lives."

A bout of doubt hit Tracy, and she couldn't help but say, "You're sure you won't be tempted to go back to LA? I really don't have any desire to move, but if you'd be happier—"

"Where?" Dex batted her eyes. "Oh, you mean that place I had to live for work? I'm pleased to say I've been transferred to the home office in Richmond, where I shall remain."

It wasn't easy, but Tracy got both arms around her, and she pulled her into her body to hold her in a tender, protective embrace. "With me," she whispered. "In our home. With our sweet girl."

"She brought us together the first time," Dex said, with her beautiful eyes filling with tears. "It's only right that she'll be here for our second act. It's going to be a loooooong one."

Epilogue

On the fifteenth day of August, Tracy grasped Dex's hand to wade into the chilly Pacific Ocean. "This *is* pretty pacific," she said, realizing her voice had climbed in pitch. "But it's colder than the Atlantic."

"Not always, but I'll admit it's a little chilly today. You know, by October it's kind of perfect. Want to stay?"

"Ha-ha. I'm giving you two days to do your voice work, then we're out of here."

"Well, I think it's a little more involved than just closing the door and driving away…"

"I've got it all planned," Tracy said, tapping her temple. "We'll spend the whole week getting your stuff packed up and loaded into the moving van. Next week we'll drive your very small electric car back to Virginia—which should be quite an adventure." She gripped Dex's shoulders, then used the buoyancy of the water to lock her legs around her, letting Dex carry her deeper into the water that didn't seem so cold now. "I can't afford to lose my job, you know. Grammy made it clear that missing a single day's work could lead to ruin, given that supporting you is going to take every cent I have."

"She honestly thinks I have no money at all!"

"Well, she thinks I'm paid by the hour. I've been unable to convince her that I get a regular salary, as well as a vacation."

"I keep thinking she might be losing it a little, but then—"

"Dexter, I'm not sure what resources she used, or how she used them, but when I spoke to her last night she suggested I should cancel my appointment with the attorney."

"The attorney?"

"The one who's supposed to advise us on how to amend Kendall's birth certificate. Grammy said that our antediluvian state has made it impossible to have a second-parent adoption unless the parties are married."

"Are you serious? I thought our legislature was coming out of the dark ages. Wait… Grammy really used that term?"

"Uh-huh. She said 'married.' Clear as day." She batted her eyes at Dex, falling a little deeper in love with her when the love-sick look that had taken up residence seemed to grow even stronger. "Are you ready to take the plunge?"

"Yes," she said, robotically nodding her head. "I will plunge any where, any time, as long as you plunge right along with me."

"I'm asking if you want to marry me, you silly girl."

Dex's eyes went wide. "You're asking me? I've been planning something, but I was waiting for a few little details to line up before I—"

"Ooo. Did I spoil your proposal?"

"Yes," she said, with her gaze growing slightly vacant. "But I won't hold it against you."

"Hold those warm breasts against me," Tracy said, shivering. "Kendall was smart to stay on your deck this morning."

"Oh, she's impervious to the cold. She's just giving us space to be alone. She's remarkably thoughtful that way." Dex touched the tip of Tracy's nose. "I'm sure she got that trait from you."

"None of us are going to have any space in that silly little car of yours, but I am honestly thrilled at the prospect of traveling across the country together. Taking a week will let us see the sights."

"Even though you think we need to spend every every moment packing, I'm sure we have time to see anything that might interest you in LA. Got a list?"

"Not that I can think of." Tracy let her head slide back, gazing up at the clear, blue sky. "What could be better than sitting on the deck of that house of yours and watching the sunset? I could start crying all over again when I think of having my arms around you and Kendall last night as the sun dipped into the water."

"Oh, it's nice," Dex agreed. "We won't have that in Richmond, you know."

"Mmm-hmm." She touched the tip of Dex's nose with her finger. "We can spend a week at the shore every summer. That will give us something to look forward to. If it was right in front of me every minute I wouldn't appreciate it as much."

"Interesting thought," Dex said, acting like she'd never heard of such a concept. "But as Oscar Wilde said, 'Nothing succeeds like excess.'"

"As Tracy Haven-Lord says, 'Live within your means.'" She gripped Dex firmly and gave her a noisy kiss. "What were you thinking when you bought such a beautiful, massive house? I'm not even going to ask what your mortgage payment is…"

"Oh, that's a good move. My accountant keeps track of all of that. I can't bear to look."

Tracy gripped her ear and tugged on it. "You've got an accountant you don't check up on? *That's* going to change."

Dex's smile grew slowly. "You can tell me what to do all day long. You've always been more of an adult when it comes to that kind of thing."

"I won't supervise you, sweetheart." She laughed. "But I will supervise your accountant." She ran her hand through Dex's hair, looking so sleek with the sun glinting off it. "You've been treated like a little princess in LA for an awfully long time. Are you sure you're ready to leave? In Richmond, you're just going to be Randy and Libby Haven's kid. The one who doesn't have a real job."

Dex's eyes twinkled when she laughed. "Very sure. My charmed second childhood has run on for long enough. There are only a few things I love about LA, and tonight I'll take you out for one of them. Kendall's—and my—favorite fish tacos are awesome. I know they have them everywhere now, but these are the best."

Tracy placed a warm, soft kiss to her lips. Was there anything better than bobbing around in the ocean while you kissed the woman you loved? If there was, she couldn't think of it…

"Other than the tacos, and never having to scrape ice off my windshield, there's nothing in LA that I can't improve on in Virginia. They definitely have the prettiest girls there," she added, grinning that devastatingly charming smile.

"I think Kendall would love to stay here for a while. Maybe a long while. I laughed when I went out this morning to see her standing at the railing, wearing a beautiful caftan that I know you bought for her. She definitely looked like a native."

Dex shrugged. "She likes to stay outside all day, and she hates to keep reapplying sunblock. Also, she says the caftan makes her feel like a movie star from the seventies. Every night at sunset, I make her a dry martini. It's a whole thing…"

"Such a doting mom. A doting, devoted, darling mom."

"I'll make you a martini, too. Heck, I'll race out and buy you a caftan if you want…"

"Let's concentrate on packing up what you have, not adding to it." She gave Dex a firm kiss. "I'm still astounded that you were going to pay your house sitter to pack up your most valuable things, then have strangers do everything else, including shipping your car. Now that you're my dependent, we're not going to spend our money like it's spewing out of a firehose."

"I'll turn over all of my assets to you. If I have twenty bucks on me in case of emergency, I'll be happy. My needs are few."

"I'm sure you believe that," Tracy said, gazing into those trusting eyes. "But don't forget the half-hour to meditate the second you wake, followed by an excellent espresso, an hour of yoga, no more than two meals a day—both at odd times. I wouldn't say you were the essence of simplicity."

"Don't forget the most important part of my schedule. Making love to the prettiest girl I've ever seen."

Tracy gave her a soft, slow kiss, then playfully rubbed her nose against Dex's. "I know I'm not even the prettiest girl on your street, but that doesn't matter. The fact that you believe it is the key." Suddenly awash in tender feelings, she wrapped her arms around Dex's shoulders and held on tight. "I don't have a single doubt about how good we're going to be together, and that's from a woman who grew up not being totally certain that the sun was going to rise."

"The sun will always rise over us, baby. I know we let some of the early morning hours of our lives pass on by, but it's not even noon. The best part of the day's waiting for us."

"And our girl. Ready to walk back and watch her read?" She gave Dex a firm hug. "I'm sorry she got the reading habit from me. It's kind of all-consuming."

"No complaints. I like looking at the top of her head." Dex was already starting for the shore. "You know, she hinted the other day that she might skip her China adventure entirely. She thinks she might be happy to travel around during her summer vacations once she gets a teaching job."

"Oh, Dex, I hope she's not afraid to try something challenging. I want her to be bold."

"I think she's plenty bold. My guess is that she's so happy we're back together that she can't bear to leave. She doesn't want to miss anything."

When they were near the shore, Tracy slid down Dex's body, then took her hand as they ran the last few feet, trying to stay in front of an incoming wave. "What do you think? Should we try to talk her into following through? She's looked forward to this for years…"

"I think she's old enough to make up her mind about living in China. But I'm almost certain she'd like a taste of the country before she makes up her mind. How would you like a built-in interpreter for our honeymoon?"

"You want to…? Really?"

"If a certain woman hadn't spoiled my plans for a pretty elaborate proposal…"

"I promise to be surprised. You're not the only actor around here, buddy. I managed to convince everyone I wasn't desperately in love with you for the last couple of decades, and believe me, that was a *demanding* role."

"I'm so glad that act is over. Let's start packing up my stuff. I'd like to be able to finish the office by three, so we can go out for tacos." She made her eyebrows pop up and down. "Beat the dinner rush."

"Three," Tracy scoffed. "You eat earlier than your grandparents do."

"This is true. But when I eat early, my dinner's all digested when we go to bed. I could even hang upside down if need be…" She lifted one of her perfectly arched eyebrows. "I don't hear you complaining then."

"And you never will, C.K. Dexter Haven-Lord. You never, ever will."

❧

Thanksgiving Day was just another Thursday in the Sichuan Province, but the breakfast at the hotel was nearly as extensive as an excellent Turkey Day feast would have been. The hotel was truly impressive, but if Tracy had been in charge, they would have been staying at a well-rated economy spot. But Grammy had miraculously found the wallet none of them had ever spotted, and offered to pay for the whole family to travel together. Obviously, the trip had been Kendall's long-term dream, but once Dex had suggested she and Tracy tag along for their honeymoon, it hadn't taken long for Libby and Randy to raise their hands, too. Once they were at five, seven didn't seem like a big leap, so here they were.

No one except Libby had ever been on a trip Grammy had organized, and that had been forty-five years earlier, when Libby was at UVA. But Grammy always knew how to do it up right. She was clearly used to being treated well, and had found an excellent travel agent who was willing to do handstands to live up to her standards. The agent was a wizard at finding attractions that appealed to each of them, catering to their separate energy levels and cultural interests.

Today, she, Dex and Kendall were going on a ten mile trek that promised not only visits to five ancient temples, but also some time at the giant Buddha statue Dex was really excited about. While Dex was meditating at such an historic place, Tracy and Kendall were going to climb a nearby peak to burn their lungs a little, while also seeing what was supposed to be a fantastic vista.

Their hotel was in Chengdu, which was known for pandas. None of them had known Grammy was avidly interested in them, but she'd made plans to spend the whole day at the main research center. Libby and Randy were venturing out to do some shopping, accompanied by a guide who was going to point out the architectural highlights, which were many.

But no matter what they did during daylight hours, the best part of the day would probably be dinner, as it had been each of the five days they'd been in China. Tracy wasn't sure if the travel agent simply knew the best places to eat, or if fantastic food was the norm, but she was looking forward to hiking briskly enough to empty her stomach completely so she could happily fill it up again.

All seven of them were still at the table, having a final cup of coffee. She was surprised to realize she was holding Dex's hand in her lap, idly sliding her thumb over the gold band that now decorated her ring finger. Dex had been intent on purchasing matching diamond eternity rings, but Tracy had talked her down, and they'd finally compromised on narrow eighteen-karat gold bands with a tiny strip of platinum on either side. It looked so nice on her hand, and constantly reminded Tracy that they were finally able to publicly celebrate the bond that had been severely frayed, but never severed.

She looked up to see Kendall gazing at them, with a tiny smile showing. Tracy was sure Kendall had paid more attention to them in the past few months than she had in the past few years. It was almost like she was a child again, intensely curious about everything she hadn't experienced yet—like true love. If Kendall wound up with someone who showered her with love like Dex had, she'd be set for life.

"We'd better get going, lovebirds," Kendall said. "We've got to stop by the concierge desk to sort a couple of things out."

"We're ready to go," Tracy said. "Finish up, honey." She put her hand on Dex's back and scratched it gently. "Kendall's in charge today."

"How's that different from every other day?" They got up and kissed everyone goodbye, then took the elevator down to the lobby. They'd both taken to following Kendall around like a pair of ducklings. When you couldn't read any of the signs, or speak a full sentence, you put your energies into keeping an eye on your guide at all times.

Two American couples were trying to speak over one another to get the attention of a member of the concierge staff who Tracy knew spoke very crisp English. But another staff member, a woman she hadn't yet interacted with, stood there silently, with a mild smile.

Kendall, who looked very American, walked up to the woman, who immediately raised her hand and pointed to the other employee. But Kendall started to speak quietly, in what must have been very serviceable Mandarin. Tracy loved to see how surprised, and pleased, people were to learn this young American had put in the years of hard work necessary to communicate effectively.

Listening to Kendall speak Mandarin was a very odd experience. Given the language was tonal, her voice rose and fell in a way that was entirely different from her norm. Tracy actually wouldn't have known it was her daughter if she hadn't been watching her lips move. They were really moving now, as she seemed to be having a slight misunderstanding with the staff member. She didn't seem frustrated, but she kept pointing to her passport, which they'd had to show much more often than Tracy would have guessed. Finally, Kendall reached into her bag and pulled out her newly amended birth certificate, the document she whipped out so often to show to friends and family it was going to be in tatters. Carefully, she pointed out that her name was on both. At least that's what Tracy thought she was saying. But if the woman didn't speak or read English, would she be able to tell that was the same set of characters? Tracy was one hundred percent sure she couldn't have done the same thing with a Chinese name, no matter how hard she tried.

She turned slightly to see the proud smile on Dex's face, clearly confident that Kendall would get this all sorted out. Tracy was confident, too, but if they couldn't hook up with the car they'd arranged for, they'd go see the pandas. Who'd complain about that?

By the time Kendall had pulled out her driver's license, Tracy started to shift her anticipation to the pandas. She was sure Grammy hadn't had to show her birth certificate to see them.

The woman finally took Kendall's documents and showed them to another man who must have just started his shift. He gave her a scowl, then nodded politely and handed everything back to Kendall. "I am sorry for the confusion," he said.

Kendall answered back in Mandarin, and they went back and forth for a minute, both of them seeming like they were apologizing to the other. Then he went to print something off, leaving the young woman, who seemed a little shook. Even though Tracy couldn't understand a word, she could see that Kendall was reassuring her that she didn't mind that the transaction had taken a while to complete. In a few seconds they were laughing together, and Tracy felt like she might burst with pride. Their daughter was consistently kind, and thoughtful, and generally very patient. Even when she was interacting with someone she'd likely never see again, those traits never failed her.

Dex leaned over and whispered, "How did we get so incredibly lucky?"

Tracy just shook her head, certain she'd tear up if she let herself linger on their great, good fortune. Of course, in an ideal world they wouldn't have squandered eighteen long years, but lingering on that was truly unproductive. Their future was stunningly bright, and they'd barely set off from the starting line.

The End

By Susan X Meagher

Novels

Arbor Vitae
All That Matters
Cherry Grove
The Lies That Bind
The Legacy
Doublecrossed
Smooth Sailing
How To Wrangle a Woman
Almost Heaven
The Crush
The Reunion
Inside Out
Out of Whack
Homecoming
The Right Time
Summer of Love
Chef's Special
Fame
Vacationland
Wait For Me
The Keeper's Daughter
Friday Night Flights
Mosaic
Full Circle

Short Story Collection

Girl Meets Girl

Serial Novel

I Found My Heart In San Francisco

Anthologies

You can contact Susan at Susan@briskpress.com

Information about all of Susan's books can be found at www.susanxmeagher.com or www.briskpress.com

To receive notification of new titles, send an email to newsletters@briskpress.com

facebook.com/susanxmeagher

twitter.com/susanx